WINGS OF SUNFIRE & DARKNESS

AWAKENED FATES
BOOK THREE

LUCINDA DARK
REBECCA GREY

Copyright © 2024 by Lucy Smoke LLC & Rebecca Grey

All rights reserved.

No part of this book may be reproduced in any form or by any electronic or mechanical means, including information storage and retrieval systems, without written permission from the author, except for the use of brief quotations in a book review.

Developmental Edits & Proofreading by Lunar Rose Services

Line Edits by Your Editing Lounge

Cover Design by Trif Book Design

CONTENTS

1.	Solomon	1
2.	Solomon	14
3.	Devonry	30
4.	Devonry	36
5.	Solomon	44
6.	Devonry	52
7.	Devonry	67
8.	Solomon	77
9.	Devonry	88
10.	Devonry	105
11.	Solomon	116
12.	Devonry	122
13.	Solomon	131
14.	Devonry	141
15.	Solomon	151
16.	Devonry	162
17.	Devonry	176
18.	Solomon	186
19.	Devonry	194
20.	Devonry	199
21.	Devonry	210
22.	Solomon	215
23.	Solomon	229
24.	Solomon	236
25.	Devonry	247
26.	Solomon	259
27.	Devonry	267
28.	Devonry	281
29.	Devonry	289
30.	Solomon	302
31.	Devonry	307

32. Devonry	316
33. Devonry	327
34. Devonry	333
35. Devonry	339
36. Solomon	347
37. Devonry	351
38. Devonry	362
39. Devonry	373
Epilogue	380
About Lucinda Dark	393
Also by Lucinda Dark	395
About Rebecca Grey	399
Also by Rebecca Grey	401

1
SOLOMON

15 years old…

The night is finally ending and dawn breaks across a battlefield full of blood and bodies. Exhaustion clings so deeply to my aching form that it invades deep into the marrow of my hollow bones. Despite the sickening sight of the fallen—enemy and ally alike—my stomach grumbles with a hunger I've been putting off for days. Amidst all of it, the dead and the gone, somehow, my body still dares to crave sustenance—for both food and blood. What is the point of food and eating save for sustaining my ability to wield a sword and command an army?

My worn boots crunch across the snow-covered grounds and over the remnants of broken barren tree branches that have, too, fallen at the edge of the field. My lips and mouth are dryer still than a hot day devoid of water. My throat tightens as my stomach grumbles once again.

Closing my eyes, I scrub my only free but dirty hand down my equally filthy face. The stench of rot and death lingers everywhere and the taste of bile and rust coats the back of my tongue. The sword I still clutch feels heavier than ever before as blood drips from its tip onto the soiled ground.

It's been a few days since I last ate, but how long has it been since I last bathed? More than days, perhaps? Is it weeks? I'm sure it's been one of the two. Certainly, it hasn't been months yet. Has it? No. Surely, one of my men would have said something if it'd gotten to that point. Then again … they aren't much better off than I am as I watch those who've survived the latest fucking battle trudge back through the woods toward camp.

"General!" I turn as a fellow soldier calls out to me. A young man of no Noble descent approaches, his own dented armor coated in blood. From the way he's limping, at least some of it must be his own. I withhold a wince at feeling as if that, too, is my fault. After all, these men are my responsibility. Their lives and deaths weigh upon me, as well as the King's expectations.

As the soldier moves closer, I search my mind for his name. "Colin," I say, finding it amidst the foggy memories collecting in my mind.

The man comes to a stop a few feet from me, breathing heavily. Despite his obvious fatigue, he beams at me at the sound of his name on my tongue, as if he's not used to someone of a higher status even bothering to learn the names of those he fights alongside. I know there are plenty of Nobles who sneer and turn their noses up at the common folk, but out here—when friendship is the difference between life and death—there are no noblemen. Only those who are dead and those who are not.

Rozentine is not a Kingdom that's often attacked nor one that's plagued by many wars. In fact, this mere skirmish likely won't even make it into the history books.

These men, my fucking men, who laid their lives before the King and their people, will be forever forgotten as lost ones in between the lines written in old leather-bound volumes too expensive for a commoner to touch, much less learn to read.

I crack my neck to the side and silently push away the disgust that rises up within me. Instead, I focus my attention on the red-haired and freckled man with eyes a dull shade of green and a face that's almost as youthful as my own. Though he's at least three years older than me, I stand taller than him and wider. Still, he must be decent with that blade that hangs at his hips, or he wouldn't have made it this far.

"The King has sent a messenger," he announces suddenly.

"Which King?" I demand. Ours ... or the Vitas Isles'?

Colin breathes through his mouth, slowly and evenly, as if he's trying to assuage some of the pain of his wounds. Despite the obvious discomfort in the way the corners of his mouth and eyes crinkle, he smiles again. His eyes alight on my own and before he answers, I already know what he's about to say. There's too much relief on his features. "The Vitas Isles' King," he says.

I nod slowly before turning back to survey our surroundings. This is it, then, I think. It's finally over. After so long away from home, these ridiculous skirmishes and the threat of the Vitas Isles' inhabitants attempting to breach our borders to make a new home for themselves not under the House of Sunfire's Divine rule have ended. The Vitas Isles' King has finally put a stop to his people's audacity. This news comes none too soon, either. My soldiers, my army, as stable and strong as they are, have been on the frontlines for longer than anyone else. They're tired, hungry, and weary. Just like me.

Sheathing the sword still gripped in my fist, I pivot away from the battlefield and march back to camp. Colin follows. I don't stop until I make it to the commander's tent —my tent—and even then, I know that sitting down doesn't mean it's truly time to rest. I wave my hand to Colin.

"Bring the messenger." I relay the order and Colin nods before quickly disappearing through the tent's open flap.

On the table in front of me are papers—letters, maps, and torn shreds of my sanity. I don't have to look at it for long because Colin returns quickly with a large, robust man in leather armor. My upper lip curls back over my teeth, and I feel my fangs throb as anger passes through me at the sight of his sword strapped to his hip. The audacity continues.

The messenger—if that even is truly what he is and not an assassin—pauses at the low growl that rumbles from me. Colin doesn't react. In fact, he straightens and his expression wipes itself clean as he senses my displeasure.

The messenger notes where I'm looking—his eyes going from my face and down to his sword before he reaches for it. Colin withdraws his blade. "You vile—"

"Stop!" I command. Colin and the messenger both freeze. God, I am so tired of death. If this man was sent here to kill me, then he'll find me far more difficult to prey upon with such a pathetic attempt.

"I plan to take it off, my Lord," the messenger says quickly, his already ruddy cheeks reddening even further. "All other messengers were lost, and I was the fastest rider among them. I meant no ill will."

I blow out a breath. "Leave your sword," I say. "It wouldn't matter if you drew it anyway. You'd be dead before you could pierce me with it." As he stares back at me, meeting my gaze, his sagging face tightens, but he nods, seeming to understand the truth in my words.

It's insulting, perhaps, to a man twice my age, but true, nonetheless. I sense no abilities from him, at least none of the Awakened kind. Therefore, I'm already stronger than him.

I wave my hand toward one of the chairs at the end of the war table. The messenger straightens and eyes the chair with barely repressed confusion.

Colin doesn't sheath his sword and instead, keeps it firmly in his grasp. I sigh and direct a look to him. "Go fetch Jacin for me," I order. "When you return, tell him to come in and then guard the tent. Do not allow another soul to enter."

Colin straightens abruptly and jerks his head in a sharp nod. Only now that he's been given another task does he finally put away his blade. Then, with a final seething glance at our enemy's messenger, he turns and strides out of the tent.

"Shall I wait for your ... fellow commander to arrive?" The messenger guesses at Jacin's status.

A chuckle rises from the back of my throat. "There is only one commander," I tell him. "I am that commander. You may relay your message to me." When he doesn't speak for a long moment, my amusement dies a quick death. "*Now*," I bark out the word, making the man jump with the ferocity of my tone.

He doesn't take the seat I've offered him. Instead, he takes a cautious step toward where I stand. His bushy brows lower over beady little eyes and the bright white and blue tunic he wears over his leather armor flutters with each inhale. I watch his movements carefully—half praying he tries something devious and half praying he doesn't—as he reaches into the satchel on the other side of his torso. From it, he withdraws a scroll and passes it over the top of the table to me. I take it and unravel it.

As I read the words on the parchment, I send a quiet, thankful prayer to the Gods. It's over. It's well and truly over. At least, I hope so—if this parchment is, in fact, truthful, then perhaps by the end of the month I'll have returned to my home or, at the very least, made it back to Sunfire Palace and back to…

I shake my head and focus on the paper in my hands. Ridding my thoughts of a certain pale-haired Princess is an effort in futility, yet, somehow, I manage it. "So," I begin, rolling up the message and tossing it to the table before me. "Your King is requesting an armistice." Metal and leather creak as I fold my arms over my chest and stare back at the messenger. "What can you do to prove the legitimacy of *this*?" I nod to the scroll.

The man inhales sharply. "If you're assuming that our King would—"

"I assume *much* of the King that rules the Vitas Isles," I growl, stopping him from saying more to insult and irritate me. "None of it is good, considering he's allowed certain tribes of his people to encroach upon Rozentine territory and attempt to claim it for their own."

"You are but a child soldier," the man boasts, angry at my insult. "You should be *grateful* that the great and honorable King Arhaan would even bother to offer your army this truce."

With a smile that I'm sure is more predatory than kind, I loosen my folded arms and lean forward. Placing my hands along the edge of the table, I feel my claws extend past my fingertips and scrape along the wood and papers strewn about, causing a rather unnerving scratching sound. The messenger's eyes bulge even more as his gaze flickers to my hands and then back to my face.

"If I am but a mere child soldier," I say slowly, "then what must that make your country's tribes who've been unable to defeat me?"

Silence hangs in the interim as the messenger struggles to calm his breathing. A pathetic excuse for a soldier if he cannot even keep his expression placid in such a tense moment. I have to wonder even further if this truce is real —even though I crave it with everything in me—if they sent him. Perhaps we truly had killed off all of their messengers if he was the best they could send.

A truce with an insult. My vision flashes red once and I blink as the color fades and then slowly reverts. Just as I'm about to snatch up the scroll and rip it to shreds and then split this man's belly open with little more than my claws, the tent's flaps slide open, and in steps my cousin.

Jacin is taller than most men, about the same height as myself. Unlike me, however, he always carries with him a certain grace and warmth. It takes no time at all for him to sense the tension within the room and I know he senses it —the brief stiffening of his spine and the quick perusal of the space from me to the messenger says as much.

He plasters on an easy smile and then approaches. "I've heard news of a messenger's arrival," he announces, striding past the man in question to me. He claps a hand on my shoulder and leans down. His voice lowers. "Your eyes are glowing," he warns me before releasing me and turning.

"I assume you are King Ahraan's messenger?" Jacin beams at the bulbous man.

The messenger's smile is relieved as he bows slightly to Jacin. "I am Baron Chandrin, sir," he announces, "and yes, I am here to deliver the good news of our King's hope for *peace.*" He enunciates his last word with a quick flash of a glare my way.

It is funny how he bows to Jacin, not seeming to understand that I am still of a higher position out here on these battlefields. I inhale a slow breath and close my eyes, counting down from ten. Once I'm sure my anger is under control, I open them and when Jacin turns back to me, he nods with an ease of his brow. My eyes must be back to normal then, I guess.

"Here are the treaty terms," I say, gesturing to the scroll.

Jacin glances down. "May I?" he asks as he takes a step closer. I nod.

Jacin's eyes rove over the page as he unfolds it and scans its contents. He hums in the back of his throat. Were we alone, I'd demand to know his thoughts. His eyes, a slightly darker red than my own, almost that of cinnamon, become overcast for a moment and then brighten. He turns to me, his brows lowering in the middle, creating a crease between his eyes. Then, with one final nod, he tells me all I need to know.

"We need to know its legitimacy still," I tell him. "Even if the terms are agreeable."

He sighs and turns back to the messenger. "Is this possible, Baron?" he inquires.

Baron Chandrin puffs up his chest. "I swear it upon my own life, sir. That document was signed by the King himself."

Jacin's gaze returns to the page. "But not sealed," he states. A trick, perhaps? One meant to make us think they are offering a truce only for the tribes to begin their invasion once more in earnest once we've left?

Chandrin blinks and appears a bit shocked. Ah, he had not been aware that the King's seal was missing. "I-I'm sure it was a mistake," he says quickly. "The King has been very tired as of late, and he—"

"Mistake or not," Jacin interrupts. "We cannot simply trust the word of your King with no seal." He offers a smile not dissimilar to my own. Jacin, too, can be predatory if need be. "You understand." It's not a question.

With newfound amusement, I open my mouth and call out for Colin to come in. The tent flap opens, and Colin approaches, glowering at Chandrin with the sword still on his belt. Jacin strides toward the Baron and hands the scroll back. "We are happy to accept these terms," he says with that same smile, "so long as the King seals it."

The meaning cannot be lost on the man—not even with his meager intellect.

"If you truly wish for peace," I tell him, earning his attention as he blinks between Jacin and the scroll and then, finally, myself, in confusion and no small amount of fear. "I suggest you ride your horse back to your King even faster than you rode it here. I will give you two days to return with the King's seal. If you are not here by dawn on the second day, I will assume your King means to continue ignoring his tribes' treachery."

"But-but you ... the King ... he's ... two days? There and back?" The man appears ready to faint.

If I assume correctly, then his King is on Rozentine soil, likely forced to come in an effort to rein in his wayward tribes. He won't need to board a ship to get to the Isles. Two days will stretch him for sure—he likely won't be able to sleep—but if he's serious about this and if he's to pay for the insult to our own Kingdom, then this is the least he can do.

"I think two days is quite generous, Blood General," Jacin says, reciting that damned moniker my soldiers have started calling me.

"B-Blood General?" Baron Chandrin glances quickly to me, the ruddy redness in his cheeks disappearing altogether as paleness invades. "I-I ..." He is at a loss for words. It's quite pathetic.

"We will also require retributions to be made on behalf of the tribe that rose up against our borders," I state.

"They did not have his Highness' permission," Baron Chandrin reminds me. Yes, that is something we are well aware of. Still...

"As a King, he is responsible for the actions of his people. Regardless of his permission or not. Retributions *will* be made."

Chandrin huffs out a shuddering breath. "If you mean to discipline those responsible for this rebellion, I assure you, the tribe leaders have been taken into custody."

I peer at him for a moment before speaking. "I assume their goal was to take land from Rozentine and use it to establish their own minor country?"

Chandrin's jaw clenches and then he casts his gaze to the floor. "You are correct, sir."

I blow out a breath. How predictable. Greedy men make the most violent of enemies. "You may return to your King now," I say with a wave of my hand. "My warriors will not attack you. Two days, I remind you. After that, this truce will end—whether it be on the other side of peace or not is up to you."

I issue a quick nod to Colin, who quickly moves forward and takes Baron Chandrin by the arm, leading him from the tent. I wait until the flap slaps down behind them before releasing a groan from my throat.

"That went well," Jacin comments.

"*Fuck.*" A curse is all I can respond with.

I'm so fucking tired, more tired than I've ever been in my life. I collapse into the chair next to the table and scrub my hand over my face once more. Child soldier? I think, recalling the Baron's words. Yes, I am. As are half of my men—or rather boys—all willing to lose their lives in a vain effort to gain some notoriety or respect from the elders of their houses or villages. All more foolish than the next. Had I been given a choice in this matter, I would have much preferred to stay back, but if it means keeping the Sunfire Palace safe ... keeping *her* safe, then I suppose I am willing to be driven into sunfire and darkness itself just to do so.

"You look rough," Jacin says.

"*Thanks,*" I mutter.

"When was the last time you had blood?" he asks.

"I don't know if you've noticed," I reply, "but there are no coffins of willing donors out here." Had we been close enough to House of Blood territory, I might have taken a quick trip back to the place where those with abilities such as mine kept their blood and, oftentimes, bedmates. "It's not as easily attainable, and I do not drink from the dead nor from my own soldiers."

"I *have* noticed," Jacin says with weary amusement.

After the energy I've expended, the dryness in the back of my throat is a constant reminder of my power and my weakness. Closing my eyes, I lean back in my chair and cup a hand over my eyes. Nights always feel eons long when they're filled with death. Now that morning has come and, with it, a potential truce, I find my exhaustion that much more unbearable.

"I shall procure a horse," he continues. The sound of his footsteps marches away from me. "You will go into a local village, and for the love of the Gods, Solo, you *will* get yourself a damned drink. You deserve it." I know he doesn't mean alcohol, but honestly, I could do with a bit of both.

His footsteps pause and the sound of his voice comes

from further away. "Rest for now, Solo. I'll be back." The tent's flap swishes again at what I assume is his exit.

Were he and I from any other House, were we anyone else, we would be at home waking from our beds. He would be hunting in the woods of our territory with Uncle Ahren, and I … I would be in the gardens of the Sunfire Palace with a certain smart-mouthed Princess. Even thinking of her brings a smile to my lips.

I miss her. This is my deepest truth.

Despite that, I know that the reason I'm the one here now and not someone with age and experience on the battlefield is because of that truth of mine. King Vernon is nothing if not aware of the emotions of his followers and with each passing day, I find it more and more difficult to shroud my feelings toward Devonry.

With my eyes still closed, I imagine the last time I was in the Sunfire Palace and the real reason that I now knew for sure King Vernon had sent me out here to keep me from Devonry.

The sun arches high above the Palace Gardens. My booted footsteps were quiet on the stone walkways as the scent of irises and fireweed seep up from the grounds. A cool breeze drifts over my left ear, ruffling my hair as I pause at the entrance to the Palace Garden stone gazebo where King Vernon sits.

"Your Majesty." I bow low and wait.

"Solomon." His acknowledgement has me standing once more, and as I do, I spot a familiar head of pale hair in the near distance. Devonry, accompanied by her Lady's maid, Sheza, sits amidst the flowers, giggling as she is taught to weave them into crowns.

It's a simple sight, one so full of peace that it takes my breath away. For a moment, I'm catapulted into a far away distant past. Where a similar face with youth stripped away to reveal a woman's maturity looked up at me. My heart is a raw and trembling creature in my chest. Full of want and need and angst and pain.

Unawakened. Unknowing. Young and blissfully unaware that her soulmate is right before her. Watching her. Caring for her. Every step she takes is both a blessing and a curse to me.

Shaking away those thoughts, I return my attention to King Vernon. Unfortunately, though, his clear blue eyes are locked on me with a knowing glint. I stiffen where I stand. He dips his head slightly, indicating with a nod that I am to sit across from him. With unwilling movements, I follow the silent command and take my seat.

"Solomon Winett." I press my lips together as he speaks my full name, dimly aware that the object of my obsession and fascination is so close by. I pray she doesn't interrupt. "You know I care for you a great deal," he says, "but it's come to my attention that you care for Devonry far more than you should."

2
SOLOMON

15 years old...

My stomach clenches and I rip myself from the old memory before he can say those vile words that I hate. *She is not for you. She is not yours.*

She is. She must be. She always has been.

Scrubbing my hand down my face, I stand from my seat and begin removing my armor. As I do, the flap of my tent flutters as someone enters. "The Messenger has been sent on his way," Colin announces.

"Good," I say. "Let the men sleep for now, but in two nights' time, we'll likely be announcing it to the others. Don't breathe a word of this before then."

Colin bows slightly. "As you command."

The flap of my tent is disturbed once again, swishing open and smacking against the side of the tent wall as my cousin returns. With a grimace, I look at his expectant face and know that he isn't letting me rest before I head into the local village to satiate my need for blood, the trade-off for using my abilities as much as I have over the last few battles.

"Thank you, Colin," Jacin says with a grin as he steps to the side and holds the tent flap open for him to exit. "That will be all tonight."

Colin's expression turns somewhat moony-eyed like a young lady half-fallen in love with any moderately good-looking gentleman who deigns to offer her his hand. As I suspected, I'm sure he's not used to Lords and Nobles even bothering to learn his name, much less use it. Thankfully, though, he doesn't say anything. Instead, he nods and takes the cue to leave. I breathe a sigh of relief when Jacin releases the tent flap and the two of us are left alone.

"Come on," he says, striding over to me and stopping just close enough to kick the leg of my chair. "Are you truly going to attempt to sleep after days without blood? You'll only wake up hungrier and even more tired."

I consider his words. I'm tired enough to pass out the moment I set my head on the pillow on my nearby cot, but I'm also well aware of the side effects of my abilities when I go too long without blood. First, it'll start with the uncontrollable vision, something that already happened tonight. Then the shortened temper—another sign from tonight—and eventually … Blood Madness. I'd really rather avoid something so viscous and terrifying. I'd only seen it occur once with one of my distant relatives. I had no desire to feel it myself.

"No," I finally answer him and lean down to unbuckle the series of clasps holding my leather armor into place. Slipping free of it, I toss the mass onto the cot. The cot creaks beneath its weight, and as I slide my sword belt off and toss that toward the rest too, Jacin strides to the cot and picks the lot up.

"Fancy yourself a squire?" I ask with a laugh as I stand and move for the bundle of clothes in the opposite corner of the tent. Bending low, my shadow throws the mass of fabrics into darkness. The light only comes from a swinging lamp and the dawning sky outside of the tent's flap. Both barely scratch the darkness. Were this tent no different from others, the dawn would be pouring in through all sides. But this is a tent fit for a General—made of animal hide far thicker to both keep out the cold and the sun when it's time for me to sleep. The thickness helps with maintaining the secrets too of conversations I've had to have regarding planning and decision making.

I find a tunic of a simple design and a substitute sword without the mark of the House of Blood. Pulling on the plain shirt and strapping the unbranded sword to my waist, I turn and face Jacin.

"Good enough?" I deadpan.

He smiles back at me as he finishes setting my leather armor out in perfect order over a chair and then sits upon my cot before reaching beneath for the leather wax canister I keep. "You look lovely, cousin," he chuckles, uncapping the canister, pulling a strip of fabric from his pocket, and dipping it inside. He nods to the tent flap. "Your horse awaits you outside, tied to an oak branch to the north. I shall be here."

I snort. "No doubt going through my things," I reply, looking pointedly at his hands as he pulls my leather armor into his lap and begins massaging the oily wax over its surface. "I can do that when I get back," I remind him.

He chuffs. "You won't," he replies. "You'll be dead asleep before you can even undress." He clicks his tongue at me and nods again to the tent flap. "Go," he orders. "Don't come back until your belly is full of blood or I swear, I'll pin you down and drain a wild turkey's blood down your throat."

"Bastard." The word comes out without any of its usual heat. No doubt he'd enjoy doing something so ridiculous. That is, if he can best me long enough to get me pinned.

"That I am—save for the fact that my parents were married long before they had me." Ever the man to have the last word, his statement is one filled with smug satisfaction.

I tighten the new belt into place. "I'll head to the village. While I'm gone, you should have the *squires* clean and wax my leather and polish my sword," I say with meaning. "*You* need sleep. With any hope, I won't need the blasted things, but we should be prepared just in case the messenger was a farce."

I turn to go, stopping when Jacin speaks again, this time his tone more even and serious.

"Do you think it was?" he asks.

"No," I say. "I don't." The rebels had gone against their own king, and he feared Rozentine as well as he should. These skirmishes and battles should not have lasted as long as they had, but regardless, at least now the impending end is in sight. Perhaps that, combined with my weariness and excitement for blood, has made me softer this morning.

I don a cloak to ward off the chill of the air outside of this tent. "If I intend to be back after dark, I'll send word," I say as I stride for the exit.

Just as Jacin had promised, my horse has been saddled and stands, waiting, at the edge of camp to the north with its reins tied around an oak branch. When the steed spots me, it snorts and pads at the snowy ground with its hoofed foot.

"Good morning," I offer him, patting his warm side as I unravel the reins. Stepping onto a root that penetrates up through the ground, I hoist myself into the saddle and click my tongue, directing the horse further north.

The ride is cold. The harsh, whipping winds burrow beneath my cloak with each step and blow forward. I bend down and bring up the fabric to cover the lower half of my face as the stinging, icy air bites at my flesh. An hour passes and then two. Dawn ends, and the day begins in earnest as I finally spot the village Jacin had been referring to. We've only been here a handful of times over the past few months to replenish our supplies—and our other needs.

I steer my horse down a narrow forest path in the direction of the village's edge. The invigorated town is bustling when I arrive and I'm pleased to find that the rebel tribe obviously hasn't made it this far since the last time we'd been here. Perhaps Baron Chandrin's claim that their leaders had been taken into custody held some merit. Had they managed to get this far, I'd be far less forgiving. Involving civilians in our battles was the height of arrogance and wicked transgression.

Stabling the horse in a nearby public stall, I toss the man managing it a few coins and head across the street to an open tavern. I hadn't expected one to find one open this early in the morning, but as I walk through the double doors, I spot a man half-sprawled on the bar top with an empty glass at his side. A tired looking barmaid passes before me and gestures to the room.

"Sit where ya like," she says. "I've got some cleaning to do, but breakfast ain't ready so if ya want something to eat, y'll have to wait." I suppose 'open' was the wrong term to use. My gaze runs down to her plump bosom and then to the steady pulse thumping in her throat. My throat tightens.

"Understood." I give her a sharp nod and contemplate between any number of tables and the bar itself. It's an unspoken rule that no one person should take a table unless expecting company, but the man mumbling to himself against the bar is sitting squarely in the center of the row of stools. With a sigh, I take a seat at the furthest end, away from him and the entrance.

The bar top is riddled with scratches and old sweat rings from large mugs of mead and ale. I run a finger over a particularly deep groove that could not have been made by anything other than a blade. What drunken squirmish had caused such damage? The calluses on my hands catch against every dip and mark. A splinter sinks into my skin as the drunkard on the bar begins to sing a particularly lascivious bawdy tune of a maid who tips her skirts up at passing Lords.

When my life here comes to an end, I wonder, will my soul look much like this bar top? Will those I have killed leave me full of blemishes, not on the outside, but on the inside? How much of my life will scar my soul? If what Chandrin said is true, we will be returning home soon. I will find my way back to the Sunfire Palace. To the Princess whose mere existence has caused mine to feel so insignificant.

Swift as the tide, anger floods me. *Mine*, the monster that lurks under my skin, sings. *Never mine*, I snarl back. King Vernon forbade it and I am nothing if not a loyal dog of the crown. If I don't want to risk the position I have at her side, I will obey that damnable command. No matter how it hurts.

The drunkard stops singing and hiccups before I catch sight of his head whirling toward me out of my periphery. "Ay, d'you know that song?"

I look up, finding one startling blue eye and one deeply brown eye staring in my direction. "Excuse me?"

The drunkard rolls his shoulders back and lifts himself

off the countertop. His clothes are covered in a fine layer of dirt, the stains of various liquids—grease, oils, and dear Gods, is that blood? I sniff the air. Sure enough, the metallic hint of blood hits my nose. I narrow my eyes, but I have no reason to suspect that this man is anything other than perhaps a hunter. No doubt he makes his kills in the nearby forest and then sells them here in town.

I watch him carefully, still, though as he shifts back, wobbling from the sticky counter on the four-legged stool under his ass. There is a gray tint to his cracked lips and a bloodshot hue to his eyes, more noticeable in the lighter colored one, but in both nonetheless. Even at this distance, I can smell the liquor on his breath. Surprisingly enough, though, he appears young. Not old. I've never seen a drunkard so close to my own age, but here he sits.

"D'you know the name of tha' song?" he asks again in earnest.

I scan the room looking for anyone playing an instrument. Only the barmaid who carries empty glasses out from the kitchen and begins to place them upon the tables can be found. Alone, the two of us are utterly alone. The room around us is painfully quiet. I'd rather not talk to this man. He's far from my idea of a meal. I'd rather not ride back to camp drunk off my ass after indulging in his blood.

"What song?" The question comes out sharply. The ire in my voice is clear, but the man doesn't flinch. If anything, it brings a smile to his face. His teeth are remarkably straight for a man who looks as though he's come from the slums. They shine out of his dark skin with a brightness that's startling.

So he's not a peasant then ... likely someone who'd at least once in his life come from money. A fallen Noble?

"The song I was sing'n." To further his point, he begins

humming the tune again. He stops just as abruptly as he started. "D'you know it?"

With a sigh, I rap my knuckles against the counter, hoping for something to drown myself in sooner rather than later. "No." A simple answer and one I hope he takes at face value.

Instead, he launches into a new song, one different from the first. This one rolls over my ears with familiarity. He sings two and a half verses, his voice surprisingly even for someone who can hardly talk through his drunkenness when he's not adding a tune to his tone. "That one?" he asks, eyeing me.

I grit my teeth. Apparently, a one word answer is not what he desires. I turn away from him and glare at the glasses set upon the shelf behind the bar top. "It's a children's song," I say.

"Something about a butterfly and carefully keeping it in your hand so as not to crush it."

In the reflection of the glass across from me, I watch the man open his mouth only to be stopped as the barmaid appears a moment later. She sets a frothing cup in front of me. "If ya want food, it'll be 'nother hour or so," she says.

"Fine," I mutter, plucking a coin from my pocket and tossing it onto the countertop. She picks it up and marches away. I sip at the rim of the mug, letting the contents warm my belly.

"My nursemaid used to sing it to me," I mutter, further answering the drunkard's question.

"'Course she did!" The man slaps his hands against the wood and then proceeds to abandon his stool and scoot across the rest of them lined up until he's within my reach.

By the Gods, it was a bad choice to stop in here before heading off to find a drink of a different kind. I'll ignore the woman's comment about food being ready in an hour and as soon as I've finished this drink, I'll go in search of what I truly need.

"I'd forgotten, but now I remember. My mother sang it to me," he says, laughing with a burst of amusement that I don't quite understand. "Don't remember much of her before she was gone other than her voice. Beautiful. She sang like a bird." He lowers his head, pressing his cheek to the scarred bar top. A moment of blessed silence passes, but then it's interrupted as he bellows out the lullaby in a deep baritone.

I slam down the mug in my fist with a hard thud. "*Could. You. Not.*" The words cut out of my throat, both threatening and annoyed. The song comes to an abrupt end.

The man peels his face from the bar top, and the smile he wore moments ago is gone. "You look miserable," he comments. The slurring has abated. I don't know if he was perhaps not as drunk as I initially thought or if he'd been pretending. Why? Did he believe me an easy mark? I glance at his hands. I hadn't felt them sneak into my cloak. Not yet, anyway.

"You're one to talk." I narrow my gaze on him. Condensation collects like little droplets of starlight on the outside of my mug before dripping slowly down to dampen my hand. Unwrapping my hand, I shake away the droplets before grabbing the mug again and taking a long swig. "But I'm quite happy, can't you tell?" I bare my teeth.

All hint of drunkenness on his expression evaporates in the next instance. I find myself face to face with a man who's as serious as they come. Had all that singing been a ruse? Why? I have to wonder. "Your face says otherwise," he murmurs.

If it was a ruse, then it was none of my business. I turn away from him, grateful only for the lack of unwanted continued song coming from him. "That's just what my face looks like."

Perhaps, at one point in time it wasn't true. Like any child, I'd been carefree once, if only for a short while. The loss of such innocence comes upon everyone, though. It's what marks the ascension from boy to man. For me, it'd simply happened sooner than most. If I had to hazard a guess—if I cared to, that is, I'd say the same happened to him. The shadows that collect in those dual-colored eyes reflect a deep, aching sorrow and pain that I know I've seen before in my own mirror.

I don't ask what caused the man's shadows. I don't care to know. Instead, I take another long pull from my drink, watching the liquid swish in front of my nose and then drain down a little more with each gulp.

What was it that had turned me into this? This half-unfeeling monster. The meeting of my heart's mate and then the realization that she was forever out of my reach? Perhaps. It was likely after all. All of this started and ended with her, the Princess. The terrifying weight of what she means to me as well as the constant danger she will have to face in her life as the heir of Rozentine rests upon my shoulders like the heaviest of burdens. Now, here I sit, with an annoying non-drunkard as a man with half a heart. What little I have left is rapidly dying away.

Gods, I hate myself.

"That's unfortunate," the man pipes up again. "You might be handsome were it not for your unholy demeanor and suppressed rage."

Suppressed rage? I turn on him, my eyes narrowing one more. "What would you know about suppressed rage?" I grit out.

Groaning, he sits himself up and swings his legs over the opposite side of his stool. His joints pop as he folds his hands together and then stretches them upward and over his head. The leather of his boots squelches against the floor when he hops off the damned chair and stands to his full height.

Tall—though still not as tall as I. Warily, I let my gaze rove over his form. Wide-shouldered, strong jawed. I'd bet my entire coin pouch that he's got muscles beneath the fabric of his clothes, honed from long years of necessary survival. He's a bit too skinny to be a soldier, and his accent is every bit Rozentine, so definitely not of the Vitas Isle tribes. The set of his broad shoulders with his smaller waist tells me that he's seen more than his fair share of hardships. He has the sight of hunger gleaming in the depths of those oddly colored eyes. The tattered coat he wears hangs down over his shoulders and arms almost to the floor.

He sways on his feet, betraying the same hint of potential drunkenness from before. A ruse. Not a ruse. There's no point in trying to figure it out any longer. Even if this man attempted to attack me here and now, I'd have his neck snapped and his body draped over this bar in an instant.

The longer he lingers, the more my hopes of him disappearing from my sight wane. Finally, he comes around to the end of the bar and stumbles against it, folding his arms as he tilts his head at me. I repress an annoyed sigh.

"Now that I'm really looking at you, you look like a soldier," he says. The man jabs his finger into my shoulder.

Soldier. I snort. *If only he knew.*

"And you look like you've drunk yourself to the bottom of a barrel," I say without any further inflection.

"I'm only *half* drunk," he corrects me, and if his words are to be believed, then his earlier atrocious singing wasn't a ruse at all.

"What's the difference?" I mutter, not really intending

for him to answer as I say the words more to myself than to him and take another swig.

"There's a whole world of difference," he insists, throwing his hands wide. His knuckles smack the counter with an audible *thwump*.

I roll my eyes. "Sure," I say. There's no use trying to convince a crazy man. They believe in their own insanities and only they can understand themselves.

The hollows of the man's cheeks are particularly shadowed as the muscles all along his jaw tense and relax over and over again. He steps back against the edge of the counter and leans down, folding his arms over the lip of the bar top and rests his chin against them. He rolls his head to the side, watching me with his cheek plastered to his arm as if he can't keep his head straight.

I dislike his eyes. I take another drink and purposefully look elsewhere. His eyes have the sheen of a desperate, broken man. I know the look all too well. Seconds pass in near silence with the only sound of the barmaid and whoever else is toward the back of the tavern performing their morning duties. Finally, I lift my gaze and meet the man's.

Our eyes connect. My crimson ones to his blue and brown. "I thought Rozentine would be different," he confesses.

I set my mug down. "Different, how?" I find myself asking.

He stares back at me, but I have the distinct impression he's not seeing me at all. His eyes are hollow, fogged over with what I assume must be some image of what brought him here to this village near the edge of Rozentine and its borders to drown himself in drink. Not Vitas ... but I suppose perhaps not completely Rozentinian either. I wait for his answer.

"I thought it would allow *me* to be different," he says.

I hum in the back of my throat. There are only a few mouthfuls left of the drink before me and I already know I'm not going to request another when the barmaid comes back, not unless I can entice her into the back of the tavern and take a nip from her vein for some sustenance. My craving for blood, despite still sitting heavy in my belly and throat, has waned in the wake of this man's presence and confessions.

I'm no priest of the Gods. I'm certainly not who he should be coming to for advice. I, myself, have asked much of the same from a slew of others. My Uncle. My cousin. King Vernon. Then, I'd learned the truth that few men knew. No one was truly there for you the way you had to be for yourself. That's when I stopped asking for advice. If they brought it to me, fine. But I would no longer seek it out.

"No Kingdom can make you something you are not," I say quietly, diverting my attention to the rim of my mug. "It was foolish to think so."

"Yes, I guess you're right," the man replies. "Now, I have no home, no loyalty, and nothing left but a few coins and the ability to hunt for my meals. I could survive off of that…"

Physically, yes, I think to myself. He could survive. But he won't. Not with the hint of defeat that cling to his words. Those with that kind of sorrow don't know how to survive past losing the will to live. Something pangs in my chest, a guilty knife sliding between my ribs and curving an upward jab at my half-frozen heart.

He is none of your business, I tell myself. *Drink your damned drink and go find a blood donor.*

I fully intend to do just that, but as I gulp down one more mouthful of the liquid, I feel a faint sense of power skittering up my spine. Young. Untapped. Full of potential. I rarely find myself in the presence of an Awakened without knowing whose House they're from.

I glance to the door, but no one has come in and the barmaid and whoever else is at the back of the tavern can't possibly ... I refocus on the man next to me. Surely not ... him?

"Have you paid your tab?" *Stupid. Ridiculous.* I curse myself up and down silently. Yes. *Him.*

Without lifting his face, he shoves a hand into the pocket of his coat. A small coin slips out a hole in the bottom of it and clangs to the floor. I look down. When he doesn't bend to pick it up and instead pulls his hand free, I direct my attention to his tightly wrapped fingers. He opens his palm, revealing a handful of currency, mostly foreign, all of the coins dark with dirt. A rotten smell clings to them, as though he'd dug them all out of the bottom of a waste heap. He drops the coins on the counter, watching them spin until they stop.

As if hearing the sound of money, the barmaid peeks out from the back. I grit my teeth and add my own polished coin to the pile and then an extra because I doubt his will be enough. I doubt they'll be happy to take foreign currency. "Stand up," I order with a released breath.

His brows furrow but he does as he's told and unfolds himself from the bar top. He rises to his full height, and the clothes under his coat are smudged with as much dirt as the coins he'd set on the table. Around the knees of his trousers are even darker stains, as though he'd kneeled in a mud puddle. He scratches at his scalp, the tight coil of curls flattened with the movement.

Grabbing ahold of his arm, I abandon my unfinished drink and drag him from the tavern and out into the sunlight-strewn street. He blinks and turns his head down as if to shield his eyes. I pull him along, never letting go and never stopping until we round a corner into a deserted alley.

"Your name." It's not a question but a command. This is a terrible idea, I recognize, but I've already come this far, and it feels too late.

"Argyle Toussaint."

I hold out my hand. "Solomon Winett." He takes my hand, his brow creased with confusion. "If you don't know who you are and haven't become who you want to be," I say, releasing him after a moment, "then you should follow me." I stride around him and start walking.

"Where are we going?" Argyle calls out. I get to the end of the alleyway and look back to find that he's turned my way but hasn't yet followed. Still, the hollowness of his eyes has been replaced with a weary defensiveness, and that, I like.

"I know a soldier who's on the outs with his House. He knows others that have been in similar *positions* as you are," I say. That power wafts from him now in nervous waves. Yes, he's an Awakened, though, not completely yet. That will come later, I assume, when he's matured a bit more. "He can point you in the right direction to get your footing again."

"Oh, I don't know if I've ever had my footing," he says with a chuckle. Then, slowly, as if testing the truth of my words, he walks toward me, shoving his hands deep into his trouser pockets. "So, you are a soldier then?" he asks.

I tilt my head to the side. "Perhaps." A nonanswer, but the best he'll get from me.

"Quite a sacrifice, fighting for your Kingdom. You must really believe in Rozentine."

I'd sacrifice a lot for Rozentine, for the great line of the Goddess Aerea, whom my House is meant to serve, for the greater good. But the greatest sacrifice and my most loyal of hearts belongs to none other than the heir of this Kingdom. I already know what awaits me in the future, for there is more that I must sacrifice. What I feel for her will be buried along with my heart. The bond between us can only be leveraged for the betterment of Rozentine. So I must lay the strength of my feelings, the power of our souls' connection, at the feet of our country. Even if it will see me dead long before my body goes into the ground.

I lower my voice to a whisper. "Tell me, Argyle Toussaint, what do you know about Ravens?"

3
DEVONRY

7 years old...

The red banners with the burning phoenix are blurry as I pass them. I'm going so fast my skirts get caught between my legs and my hair tangles behind me. Sheza warned me to slow down, but my feet don't listen as I race through the halls. My slippers make me quiet, but Sheza's footsteps are loud behind me.

She sighs when I reach my mother's door, but I don't stop. The guardsman turns at the sound of my approach. His hand hovers at his hip for a moment before he recognizes me and he bows. The leathers he wears creak and groan when he stands up.

I've been so worried about my mother that it makes my chest hurt, but I'm so excited to see her now. *All will be well soon enough*, is what Sheza said. I hope so. She's never been wrong before.

Mother's door is so heavy, but I push into it with all my strength and it opens slowly, just enough for me to squeeze past it. I'm probably going to be in trouble later for barging into Mother's room, but I don't care. I want to see my mother. I need to see her.

My mother's room is always bright with sun in the morning and there's a cool breeze. I can smell the rose garden below, and I take a breath of it as I look for her. I blink. Underneath the smell of roses is something else, something bitter and salty.

"Devonry." My mother smiles when she speaks my name and the hurt in my chest feels better. Her red robe, with gold stitching, sparkles as she reaches out to me from her seat at the vanity.

"Gently," Sheza says in warning as she follows behind me.

But I'm already running to her and colliding into her open arms, curling around her and not wanting to let go.

It's been four days that I have not been allowed to see my mother. It feels like so much longer. Things in the palace were different when I couldn't see her. People came and went from her room all the time, but I couldn't. Strangers carrying cases who called themselves healers. I don't know why these men were any better than the healer who stays at the palace. Now, even when my father smiles, he looks worried.

She looks different, I think, noticing she's not as soft as she used to be as I squeeze her.

My tummy hurts with how strange she feels. I try to ignore it though, as I bury my face against her and lock my arms.

She runs a shaky hand through my hair, squeezing me so tight in return with her other arm. She smells like Father's soap, with the strong scent of patchouli, but there is still that other smell underneath, the salty, bitter one.

"Sheza said you wanted to do my hair," I say softly against her. "Are you feeling well again?"

The hand stroking my hair slows at my muffled question. "I am feeling well *today*."

Just today?

I pull away, even though I don't want to. I immediately miss her warmth and how comforting her touch is. Her eyes are pink and dark, but she's still the most beautiful person in the world. No one compares to my mother. Carefully, I pick up a few strands of her white-blonde hair and notice it looks thinner than it used to, but the softness reminds me and I straighten.

"Sheza taught me how to braid! Can I show you?" I ask, though I'm already dividing a section of her hair into thirds and passing the strands between my fingers. The hair at the base of her neck is wet, but I don't say anything.

She'll be proud, I know it. Mother always loves when I learn something new. The more I know, the better I can one day keep the peace without lifting a weapon, just as she has.

Her laugh turns into a cough, but she nods her head, seeming just as excited to see as I am to show her. Her eyes are big as I twist the strands of her hair making a braid down to her waist. "My sweet girl, what a beautiful talent you have already." She runs her fingers over the braid and I beam at her words. "Now, it is my turn. May I?"

I nod and turn to give her my back. My hair is only just past my shoulders, but I hope for it to be as long as Mother's one day.

I swear I brushed her hair before we came." Sheza chuckles as she sits down in one of Mother's reading chairs.

"A bit excited this morning? Was it your pitter-patter of feet I heard coming so swiftly down my hall?" Mother coos.

"A bit too excited," Sheza adds and my cheeks heat.

"I'm sorry, I shouldn't have been running in the halls." I lower my chin, digging my teeth into my lower lip while Mother works a brush through my hair.

"Don't worry too much, my dear. Rule-breaking is in our blood. For what can be changed if it is not first challenged and tested? A stagnant ruler is not one who builds a thriving Kingdom."

I will never be a stagnant ruler, I swear to myself, then ask, "What does stagnant mean?"

Mother hums for a moment before speaking. "To be stagnant is to be standing still. It is the absence of growth and betterment." She pauses. "Are you often a rule breaker, Devonry?" Mother asks, her words more quiet than before.

I shrug, not sure how to answer. "I try to follow most rules. Solomon says that's my job as a Princess, but sometimes he breaks the rules with me." I pause, panic suddenly making my throat tight. "But don't tell, Father. Solomon will get in trouble."

She sets the brush on the vanity, her fingers parting my hair gently before she speaks again. "You and Solomon are good friends."

I dip my head in agreement. "Solomon is nice to me but not in the same way other people are nice to me. I think he actually means it. I really like when we get to play together too. When I'm with him..." I twist my hands together trying to find the words to describe what it's like to be around him. "When I'm with him, I'm happy. My body feels jittery, like there are a bunch of little bugs under my skin ... but in a good way, not a scary way. Like the bugs are supposed to be there."

Sheza sits forward in the seat, her attention moving from me to Mother. Did I say something wrong? Will I get Solomon in trouble? Worry has me grinding my teeth.

"Oh?" Mother leans toward me, planting a small kiss on my cheeks before she moves to braid the other half of my hair. "So you like Solomon very much?"

"Yes, but I don't think I'm supposed to," I admit, "Father frowns if we play together too much."

"You know, it's okay for you to like him." She hums a moment as she finishes the braid before she spins me to face her again. "Solomon has and will always like you back."

My heart does a little dance in my chest. A fresh wave of warmth passes over my chest and face at the very idea that Solomon may like me in the way I think I like him. But it can't be true, can it? Sometimes Solomon gets upset at me when I run off and he has to drag me back. Father will look at him with those upset brows, and then Solomon acts as though playing with me is beneath him.

"Really?" I smile up at her.

She runs her fingers along my face, tipping my chin up further. "Really. Did you know there is a story of our Goddess Aerea and her love of Levim, who birthed the House of Blood? They sacrificed a great deal to be together. It is in our very nature to be bonded to the descendants of Levim and them to those who came from Aerea."

I've heard these stories before. In some stories, Levim sacrifices himself to save Aerea. Others say that neither of them passed, and their love for each other binds them to their bloodlines so that they can be reborn and finally be together like they're supposed to be.

"I think when I grow up, I want to marry him. Then we can be like you and Father. Even if I never Awaken, everything will be okay as long as he is with me." Pulling my shoulders back, I stand taller knowing Mother says it's okay.

"You are a long way away from marriage." She chuckles, but the sound becomes rough. Her breathing sounds funny, like she needs to cough, and then she does, violently. All I can do is stare as she brings her hand to her mouth to catch the sound. Her body shakes and I plant my hand on her leg hoping it's of some comfort.

When she pulls her hand away, she looks down at her palm before closing her fingers tightly and looking up to Sheza with an expression I've never seen on her face before. Fear? But that can't be because my mother isn't afraid of anyone or anything. She's the strongest person I know.

With just the one look I don't understand, Sheza is off her feet and taking my wrist in her hand. Her fingers are tight, not allowing any give as she tugs me toward the door.

"You look darling, my Princess. We must be off now for your lessons before you're late." Sheza's too strong and drags my unmoving feet easily over the tiles.

"But—" I start, flinching when Mother coughs again, her body bending in half.

She takes a breath that makes a terrible wheezing noise. "Have a good day, Devonry, I love you." Her parting words are a whisper, but I cling to the sound of her voice even as her door closes behind us.

4
DEVONRY

Present Day…

In my twenty years in this life, I never *ever* would have expected to find myself—*me*, a Royal Princess and Queen of Rozentine—hiding from soldiers in a brothel. The sharp scent of burning sage and the smoky hue that surrounds us makes my nostrils twitch and my eyes burn, but I maintain my dignity as best I can. Cupping my hands over my lips and nose, I hunker down further behind a pile of crates as the woman in the doorway coos to the soldiers passing by.

"I can show you a good time, handsome," she calls out. "You can come see me after your shift, can't you?"

"No, madam." The soldier's response is direct and cold—very much like Solomon's I imagined were he in the same situation. Unfortunately, Solomon isn't here. If he were, he'd likely have thought of a better plan than hiding in a rank smelling room where the sage is desperately trying to cover up the scent of sex. "Now, I'll ask again. Have you seen this man or woman?"

The crinkling of paper as it's waved in front of the woman's face sounds and I hear her puff out a breath of exasperation. "Ugh, I already told you no." She lies easily, her tone sounding more put out by his rejection than I imagine she actually is. Had the soldier taken her up on the offer, we would be in a very different predicament. "If you're not going to sponsor my establishment, then shoo. My girls and I have work to do."

I peek my head over the top crate, making sure the cloak's hood remains over my hair, to see the soldier roll up the paper, nod at her, and then stride away. Only when the woman steps back and slams the door do I release a sigh of relief.

"You can come out now," Rita calls out. "He's gone."

My head rises above the crate entirely. "Are you sure?" I ask. "What if he comes back?"

Her beautiful red-painted lips twist. "A man like that?" She scoffs. "Doubtful. Too sanctimonious. I bet he's never even bedded a woman." Her coal-lined eyes glance down to her bountiful breasts that look as if they're ready to pop out of her corset at any moment. "No one can resist these. Perhaps he prefers male company." She taps one finger on her chin. "Yes, that would make more sense."

I sigh, letting her muse to herself as I direct my gaze back to the *other* problem at hand and the reason that both Solomon and Argyle are away at the moment. Bending down, I press the back of my hand to Celine's face. Sweat clings to her reddened cheeks and forehead. She groans lightly, curling into herself.

Two weeks at sea hadn't been nearly as bad as the sudden epidemic that seems to be sweeping through the coastal cities of Rozentine. Rita rounds the crates and frowns at Celine's prone form. "I can't keep her here if she's got the plague," she snaps.

"She doesn't have a plague," I reply sharply. "It's just a bit of influenza."

Rita narrows her gaze on first me and then Celine before humming in the back of her throat. "You know the only reason I even let the two of you stay here is because of Argyle," she says. "If he's not back by the end of the day, you'll have to find somewhere else to hide."

I repress the urge to hurl obscenities at the woman, reminding myself that she is, in fact, offering us sanctuary based on nothing but Argyle's good word—whatever use that is. Then again, it must be decently useful since he's managed to keep us hidden for the last several days upon our return to the Rozentine borders and ever since Celine began showing symptoms of this strange epidemic within days of us landing. The problem now is finding our way to Lord Frederic's territory and then devising a plan to take back the Kingdom with as few casualties as possible.

Too many people have already lost their lives as a result of what I now call the Bloody Night—the night my father was murdered and Solomon and I were sent on the run. I can't lose anyone else. Which means I have to be particularly careful about how I go about getting back into the Sunfire Palace after the fiasco that ended my relationship with my enemy's brother—as it stands, The Bartoli Empire is no longer an allied nation with Rozentine. In my eyes, they're just as bad as Nasir.

"Argyle will be back," I say quietly, gently shaking Celine awake and urging her onto her feet. "As will Solomon. For now, is there a room we can hide in that's further from the street?"

Rita blinks blandly at me before sighing and then shoving her way through another open doorway, draped in moth-eaten fabrics and faded silks that, maybe once, long ago, had been extravagant and expensive. Now, though, they're so thin and worn that they wouldn't even be used as dish rags.

"D-don't worry about me, Y-Your High—" I quickly cover Celine's mouth with my hand. I still don't know how much this woman knows. I doubt Argyle has confessed my identity to her, and with Celine half delirious from her fever, there's no doubt she doesn't realize her mistake. As if to support that thought, a shudder works through her and her teeth begin to chatter behind my palm.

"None of that, Celine," I urge her quietly, lifting one arm over both of my shoulders as I help her shuffle after the woman housing us.

Celine must really be out of it because instead of insisting, she merely nods and sags against me. Together, the two of us manage to get through the doorway and into what looks like a storage room full of more crates, though these ones are actually packed high with things—such as faded dresses and musky-smelling sheets. The ones out in the main room had likely been meant to be thrown out as they'd been empty.

"Do you have any water?" I ask as I gently help Celine lower herself to the ground in a corner of the room. "Surely you have a bathing room somewhere in here?" Dust coats half of the objects as well as most of the floor. It can't be the best place for a sick person, but it's what we've got. The least I can do is try to clean it up in the hopes that Celine doesn't get any worse.

Rita snorts from where she still stands in the open doorway. "You must be an ex-Noble," she says before jerking her thumb over her shoulder. "There ain't no bathing room in this place. If you want to wash or grab water, you'll have to go pull it up from the well out back yourself."

I contemplate that. While I don't like the idea of

leaving Celine in here by herself, I also can't conceive of trying to get her better in a room so filthy. Rita's expression when I turn to face her is one of cold amusement. Yes, I suppose she would think of me as an ex-Noble. As it stands, I have virtually no common knowledge that those of the lower classes would have. I try not to let it show that I'm shocked by the lack of a washroom in the building and merely give her a succinct nod.

"Thank you. I'll do that."

She eyes me for a moment more, shifting against the doorframe before rolling her eyes, turning around, and flouncing away. I release a sigh and return my attention to Celine. As it stands, she's fallen back into her feverish exhaustion, slumped right where she is. Glancing from her to the stacked crates, I decide to make her a pallet on the floor to lie on. The soldiers have already passed by this place and no doubt they're not going to search inside. No one would ever expect me to be here. It shouldn't be too dangerous to air out a few of the sheets in the crates and bring in a bucket of water.

With nothing else to do for her, I leave Celine where she is and get to work. I pick through the crates, grab a few of the thicker sheets and blankets, and cart them through the downstairs of the brothel and out into the courtyard out back to beat them free of the dust. I let them soak in the warmth of the sun as they hang over the ledge that divides the courtyard between the other three buildings that back it.

In the center sits the well that Rita had mentioned earlier. An old wooden bucket with a metal band holding it together rests against its stone side. Hurrying toward it once I'm done with the blankets, I toss the bucket down into the darkness of the well's hole and wait until I hear it hit the water below with a sloshing *plop* before I drag it back up.

With a bucket of water in one hand and the marginally cleaner sheets under the other arm, I hobble back into the slanting wood and white brick building. Sweat coats the back of my neck, sliding down my spine under my cloak and dress.

Celine is in much the same position when I return, her face still flushed and her chest rising and falling in rapid beats where she leans against the wall. Hurriedly dropping the bucket of water inside the doorway, I haul the blankets over to a corner of the room and lay them out. I stack a few into piles, twisting and folding them toward the head of the makeshift bed before standing and removing my cloak.

Even with the extra fabric off of my body, I still feel overwhelmingly hot. I ignore the discomfort and go back to where Celine lies propped against the wall and rouse her from her slumber. "Come on," I urge her, grabbing one of her arms and pulling it over my shoulders. "I've got a bed set up for you. Can you stand?"

Celine jerks in my arms and moans in what I assume is discomfort. Her eyelids lift slowly as if they're weighed down by thousands of pounds and she peers back at me, unseeingly. I force a smile I don't feel, hoping she can't sense my mounting worry. "Try to get your feet under you," I order, pulling her up and away from the wall.

Her weight slams into me, nearly sending the both of us toppling in the opposite direction. I plant my feet and halt the impending crash. Another moan echoes out of her throat, sounding drier and drier each time. With gritted teeth, I help her get to her feet and we stumble the last few steps to the pallet on the floor in the corner of the room where I lay her own.

Once she's down on the relatively softer ground, Celine promptly passes back out. A part of me envies her that ability right now, though I'm sure she wouldn't agree. She's far too fastidious for that. Sweat clings to her face, making the darker strands of her brown hair at the edges of her face curl into tiny corkscrews.

A single slit of a window sits horizontally above the pallet I've made on the floor. Hopefully, it'll provide a bit more airflow for Celine when I get her into place. I grab the bucket I'd brought in with me and carry it closer, finding a semi-clean rag amidst the stuff in the crates and dip it inside. With careful and gentle strokes, I wipe Celine's face and neck. Pulling her hair away from her skin, I braid it and set it to the side so that the strands don't cling to her. If I had more strength, I'd even try to rouse her back from sleep and get her to wash a bit, but I don't know when Argyle or Solomon will return and I wouldn't want anyone walking in on her in any state of undress.

Instead, I wait for the time to pass by cleaning up the room we're in. I move several of the crates to the furthest side of the room, stacking them against the wall instead of in piles throughout the room. I grab a few more clothes, shake them out, and try to mop the dirt and grime from the floor, starting where Celine lies sleeping and moving outward.

Hours pass like that until there's nothing left for me to do and my muscles are sore. Without medicine to counteract the effects of Celine's illness, I'm forced to wipe her down repeatedly. I collapse against the wall at Celine's side and stare at the light from the window above us as it slowly rises up the wall and then disappears entirely.

The day is over, but Rita doesn't come back. I suppose her earlier threat to kick us out if Argyle wasn't back by the end of the day was just that … a threat, and an empty one at that. To say I'm relieved would be an understatement. Even with that minor anxiety assuaged, though, I find myself unable to sleep.

Outside, the bustling of people grows louder. Not surprising considering we're in what many would consider the red-light district. Lamps glow in reds and whites outside of the window. The deep rumble of drunken voices and cooing women echoes from the other side of the walls —even though we're a bit further from the street than before.

Lights illuminate on the other side of the doorway as many women who were previously sleeping before—or entertaining their daytime guests—have risen to work the night. Once the sun is gone and darkness consumes the room, I find a hidden half-used candle in one of the crates, and set it next to me, and use my ability to make a flame bloom to life. As it flickers, casting monstrous shadows on the wooden walls, I lean against a crate and sigh.

Waiting, I find, is an impossible task made possible only by the fact that once you start, there is no stopping. I only hope Argyle and Solomon don't torture us with it for much longer.

5
SOLOMON

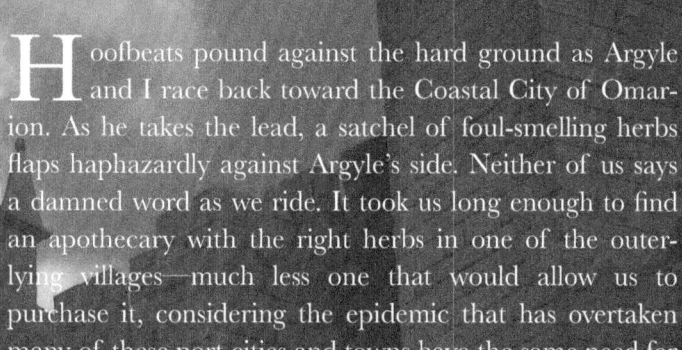

Hoofbeats pound against the hard ground as Argyle and I race back toward the Coastal City of Omarion. As he takes the lead, a satchel of foul-smelling herbs flaps haphazardly against Argyle's side. Neither of us says a damned word as we ride. It took us long enough to find an apothecary with the right herbs in one of the outerlying villages—much less one that would allow us to purchase it, considering the epidemic that has overtaken many of these port cities and towns have the same need for them that we do.

The moon rises higher into the night sky as the two of us come to a grinding halt over a cliffside that peers into Omarion. Little pebbles flick over the edge, clacking down the cliffside as dust kicks up against the hooves of our horses. In the near distance, I spot the quartette of tall buildings surrounding a small courtyard close to the slums. It's far to the back of the small city, further from the ocean, but not so far that the scent of seawater doesn't still permeate the air. My stomach tightens with displeasure.

Forcing Devonry to take refuge in such places curls vicious blades of distaste in my gut.

"Almost there," Argyle says, panting hard enough that the edges of his mouth are strained and sweat beads his dark brow. His back is as ramrod straight as any soldier looking out over a battlefield, but the tension in his body mirrors my own. Concern. Worry. It's all etched there in his face, shadowed by a slight beard that has been growing for several days. "Let's keep going." I twist my head and look at him—at the stoic, emotionless mask he's worn since that first night we arrived in Rozentine. The night that had been plagued with Celine's low, wet coughs. Were I him and were it Devonry in Celine's place, I'd be much the same.

Without another word, we both turn our horses back to the path ahead. I offer my silent agreement with his words by way of kicking the animal into a fast-paced clip. He follows and soon enough, we're down the twisting hillside pathway and back into the city of Omarion, taking the side streets as fast as we're able and avoiding the night crowd for the most part until we reach the red-light district.

Argyle jumps from his horse before me. He practically rips the herbs from their ties on the satchel and hands the reins over as he lifts his head. "I'll meet you there," is all he manages to get out before he takes off running down the street and into the crowd of men smelling of liquor and women with more skin showing than clothes.

I blow out a breath. As much as I want to return to Devonry's side, I can understand his haste. Devonry isn't the one ill. So, I let him go without argument and slide off of my own horse, taking both by the reins as I lead them to the stables at the end of the row of tall wood and stone buildings that are half-slanting and dilapidated.

Stabling the horses and tossing the man at the entrance more than enough coin for the night, I hurry down the street and slip into the side entrance of the brothel we'd left the girls in earlier today. The place, although not one I've ever patronized, is close enough to the coast, well built amongst the stacks of other ramshackle red-light district businesses, and inconspicuous enough to blend into the rest of the slums, that it hadn't been too far to travel once Celine had begun showing severe symptoms of the disease. That, combined with Argyle's subtle working relationship with the owner, is the only reason I'd felt secure enough to leave them unattended.

Prostitutes stumble up and down the back stairway in various manner of dress as I step inside. Some have bruises and keep their heads down, eyes away from ours, but several more grin and prop their hands on their hips as they offer sly smiles and heavy breaths that heave up their breasts against their plunging necklines. I bypass them without a second glance and trail Argyle's wide back. What patience either of us had has waned through the day and become nonexistent.

The smell of the herbs Argyle carries with him filters back to me as he takes a staircase up to the first floor, turns down a long corridor, and then takes a second staircase to another lower floor facing the opposite street. Our booted steps grow softer and quieter as we slow down and reach a back room. Both Argyle and I cast a look to either side before spotting an open doorway with hung fabrics and a low feminine voice beyond.

He doesn't look back, but he also doesn't hesitate as he moves for it, disappearing within. The moment I step inside behind him, ducking beneath the hanging fabrics, I finally feel my heart begin to calm. In the corner, a familiar pale face surrounded by varying lengths of strawberry blonde hair peers back at us. She spots Argyle and quickly scoots away from the body she's sitting alongside—the woman she'd been softly murmuring to.

Argyle leans over a pallet laid out on the floor, and as he begins to talk in a quiet, gentle tone I've rarely heard from him, Celine's eyes crack open and gaze up at him. My attention drifts back to the woman I'd been worried about the whole time I'd been gone. Devonry's eyes meet mine, and as quietly as she's able, she rises to her feet and skirts around Argyle and Celine to get to me.

I inhale sharply at the glimmer of fear and concern that penetrates from the dim blue-hazel of her eyes. I open my arms and she burrows against my chest immediately, letting me pull her close in an effort of comfort. These last few weeks fleeing Bartoli and returning to Rozentine only to be met with this awful plague have been more than dampening on our hopes. Yet, in this moment, I can't deny that the warmth and scent of her cools the worst of my lingering apprehension. It feels right to have her against my side. Her body fits perfectly, and the scent of her erases the sour smell of the herbs Argyle is currently crushing up on the other side of the room.

"Come," I say, pulling Devonry back toward the open doorway. "Let's give them some space."

Her head lifts and she glances over her shoulder once more. She senses it too. She must. After all, it's becoming increasingly obvious—the care and spark of interest between Argyle and Celine has slowly grown over the last few weeks. Instead of commenting, however, she dutifully follows me out of the room, through the next, down a darkened hallway, and out into the courtyard backing the buildings nearby. Overhead, clouds clutter the ebony skies, only their edges visible in the moonlight.

"So," she begins, voice tight, "is it…?" She trails off as if she doesn't even want to verbalize the possibility, but I know what she's asking. She wants to know if Celine has contracted the strange disease that's permeated the coastal cities of Rozentine.

I cup my hand over her shoulder and shake my head. "I don't think so. It's similar, but from the looks of it—she hasn't gotten any worse since we left. Those who've contracted this new disease are usually dead within days. She would have gone downhill quite rapidly."

Devonry breathes a sigh of relief and I hope that my words are truthful. As far as we know—from what information Argyle and I managed to glean from nearby towns and the apothecaries we visited—this disease is like nothing anyone has seen before. It's entirely possible that this could be a different strain. We won't know, though, until Celine reacts to the herbs. If she gets better, then all will be well, and if she doesn't ... well, even I don't want to consider that possibility.

"This is going to interrupt our journey to Frederic's territory, isn't it?" Devonry asks, and though I'm sure she already knows the answer, I still nod.

"While Argyle was getting the medicine," I say, "I sent a messenger to the Caladrius territory. Gods willing, we will hear back within a fortnight."

Cloudy blue eyes peer up at me from beneath dark blonde lashes. "Do you think it'll take that long?" she asks.

"I hope not," I answer, "but we have to keep in mind that with the soldiers scouring the country for us, messenger routes may have been compromised. The message I sent was under a pseudonym, but Frederic is a smart man. He'll understand who it's from." *If he receives it, anyway.* But I don't say as much. I don't want to worry her more than she already is.

Devonry blows out a low breath and steps away from me to reach up and rub her thumb between her brows. In the dim lighting of the courtyard, her choppy waves appear darker around her face. For a moment, my vision blinks from normal to the black and white of my Bloodlust and her hair transforms from a muddle of reddish-blonde to a bright ruby color. I blink again and my normal vision returns.

Shaking my head, I scrub a hand down my face. I must be more tired than I thought.

"You must be tired," I say. "I think after we've waited enough time, we can go back in and see about crashing for the evening."

"Honestly?" Devonry leans back and groans as she stretches, her arms arching up over her head as she laces her fingers together. "I'm exhausted, but I'd rather have a bath than sleep. I feel filthy." She drops back down and looks pointedly at the marks on her hands and forearms. "I tried cleaning that room as much as I could while I waited for you to get back. I didn't think it'd be good for Celine if she was sleeping in a room filled with that much dust."

I consider her words. A sharp ache stabs at my chest. I know it for what it is. It's guilt. I think back to the route Argyle and I had taken to the towns surrounding Omarion. I distinctly remember passing a river that had led up from the city. I'm sure if we follow it enough, there's bound to be a section secluded from the rest. Though I'd love nothing more than to take her to a bathhouse, we're low on funds—relying on Argyle's connections to keep us safe for the night. A river bath will simply have to do.

"Come with me," I say, reaching out and snagging her arm. Devonry stumbles a little bit as I pull her forward, but soon enough she's striding at my side, following me willingly. Enough so that I drop her arm and let her trail me more naturally as I lead her from the courtyard and back into the storage rooms of the brothel. I stop her before she enters the room with Celine and Argyle. "Wait here."

"But—" Her wide, confused gaze peers up at me, but I don't give her a chance to finish. I disappear into the room, finding her cloak and grabbing it. In the corner, Argyle is seated with his back to the wall and Celine propped on his chest as he feeds her herbs and water from the bucket alongside the pallet I suspect Devonry had made.

"I'm taking Devonry out," I inform him. "We'll be back by morning."

Argyle hardly looks up from Celine, but when he does, his brow is creased with exhaustion and concern. His one blue eye glitters like a light in the near darkness of the room. "As long as she's well by dawn, we'll leave for the next place," he replies. "I want to get the fuck away from the coast as fast as we can."

I pause and sigh. "You know there's no outrunning an epidemic, my friend," I say. "But if it eases your concern, we will get her to Caladrius and we will get her well."

Argyle turns his attention back to the woman in his arms. "Yes," he agrees. "We will." As if that's the only outcome he'll accept.

With that, I leave the room and snatch up Devonry's hand as I do. The sound of her rushing footsteps echo up to my ears as she hurries to catch up and meet the pace I've set. "Solo?" She tugs back on my hand, but I keep going, dragging her out of the brothel and down an alleyway where I sling her cloak around her and flip up the hood before taking her hand again.

"Solo!" she tries again. "What's wrong? Where are we going?"

I don't answer. I'm in too much of a rush to be away from the prying eyes of those on the streets of the red-light district. Cooing women and rambunctious men cackling echo into the air all around us. I feel the skin over my back tighten more and more. It isn't until we reach the stables that I feel even a margin of relief.

Devonry has since seemed to give up on getting me to talk. With a frustrated scowl on her face, she allows me to pull her along and even help lift her into the saddle of my horse. Though she's gotten proficient at riding herself, I leave Argyle's horse behind in case he needs it. Gripping the front of the saddle and hooking my foot into the stirrup, I swing my body behind Devonry's.

Immediately, she leans back into my chest. My heartbeat speeds up. So instinctive. So easy. A thick knot forms in my throat. The line between us has already been crossed, but neither of us has truly discussed what it means. The way her body naturally falls in tune with my own makes me hopeful. Curving my hand around her waist, I yank her back harder still, earning a gasp from her lips.

Her head pivots and blue eyes glare up at me. I fight the urge to grin as I spread my palm over her lower belly—letting her feel my heat—and kick the horse into a clip that leads us out of the stables and down the street. The repetitive back and forth of the horse's movements makes me imperceptibly aware of the rounded ass against my groin.

Soon, I promise myself. *Very soon.*

There's no doubt in my mind that this bath Devonry's requested will lead to something more. And if she doesn't have an inclination yet, she will realize by the time we arrive as my resistance to her scent and the feel of her cushioned backside rubbing on my cock wanes. After all, I am only a man, and Argyle's apprehension over Celine's illness has made me need her all the more tonight—if only to assure myself that she's well.

6
DEVONRY

Solo remains quiet as he directs the horse further away from the city and up into the treeline that sits above it. He sits like a statue at my back, as solid and unmoving as stone. The only difference between him and a relic is the warmth of his beating heart that races against my spine. I've long since given in to whatever he plans and find myself leaning into his broad chest, relaxing as I let him take the lead. He makes it so easy to let go sometimes. I know I can trust him to take care of me, and so my mind takes a break and I let my thoughts wander.

Over the course of events that have led us to where we are now. My father's death. My journey to the Bartoli Empire. Escaping Enver. Each and every event has resulted in Solo and I being placed right here where we are now. I wonder, briefly, if I had made one choice differently, would we still have ended up here? Would I have still given him my virginity? Would I be back in Bartoli, married to Enver? Would I have been captured by Nasir? There are so many 'what ifs' that it's dizzying.

The tension in Solo's body is what draws me out of my

thoughts. More than that, it's also the hardness pressing against the curve of my ass and my lower back. I blink and hazard a glance back.

"Solo?"

His face remains trained forward and his jaw practically pulses with tightness.

Oh. Oh! Heat begins to arch up my throat, reaching for my face and I quickly face forward once more. The horse clomps onward and neither Solo nor I say another word. I can't. The words are stuck in my throat, along with the unerring knowledge that something else is bound to happen tonight. My stomach does little flips, anticipation and guilt warring within me. I want him, but at the same time, it feels wrong to steal a little piece of time for ourselves with everything happening.

The further from the city we get, the darker it grows. Once we're in the forest, scant moon rays peeking in through the overhead branches light our way. My heart pounds inside my chest, a fidgety thing. I swallow down the emotions, fears, and desires building inside of me, only releasing them on a long breath when Solomon's horse finally slows its steps and Solo steers him off the beaten path.

He jumps down first, reaching back, and though a part of me wants to insist I can get down myself, I let him take me by the waist—his wide hands as hot as ever on my sides—and help bring me slowly to the ground. My body slides against his, the feel of our chests rubbing against each other has me catching my breath and, for a moment, after my feet touch the dirt, I'm held suspended. I don't want to move away.

I tip my head back and this time, Solo looks back at me. The dark streaks of his hair falling over his forehead throw shadows down over the crimson eyes I know are there. The slender beams of light that pierce the darkness only illuminate the lower half of his face and parts of his body—his shoulder, his chest, his hip. My attention trails down, fixating on the expanse of chest hidden behind fabric and leather, a chest that had warmed my back as we rode. My lips part. "What are we doing?" I ask.

"You said you wanted to bathe," he replies gruffly.

I glance around us. "So you brought me to the forest?" I counter. "I know I've grown used to 'roughing it' as Argyle puts it, but *really*?"

His lips twitch. "You'll see," he promises, taking a step back and grabbing ahold of the horse's reins to lead the creature further into the darkness. As Solomon leaves me, my body sways toward his retreating back. I catch myself and ball my hands into fists, giving him a head start as I watch him walk away through the peering moonlight above us. Once he's a few yards ahead and out of my immediate reach, I follow him.

My feet move quietly through the underbrush. I've grown accustomed to walking through nature like this, but I still feel almost naked without the bow and arrow I've gotten so used to carrying with me on my back. It, along with the rest of our supplies, I suspect, are back in the stables with Argyle's horse. After all, if Solomon is here, I don't really have need for it. Even if I do have to fight out here though, I have my fire now.

That reminder has me lifting my hand and conjuring a small flame to the center of my palm, holding it before me to help guide my steps. Ahead, Solo pauses and glances back for a brief moment. As I march toward him, he turns and hooks the reins of the horse onto a nearby branch, tying it around the tree with enough give for the horse to be able to bend down if it needs.

"This way," Solo calls, not waiting for me to catch up

to him before he pivots and disappears between two leaning trees that smell of moss and oak. I curse and scramble after him.

The fire in my palm extinguishes as I dive between the trees and come out on the other side, nearly falling down a slope at the sudden incline of the ground beneath my feet. Two thick arms come around me, lifting me off my feet, and cradle me against a familiar chest.

"Careful." Solo's voice lowers. "You wouldn't want to fall and break your pretty regal neck."

A snort escapes my nostrils, but I reach up and link my arms around his neck as he carries me down the hill toward what sounds like a bubbling stream. "Sometimes, I wonder if you wouldn't like to see that," I reply. "I've become enough of a hassle for you."

"You've always been a hassle," Solo replies, the sound of his voice soft but amused.

Even if he is teasing me just to elicit a reaction, I can't help but give in. Pulling one hand from his neck, I slap his chest. "Ass."

His only response is to keep walking and the two of us settle into a comfortable silence as I let him carry me down the slope until we reach a river as wide as a street. Bits and pieces of the still water shine and reflect the moonlight. From the trees and boulders poking up out of the surface along the edge, too, it's deep enough to bathe in. The arm beneath my legs slides away, allowing my feet to touch rock and dirt as my body sways back into Solomon's chest. He places both hands on my shoulders and gives me a careful nudge toward the stream.

"Go," he orders. "Bathe. I'll keep watch."

I hesitate. Not because I don't want a bath, but because I don't want him to step back into the dark and 'keep watch.' My mouth suddenly dries up. My tongue swells until I fear it's going to choke me. As he turns to walk away, I spin on my heel and snag onto the sleeve of his jacket, stopping him in his tracks.

Silence echoes all around us, filled only by the night underbrush creatures—skittering here and there as they dash through bushes and the current of the river at our backs. I lick my dry lips and swallow roughly. Before I can get a single syllable out, though, Solomon speaks.

"Devonry." My name is a warning on his tongue. "If you know what's good for you, you'll let me go."

I cough out a quiet laugh. "What's good for me?" I repeat the phrase. How funny it is. "I thought Nasir was good for me. I thought Bartoli and Enver were good for me. "I think we both know I don't know what is good for me anymore." So, I'll take what I know to be bad for me. I'll take it and hope to the Gods that I'm right this time.

Slowly, so excruciatingly slowly, Solo turns back to me and as I gaze up into his angled face, the red of his eyes glows brighter. "What do you want, Devonry?" he asks.

I dip my head, staring at the shadows at our feet. "I..." I want a lot of things that I know I shouldn't. I want a lot of things that are impossible tasks. But most of all, I want a break. I want this moment. "Solo ... I—"

My words are cut off as his finger touches the underside of my chin and tips my head. My heart races inside my skin, fluttering like the beating wings of a bird getting ready to take flight.

"Whatever it is," Solo begins, leaning down so I can feel the hot rush of his breath over my face, "I'll give it to you. All you have to do is ask and it's yours."

Tipping my head back further, I stare up into the illumination of his red gaze. Slowly, purposefully, I reach up and undo the drawstring ties of my corset—a commoner's corset, I've learned is far less restrictive. It takes no time at all for me to loosen the ties and slide them off my form, tossing the fabric over a nearby rock.

Solomon's hands drop away, but his eyes are locked on me. Unable to leave my form, I assume, with no small amount of pride. I continue to make my way backward, undoing the rest of my clothes as I go, toeing off my boots until I'm completely and utterly nude before him. My heart beats faster, as if it could burst from my chest and run away.

"Devonry." Solo's voice is gruff. Hoarse.

I step into the water, not stopping until I'm almost up to my waist. Only then do I lift my hand and wave him forward. "Join me, Solo," I say, pleased that my voice doesn't betray my nerves. "I'm sure you're as tired and coated in sweat as I am."

Solo doesn't speak as he stares back at me. His gaze is piercing. Hungry. The red swirling in misty circles as he watches me. A beat passes and then another and another. The silence is broken when he finally curses in a low voice —almost to himself—and then begins to divest himself.

Sinking further into the water and shivering at its chill, I watch, enrapt, as Solo reveals the lines of his muscles inch by inch. He drags the stained tunic he wears over his head, ruffling the dark curls at the top before tossing it on top of my corset. His hands move to the ties of his breeches and my breath hitches. My insides flutter.

Even in the moonlit space we're in, I'm able to see the dips and curves of his abdomen. The shadows play with my mind as he shifts, half turning and drops his trousers. I'm graced with the solid line of his side profile. My hands itch to touch him, to run my palms up the expanse of his chest and then down ... down ... until I—I cut that thought off and whirl around, swallowing as I try to tamp down the fire in my bloodstream. Want and need are twins that slither through me, burning me up from the inside. But really, is now the right time? The water ripples with my sharp turn, flowing and sliding around my legs and lower belly.

Is this a mistake? The thought penetrates my mind a split second before the sound of water splashing at the edge of the stream reaches my ears, letting me know he's entering. *Even if it is,* I think, *it's too late now.*

I turn back just in time for Solomon's waist to disappear beneath the surface of the water and release a breath that I hadn't realized I'd been holding. Solo tracks me through the river, eyes set on me. I tip my head back as he approaches and once more, we're pressed chest to chest. Breath to breath.

"Now what, Princess?" The corner of his mouth curves up as he asks his question. My title sounds like both a confession and a reminder on his lips.

Despite the coldness of the water that surrounds us, his chest radiates heat. I reach up, hesitantly at first, and then with more nerve, I touch him. He freezes at the first graze of my fingertips over his chest. Hard brown nipples tip his pecs and a small smattering of dark hair mars otherwise smooth flesh. Every once in a while as we sway in the current beneath the river's surface, a beam of moonlight slides over his body and I spot a scar or two.

When I see them, I find myself drawn to them. My fingers move over lines on his shoulders and down his arms. The more I touch him, the more taut Solomon's body grows. This is my effect on him.

After one hand draws impossibly close to the line where the water meets his stomach, he reaches down and snatches it away, holding it up between us. "Devonry."

Despite the firm grip he has on me, it doesn't hurt. He would never hurt me. "You asked me what we're supposed to do now," I murmur before lifting my eyes to meet his. "I think you already know the answer."

His face is tight. His jaw rock solid as a small muscle ticks beneath the flesh both there and at the top of his forehead. Unable and unwilling to stop this forward momentum, I go up onto my tiptoes and press a chaste kiss to his chin. When he doesn't respond immediately or dip his head to meet my mouth, I part my lips and nibble at him. Still nothing, so I drop down and lean forward—pressing my face into his throat.

"Princess…" I've never heard Solomon Winett sound so breathless. Now he is, *because of me*. I think I like having this kind of power over him.

My teeth sink into the flesh of his throat, not hard enough to pierce but enough to let him know that I'm not backing down. A low growl rumbles from his chest against my own.

"Let go, Solo," I whisper, releasing his skin to lick at the marks I've made. "For tonight, let's just do what we want." I look up at him again and he meets my gaze. "I think we've both earned that, haven't we?"

Solo is quiet for a long time. I can see the battle on his face. Just like me, he must be wondering if this is right. If we should allow ourselves this bit of intimacy. Even if we can't take back what we've already done … is it right to continue this relationship knowing we may not be able to see it through to the end? His eyes glow before dimming and then glow again. His lips part to reveal gritted teeth. I wait, already knowing where his mind will lead him. It's not like we haven't already crossed the path of no return. I don't know why he thinks it's still necessary to fight, but I'll be patient because I know, in the end, I'll still get what I want.

"*Fuck.*" The word slips through Solo's teeth a split

second before his head comes down. His mouth crashes against mine with a familiar ferocity and I close my eyes as his hand cups the back of my skull. His body moves harder into mine until I can feel the evidence of his arousal against my stomach.

Long and thick and throbbing, Solo's cock strains between us as his tongue invades my mouth. He pulls away for a single moment only to reach down, releasing my head as he hooks his hands behind my thighs and yanks me up. My feet leave the muddy, rocky river floor as I'm catapulted against him. My arms encircle his shoulders, and I feel the hardness of him right at my core.

"Solo!" He doesn't stop at my cry of surprise but instead arches me higher—just enough so that the head of him slips into my entrance. A gasp leaves my lips and then he's there, sliding into my pussy with excruciating slowness.

"You wanted this, Princess," Solo spits between clenched teeth. "So take it. Take my cock." A whimper leaves my lips as he spreads me open. The thickness of him stretches my inner walls until they burn in the most delicious way. "Yes," he hisses. "Just like that. Fuck, you feel so good."

More whimpers echo out of my throat. My nails rake against his shoulder and over his back as I cling to him. Whatever magic keeps the two of us grounded to this Earthly Plane works over us, forcing me to slip further and further down until Solo's cock is seated inside me all the way to the hilt. I feel desperately full—like my insides have formed around him. He slides right into my body as if he's always belonged here.

"No regrets..." Solo whispers against the side of my face. I don't know if it's a question or an oath for himself, but I agree readily.

"No," I reply, my voice craning to be heard. "No regrets."

My body bows against him, as if I'm trying to get close enough that I can crawl into his skin. It isn't enough for him to be inside of me like this. *I* want to be inside of *him*.

"Shhhh." Gently, too fucking gently if you ask me, Solo shushes me and once more cups the back of my head as he presses my face to his massive chest while my legs lock around his waist. My insides burn and stretch as he takes a step forward. A moan bubbles up out of my throat.

I don't know what he's doing—what he's planning—but every step he takes jostles the length of his cock inside of me and scrapes his pubic bone against my clit. My eyes slide shut and sparks dance behind my eyelids. They burst faster and faster as he hastens his speed. I pant, I squirm against him, feeling his hands—one on my head and the other beneath my ass now—holding me close.

They feel hot—like scalding brands placed against my skin. I like it, but I want more. It's not enough. Something cold touches my lower back—smooth but icy—and a shriek escapes my lips as Solomon drops me down. My eyes burst open and I look back to see that he's placed me on a boulder. When my eyes return to the man before me, it's to find his eyes glowing once more. The red is deeper and with his lips parted, I can see the points of his fangs as they peek through.

My pussy clenches instinctively around the massive rod inside of me. Solo's face goes slack with the shock of pleasure and then the hand that had been underneath my ass a moment ago punches into the rock beneath me. The loud *crack* of his fist making contact echoes into the otherwise quiet forest air.

Breathing raggedly, I glance down to find a fissure created right beneath his knuckles. My eyes widen and I peer back at him. The strength it would take for him to crack a boulder as big as this...

With an impenetrable glare, Solomon bites out two words. "Don't. Move."

As much as it would please me to torment him with some snarky comeback, I find that I'm fresh out. Not a single one comes to mind. The only thing I can think of is that I've taunted a beast and now he's hungry. A shiver slithers up my spine. Solomon's other hand finally leaves my head. After several moments, I reach my hand back, inching along the boulder in increments until I've placed my palm flat and adjusted my body so that I can rest my weight on that arm.

He doesn't move though. Not once the entire time. It's as if Solo has become a statue before me with his cock firmly locked into my pussy. He doesn't withdraw or thrust but just stands there as if he's trying to open me up so that he can crawl inside, soul and all. I'd be lying if I didn't feel the smallest bit of fear. Not fear that I'll be wounded by him. Fear that I've pushed him too far.

As much as I find pleasure in this act, I want him to find it too. Reaching up with my free hand. It lands on his chest between his pecs and slides up until my thumb brushes the base of his throat.

"Devonry," my name is a warning on his lips.

I can't help but smile. "Solo," I respond mockingly.

"Do not test me, Princess," he growls. "I could tear you apart if you're not careful."

"You'd never do that," I tell him. "So don't even try to scare me."

"You could do with a little scaring," he says.

I laugh, the sound louder than I intended as it bounces off the trees and the surface of the river behind him. I'm suddenly reminded that now that he's moved us and lifted me onto his boulder, I'm no longer half-hidden beneath the surface of the water and neither is he. I glance down with wide eyes and gasp as I see the base of his cock jutting out from where he's inside of me.

My insides clamp down again in awareness and Solo drops his head to my shoulder, a groan rumbling up his chest. "You torture me, Princess," he mutters. "Your cruelty knows no bounds."

Needing to reassure him, I lift my hand from his throat and move it to the back of his head. I let my fingers slip through the dark locks of his hair, inky black against the paleness of his skin. I scrape my nails over his scalp in gentle scratches, earning a shudder from him.

"You're the one torturing me," I murmur. "You may have entered me, but you haven't fucked—ah!"

Hard palms grip my hips as Solo suddenly withdraws from my pussy and slams back inside, interrupting the flow of my words. My hand leaves his head, snapping out to keep me up on the boulder as flames erupt beneath my flesh.

"You were saying, *Princess*?" Solo looks up at me and smirks, the tips of his fangs poking through.

"*Bastard*," I gasp.

In response to my curse, Solo withdraws and thrusts back into me, his fingers branding my sides with the strength he possesses. Another cry lodges in my throat and this time, it gets stuck, rendering me silent as my eyes burn with unshed tears.

With the icy chill of the boulder against my back, Solomon's heat at my front, and his cock powering into my insides, I lose my ability to speak. Solo takes full advantage. He groans as he fucks into me, thrusting the length of his cock into my inner walls and stretching them apart with a quick burn that bursts to life beneath my skin.

The sky above twists and changes. The branches fade from my vision as I feel something otherworldly overwhelm my senses. It hurts. It feels good. No, it feels ... euphoric. Addictive. I arch my back, reaching down and latching onto his wrists as he holds me in place for his thrusts. Again and again. Over and over. He takes me higher with each push.

When Solo's head moves down, and the soft, feathery feeling of his hair touches my breast a moment before his lips close around my nipple penetrating my fogged over mind, I finally find my voice again. High pitched and whining, I keen and squirm. It's too much. The feel of him fucking me below and curling his tongue around my sensitive nipple is too much. His teeth scrape my flesh, flooding my nerves with lightning.

"Solo!" I cry out his name, hoping and praying he gives me release, but he's too cruel for that. I know because I can feel the corners of his mouth tilt up as he bites down on my flesh and sends another bolt of pleasure through me.

With my breasts against his face and his cock in my pussy, I encircle his head with my arms. "Please ... please ... oh, please, Solo..." I don't care if I'm begging, but I need something to break. There are so many emotions, so much feeling buried beneath my skin, and if it doesn't come out soon, I fear I'll burst apart. I'm going to rip at the seams, and then no one will be able to put me back together.

Solo's lips release my nipple, moving to the other one. "You say my name so sweetly when you're like this, Princess," he murmurs just as he closes his mouth over his second target. A groan arches up my throat and I wiggle in denial.

"I need ... please, Solomon, for the love of the Gods, stop tormenting me!" I cry out.

His responding chuckle is low and vibrating. "Ah, but I love to see you in the throes of your torment."

Those unshed tears from earlier break free and slide down the sides of my face. I sniffle weakly. Solomon's lower body rolls into mine. His head bends forward, and a gasp escapes me a moment after his warm breath grazes my cheek. Then his tongue touches the soft skin there as he licks the tears from my face. My insides turn molten. The shock of the action ends with his lips brushing lightly on my brow. His cock scrapes at the top of my pussy, pushing in and out, thrusting and nearly leaving me entirely with each pull and push. Words stick in my throat, clogging my airways. My lashes flutter.

Each thrust brings his pubic bone right against my clit. At first, the movements are slow and then they pick up the pace, moving faster as he releases my nipple and arches up over me. Glowing blood-red eyes peer down at my face and body. My lips part and I whimper, begging.

He dips his head, understanding my craving as he meets my lips with his. Our tongues tangle, dueling and then sliding along each other. My chest rises and falls rapidly as he fucks into me. Strong hands lift my hips, canting my lower body in a new way that causes the cock thrusting into my core to slam into a point deep inside me that I've never felt before. My nails claw at his arms as I rip my mouth from his.

"Oh Gods!" I scream, eyes slamming shut. All at once, Solo stops moving. My eyes pop open. "No!" I cry out.

His hand cups my face, holding my chin in an unbreakable grip. "Look at me," he commands. "Look at who's making you come. Say it—say my name."

My mouth opens on a fresh cry as pain assails me. The cramping of the release that had been just on the precipice spreads through my stomach. "Solo," I beg. "Please…"

His cock thrusts back into me, powering forth until he bottoms out inside of me and then a thumb moves across the bundle of nerves between my legs, pressing down and circling in hard fast movements that send me over that cliff's edge. A scream shoots up my throat. All the while, Solomon holds himself still, his teeth bare and elongated as he glowers down at me.

The hot pulse of his cock throbs against my insides. One second passes. Two. Three. In total, ten seconds pass before Solo sags forward, his arms closing around me as he holds me against him. Fresh air wafts over my bare, wet flesh. I shiver in his arms, curling closer to steal some of his warmth.

Panting and covered in fresh sweat, a long while passes before Solo eases himself from my sore insides. Once he does, though, the two of us don't say a word as we return to the center of the river and begin to wash away the evidence of our actions.

My heart takes longer to slow its rapid beat. By the time we exit the water, my thighs feel somewhat more stable—though my pussy remains sore. I wring my hair dry and braid it to the side before redressing. As quickly as the need for Solo had come on, the reminder that we have other—far more important—duties to see to returns.

For however long it lasted, though, these few moments in the moonlight river were ours, and I know it'll keep me going for that much longer.

7
DEVONRY

Every rock of our bodies as the horse canters back toward the stables sends shockwaves through me. They're reminders of what we've done. Sometimes, the voices of those who raised me still creep into the back of my mind. Despite the way my body shivers at the memory of Solomon's lips on me, of the heat of his body against mine, they tell me that all of this is wrong. A Princess is meant to be a certain way and dallying with her bodyguard in a forest is not the path that I was meant for. Each day, though, it gets easier to ignore those thoughts and voices. If there is still a part of me that feels guilt over the loss of my virginity, I can't seem to find it within myself. The lingering ache only brings with it this quiet joy of being *something* with Solomon.

The nearness of him brings my body alive in ways I'd never realized were possible. Perhaps it is only the throes of lust that I've been well-warned of my entire life. However, I am not entirely convinced that it isn't something more. There are feelings there. A well of them that I'd pushed away, but now, in my Awakened state, those same emotions draw my power as easily as breathing.

As if thinking his name brings me back to the present, I stiffen and then sigh as his warm breath fans against my cheek. The horse crests a particularly steep hill and I'm forced to recline and lean back into him while he clicks his tongue at the animal and directs it down into Omarion. Soft earth becomes hard cobblestones. The further we get from that secret place in the woods, the heavier my shoulders feel—as if the burden we'd both set down for those few moments is being returned to us. When we finally stop, his hand falls to my hip, fingers digging into the curve of my body like a brand before promptly letting go.

With a grunt, he swings down off the horse and offers me his hand. His palm lingers in the air between us, an offering, a surrender, and a promise. I stare at the few small scars that litter his hand. With a slight smile, I place my fingers in his. The warmth he always carries seeps into me and I grin as he guides me back to my feet. Our breaths mingle in the slender space between us.

"Thank you," I whisper, unable to move from where I stand. The press of our bodies renews the flutter of desire between my legs.

"For the bath or for the orgasm?"

My eyes shoot up to his, my brows rising in utter surprise. A smirk lifts one side of his mouth, making him seem more boyish than man. Rebellious, teasing, and wild —like we'd both once been long ago. My eyes catch on the way he runs his tongue over the tip of his fangs for the briefest second. The same tongue that's done dangerously delicious things to me. The same fangs that had sunk into my flesh and drank from my veins.

Fresh heat burns my cheeks all the way up to the tips of my ears. "I *meant* for the help getting off the horse," I say, emphasizing my words. I swallow and try to appease the sudden dryness in my throat as I step all the more closer and look up at him from beneath my lashes. "But ... I suppose I should thank you for that too, shouldn't I?"

Two can play this game, I think.

That half smile never leaves his face. Even so, Solomon steps back, allowing me space to move around him. I have no doubt that both of us would love nothing more than to lose ourselves in those woods once more, but our reprieve —however short—is just that. A reprieve. It's not forever. It can't be.

His light hum of laughter is deep, rumbling over my ears with a clear, precise sound. It's a nice respite from his usual stern expressions. I still, wanting with all my might to stay in this moment to soak in the sound of his amusement. *Just one more moment*, I beg the Gods. If only I could stop time. I would refuse the world if it meant I got to be here and now with him for a while longer. But the world does not wait, not even for me.

The moment is there and then it's gone.

"Come, let's check on our friends," Solomon says, offering the reins to a stable boy who walks swiftly to meet us. A bit of coin jingles in his pocket as he digs to pull out a small piece and tosses it toward the child. The boy, covered in enough dirt and dust to disguise his complexion, scurries to catch it with a beaming grin that is missing several teeth. I hate that I now know just how much one singular coin is to a boy like him—especially right now when Rozentine is on the precipice of something disastrous. If we fail to get the throne back or worse, if I don't return at all, then there's no telling what Nasir will do with my people. So, there is no choice in the end. Not for me. Not anymore.

I pull my hood tighter around my features when we stride away. The musty scent of the stables is replaced with the lingering scent of urine and stale ale. As many men as before, if not more, remain in small groups outside of the brothel establishments that line the streets filled with more filth than even a trash heap. Fewer women drape themselves between them, but the night is far from over. They speak loudly, their words slurring into a string of unidentifiable words, and crow their amusement in an uproar of laughter.

Solomon's hulking form keeps pace at my side. His head remains on a constant swivel, eyes searching every darkened corner. I try to look for threats with the same determined attention he gives, but my eyes often drift back to him. As though he feels the heat of my gaze, his hand flicks back the side of my cloak and slips in enough to interlace his fingers with mine. Despite my words, spoken so many nights ago, of how none of this can continue after this journey is over, I find myself holding on, not wanting to let go.

A shiver travels the length of my spine when his thumb strokes along my skin. The flickering lantern lights that illuminate the street of brothels hang over us as we walk with quiet determination back toward where Argyle and Celine are amongst one of the many Houses of ill repute. Under each lantern, our shadows stretch our figures at odd angles against the buildings and cobblestone roads.

Eyes follow us as we move. I squeeze his hand tighter, my gaze narrowing on every figure we pass. Upon the women, the ones draped in open doorways in nothing but bustiers and practically transparent skirts, I frown. Not one of them says a word. They don't bother to approach or offer their services. I don't care to know if it's me or the imposing cut Solo makes of himself along the streets filled with pot-bellied men and those too drunk to appear even remotely attractive. So long as I don't have to witness one of them shoving their bosom in his face again, I'm happy to keep walking right through them.

"But *you* can stay," Rita's familiar voice carries through the night pulling our attention to the stone steps of the brothel we'd left hours before.

Argyle's arm circles Celine's slender waist, holding her against him. My lips tighten. Despite the fact that her eyes are open and somewhat aware, far more than they had been earlier, she still appears just as pale and weak as ever. Argyle's ever-present caustic and amused expression is gone, and in its place is one of somber anger. Tension puckers his lips as he shakes his head.

Celine brushes a hand against his chest, drawing his gaze away. Her eyes pass him, though, until the dull brown of her irises cut through the darkness, locking on Solo and me as we close the distance that separates us. A flush of fever still darkens her cheeks. Despite that, her breaths appear normal, and the sheen of sweat is no longer coating her skin. A relieved sigh escapes me.

"I told you before," Argyle practically seethes out the words, sounding more angry than I've ever heard him— even toward me when we'd first met. "We are a package deal, Rita. While I *appreciate*"—he doesn't sound all that appreciative at all, but he's trying to be polite despite the waves of rage that are pouring off of him— "all that you've done. We've obviously overstayed our welcome and we will be on our way."

Rita *harrumphs* and folds her arms over her ample chest. "On your way to the grave, Argyle," she snaps. "The only place you should be going with that woman is to a healer. If that illness starts spreading through my girls, you can bet I'll be looking for you."

"Send a letter if that ever comes to fruition." Argyle grits out the words before taking the last of the steps with

Celine. On the bottom step, Celine stumbles, the edge of her foot, back in her worn riding boots catching on an uneven stone. Argyle doesn't even hesitate as he catches her quickly and hauls her against his chest. He doesn't look back at Rita as she flips him a rather rude gesture with her hands before stalking back inside.

"Celine." I breathe her name, loosening my hand from Solo's and hurrying to Celine's other side. "You're awake. How are you feeling?"

"Like walking death." Celine forces a small smile and though it's weak, it's a beautiful sight to see.

The stomp of Solomon's heavy boots passes us as he marches up to the door Rita just went into. I blink after him with one of my hands on Celine's shoulder as he withdraws a pouch of coins. He disappears through the interior, and when he comes back out, that pouch is gone. What had he asked of her? Did he threaten her to keep quiet? Or was it a bribe? A deal?

I don't have time to ask as he steps down the short three steps into the street. Whatever he'd done, I pray that it buys us time and protection. We're already running short on funds as it is, and there are only so many animals he and Argyle can hunt, kill, and sell along our journey to keep us going when we have to hurry. Just as Solo steps off the curb, the door opens slightly and Rita sticks her head out once more. Her gaze, sharp and full of bitter venom, settles on Argyle.

Sticking her nose in the air, she huffs out a breath. A fresh look of offense puckers her features. "We'll be in touch, Argyle," she says to the four of us, "but your debt is paid." I expect her to slam the door in our faces once more, but instead, her gaze drifts to Celine and her mouth turns down into a deep frown. "And get that girl to a damned healer," she hisses before giving us her back and slamming the door behind her once again.

Argyle shakes his head and drags a hand over his face. "Thank the Gods you returned. I was only minutes away from searching you two out myself," he says. "She is well enough to travel now, and I want to be in Caladrius territory as soon as physically possible."

I stretch, sparing only one more glance at the brothel. Muscles all along my back protest at the motion. The place between my thighs twinges with a different kind of soreness, a delicious sort of pain. I drop my arms immediately and flash a look to Solo before looking to the ground at my feet. That storage room and the hard, uneven floors will not be missed by me. However, as that thought crosses my mind, a new disappointment registers. If we're to be on our way once more, then there will be no room to sleep in tonight at all, and likely not again for a few more nights. Nothing but the even harder ground of the softened earth.

Exhaustion makes the entirety of my body heavy and my eyes sting with the need to close them. There was always a time limit on our stay here in Omarion. Now, we've finally met it.

"If you are well enough…" Solomon begins, his words drifting off into an unfinished question as he looks to Celine for confirmation.

"I am." She dips her chin and straightens, standing a little taller than before even when her knees threaten to buckle. Argyle's grip on her tightens, wrinkling her gray-brown mismatched dress and cloak under his fingers.

"Then, we will go," Solomon decides.

Walking in a slower stride with Celine, the four of us move together back to the stables where Solomon and I had just left the horse with Argyle's. The same boy from before quickly drops the brush he'd been running through a sable-colored horse's coat as we enter. He pushes the hair that falls into his face back and gives another toothless grin.

"Back so soon?" he asks, directing the question to Solo.

"Your lucky day." Solomon flicks him another coin. "I'll give you another if you ready their horse for us," he says, nodding to Argyle and Celine.

That offer is more than enough to send the child in a flurry to saddle Argyle's horse while Solomon redresses ours. More and more coin gone and yet, I can't find the will in me to mind even if it likely means that there will be less to eat and fewer inns to stay in on the road. Maybe I've become accustomed to sleeping under the stars, but I'd do it every night of my life if it brought the same bright joy upon all of the people of Rozentine as the thought of more coin does to the stable hand.

The longer it takes to saddle up the horses once more, however, the more I feel the weight of my fatigue pass over me. The sounds of horse nickering and stomping hoofbeats, along with the now familiar scent of hay, infiltrate my ears and nose. Back and forth, my body sways with exhaustion. Too little sleep. Too much pressure and concern. It hits me with such ferocity, my eyes threaten to flutter closed. I force them open and lean against one of the nearby stalls, reaching up and locking my fingers over the top.

A few minutes pass, and the boy approaches us, holding the reins out for Argyle, who shakes his head. "Hold him for me," Argyle says before turning to Celine.

She parts her lip in protest, but the moment she tries to push away from his arms, she nearly goes down onto her knees. I jerk forward, wide awake, as concern bolts through me. Thankfully, though, Argyle catches her with a curse. "Stubborn broad," he mutters in irritation. "Let a man help you, woman." He practically growls out the words. "Unless you'd prefer to break your pretty little neck."

Celine glares at him but says nothing as he sweeps her into his arms. He kicks a nearby stool closer to the horse's side and then steps onto it, lifting her into the saddle. Only when she's firmly atop the beast does she finally speak. "I'll thank you to mind any other woman's neck but my own," she snaps. I bite down on my lower lip to keep from laughing as Argyle tightens one of the straps of the horse's saddle.

"Now, why would I want to do a fool thing like that, sweetheart?" Argyle replies coolly. "Your neck is the prettiest I've ever seen. If you keep it open to me like that, a man like me might just take a bite."

Celine's eyes widen and before she can reply, he reaches up, his hand curling over the horn of the saddle and then he hefts himself onto the horse right behind her. Argyle's lips twitch with amusement, his somber anger gone for the moment. Despite Celine's words though, her forehead is speckled with little beads of sweat and she sways forward before being dragged back against Argyle's chest with one of his hands. She doesn't try to move away.

Solo comes down the aisle, leading our horse, also now saddled once more. As soon as he gets close, I follow suit and use the stool to climb atop the horse. My thighs scream in aching pain when I tighten them around the horse's sides as I keep myself in place when the animal shifts under me. Solomon's gaze is distant as he works in silence, attaching my bow and arrow to our horse and climbing up behind me.

The stable boy lingers nearby and the second Solo procures another coin, tossing it his way, he grabs it and scuttles away. Then we're on the move. Within a short time, the city of Omarion is replaced with dirt paths and nothing but forest, forest, and more forest. The longer we ride, the longer my blinks become and the more lax my body is against Solomon's. Not a single cloud lingers in the sky, allowing the moon to cast a gentle blue glow over the land. Several miles away, the mountains stand stark and ominous against the starry night.

My breath fogs in front of me. Cold cuts through my clothing and into my bones. Only Solomon's heat keeps me from shivering with every pass of the wind. Finally, the heat of summer is waning and the threat of winter comes all too quick.

"This way," Argyle says, pointing us down the next trail.

"How do you know about all of these backroads?" I ask, adjusting my cloak around me.

"The House of Ravens is often on the run from the law ... after a few years, you get familiar with the safest least traveled routes and shortcuts. I—"

Celine coughs into her sleeve. Argyle's entire body, all six feet of him, freezes until she whispers, "I'm alright."

In answer, Argyle buries his face in her neck and sighs. I smile softly at the image of them and tilt my head up to Solomon. He leans his cheek against my forehead but says nothing.

"We'll be in Caladrius territory soon, right?" Worry tinges my question to Solomon. It eats a hole in my stomach and makes my heart heavy.

"Soon enough," is the only response I get.

8

SOLOMON

The mountains are an unyielding cold that slices through the many layers of our clothes. Thick cloaks and the press of our bodies together atop the horses are no match for the elements during the long hours we ride these winding trails. As if the mountainous air senses my distaste for the chill, an icy wind carries with it a fresh current of rain. Sporadic downpours come and go, making our path more mud than anything else. Every step the horses take comes with a suctioning sound as we push them relentlessly onward.

In the circle of my arms, Devonry shivers. The dampness of her hood and the wind-whipped strands of her hair occasionally brush against my cheek, causing my skin to prickle. Her weight against my chest is a welcomed comfort though. I soak in what little heat builds between us and savor it. As I savor her nearness, her scent, and the constant healthy thrumming of the blood rushing through her veins.

I suspect she's more miserable than any of us, but she keeps her lips sealed. A far cry from the privileged Princess of the Sunfire Palace, she faces the cold and rain and exhaustion like a war-worn soldier. Better than most soldiers actually. Many fine men would have already given themselves over to their sullen thoughts. Though it swells my chest with pride, her perseverance is akin to red wine marring a wedding dress. A precious, innocent thing brought down by a world that's stained her crimson.

When the wind dies down and the rain stops, she lifts her fingers. Orange flames dance across her palm and up her fingers. Rain hisses and turns to mist when it touches flesh. Power fills her eyes with gold as she lets the fire rage against her, large enough to warm the air but small enough for her control. Her trembling stops. I press myself tighter around her and purse my lips at the tenderness in which she rests against me.

Time away from her life within the tall sheltering walls of the Sunfire Palace seems to have only fed her need for independence. What freedom she craved before was the kindling that easily ignited during our travels.

Devonry doesn't need me for her warmth; she creates it on her own.

I hope her father would be proud of the woman she's becoming. My strong, capable, self-reliant Queen. Part of me longs for a world where he might have been proud of me too, but that piece of me is tattered at the edges, weather-worn, and bare-threaded. For I am King Vernon's greatest failure. A match for his daughter I may be, but I'd never been intended for her bed.

The taste of her tender flesh under my fangs and the hot grip of her cunt around my length is not something I can so easily forget. Her attention and the desire for a place in her heart is like a war cry in my mind. I am mesmerized by her, ruined for all others.

Sighing, I rest my cheek against her head. Through the

earthy scent of travel on her skin, there still remains the soft floral smell she's always carried. The idea of nuzzling my nose into her hair and the crook of her neck comes with desperate need.

Had King Vernon loved his Saintess Queen with the same passion I have for their daughter? Would the Queen, should she still live today, see the strength this country needs in Devonry? I have little doubt from what I remember of the Saintess that she would be oozing pride for her daughter. Though she valued passive peace, she'd always had a way of seeing people for who they truly were. The Queen Mother had known her daughter before her daughter even knew herself. If I am King Vernon's failure, then she is the Queen's victory.

And even if, for whatever reason, they wouldn't be, *I* am proud.

I only hope that I am enough.

For several miles, my mind spins from what ifs and maybes to all our problems that are far from solved. So much so that an ache has begun between my eyes where my brows may perpetually be furrowed.

"Let's make camp before we lose the last of the light." Argyle slows his steed. I tug gently at the reins of mine, hurtling back into the consciousness of my physical body. "This looks as good a camp as any."

With a wave of his hand, he motions toward an alcove of rocks and the bit of space where the trees are thinned. It will do well to protect us from the wind and provide us with some coverage. I look to the darkening sky. We'll have just enough time to check the surrounding woods and warm some food before night truly takes.

Argyle looks to us before trailing ahead, then returning again with a crease forming between his brows. "Are you well?"

Has the distance of my mind shown so plainly on my face?

Devonry twists in the saddle at the question, her wet clothing squeaks against the leather under us with the movement. Pink kisses her cheeks from the lashings of the persistent wind and it makes her eyes look several shades brighter. She blinks up at me, those long lashes brushing her brow bone.

"I am in good health." I inhale slowly, exhaling the rest of my words. "Only lost in my thoughts."

"You swear it?" Devonry demands.

A slight smirk tugs at my lips. How adorable she is when she lets a bit of her ferocity out. Like a small animal too cute to seem feral, thus hiding the enormity of her bite. And for her to be such a way regarding my health? I fear I may have died and passed on with the Gods, for less than a year ago, she'd have loved for me to have fallen ill for days just to be rid of me.

"It is only the darkness of my own mind that plagues me," I answer. "I swear it."

Argyle's laughter is short and bitter, but the lines of worry have smoothed on his features. "You are not alone, brother."

Leaning away from Devonry's body heat, I drag my leg over the backside of the horse and drop to the ground. My boots squelch in the mud. Once these boots had been cleaned nightly, polished with the care of a man who knew the value of taking care of his things. Now they are scuffed and dirty and I have no intention of doing anything about it until we reach House of Caladrius territory.

Ignoring the way my weight sinks into the earth, I stretch my hand out for Devonry. Blue-gray eyes made more icy by the flush on her face, look me over before settling on my palm. A slight smile lifts the edges of her mouth. Is that ... is she smirking at me?

With satisfaction written all over her pretty face, Devonry swings her leg over the saddle and lowers to the ground.

"I'll stay with Celine and start a fire." Devonry pats the horse's neck, looking up from under her lashes. Raindrops still linger on the hairs that curl around the edges of her cloak's hood. "You and Argyle want to set a perimeter?"

I watch the way her mouth shapes the words, wondering just how many hours it's been since I've kissed those lips. My tongue traces my own lower lip, searching for any remnants of her taste. I fight a scowl when all I taste is rainwater and sweat.

"She sure is starting to sound like a Queen," Argyle muses, carefully helping Celine out of the saddle. She sways and grips his arms so tightly she squeezes moisture from the cloth. When she's steady on her feet, he adjusts his sword belt over his hips and watches her. Celine watches him back as though they've begun a conversation that only the two of them can hear. After a moment, Argyle exhales and moves to tie his horse loosely to the nearest tree.

"As you say, my Queen." I offer her a bow that earns me the roll of her pretty gray eyes. With the prickling sensation of her gaze on my flesh, I turn and make quick work of tying up our horse. Devonry still watches me when I face Argyle and say, "Shall we?"

Argyle wearily stares out at the surrounding trees. "May I escort you through the woods, where I'll endeavor to take the last of your innocence?" he asks, his tone light despite the hardness of his gaze. Somehow in the dimming evening light, he looks older. I can't place the how of it. There are no obvious lines wrinkling his skin or a sudden patch of gray hair to show the passage of time, but there is a weight upon his shoulders. One that's begun to rip his youth away from him. Even as he tries to smile, I search for the lost boy I'd found in that tavern years ago.

Between Celine's illness, the exhaustion of traveling, and things I'm surely unaware of, it's clear life is wearing on him.

"I'm afraid my innocence is long gone." Needles and leaves from the evergreen trees grind under my feet. Their crisp scent mingles with earthy musk and the lingering smell of wild animals. The wind still finds its way through the trees to ruffle my hair.

I spare one last glance at the women as they make their way closer to the rock. Devonry pushes her hood back, tipping her face to the sky. From where I stand, I can't quite make out her expression, but somehow I know she's smiling. Though there are a thousand reasons not to, she still has hope. Perhaps she's given me some as well.

Argyle pushes aside branches as we begin to move in arching circles around our soon-to-be camp. It's only us and the crunch of brush underfoot. The quiet is thick with our even breaths and I catch his eye, not for the first time. I squint through the last of the sun's rays, watching through the cracks of the forest for signs of man or beast alike. My eyes return to Argyle's lingering gaze the farther we move.

"What is it? What's on your mind?" I grunt. Thorns snag and dig into my clothes from the nearest bush. Their prickly ends push past the material of my pants and scratch against my skin. I yank the branch away, ignoring the bite of the thorns in my palm.

"Why must something be on my mind?" He skirts around the same bush, giving it a wide berth.

"You keep staring at me."

"You've got a good face."

I snort. A fine face, indeed, but I highly doubt it is my

face that has him so lost to his thoughts. "Quit jesting and speak."

"You should be flattered."

A bird caws and bursts from the nearest tree. Both our heads snap up. Two other birds follow its lead, breaking from the canopy above with a flourish of falling leaves. Argyle is at my side, silent and unmoving. My attention drifts around the woods, my ears straining to catch any other noise. Every twitch of the forest draws my gaze as I scent the air.

"I am immune to your charms, friend." I lay a hand on his shoulder, both of us relaxing as the area falls into the steady heartbeat of nature once more. Argyle presses his mouth into a firm line. "How do you think she is fairing?"

"Celine?"

"No, the other woman you've been pining after who's fallen ill recently." I deadpan. At this distance from camp, I can hardly make out the vague mumbling of Devonry and Celine's conversation, though I can't see around the rise of rock and tree between us. I turn, angling us farther in more looping circles.

"She seems much better." Argyle sighs. "Though I think she fronts as to how well she is doing. She doesn't want to concern the Princess." He snaps a small branch from a tree and rolls the wood in his hand for a moment before dropping it to the ground.

"We're lucky it wasn't the same thing sweeping the coast." I mean my words as a comfort for my friend, but he flinches at the notion as though he's thought about it far more than even I have dared. Celine has been lucky. We all have.

"I am thankful. Surely, she is too. Though this rapid and deadly *disease*, or plague as others already call it, is cause for concern."

"Another thing our nation must come together to fight against." I nod to the sentiment, pushing a low-hanging branch from our path. Mentally, I add it to my ever-growing list of worries. One more thing to protect Devonry from. How does one fight something so unseen as illness?

"Where do you think this ailment has swept in from? Celine thinks it is a punishment from the Gods since Aerea's line is not sitting in its rightful place."

"Nasir." I spit his name like the vile thing it is. "That scheming bastard holds our palace and our country, but even he is nothing but a fly to the Gods. I doubt they care much over the trivial blip of his life." My fingers circle over the hilt of my sword as if I might draw it on that wicked man though we are miles apart. I look to my friend, who fiddles with yet another stick. "Celine gives him more credit than he is due. Devonry is far from defeated. This disease is likely to be something brought in from traveling merchants."

There is reason to be found in my statement. Wise men and healers across our great country have said time and time again how easy it is for those who travel to bring with them new blights. A plague brought by merchants is an easy answer. A practical one.

"I am always surprised at how often you make sense," Argyle says with a tight-lipped smile.

"Yet it does not ease your worry," I point out. "And it will be another obstacle in our way."

"As are the guardsmen that hunt her on her own soil. Are we so certain they have any loyalty to Nasir? How can he have the country in such a hold so quickly? I'm keen to meet with other Ravens to hear our nation's gossip."

What little light we'd had when we'd arrived is nearly nonexistent now. The moon can be seen through the branches and the stir of wildlife rising begins around us. A hum of chirping insects signals the end of another day. I scratch at the stubble on my cheeks, feeling the weariness of our travels clear down to my bones. It's an annoying sensation I've learned over and over in my life to ignore. For the body is far greater than the limits we place upon it.

"Not every man can be so sure of Nasir. There are smart men in those ranks, good men." *But Nasir is Awakened. I am sure. The extent to which is still to be determined, but the poison he spills with his abilities is affecting many. Perhaps he* is *the plague upon us.*

Argyle hums and nods. Yet his uncertainty comes off of him in waves. He trusts the noble Houses very little and rightfully so. What faith he has in our country rests solely in his relationship with myself and our Queen.

Lost to the torment of our thoughts, we split up and finish circling the camp. When we both return, a small pile of wood is already ablaze and warming the circle of rock. I can taste the smoke on my tongue as I walk through the last of the wind and find my bedroll already laid out next to another.

I lift a brow and find Devonry watching me from the other side of the flames. The glow of the embers reflects in the pool of her eyes. Between us, the burning wood cracks and pops.

Celine stretches her feet toward the warmth. Though she does not turn her face, her eyes follow Argyle as he makes his way to my side and lowers onto a waiting log. In his hands, bark crumbles from a thick bit of wood. He pulls a small knife from his boot and watches the fire light dance in the blade.

"Did the two of you drag this log here?" he asks, adjusting himself over it.

"We're stronger than we look." Celine pats the log

underneath her with a smile. There are dark circles under her eyes that shine with mischief.

"You should still be resting." Argyle clicks his tongue at her. His brows lower, his shoulders hunching forward. "Next time, I'll carry the heavy log."

"Hopefully there aren't too many next times to worry about." She pulls her legs up to her chest and folds her arms over her knees.

All the while, Devonry's gaze has yet to leave my face. I can feel her watching me as though she's lit another flame against my skin. Drawn to her, I can do nothing to stop myself from meeting her attention and drinking it all in.

"All is well. We should sleep decently tonight so long as the last of the rain has passed," I say, stretching my arms overhead. The hem of my shirt pulls from where it has been tucked into my pants. The chilled evening air licks at the veering muscles of my abdomen. Devonry's eyes pull from my face and travel down my torso. I grin at her when she finally manages to hold my gaze again.

"We should be getting to bed then. It'll be another early morning." Devonry rises from her seat, pulling the blanket wrapped around her shoulders tighter. Celine nods, her own bedroll set just inside the curve of rock, Argyle's a few feet away.

As she comes to my side, I lean down, keeping my voice soft. "A case of wandering eyes, my Queen?"

She sniffs and shoves her elbow into my side. "I'm going to sleep, Solo. Goodnight."

I take it with a hiss of breath and chuckle. Her wicked tongue could get us both into a handful of trouble. It's happened a time or two before, and out here in these woods there is even less to stop us. "If you have trouble sleeping, I might know a thing or two that will help exhaust you."

"Keep your hands to yourself tonight, guardsman," she quips back, though that smile of hers betrays her as does the clear hunger in her eyes.

I might never be able to keep my hands to myself again. Not with her. I am a changed man with my soul's match at my side. So I watch her as she lays herself down and then I lower myself to my own bedroll, curious if I'll dream of the sweet curves of her body or the sinfully delicious taste of her cunt on my tongue.

9
DEVONRY

I'm dimly aware that I'm dreaming, but that doesn't stop the following events from happening. Rather than resigned to the course of what's about to happen, though, the awareness only seems to make me even more frightened of them.

The dock sways beneath my feet. Cool air slaps at my cheeks and above my head, and the moonlight pours down over the trembling waters of Carion City's port. Across my shoulders, a fire burns hot and heavy. The bow and arrow in my hands feel as though they've been molded to my body. They've become one with my flesh. I couldn't let them go even if I wanted to.

My head pounds as the sea ripples with waves and the sky overhead rumbles with thunder. Clouds slide back and forth across the moon, cutting out its brilliant light until all that remains are the lightning flashes within the darkness and the raging inferno of the slave trader's ship.

Another flash of blinding lightning appears across the top of the sky. This time it illuminates the man standing in the small boat several yards out, fleeing from the larger ship with hurried movements as he forces his arms to row harder and harder. My lips part. Air squeezes into my lungs. It's hot and tastes of ash and desperation. As *if by memory alone, my arm draws back the bow, the arrow notching against the wood and string. My heart pounds, galloping like a racing horse in my chest. The thunder above echoes in my ears. Over and over again until it's all I can hear.*

It reverberates through my bones.

Confusion swarms me. Why this? *I wonder.* Why am I dreaming this? Is it a reminder of what I've done? *I already know that I cannot turn back the clock. I cannot take back a life that has already been taken. Even if I could ... I'm not sure that I would. This man is—was—evil. Wicked. Cruel. Monstrous in his greed. He doesn't—didn't—deserve my pity or my mercy.*

My face feels unmovable. All the emotions rioting against my insides in much the same way the storm beats against the land and water. My shoulders ache with how tight I draw my arrow back and further back until the string and feathers of the arrow are almost touching my lips.

In the distance, the face of the slave trader—the vile man who tried to escape me once before—morphs into a new face. A different man of far more importance. The stone-like emotion in my facial muscles goes slack with shock. My fingers slip free, loosing the arrow unintentionally.

No. *My eyes widen.* This isn't supposed to happen. This isn't what *did* happen. *My lips part and as the arrow flies, I drop the bow and reach out as if I could yank it back out of the air, reverse time, and reclaim my hold.*

Even in dreams, though, that's impossible. So, instead, I watch as the arrow soars into the night—aimed directly at the man standing in the boat. The man who is no longer a slave trader but the exact replica of my father. Tall. Proud. With a golden crown encircling his head and the Royal robes covering his body. He stands rather still amidst all the chaos surrounding us.

"No!" My scream arches into the empty darkness. My heart leaps into my throat, and the pounding of its vessels fills my ears, drowning out the thunderous skies. I can't hear anything. Not the sea. Not the

shouting of Solomon I know should be behind me. All I hear is the thumping beat of my own insides as the arrow I shot flies through the air and pierces my father's chest.

The blossom of red starts in the very center of him and spreads outward, a grotesque flower of blood blooming against his body as the arrow digs deeper and steals his life. A pang slams into my chest and I crumple onto the wooden slats of the dock, swaying as I look down, sure that I, too, had been hit with something sharp. Where I expect there should be blood, though, there is nothing. My hand moves across the space between my breasts, coming away clean of anything save for rainwater.

It falls into my face, clinging to my lashes. I slowly lift my head and see that across the waves my father stands still in the center of the boat. The wooden shaft of my arrow jutting straight out from his chest. My eyes burn in horror.

What have I done? *My skin crawls with ice and tingles. My breath chokes in my throat. I press one hand flat to the dock's surface and shuffle forward on my knees. No. He's already dead. I didn't ... I didn't kill him. I could never. I...*

Arms wrap around me from behind, so hot that they scald me. I struggle against their grip as my father sways one way and then another before eventually toppling into the black sea. "No!" Another scream is ripped from me, but it disappears just as quickly and I'm left to fight against the bands of iron that control me, lifting me up and away from the scene.

More arms, liquid and strong, wrap around me. Again and again, holding me down. I kick. I thrash. I gasp for breath that simply won't come. His arms tighten, growing hotter and hotter. Fire licks against my skin, burning away my clothes and scorching my flesh.

My cries dissolve into whimpers. The pain on the outside is nothing compared to the agony in my guts as the thought that I am the one who killed my own father whips through me. I shake my head. It's not real. None of this is real. But why then? Why would I...

. . .

My eyes shoot open as I fight against the blanket that surrounds me. Somehow, during my slumber, someone had tucked it neatly around me, but now I realize that this is what had been squeezing me and I can't get it off fast enough. With where my pallet is stationed so close to the lit fire, heat pours over me. Sweat clings to my skin, wetting the small baby hairs at the nape of my neck and making them stick to my body.

I rip at the frayed edges, nails digging into the dark swath around me as I tear at the fabric that encases me. I practically hiss with fury and fear at the difficulty of it. Little beads of wetness, not yet cooled, slide over my temple and down the side of my face. Panting, I finally manage to fling the blanket off of me and onto a pile of wood and leaves, the rustling sound loud in the quiet clearing. The soft murmuring of masculine voices halts abruptly.

"Devonry?" Solomon's deep baritone rolls over my ears, calming me slightly.

I ignore his call. Putting a hand to my chest, I look down over my body, checking myself. Relief floods me when I see no evidence of my dream's truth. No blood. No burning. I'm much the same as I had been when I'd fallen asleep. Yet, still, the image of my father remains at the forefront of my memory like a hovering shadow of death that cannot be waved away. I close my eyes as a shudder works through me. Pressing my lips together, I fight back the sour and bitter bile that collects in the back of my throat, threatening to spew forth.

The soft sound of leaves crunching underfoot and fabric swishing reaches my ears a split second before a warm and firm hand comes down on my shoulder. "Are you alright?"

I inhale and slowly release the breath, counting down

the exhale until I swear there's nothing left in my chest before I nod. "Yes," I say.

No! My mind and heart cry.

I wipe the sweat on my brow with the back of my hand. "I-I'm fine. It was just a dream." Before he can take his hand back, I gently brush Solo's arm away and push the rest of my pallet down my legs. Normally, I wouldn't mind his comfort, yet for some reason, the feeling of his skin so close to mine makes me feel ... dirty. As if I can't bear the thought of him touching me with the image of my own arrow jutting from my father's chest still lingering in my mind.

The crackling sounds of the fire fill the small camp that we've made for the night. The flickering red-gold glow dances over the ground and the trunks of the trees. On the other side of the fire, Celine's sleeping form continues to rest. I glance over, noting that Argyle is sitting on a nearby log. He lifts a brow when I meet his gaze, but I don't respond to it. Instead, my eyes drop to the small piece of wood in his grip and the knife he's using to carve at it. The wooden shard is hardly even the size of my pinky.

"It's not yet dawn," Solo says, dropping his voice in an effort, I guess, not to wake Celine. "You should try to get some more rest. It'll be a bit longer before we reach our destination."

I shake my head as I get to my feet. "No." If I try to close my eyes again, all I'll see is my father's bloody chest and my arrow sticking out of him as he falls into the black sea. Reaching up, I drag the sweaty and straggly strands of my choppy, uneven hair off of my nape and yank it up, tying it off with the band of leather I've kept around my wrist the last few days for just this purpose. "I can't fall asleep right now if I tried," I say.

My stomach churns and my head throbs. That bile still

sits in my throat, practically burning a hole with its need to come up. With my back to Solo, I sense more than see the look he shares with Argyle. There's no real reason I suspect they're silently communicating save for the unusual silence that follows my words and the long pause before anyone speaks. I reach for the blanket I'd flung off of me earlier.

"Perhaps you need something to exhaust your mind," Argyle says.

Now that's an idea. "Yes." I swallow and turn toward my pack. It's still where I left it, leaning against the base of a nearby oak tree, along with my quiver of arrows and my bow. "I think exhausting my mind is exactly what I need."

Before I can think better of it, I've crossed the space between me and my things. I snatch my bow off of the ground, gripping my quiver along with it and slinging it over my back.

"Devonry!" Solo calls out, and I pause at the mouth of our camp, between two trees, and turning back slightly,

"I won't go far," I assure him without ever truly looking at his face.

"Let her go, my friend," Argyle says. "We've set up a perimeter. There's no one in the area." My gaze shoots to Argyle's face and he smiles. "Besides—I suspect if someone did happen across your Princess right now, she'd likely make them regret it." The words are said with a smirk and a teasing lilt, but I wince at the comment.

It's a fair assumption, I suppose. I must look more than a little on edge, and it's true: I'm not the same Princess I once was. I now know what it's like to hold a weapon in my hand, to wield it, to kill with it. I step toward the tree line again, hastening my feet as if getting away from camp will be the same as fleeing from my own dream and memories. I'd like it if I could actually run away from it all, but I can't. So, I'll have to make do with the next best thing.

Getting away from their curious and concerned gazes, away from the dream, away from my own fears, and just … forgetting.

As I make my way into the darker shadows of the forest, the smell of wet pine and soil grow richer with each passing moment. I don't hear Solo's footsteps following after me, and I'm grateful for Argyle's words as they seem to do the trick. Once I'm far enough away from the camp and the fire that I'm shrouded in darkness and it's hard to see, I lift my palm. Almost immediately, light and flame lick at my fingertips, glowing brightly as they illuminate my way. I keep walking, seconds passing into minutes until I find a space far enough away that I know I won't accidentally send an arrow flying back toward camp, but close enough that I know I can call for help if need be.

Argyle was right. I don't know how he recognized the need within me, but he had. With the uproar of emotions swirling inside of me and the need to let it all pour out, I doubt I'll need any of that help, even if I am attacked out here. I feel every inch the bloodied girl in my dream, in my not-so-distant past. It's both relieving and frightening.

Setting down my bow against the skinny trunk of a pine tree, whose little stringy needles litter the ground at my feet along with the star-shaped oak leaves that have fallen during the cold season, I clear away a path from one tree to another. Using my boots, I kick away some of the leaves, revealing fresh dirt, and then bend to find a few sticks tall enough to be jabbed into the ground. I try not to think as I work, just focusing on the movements of my body and arms.

Physical labor does that, I've learned in the last few months. You can't really think all that hard when you're driving your own limbs into aching numbness with work.

This will be good practice in multiple ways, I think, as I finish lining the area with sticks and then retrieve my weapon.

I stand slowly, measuring my work with a glance. It will have to do, I decide. With slow, careful steps, I move several paces away from the widest tree of the bunch, the one I cleared a path toward as if to give my eyes a direct line to follow with my arrows. Stopping far enough back, the simple wide trunk becomes an actual target. I swallow down my breath and focus my energy. The heat beneath my skin rises to the surface. It grows hotter and hotter, spreading along my limbs, down my arms and up my legs. Once I feel like it's surrounding me, I open my eyes and focus on the line of dirt I've revealed beneath the bed of leaves and needles of the forest.

All around me, the sticks I'd marked spark and flare, fires bursting to life to illuminate my surroundings. Without oil, without so much as a match or cloth to be lit aflame, these fires are set and controlled by nothing more than my will. Another addition to my training I've decided to include. Holding onto fire is like holding onto the will of a wild beast. She bucks and cranes under the weight of my power, but at the end of it all, she will concede to me as I am her Master. Fresh sweat beads pop up along my temples and at the base of my throat, but I clench my teeth and keep my focus.

Controlling the fires is hard enough. Being able to shoot simultaneously while maintaining every flame will most certainly raise the difficulty level. It's good practice, I remind myself as I swallow another breath, sucking down some of the frosty air lingering in the woods. It'll be necessary as we get closer and closer to our goal.

As much as I don't want to admit it, my dream reminded me of something I had almost forgotten. Something I wish I could forget even now, though doing so would be an insult to all that I've risked, all that everyone with me has risked to get this far. The end of our journey and struggles will come with a price. Retaking my throne and my palace is not going to be an easy task. It's entirely possible I'll have to kill again. That I'll have to kill Nasir myself.

I lift my arms and remove an arrow from my quiver. Despite the similarity of feeling, the physical movement of drawing my bow seems to cause the memory in my dreams to fade faster. Thank the Gods.

One. *Breathe.* Draw. *Tighten.* Loosen. *Release.*

Step by step, I let my arrows fly—aiming at the base of the tree several paces away. Every once in a while, one of my fires goes out—smoke smoldering as it drifts into the darkness. Whenever that happens, I have to stop and refocus my attention. It's harder than I expected to keep up so many small fires—just bright enough to shed light, but not so bright or hot as to catch against other leaves or trees or underbrush. That, combined with the arrows I'm shooting, leaves my entire body aching with soreness.

By the time I take my last arrow from my quiver and send it sailing toward my target, perspiration slides over my skin and the flesh over my forearm feels shredded. Exhaustion overwhelms me, washing away the icky memory of that dream. If I could allow myself to stay here, I'd collapse on the ground right where I stand. But I need to gather my arrows. There's no telling when we'll be able to procure more.

My body is coated in a thin layer of sticky sweat beneath my clothes and the loose fabric of the trousers I'd traded my skirts for some time after we'd left Omarion sticks to my skin. I rock back on my heels. The muscles of my back and shoulders spasm with use. More air slips into my raw throat, shredding a path into my lungs.

For several moments, I stand there just like that—head back, body still, as I just breathe. Despite the heat that burns within me, a visual reference to the fires still flickering all around me, the tips of my fingers, as well as my nose, feel ice cold.

It is only the sound of a twig snapping under booted feet nearby that draws me out of my silent trance. Jerking upward, I take a step toward my target and spin in the direction of the sound, holding my bow up as if it's a club since I lack arrows in my hand. From the shadows, a man's figure appears. Covered in darkness at first, he becomes more and more clear until he steps into the path of my makeshift training ground entirely. A sigh of relief escapes me. I lower my bow.

"You couldn't announce yourself?" I ask with tartness as I turn my back on Argyle and move to my makeshift target.

"I did," he replies with a gentle and amused tone. "You heard me coming, didn't you?"

A scowl ripples across my lips as I rip the first arrow out of the now-scarred tree trunk and slide it into my quiver. "I can't tell who's approaching based on their footsteps," I snap back. "No one can."

"Wrong," Argyle says, his amusement rising further. "I'm pretty sure Solomon can."

That … I can't deny. Solo does have a sort of strange preternatural sense when it comes to that, so it's not like I can disagree with him.

"He's the Blood General," I say. "He can do anything." A fact that I hated as a teenager and that now, I no longer find annoying but instead, reassuring. As if he'll never let anyone sneak up on me or hurt me.

Argyle's responding snort is more caustic than anything I've heard from him before. Turning my head, I watch him as I continue to pry my arrows from where they landed and place them back into my quiver. Without another word, Argyle moves into the space I've created and looks around, his eyes fixating on the fire sticks.

Seconds pass, one after the other and he doesn't speak again or look at me until I've finished my task and pivoted to fully face him. "You're getting stronger, it seems," he murmurs almost thoughtfully. "And you're getting better at this." He nods to the arrows in my hand as I shove them back into my quiver.

Rounding on him, I place my hands on my hips, and then, because the position makes me feel too vulnerable, I cross my arms over my chest as I glower at him. My forearms twinge, but I don't look down.

"I thought it'd be good practice," I say sharply.

He chuckles. "No need to be defensive," he replies, before gesturing to the fires. "Can you put them out and light them with ease now?"

My attention moves to the fires. "It still takes focus," I answer him, lifting one hand away from my crossed arms and letting the other fall. As I do, one side of the path goes dark, the fires dispersing in less than a moment.

Argyle hums in the back of his throat, his expression thoughtful and musing. When he finally graces me with a look, his eyes fall to my arms and he frowns. "You're hurt," he says.

I blink and follow the path of his gaze, finding that my forearm, the one I used to pull my bow back is lined with red welts. Some are so swollen that the flesh has been split and droplets of blood ooze out. I've been at it so long, though, that more than half of the wounds have already stopped bleeding. "I was focusing," I say. "I didn't notice that I—" What? That I'd been repeatedly opening my flesh over and over again? Would he believe that I hadn't even felt the blood as it slipped down my skin toward my elbow and then to my wrist as I lifted and raised my arms? I bite my lip.

Argyle strides toward me, quickly closing the distance between us. When he stops in front of me, he grabs ahold of my wrist, pulling my arm out and twisting it upward. "Your skills have definitely gotten better, but if you're not careful with how you draw your bow, the string will ricochet and snap your forearm. These aren't too bad, but I suspect you'll feel them more in a few hours. The area will bruise."

More than his fingers on my wrist, my obliviousness of hurting myself—the fact that I hadn't even noticed—as I'd practiced makes my cheeks burn with embarrassment. I tug against his hold. "It'll be fine," I say quickly.

Argyle's grip tightens and when I expect him to release me, he doesn't. My eyes flash up to his face. "You shouldn't injure yourself just to take your mind off of things you'd rather not think about."

His words strike something in my chest. I grit my teeth. "That's not what this is," I insist.

Argyle's brows lift and the unchanging expression on his face tells me he doesn't believe me. "It's good to practice and get better at controlling our abilities—both Gods given and learned—but once you start hurting yourself for your goals, you'll find it too difficult to stop."

I pull against my arm once more. "I told you—*that's not what this is.*"

"If not, then let me help." Argyle's response shocks me more than anything else. Before I can formulate my refusal, he's pulling me to the side and pushing me down onto a fallen log. My ass plops down, the cold and prickly wood stabbing at my backside as he finally releases me only to reach into the satchel at his side.

"I'd rather not listen to Solo's complaining if you come back to camp bleeding," he continues, removing a small glass vial and a strip of fabric.

"Do you always carry medicine and supplies with you like that?" He doesn't strike me as the type, but then again —it's already been proven time and time again that I am not the best judge of a person's character.

Argyle's lips twitch and then shift into a smirk as he crouches before me, getting to one knee as he takes my arm back into his grip. "With Celine the way she is right now, I didn't think carrying extra medicines and supplies could hurt," he replies.

He pushes up the sleeves of my tunic a bit more. I had done just that myself as I'd trained. An obvious mistake because it had left my forearms bare to the stinging bite of my bow's string. Thankfully, as I look down, the welts don't appear that bad. Only a few are truly deep and bleeding. The rest are merely red and swollen.

Placing the cap of the bottle between his teeth, Argyle opens it and then drips a few drops of translucent green goo from the container onto my forearm. Recapping the bottle and stashing it back in his bag, he smoothes two fingers up and down over my welts, rubbing the medicine into my flesh. I wince as it begins to tingle.

"You seem to really worry about her, don't you?"

Dual-colored eyes lift back to my face. There's no doubt who we're talking about. For a moment, though, I still think he'll deny it. Instead, however, he surprises me again. "I do."

Two words. So simple and yet within them, they hold substantial meaning. I wonder if Argyle has ever admitted to anyone whether or not he cares for someone other than himself. I know he's friends with Solo, but Solo isn't the type to inspire concern. Celine is different. She's strong in her own way—mentally, spiritually even—but physically, she makes even someone as weak as I want to protect her. For someone like Argyle, she must be a confusing existence.

"I'd rather talk about something else though," he starts as he finishes smearing the medicine into my skin. "You want to tell me what you dreamed about that made you want to come out here and train until you were nearly falling over?"

My back muscles tighten and then, as a result, scream in pain when I tense. I turn my head away from Argyle. "It's nothing."

"Doesn't seem like nothing," he says calmly.

Cloth touches my wrist, causing me to jump slightly as his thumb presses over my pulse there and holds me steady.

"How did you even know it was a dream?" I ask instead.

The breath he blows out is loud in the near quiet of the forest. "You were whimpering in your sleep," he tells me. "Solo was ready to wake you and I suspect he would have had you not woken yourself."

As he wraps my arm in the cloth, trapping the medicine inside and covering the welts, I dip my head and turn to watch his movements. I can't look at his face if I'm going to talk about this so I focus on the repetitive motions of Argyle's fingers as he lifts my arm again and again, twisting the fabric around my forearm from wrist to my elbow.

"My mother was a Saintess," I hear the words before I realize I've spoken them. Now that they've been released, I know there's no stopping them. "She thought that all life was precious. She taught me that. But ... after everything that's happened, I don't know if she was right."

"Did you dream about her?" Argyle asks.

I shake my head. "No," I admit. "I dreamed about the slave trader back in Carion City. Except in my dream, before I killed him, he turned into my father."

"And you think that has something to do with your mother?"

My brow furrows. "She believed in *all* life," I say, emphasizing the word 'all.' "The life of a slave trader would've been no exception. I think ... taking his life was like betraying my family. Betraying both her and my father —maybe that's why he turned into him." And the action of killing is something that can't be taken back once it's been done.

Argyle hums in the back of his throat, continuing his movements. "But you're questioning whether she was right or not?"

I grit my teeth and my hand clenches into a fist. I hate it but yes. "If Nasir had been killed before then my father would still be alive." So would Jacin. "I've killed, and I'll have to kill again. Even if it's to protect others, my mother ... she would be ashamed of me." Even if that is the case, though, I find myself unable to see another path. One without death. If killing is what I have to do, I know now that I'll do it. Regardless of her beliefs and teachings.

It's a betrayal and one I'm walking into with eyes wide open.

Argyle's hands finally still after what feels like a lifetime of wrapping, and he carefully tucks the last edge of the cloth into itself before looking up at me. "Listen, Princess," he begins, still crouched before me, our eyes level with each other. "Some people think that killing gets easier the more you do it. Some say that it's the opposite."

Curiosity rises in me at those words. "Have you ever

killed someone before?" I feel like I already know the answer, but what I want to know now is how he'll respond.

Argyle's smile is small and it doesn't reach his eyes. The lines of his dark face, as close to night as I've ever seen another living being, are drawn. "I've killed my fair share," he says. "Probably more than. The point is to not let any life be in vain—no matter if they're a prostitute, slave trader, or King. The value of life is decided upon by the people who live it."

"For you," he continues, "killing isn't about fun. It's for survival and protection. That's admirable." He cups my shoulder with one hand and rubs the pad of his thumb over the pulse point beneath the fabric now covering my welts. "Your mother was free to make decisions for herself in her lifetime, and as much as you might have cherished her in life, perhaps even revere her in death, her decisions cannot be yours and yours cannot be hers. What you face are two different lives."

Somehow, I find myself unable to tear my gaze away from his bi-colored eyes. They hold steady on my face.

"It's okay to be sad about losing the life you thought you were meant to live." His words are quiet. Gentle but firm. "Don't let that sorrow tear away the ability to live the life that's set before you. It's all too easy to lose the will to live on after tragedies like the ones we've—you've faced. If you give in, *they* win. And I don't know about you, Princess,"—the way he says my title was once so antagonizing, as if he was taunting me for it. Now, it feels like an endearment— "but I'm not willing to let the choices I've made in the past define my future."

Argyle releases my shoulder at that sage advice and nudges my chin with his knuckles. "Now, let's head back to camp. Dawn will be coming soon."

With that, Argyle releases me and straightens, standing

to his full height. I let him reach down and take my hand, helping me up. His words continue to replay as the two of us make our way back to camp. *I'm not willing to let the choices I've made in the past define my future.* Was that what I'd been doing? What I'm *still* doing? Maybe ... maybe he's right.

Putting one foot in front of the other as the sky above our heads lightens, I look up ahead of us and release a breath I hadn't realized I'd been holding. The feminine sound of Celine's light tone reaches us just before we step into the warm circle of our camp. She spins toward us, her mismatched skirts, a patchwork of different fabrics sewn together to hide old tears, swishing around her calves. Her face—which had, for so long been drained of color as she fought her illness—brightens.

"Welcome back," she says. "We've got breakfast ready."

I come to a stop as Argyle moves toward her and I take in the scene before me. Argyle's earlier words penetrate my mind with more meaning this time.

Had things played out differently, I wouldn't be here right now. I wouldn't have known Argyle or Celine. At the very least, even if I've gone against everything my mother wanted, I know that I won't regret protecting their lives. Theirs or—I turn and meet a ruby-red gaze—*his*.

10
DEVONRY

Solomon's fingers curl and uncurl against the rounded muscle of my thighs. He works his thumbs in circles as I hold the reins. In time with his movements, I stroke the old worn leather in my grip. Several areas have gone soft and pale with use and the feeling of it against the pads of my fingers is as much a comfort as the control I have guiding the horse along its path.

The nip of the mountain air has lessened, and humidity has taken its place. Every exposed part of my skin is sticky with it. The thinner hairs around my face curl with the excess moisture.

Solo pauses the kneading of my leg to wrap a strand around his finger and gently tug. "Second summer," he murmurs before pushing his sleeves up his forearms. My own greedy gaze eats up the definition of his arms and the veins so clearly visible underneath his skin.

"Second summer?" I let my head fall back against his shoulder. The rough hair of his chin scratches against my forehead. His lips, so full and stained with the memory of our kisses, brush against me as he responds.

Gods, I want to kiss him again. And again.

"Much of the House of Caladrius territory experiences it, a brief wave of summer heat, before the season finally gives way to fall and winter."

I hum and nod, though this is far from the true Rozentine heat I've experienced; it is much warmer than I might consider normal for the season. But compared to the cold we'd fought for days across the mountains, this is practically a day at the beach.

The familiar *caw* of a bird breaks the following silence. I swat away a bug as Solomon sits taller in his seat and Argyle's attention finally lifts from the path before us. A shadow circles above our heads, the dark swath of wings flapping as the creature descends further and further, grazing the edges of the tops of the trees. My own gaze is drawn to follow that of the men to find the creature that swoops below the tree branches. Black feathers with the sheen of blue darts between us. Our horse huffs and digs its heels into the ground.

"A raven," Argyle whispers, then louder says, "Follow it."

"We're close." Solo agrees and slips his hands around mine. The horse's hooves stomp against the dirt as it picks up the pace.

The raven caws again. All at once, my body tingles with relief as much as with anticipation. After days of travel, we'll be somewhere relatively safe … with a warm bath. I practically groan at the thought of water not coated in frost. I can't remember the last time I had such a luxury.

It's not just the thought of a bath that has my muscles tensing with expectation and excitement. It's also the thought of seeing Frederic, a familiar face I didn't realize how much I've missed until this moment.

A steady stream of anticipatory excitement lingers

inside my mind as we follow behind the raven that guides us. When the covering of trees finally falls away to reveal the large courtyard leading to the white stone mansion with vines and leaves climbing its side, I'm practically falling out of my seat.

House of Caladrius. Lord Frederic's estate. Had it just been a few months since we'd been here, Solo and I, recovering from that horrific dive over the cliffside? It feels like a lifetime ago.

Pillars hold up the large awning that casts its shade over the man who stands with his hands deep in his pockets. At first, his eyes are directed skyward, but when he sees the raven streaking through the tops of the trees, his eyes turn down. Toward us.

Lord Frederic steps out of the shade to squint at our party as the horses trot the last of the distance. My heart thunders in my chest, getting louder and louder with each passing second. The sun shines off the light blond of his hair and catches in the brilliant blue of his eyes. Those ocean eyes roam over us, concern crinkling the skin around the edges before relief eases them. His attention settles back on us as we slow to a stop. Frederic smiles, revealing a dimple in his freshly shaven cheek.

"Your Highness, Lord Solomon," he calls, opening his arms in welcome before dropping into a deep bow. "You have no idea how relieved I am to see you well." His gaze shifts behind us slightly. "And you've brought friends." He offers Argyle and Celine a quick dip of his chin, a respectful acknowledgment, before he settles his hand over his chest and smoothes down the moss-colored shirt tucked neatly into his brown trousers.

Argyle's eyes shift quickly from the raven that disappears behind the manor to Frederic. His jaw tightens as he watches how Frederic moves toward us as though he's waiting for him to pull forth a blade and slit all of our throats. It'd anger me if I didn't know now, just how protective Argyle is, especially because of Celine's recent illness. I, however, am more than overjoyed to see Frederic.

"Lord Frederic." His name springs from my lips as the horse slows and stops. I don't even wait for Solomon to get down before I'm already sliding from the horse. Solomon curses quietly and snaps out a hand, grabbing ahold of me to slow my fast descent. My feet hit the ground, kicking up a small, low cloud of dirt around my worn boots. I release Solo's grip and rush toward Frederic. I stop before him, my insides clenching with the desire to throw my arms around him. I hold it back. "It's good to see you," I say. "You have no idea. Thank you for welcoming us again."

New lines mar the sides of Frederic's face. Stress lines. Still, his smile is radiant as he offers it. "No thanks are required for helping my Queen." Taking my hand in his, he brings his lips to my knuckles and brushes a soft kiss there. The smile on his lips falls a fraction as his attention flicks over to my side. "It would seem our great Blood General has done masterfully in his duties and you've returned back to Rozentine unscathed."

Solomon stands tall and stiff while he watches our host. A polite but tense smile is at odds with the way his jaw clenches. The heat of his hand hovers behind me as though he means to guide me away.

My fingers slip from Frederic's. "I am well," I assure him. "Solo wouldn't let me be anything else." Lord Frederic chuckles at that but doesn't disagree. I gesture back toward where Argyle is currently helping a pale-faced Celine off of their horse. Despite her improvement, the ride and journey has taken its toll. "But we are in need of your healing skills. My friend, Celine, is suffering the lingering effects of an illness, and we were hoping…" I don't have to finish my statement. I can tell from the way his head lifts that he already knows what I'm asking.

With one long finger, Frederic pushes at the center of his rounded spectacles. He tips his head, looking past us to where Argyle grips Celine's waist and finishes easing her onto the ground. "She is still ill."

"On the mend, we hope, but it would do a great deal for my own worry if you were to look her over."

"Happily." He motions toward his home. "My staff is waiting to help you find your rooms and settle. Warm baths will be drawn and I, of course, will personally see to—"

"Celine Dayon." Celine dips in a shaky curtsy.

Frederic's brows rise. "The House of Starfall?"

"Ravens," she whispers, the wind tousling the waves of hair that have fallen from her braids. At her side, Argyle stares at Frederic as if daring him to insult her bastard lineage. I know Frederic, but Argyle doesn't. I can't fault Argyle for being so on edge.

The Lord of the House of Caladrius pauses, taking the information in. He clears his throat and waves us all forward. "Any friend of Princess Devonry is a friend of mine. Once everyone is sorted, dinner will be served in the hall."

Inside the proud manor, his staff waits for us, as promised. Someone takes the horses back to the stables while others guide us back to our all-too-familiar rooms. In my chambers, I nearly melt out of my clothing and into the tub. Only when my flesh is pink from scrubbing and my fingertips have pruned do I finally step out to dress.

In the colors of my House, I finally emerge from my room. My stomach growls loud enough to make me blush when I find someone waiting outside my door. Solomon's arms are folded over his broad chest, his ankles crossed, as he leans against the opposite wall. Blood-red eyes scan me from head to toe before he pulls himself away and offers his arm.

"You didn't need to wait for me. I'm sure you're quite hungry yourself." I rest my hand against his forearm.

"Starved." He runs his tongue over the tip of his fangs. I tremble with the reminder of the sensation of having them plunged into my skin and the fiery pleasure that came with it. Solo smirks as though he's read my thoughts.

The sound of our steps accompanies us to dinner, the soft chatter of voices only reaching us when the dining hall comes into view. Candles flicker from the chandelier that hangs from the tall ceiling, and the last of the sun shines through the large windows behind the head of the table, where it outlines Frederic's silhouette as he stands.

With the scrape of the chairs against the floor, Celine & Argyle rise as we enter. A vibrancy has returned to Celine's features. Her tightly cinched dress shows the slender curve of her waist and displays the weight she'd lost while sick. In her hand, wine sloshes in a glass and she beams.

I grin back and look to Frederic to give my thanks. He smiles softly in return. With his blond hair pulled back into a ponytail at the nap of his neck, it is easy to appreciate the man's beauty. From his defined jaw, full lips, and the strong line of his nose, it is a wonder he hasn't yet married. But I remember that he'd once been a contender for my hand and pull my gaze away.

"Celine, you are looking well. I assume our host has made good on *his* promise to look after you," Solomon says, letting go of my arm only to pull my seat out for me.

"I have never felt better. I can't thank him enough." She sips her wine and sits.

Argyle settles next to her and drapes his arm across the back of her chair, leaning toward her but never touching.

With his free hand, he circles the rim of his own glass. His travel-worn clothes have been replaced by a loose tunic tucked into dark trousers. Though we sit safely within Frederic's manor, a bandolier of daggers is strapped across his chest. Perhaps the first time I've ever seen him dressed in weapons. I know without asking that he's been training himself, preparing as we've all been preparing for what is most likely to come over the next few weeks.

I redirect my attention to Celine and respond to her comment. "It's such a relief to hear that." I reach across the table to clasp her hand. She squeezes my fingers before leaning back into her seat. She takes no notice of the way Argyle angles his body, a bit possessively, as his eyes scan her frame.

"I hope the four of you find everything comfortable while you're here," Frederic says lightly with a small, albeit a little tense, smile on his lips.

"Everything is lovely," I assure him, picking up a spoon as a bowl of soup is placed before me.

"Have you heard any more from Sunfire Palace?" Solomon asks, his tone grim. What little ease within the room dries up immediately. Though no one had wished to begin this conversation, I'm not surprised that he's the first. I also don't have any reason to scold him because, after all, that's exactly why we're here. To gather information. To share knowledge. To prepare and plan.

I say nothing as Solo swirls the glass of crimson liquid —much darker than those of us with wine—in his hand. I don't have to ask what it is, but not knowing what Frederic has prepared for Solo has me sliding a glance his way.

Lord Frederic smooths a napkin in his lap, his glasses sliding against his nose as he looks down. "According to my sources, with the plague darkening the corners of Rozentine, Prince Nasir hasn't left the palace in several days. No more commands have been sent, but there are … whisperings of Nobles who still support a marriage between Rozentine and Bartoli, even to the younger Prince. Most, such as myself, are unable to look past the death of our great King. I've been in correspondence with most Houses, trying to get a feel for loyalties. Your return, my Princess, is greatly welcomed." The look he graces me with is full of repressed warmth and no minor amount of relief.

"Speaking of the Houses." I pull my shoulders back and set down my spoon. "With your help, I would like to call a meeting with representatives from each House. Quietly, of course. We can't have Prince Nasir getting wind of what we plan to do, but if we're to defeat him then we'll need each other and our allies."

Frederic pushes his glasses back up his nose, his expression hardening as he considers my words. "I believe it can be done," he states. "I'm not sure if everyone will come if called, especially since I can't explain that *you* are the true reason for a meeting of the Houses, but I'll send word tonight."

"Not to the House of Daemonium though," I correct myself. Frederic's eyes widen, and he looks at me with both expectation and curiosity. With tightness in my throat, I explain. "I am concerned that their loyalty has been compromised and the betrayal of Bartoli expands to that House." That's all I can say, but in my mind, the memories of Prince Enver, Nasir's brother, and Lord Bryon run rampant. It heats my blood and I curl my hands into fists to tamp down the energy swirling beneath my palms, the fire building.

"I see." For a moment, that's all Frederic says, and then, "If I may, Your Highness, I do have a contact within the House of Daemonium—one that is not an heir—that I can vouch for. He has my respect and I am convinced of his loyalty."

I fiddle with my own napkin. What Lord Byron did cannot be taken lightly. The poison the Galeano family spews seems to go far and wide. Not just their words, but the actions of their second-born son. How can I be so sure that it has not ruined the entire House of Daemonium? Every chance I take might be one that costs me my throne and my country. Though to refuse a seat within a House has been unheard of. It is akin to rejecting the Goddess of the Afterworld, Etia. Something in my chest pulses in pain and the thought of the clear rejection.

Solomon's glass chimes against his plate as he sets it down. I glance at him as he speaks. "I have faith in Lord Frederic's judgment. I think it is wise to consider including someone to represent the House."

I exhale slowly, surprised at Solomon's endorsement. It seems to contrast with the way his features tense when we are near Frederic. Unlike the courtiers of the Bartoli Palace, Solomon trusts and respects Lord Frederic, but trust and respect is a far cry from actual fondness. My teeth worry my lip as I ponder their words.

After everything Frederic has done for us, I, too, have faith in him. And if Solomon trusts that the House of Daemonium isn't entirely rotted, then perhaps I should give this non-heir a chance. I would hate to have to see one of my Kingdom's Houses fall simply because of the failures and false loyalties of its ruling family. There are several branches of the House of Daemonium that could take their place if I let them.

"Then, we will put our faith in you and your contact, Lord Frederic. He will be allowed. I look forward to meeting him along with those of the other Houses. I want them to be witnesses to the official instatement of a new

Rozentine House." I hold Frederic's questioning gaze, fully aware of the frozen stillness that has taken over the rest of the table and my companions.

"A *new* House?" Frederic's words are ripe with confusion as well as curiosity. No denial. No rage. A good sign.

"The House of Ravens." Celine's lips round into a perfect circle as the words leave my lips. Argyle blinks several times before leaning forward in his seat and gripping the edge of the table. I turn my attention fully to them. "I was hoping the two of you might represent this new Rozentine House."

"Your Highness," Celine brings a hand to rest over her heart as she speaks a bit breathlessly, "it would be my honor."

I slide my gaze to Argyle. "And you?" I ask.

His throat bobs as he swallows and his attention shifts from one person to the next. "You want to make the House of Ravens official?" he clarifies.

"Yes, but you don't need to answer my question tonight. If you're unsure, all I ask is that you think on it." Though it would be better to have both him and Celine as witnesses and representatives rather than *just* Celine. Argyle's uncertain heritage and the fact that it's clear he's only partially of Rozentine descent would be a statement within itself. That anyone can be a Rozentinian. Loyalty above purity.

"Though I wish it was under better circumstances, I think that's a fine idea," Lord Frederic says, his confusion cleared away to reveal beaming pride as he looks back at me, meeting my gaze. "This will be a joyous occasion. All of the Houses united under our ruler with the start of a new House." Frederic lifts his drink. "I think a toast is in order. To our future Queen and to a future with the House of Ravens!"

One by one, our glasses rise, and though unsure and perhaps a bit shaky, Argyle's is the last to join. But it still joins. The echo of the sentiment rings through the dining hall. All the while, Argyle watches me, his mismatched gaze glazed over with a mixture of emotion I've yet to place. I can only hope the rest of the Houses are as accepting as Frederic and the House of Caladrius.

11
SOLOMON

Wine and blood fill my stomach and soften my senses. The fear that lingered most of our days is lessened if only a fraction while beneath Lord Frederic's roof. He's kept his word and our secrets. For now, House Caladrius has my hard-earned trust. If the other Houses are to be trusted, it will be determined soon enough.

The quiet halls of the manor lend my mind the ease of deep thought. Devonry had made a statement tonight. While it was only announced to our small group, the magnitude of such an announcement will be felt all across Rozentine. The impact of such is possibly even broader than such changes often have. The House of Ravens is to be recognized as an official House. A place where the outcasts can find themselves again. A community of those rejected from their original birthrights and thrust upon the streets. But with their legitimacy comes their safety.

Yet still, Argyle hesitates. From the drink in his hand to the twist of his features, for a moment at dinner, he'd been the young man I'd found half dead at a bar. He was raw, broken, and clinging to life in the same desperate way he clung to his drinks.

His drunken lips have led to many confessions. A childhood cloaked in darkness, the bravery of an illegitimate child nearly killed by his own family, and finding a home upon a ship of misfits. Argyle is the House of Ravens. He's everything they stand for; he's their miserable pasts and the courage of pulling oneself up by their bootstraps all wrapped up into one. He is, though I loathe to admit it out loud, my best friend.

It is these thoughts, these worries, that lead me to my friend's borrowed chambers. I pause at the door long enough to knock before letting myself in, leaving the door ajar behind me. Only a couple of candles, near burning out, light the room. Thick moss-colored curtains are pulled closed over the windows, blocking out the fullness of the moon.

Argyle's body is a shadowed form that turns rigid as the heavy *thump* of my boots approaches from behind. A half-empty wine bottle sits on the floor, not even a full foot away from his scuffed shoes. Red liquid leaves a ring at its base and drips down the bottle.

The flicker of a candle's flame flashes in the reflection of a small dagger's blade before the weapon is tossed through the air. It whistles as it makes two rotations before the dagger sinks into the smooth canvas of a painting hanging next to the large bed. I count the slices made in the art as another, lighter set of steps enter the room. This time, the door is pulled closed with a definitive click.

"What did this unfortunate man ever do to you?" I grunt, walking around Argyle, careful not to kick his wine, before I pull the dagger from the canvas. The tear in the material gives the gentleman painted upon it the appearance of a dark scar on his cheek. The other rips littered around his face or through his chest of armor.

"It would seem he has the curse of being in the wrong place at the wrong time," Argyle says, sliding the dagger in his hand back into the sheath across his chest.

"That would be my Great Uncle Ulich." Frederic slides his hands into his pocket, bouncing on the tip of his toes as he speaks. "He was a cranky old man. I never liked him much."

"Still, to defile the art in the home of our host…" Argyle looks away as I point my ire at him but takes the dagger I'd pulled free and sheathes it as well.

"My *greatest* apologies, my Lord," he mumbles, stooping to pick up the wine bottle. A line of crimson drips down his chin as he drinks directly from the bottle and he wipes it away with the back of his sleeve.

While my mouth pulls down into a stern frown, Frederic does nothing but smile gently. He looks from Argyle and back to the painting before clearing his throat and saying, "We have other paintings should you need more target practice. Come to think of it, there is one of his wife, my Aunt Ethal, somewhere that would be perfect for such an occasion."

Argyle huffs a laugh, managing to finally lift his gaze. "You are not like other Nobles I've known."

Frederic's gaze is distant as he stares into the now-marred face of his late uncle. After a second, he shrugs and lowers himself into a wingback chair angled before the unlit hearth. "I try very hard not to be like my father. I'm sure he was exactly like the Nobles you're referring to. I'll take what you say then as a compliment." He stretches his legs out, crossing them at his ankles.

"From him, that's high praise," I answer to fill up

Argyle's silence. In only a few steps, I join Lord Frederic and lean myself against the mantle.

Argyle lingers where he stood throwing the daggers before the defiled portrait. His typically proud height is stunted by the hunch of his shoulders as he shuffles in our direction and drops into the armchair next to Frederic. He blows out a long breath, rolling his eyes up to the ceiling.

"So dinner was eventful." Frederic runs his finger over the stitching of the chair's fabric. His attention follows the movement. "Our Princess has many grand ideas. One might think you'd be happy about it, yet I've not witnessed a more distraught man since Solomon was last here."

I exhale, all too familiar with the broken, desperate, and sad man who'd been healed in this very home. Devonry had been my dream then, the one I was desperate to have and determined to never truly get.

Frederic had not so subtly insinuated that if I didn't claim her, he might be likely to step into that role for our Princess. It had awoken something inside of me. Hope perhaps.

Though the parameters of the relationship between Devonry have yet to be set, every stolen second I get with her is like falling from that cliff all over again. The two of us against the world, clinging to each other as the winds try to tear us apart.

Argyle groans and I blink away the trail of my thoughts. I'm not sure it's possible, but somehow, he manages to slouch even deeper into the chair. "I do not wish to be one of them," he says, squeezing his eyes shut.

"With legitimacy comes the power to make a difference." Frederic leans forward, propping his elbows on his knees, only to straighten as Argyle swiftly rises from his seat.

"The House of Ravens already makes a difference,

Lord Frederic." Something dangerous and wild flares in Argyle's gaze. I recognize the swift rise of uncontrollable anger. "Every damn day, we make a difference. We might not be changing the country with a snap of our fingers or passing laws as we sip our morning tea, but when we take in another person cast from their House and shrouded in their own shame … make no mistake, we have changed the world for them. We give them a home, a purpose, a new family. We fight against the evils of Rozentine that the Houses would rather pretend don't exist." He sniffles and runs his sleeve under his nose as he pulls his shoulders back and continues. "I have little interest in being one of *them*."

"One of us, you mean." I pull myself away from the hearth. "Is there no part of you who could agree to head this House? Because whether or not you want it to happen, it needs to. For the safety of all like you and the good of Rozentine."

"I was never meant to be a Noble," Argyle whispers. "No matter what is in my blood."

A drop of red slips from the end of the bottle in his hand. Wine mars the hardwood floor and Argyle rubs the toe of his boot over it to wipe it away. Still, the crimson spot remains. Much like the sins of this country will after Devonry is crowned. Like ghosts, the misdeeds of those before us will haunt us as they haunt my friend now.

"It's not what is in your blood that matters." I place a hand on his shoulder, my fingers curling against the thick material of his shirt until I feel the warmth of his flesh beneath it. "What matters is what is within your heart. No matter what becomes of the Ravens, Argyle, you are good. Your heart is good. Rozentine needs more of it."

Argyle hands me the wine bottle and runs a hand over his face. The neck of the bottle is sticky with liquid and I frown as I set it on the mantle. His mouth is pressed into a firm line, eyes narrowed but still full of the ghosts from his past.

Frederic rises. With a single step, he stands before us, bringing with him a medicinal but herbal scent as if his abilities have manifested in the smell of his skin. I'm not sure if I prefer it to the sickly sweet scent of the wine.

"Princess Devonry wants to usher in a new era when she claims her throne. Legitimizing the House of Ravens is a fine idea. Argyle as its Lord, perhaps even finer. It seems as if the time for traditions to be changed has come, and I, for one, support it," Frederic says as he places his hand on Argyle's other shoulder.

My friend sways beneath the weight of our hands, but he nods and says, "I will think on it."

"That's all we can ask." Frederic offers a small bow before turning to the door. He pauses. "You know, typically, those who do not wish for power make the greatest leaders." With one last flash of his smile, he dismisses himself from the room.

If it was anyone else I might do the same and let them wallow in their miseries alone. But when I look at Argyle, I see the boy I found on that bar top, the one who claims I saved him, when I'm quite certain it was he who saved me. So I set myself to lighting a fire before I claim Frederic's now empty armchair and stay.

12
DEVONRY

Wind tussles my curtains as I pull my stocking up my leg. I stare at the way the material flutters against the walls, my mind playing tricks on me. The rise of the sun has begun to cast a shadow and in the haze of my early morning thoughts, there is a flicker of strange movement. The shine of scales slipping over the window's edge. The twitch of a serpent's tail.

My palms warm but never turn to flame as I stand to my full height and cross the room. The breeze smells of frost and pine. It blows the strands of my hair away from my face as I squint into the sun. Boards creak under the weight of my footfalls. The curtain flutters again, rising up to graze my leg before it stills once more. Silken and smooth the material ripples like water as I brush it aside and stare out at the House of Caladrius' land.

Frost shines on each blade of grass, a sign of autumn and the return of winter. The nights foretell the bitter cold to come, but the days still hold onto summer, not quite ready to let it go. A shiver leaves behind goosebumps on my arms as I lean forward, eyes searching for movement or shadow.

It's not possible. I tell myself. *It's only your imagination.*

Vivid and stark are the games my mind plays, fueled by paranoia and fear that always seem to wait until the day is quiet and I'm all alone. I bite into my lip. The small spark of pain is the reminder that I'm still alive and hope remains.

I let my attention roll out over the yard. The only shadows found, lurk at the edge of the property where the trees grow thick and the road into town leads away from the manor. Only birds, rabbits, and other small animals move about, not man or monster. There is no shine of reptilian scales. No purple-hued eyes waiting to betray me. Nothing.

The race of my pulse slows as I let out a long breath. Yet, I still find myself leaning further out the window, daring to look beyond what I am capable of to remind myself I'm safe.

"Don't lean out too far, or you'll fall on that pretty little head of yours, and this will all be for naught."

My heart leaps into my throat and my fingertips turn to flames. I spin, pinning the curtains between me and the window's frame. The sizzle of flames in my hand dies at the sight of the crimson gaze settled on me. The hint of a lopsided smile graces his full lips. The dark strands of his hair, grown long enough to fall forward into his eyes, are sprawled over his forehead.

"Solomon, you startled me." I press my fingers to my chest, the beating of my heart steady underneath. "I didn't hear you come in. Why didn't you announce yourself?"

"I did," he says, taking another step closer. "I knocked. Twice."

Had he? How had I not heard him?

I smooth my fingers over the reddish brown gown I'd slipped into. The bodice is suddenly too tight at the sight of Solo watching me with such brazen intensity. His attention slides down my frame. The dress is simple, somewhere between a commoner's garb and the finery one would assume a future Queen ought to wear. All I can do is watch as his tongue slides out across his full bottom lip and he raises a singular brow.

"Oh." I manage, pulling myself away from the curtains.

"What were you doing?" The floorboards groan as he walks by me to peer out the window. He pushes a hand through his hair, only for the strands to fall back over his face as he leans out and looks one way and then the next.

"I thought I saw something." I wave a hand as if to prove that even the vague thought was silly. I am being strange, this much I know. It's hard not to find myself reliving these past few months.

But Solo cocks his head, his features turning down and thinning with seriousness. He takes another glance out the window; this time, it looks like his red eyes are tracking over every darkened space a person could hide. He tips himself further still, looking up and down the edge of the building.

My body warms. His body is firm under my palm as I place a hand on his back. "It was just a trick of the light. I think I was being overly suspicious."

"I take all threats to your safety seriously. Even…" He straightens and tucks a strand of my hair behind my ear. The warmth of his fingers lingers against my cheek before his hand falls back to his side. "Even if it's all in your head."

"I suppose that is what you took your oath for," I answer, missing the warmth of his touch already.

"I would protect you even if I was not bound to an oath. Though I'll admit, I quite enjoy the idea of you protecting yourself." He looked down to where I'd clasped my hand in front of me. "You were really quick to draw your flames. Your abilities have come far in a short time."

"A compliment? From Solomon Winett?" I fan myself, grinning at him. He rolls his eyes as I stroll past him to my slippers and slide my feet inside. "How gracious of you."

In turn, he mocks a bow. "I only endeavor to please my Queen." As if on cue, my stomach growls as he finishes the sentiment. "And apparently, what will please my Queen is a healthy meal. Shall we?"

He offers his arm, his shoulders pulling back as my hand slips onto his forearm. In another world, walking arm in arm together would be as familiar as breathing, but in this world, I can still feel that twinge of guilt left over from a childhood of keeping us apart. This togetherness, as small as the gesture is, would have the entire Court staring and gossiping. Not just something frowned upon between a Princess and her guard but something once forbidden by the King.

But I'm the Queen now. I remind myself, lifting my chin in defiance against the still niggling feelings.

A comfortable silence falls between us, though it grows less comfortable when my stomach growls again and Solo chuckles quietly to himself. My cheeks heat with that ever-persistent blush I can't seem to shake when it comes to him. I look at him, ready to shush him with something witty I haven't quite come up with yet, but what little words I have get stuck in my throat when I catch the way he stares so intently down at me.

"What?" I ask softly.

"Nothing, just waiting to hear what that smart mouth has to say."

A woman rounds the corner ahead, several fine shirts hung over her arm. A maid, then. She slows as she approaches, dropping into a quick curtsey. The halls of Frederic's manor are not as large as the ones in the Sunfire Palace, which leaves little to no room for either of us to pass the other. Solomon drops my hand only to bring his arm around my waist and pull me closer to him to create the needed space.

My curves flatten against him, my steps stuttering only to be forced forward by Solomon's unrelenting strength. His heat seers through my clothing, setting every part of my skin buzzing with a prickly sort of energy. *Damn him*, I think, only to be rewarded with a teasing smirk as he sets me right again. *Will there be a day when my body doesn't melt at his touch?*

I'm saved by the flurry of movement as we turn. A flash of blond hair and icy blue eyes is hidden behind a dark cloak quickly thrown over broad shoulders. Frederic points a finger to a small chest before a man scurries to pick it up and carry it outside. There is a flush to his cheeks and a light sheen of sweat over his forehead as though Frederic had been running these halls not a moment before.

"Lord Frederic." I pause and Solomon's fingers curl tighter against my hip instead of falling away. "Where are you off so early this morning? I thought we might see you for breakfast."

"Oh," he says, his words breathless as he slings a pack over his shoulder. "That would have been lovely, but I'm afraid there are a few things I must attend to this morning. There should be food ready and waiting for you in the dining hall."

"What things must you attend to that have you leaving so quickly?" Solomon's tone is harsh, untrusting, even though his expression remains free of his usual scowl. It takes some strength on my part not to shove my elbow into his ribs for prying. Yet I find my own anxiety rising at the uncertainty.

Frederic's eyes slide from Solomon's face to mine. Whatever he sees gives him enough pause. He inhales slowly, adjusting the bag on his shoulder. "My apologies, you're right, this does appear quite frantic of me. Let me explain myself." His attention slides down to where Solomon's hand still holds my waist. "This epidemic has spread amongst my own territories. I was just headed out to a few villages to offer aid and services for those affected."

My chest tightens. How far and how fast has this plague spread? How many lives has it claimed already? On their own accord, my feet carry me a step forward and out of Solomon's embrace. I look down to the other bags and chests waiting to be taken to those in need.

"Does the power of the House of Caladrius rid people of this illness?"

The sound of Solomon's leathers as he moves is loud following my question. I don't need to turn around to know that he's crossing his arms over his chest, waiting as if he already knows what I'll be asking next.

"It can lessen the symptoms. I have family who've traveled to help other Houses affected. We do what we can, but it is ultimately up to the Gods if the person is to survive." Frederic sighs and grabs for a chest, pulling it up against him. The shuttering of glass vials gently chiming against one another follows the movement.

"Could I come and help?" I'm already reaching for the last wooden crate. My fingers brush the wood when Solomon's heavy boot lands on top, rattling the contents.

"Did you just ask if you could go to a village riddled

with a plague that has been taking lives all across Rozentine?" My guard stares down at me, the darkness of his disapproval shining crimson.

"I want to help." I grunt with the effort it takes to push his foot aside. Still, he stands as a looming, warming over me as I heft the crate up into my arms. A bitter scent that wrinkles my nose wafts through the slats. "And if Lord Frederic would be so kind as to allow me to accompany him, I will do just that."

Because this is the kind of Queen I want to be. This is the kind of woman I want to be. Someone who doesn't hide from the ugly parts of this country but faces them head-on. There may be a lot of things I can't do in the position I'm in, but this is *something*.

"It would be my honor." Frederic's bow is awkward with the chest in his hands, but he manages well enough.

"You cannot be persuaded to stay here, where it is safe?" Solomon eyes my white knuckles as I hold the supplies against me.

"I cannot."

A growl rumbles out of his chest as he exhales and drops his arms in defeat. I smile a little at that, but the red of his gaze flares for a moment before he takes the crate out of my arms. "I would just like to say that I think this is a terrible idea." He turns toward Frederic. "You've got room for two?" My grin widens.

Frederic nods. "I'll have someone bring a horse from the stables."

Less than ten minutes later, I'm seated upon a steed with thick packs of supplies strapped to the animal's hind side. Solomon settles into the saddle behind me.

"I still think this is a terrible idea." He speaks softly into my ear. His breath tickles down the side of my neck. I lean back into him as he circles his arms around me, reaching for the reins with one hand, the other holding a small cloth-wrapped item. "For you."

"For me?" I take the small bundle from his hand. Warm and cradled in my palm, I peel back the folded material. A warm pastry and a few strips of meat are enough to make my heart flood with joy. "Thank you."

His lips brush my cheek, but he says nothing in return, only guiding our horse behind the wagon, practically overflowing with supplies. Frederic sets the last of his packages in the seat next to him before turning toward us.

"When we get there, as a precaution, you'll need to cover your faces when we attend to those in need. Are you ready, Princess?"

"Yes," I say, though I worry that I'll never be ready enough to witness the toll this disease is taking on my country.

The ride into town isn't a long one, not when compared to the days we'd spent on horseback previously. Our journey is silent, though excitement runs through my veins at the prospect of being helpful.

The first rotting body we see is half a mile from the village. A dark gray color darkens their flesh, dried blood a ring around their mouth, and their ribs jut out over a deflated stomach already picked open by wildlife. After that, the first of the houses come into view and I swear even the vibrancy of the surrounding trees is dulled the nearer we ride. A sickly scent lingers in the streets, a mixture of death and bile stretching in every direction like a thick fog.

My excitement dims the further we go. I point to a home with a red line painted across the front door. A woman with a thin scrap of a blanket thrown over her shoulders huddles on the steps, her cheeks sunken with dark circles under her eyes. "What is that mark?"

"A home that has the plague, likely," Solomon answers.

The farther we ride, the more houses we find with the markings on their doors. Villagers huddle outside of the affected homes as the few who remain healthy try to distance themselves. The pounding of a hammer reaches my ears. A man with his face wrapped in a scarf places nails in a long board over the door of a home with that same red marking.

I watch in horror as another man, walking on the side of the road, slumps forward before his body topples over. His head is turned toward us, his eyes distant, his chest still. Dead.

This disease is eating away at my home, my country. If this place, newly affected, is as terrible as this, then what are the cities hit sooner, filled with so many more people looking like? I shudder to think.

13
SOLOMON

The village is one of the worst I've seen since our return to Rozentine, but there are signs that it was not always this way. Despite the lack of people walking through the streets and the clear miasma of disease that hangs in the air, there are tools laid beside doors and overgrowth along the edges of houses. The streets, however, remain clear and there are still supplies and stacks of firewood outside of the houses that tell me things were not always this poor.

Gently, I settle my hand on Devonry's shoulder as the horse beneath us clomps forward. "Bring your face covering up," I advise her as I lift my own and tie it firmly around my head.

Devonry hurries to follow my command as I direct the horse to follow after Frederic's covered caravan full of supplies. The moment it stops, he disembarks, jumping from the front and rounding to the back while calling out orders to those who've come with us. All at once, from silence to sound, there is a flurry of movement.

Men and women from the Caladrius House cover their

noses and mouths with tied cloths and get to work. I steer the horse to the side and quickly jump down. Before I can turn and reach up to help Devonry, she's already thrown one leg over the saddle to join the other and is sliding over its side. I capture her quickly, with my hands around her waist, and lower her the rest of the way.

"These poor people," she murmurs in horror as doors start to open and those that are healthy enough to walk peer out of windows.

"My Lord!" a woman cries out from the opening of one hut. She dissolves into a harsh coughing fit a moment later. "Oh ... thank ... the Gods..." she says between bouts.

"Be careful," I warn Devonry with my eyes set on the woman before turning to the rest of the village. "Don't get too close if you can help it."

Devonry's body stiffens at my side. "I came here to help, Solomon," she snaps in response. "I will not treat them like pariahs."

My attention focuses on her face and I can tell, even with the cloth covering half of it, she's scowling at me. The little pinch between her brows is enough of a sign. "Do what you can to help," I say, "but remember that you are an important figure and if you want these people to have better lives, we can't have you get ill. I should not have allowed this in the first place."

She steps up to me and my hands release her waist as she pokes me in the chest. "You are not my commander, Solomon Winett," she growls. "I am yours—don't act like you're doing me a favor."

There's no chance for me to remind her that I very much am her commander and that if I think she's in danger, I don't care if it'll piss her off; I'll whisk her away without a moment's notice. And I certainly won't listen to her complaints if it comes to her safety—whether we're battling a man or an illness. Before I have an opportunity, she turns away from me and strides toward the back of the caravan.

I watch her for a moment with narrowed eyes, making sure she's taking on jobs that don't bring her into contact with the ill. Frederic lifts his head, as if sensing my attention, and glances at me. A silent exchange passes between us and he nods his understanding. As the Lord in charge of this territory, even if she is the Princess, Devonry will bow to his orders and follow them.

Within minutes, he has her unloading supplies and stacking them in areas that are easy to access. She, along with many others, set up an emergency shelter to begin the proceedings. Left with little else to do, I follow the larger members of Frederic's party and begin to ready medicines for dispensing.

Though it's not hard work, it is long and seemingly never-ending. The day grows long, and eventually, I find myself entering the houses of the diseased, carrying many objects for the healers and apothecaries who have joined us to do their duties. Unlike what we'd witnessed with Celine, these villagers have even worse symptoms.

Haggard faces covered in graying skin peer out from beneath torn sheets and worn blankets. The sound of hacking coughs and wheezing breaths echo into my ears. Each house seems worse than the last. Some of the villagers are even too far gone for medicine and when that happens, the healers and apothecaries simply exchange the herbs for coughing and breathing to ones of pain relieving nature.

Sorrow and sympathy fill me as the healer I'm with bows her head over the man lying with his eyes closed in a cot in a darkened and dusty hut. Her soft sniffles hurt my chest and I'm more thankful than ever that I didn't allow Devonry to see this. It would have broken her heart.

The man coughs once, his entire body seizing with the movement as it wracks his old frame. The healer cries harder and finally, I can take it no longer. Cupping her shoulder, I nudge her back. "Go outside," I urge the woman with fraying hair and a smattering of freckles over what I can see of her nose and cheeks and forehead. "I shall attend to him."

Watery brown eyes look up at me. "There's no medicine for this," she says. I know what she means.

"I shall stay with him," I assure her. It's the least anyone can do for someone who is too far gone for a cure or treatment.

A battle of responsibility wars across her expression. She looks from me and back to the old man. I give her a few moments for the illusion of a decision on her part, but in the end, I know that if she denies me, I'll simply lift her and carry her out only to return for the man not to be alone as he passes. Thankfully, however, she doesn't force me to do that.

Instead, she nods and then gets to her feet, handing me the rag she'd been using to pat the sweat from the old man's face. "Don't…" She sucks in a breath that forces the cloth over her face to mold itself to her lower half.

"I won't leave him alone," I tell her, guessing her intentions.

She blows out a breath and the cloth moves away from her face slightly. I know I've guessed right when she nods sharply, turns, and flees the room. With a sigh of my own, I pick up the discarded rag, dip it into the bowl of water that the healer had set nearby, and then wring it out. I pat the old man's face, and as I do, his eyes crack open.

"Richard?" The old man leans up as he stares at me. "Oh, Son. You've come back. Oh bless the Gods…"

I bite down on my tongue to keep myself from correcting the man. I don't know if it's a cruelty or a kindness to tell him the truth. It's clear the man is excited and animated by the prospect of seeing his son on his deathbed. If he thinks that son is me, then who am I to deny him that final wish?

"I"—cough—"wanted"—cough—"Oh Gods…" Unable to string a sentence together in the midst of his coughing fit, I carefully help the man sit forward as much as he has the strength for. Unfortunately, the coughing doesn't stop even with the movement. It only gets worse.

His body bows and contracts with each harsh breath as he hacks and hacks. I close my eyes, fighting through my own emotions to find the place I know well. A place so far back in the recesses of my mind that nothing can reach me. I developed it when in battle. A safe haven that keeps me grounded even in the middle of death and destruction. I need it now, I realize, even without bodies falling around me and blood spewing from swords and arrows.

These are battles of a different nature but will end in much the same way. "It's alright," I say to the old man, my hand smoothing down his back.

So focused on my task of holding him, I don't realize the old man's sudden burst of strength. Before I can stop him, he reaches out and snags a hold of the cloth over my face. He yanks it down and leans forward, eyes wide and mouth open. Instead of words, however, upon his next cough, a spray of blood comes out.

I blink and jerk back, but it's too late. The blood speckles my face and the old man cranes over the side of his bed before collapsing back, wheezing out one final breath as he reaches up to the ceiling of his hut.

"Richard..." That one word, that begging call, rings with finality a second before the old man closes his eyes and then is gone.

"Shit." I jerk to my feet and rip the cloth off my throat, using it to mop up the blood. I'm not angry at the old man for endangering me. No, but I am filled with a deep void of worry.

"Sir Solo." The sound of the healer's voice in the doorway returns. "Is the old man—"

"Don't!" I call out, holding up a hand behind me. "Don't come any closer."

The cloth in my hand comes away with the blood of the deceased and another curse falls from my lips. Without turning to face the woman, I let my hand drop to my chest.

"What's happened?" she asks, sounding scared.

She should be, damn it. And so should I. I never should have let Devonry come here. I never should have come here either.

"Please inform Lord Frederic to take Devonry back to his manor immediately," I command.

"W-what?" The woman's confusion is clear in her voice.

I don't want to turn and face her, but I do so anyway, and when I do, she cups her hands over her mouth—despite the fact that it's still hidden by her face covering. "Oh no..." I don't have to look in the mirror to know that I haven't cleaned up all of the blood on my face, and it doesn't take but another moment for her to realize the reality of my situation.

"I-I'll go inform Lord Frederic right away, Sir Solo," she says. "St-stay—please stay here. You should put your mouth covering back on."

"I think I'll need a new one," I say, holding up the blood-stained cloth. Even if it feels pointless, I should do so just in case. This horrid disease has done far too much. Even if Frederic allows me back in his manor, I'll need to be quarantined and at that point, there's nothing more to do than pray to the Gods that they won't steal me away from Devonry before my purpose has been fulfilled.

"Yes, of course," the woman stumbles back, nearly falling as she hits the lip in the doorway. Instinct has me reaching forward, only to stop and pull back once more, curling my hand into a fist as I let it drop back to my side.

"Hurry," I urge her. "*Now.*"

With a quick nod, the healer rights herself, turns, and sprints away, leaving me alone in the old man's hut. Slowly, I turn back to face the man. In death, his face is much more serene. No longer wracked with pain. That, at least, is a blessing.

I close my eyes briefly, and when I open them, I reach forward, grabbing hold of the edge of the sheets he'd attempted to throw off in an effort to get to me. With gentle hands, I draw it up and over him—covering the old man's face and his peaceful expression. I hope, for his sake, that his last thoughts of his son were good ones. I hope, if the son has since passed on as well, that the two will meet each other in the Afterworld.

That is the last hope I can have for them as I take a few steps away from the cot and slide down the wall. My knees point upward, bent, as I settle my elbows on top of them and hang my head.

This disease is the last thing we needed.

It doesn't take long for the healer to fetch and alert Frederic to the circumstances. A knock sounds upon the doorway of the hut several minutes later and I lift my head from where I sit. Frederic's figure stands just on the other side, but he's smart enough not to enter.

"I need a horse," is all I say.

A moment passes, and then he nods. "You'll have to return alone," he says. "I've already sent a messenger ahead to the manor."

I blow out a breath. "What will be done?" I ask. I could guess, but I'm curious to know if he'll take this as seriously as I would.

"The healers recommend isolation for two weeks," he states. "I've ordered the servants to remove most of the furnishings in your room. I'll have food delivered twice a day if that's acceptable as we wait…"

He doesn't say it, but I know what he's thinking—as they wait to see if I'll catch this disease and perish the same way the dead man behind me did. My head sinks back on my shoulders and I stare up at the hut's ceiling. It's thin, barely a barrier to the elements at all with various slats of wood mismatched and uneven, allowing small tendrils of light to pierce through. I pity the man who lived here and yet, at the same time, I don't regret allowing him to think of me as his son before his passing. Wherever he is now, I hope it's a much better place than this one. I hope he's no longer in any pain.

"Don't tell the Princess," I say as I slowly climb to my feet. "Leave a horse outside of the hut and make sure everyone stays clear."

I don't have to see Frederic's face to know that he's making a rather surprised expression. His voice upon his next words is enough to tell me he's rather shocked by my words. "You want to keep it from her?"

"Yes."

"You know that's not possible," he argues. "She's going

to notice that you're not around when we return to the manor."

I know he's right. "You can keep her from worrying for the time being by lying to her," I snap. "Tell her I ventured ahead."

"And in the morning?" he prompts. "When she realizes you've yet to come out of your room? She will have questions, Solomon."

"I'll cross that bridge when I come to it," I reply.

Yes, Devonry won't be unaware of my problem for long, but for at least this next day or so, I can ease her mind. Inevitably, she will blame herself for this. I know her well enough to know that. If I can stave off her pain and guilt for however long it takes for her to find out, then I will.

"This is preposterous, Solomon," Frederic snaps, his voice turning angry. "I will not be *lying* to my liege, and certainly not for you."

"Don't think of it as a lie then," I tell him. "Just keep the information for now. As you said, she'll find out soon enough. At least let her finish her duties today."

Tension fills the space between us. Careful as he is not to enter the hut and come near me, Frederic is also not pleased with the situation. No one would be. Finally, after a beat, he responds. "I will respect your wishes for now, Lord Solomon," he says through gritted teeth. "A horse will be called over and placed outside for you to take back to the manor. At the very least, I will alert your friend, Argyle, of the situation."

That, I suppose, is as much as I can ask for from him. I nod my acquiescence and watch as he turns around and disappears once more. A little while later, the sound of a horse's neighing draws me to the window and I watch from the distance and relative safety of the hut as Frederic, himself, ties a horse to a nearby tree branch. When he finishes, he looks up and catches my gaze.

He's not pleased, that much is for sure. He nods once before glancing back to the horse, turning, and then striding off. The second he's gone, and I've made sure there isn't anyone in the vicinity, I dart out of the hut and make my way to the tree line.

The horse nickers at me as I unwind its lead and then place my foot in the stirrups. It's been minutes, not days, but already I feel my mind roiling with worry. What if I am, in fact, ill? What will happen to Devonry if I die here?

I lift myself onto the horse's back, straddling the saddle as I steer the creature the same way I'd come not long before. Who would have known that I'd be returning like this, as if the hounds of the Afterworld were on my tail?

Perhaps Celine had overcome it—and yes, we had been around her without getting ill ourselves—but it's clear that the disease has taken a new, dire path. She had never coughed blood. Kicking the horse into a gallop, I lean down and send a prayer up to the Gods. Please, I beg. Please let these next two weeks pass by without a sign of disease. Let her be safe while I cannot watch over her.

I can't leave Devonry. Not now. Not when she needs me most.

14
DEVONRY

"Where's Solo?" Several heads lift and turn toward me as I voice my question. A few of the healers exchange a pregnant glance, but what they say, I'll never know because before I can ask, Frederic appears before me.

"He went on ahead to the manor," Frederic says. "You'll be riding back with me."

"He did?" I frown as I allow Frederic to take my arm and lead me over to one of the wagons now being piled high with the others who came from the manor to attend to the villagers. "Why didn't he say anything before he left?"

"The matter was urgent," is all Frederic says.

I frown at him. *What could that mean?* Once more, I don't get an opportunity to ask as several servants and healers pass by us, their forms downtrodden and shoulders slumped in exhaustion. It's been a long day, and even now, as the sun descends beyond the horizon, I can feel the exertions of the day taking their toll.

Lord Frederic assists me into the front seat of the

wagon and then takes his place next to me, lifting the reins. Dust kicks up as he clicks at the horses and they begin to move forward.

My fingertips are cold from the air and my cheeks feel flushed. My head aches from lack of hydration. I'd forgone any sort of break due to the dire straits of the village. This disease is nothing like anything we've ever known before. It's curious and also deadly. How fast it's spread, and how quickly it's changed. As we make our way back to the Caladrius manor, I contemplate what I know of it. Celine had gotten it early on as we'd arrived in one of the port towns. The Caladrius territory, though, despite its vast trade routes, is far enough from the larger port cities that it shouldn't have been hit this hard. At least not yet.

I try to think back to my lessons with imperial tutors. Closing my eyes, I rest my head back on my shoulders and draw from my memories. As the sole heir to the Kingdom of Rozentine, I'd been taught everything from economics, etiquette, and political policies to art, history, and literature. Illness was an inevitability in life, but so rare was it this bad that it would destroy entire villages and disrupt a country's daily life. It can't be a coincidence that something like this would coincide with the disarray of the political climate we're currently living in.

The Kingdom is run not by its true heir but by a usurper.

My eyes pop open as the wagon lurches side to side and I turn my head to Frederic. "Tell me something, Lord Frederic," I say.

Cool blue eyes turn my way. "Yes, My Lady?"

"How has Rozentine been in my absence?" I ask.

He stiffens as if the question has thrown him. I admit, it's a rather startling question to even myself, but one that must be asked. In history, a sudden change of a sovereign

—especially after an assassination—is met with riots and upheaval.

"It's…" Frederic begins only to trail off as his expression turns contemplative. "It's been … rather quiet, actually," he admits, lowering his voice. "Other than a few notices from the palace and some obvious, underhanded threats, Prince Nasir hasn't done anything to change the policies and such of Rozentine. Everything I've noticed that he's done specifically has all been in search of you, Your Highness."

Just what I thought. I lift a hand and tap my chin. My finger edges up a little bit at a time until I pull my nail into my mouth and bite down. It's a nasty habit I'd had as a child, and yet somehow, it's returned. I jerk my hand from my mouth the second I realize what I'm doing.

"So, other than his search for me, you're saying Nasir hasn't done anything else? He's not placed new policies? What about with his home country?" I demand.

Frederic turns his gaze forward once more, his jawline tightening as he clenches his teeth. The skin over his knuckles whitens as he pulls the reins in his grip taut. "My sources say that he was in contact with the Bartoli Court while you were there," he says, his tone low, quiet and seething. "My guess is that he was more than happy to learn that you'd survived that cliff fall he'd once thought took your life."

"Do you think he was in cahoots with them?" I ask.

Curious eyes cut toward me once more. "Do *you* think so?"

No. I shake my head. "They wanted me to marry his brother," I state. "I think they wanted me as well as Rozentine. With Nasir in control of Rozentine and his brother married to me … they would have everything they wanted and I'd be nothing more than a puppet Queen."

Frederic nods at that. "I could see that being the case."

"If he was in contact with the Bartoli Court while I was gone, other than finding out I was still alive … what would he want? Information?" There's still so much I don't know and so much I don't understand about Nasir's reasoning. More than that, though, I have to wonder why the people of Rozentine's lives have hardly changed. He's done nothing but search for me, but even if that's the case—Rozentine and the Sunfire lineage is based on the Gods' bloodline. No one in Rozentine would allow an outsider to take the throne—not without a fight.

Yet, there's been no fight. No battle. No war. Weeks. Months have passed since my father's death. I'm missing something, but what I can't say. "I have to talk to Solomon when I get back," I finally decide.

At the mention of Solo's name, Frederic's body goes rigid at my side. With a frown, I turn to him. "Frederic? Are you alright?"

His lips press together into a flat line as we crest a hill and the top of the Caladrius manor appears before us. "Perhaps it would be better for you to rest on it tonight," he says, enigmatically.

"I mean, I suppose I could," I say, rather startled by his abrupt shift of attitude. "I do want to figure this out before our meeting with the Houses, however."

Still tense, Frederic nods. "I understand, Your Highness, but sleep is also important. You must take care of your health."

I sigh. "Are you upset with me for coming today too?" I ask, and then before he can answer, I launch into my defenses. "I know Solo was against it, but if I'm a Queen, I need to see how my people live. It's my responsibility as a Royal to take care of them. They rely on me, and what use is a Queen who doesn't even care for her people—"

"I am not saying you did anything wrong today, Your Highness," Frederic cuts me off as more and more of the Caladrius manor comes into sight. The windows glint with the lowering rays of twilight, and the gates are already open, with the guards standing vigilant as we come up to it and pass through. More dust and dirt kick up around the horses' feet and the wheels of the wagon as we draw to a slow stop.

"Then, what—" Frederic snaps the reins back, halting the wagon from going any further and I lurch forward, catching myself on the lip of the seat to stop from flying off completely. *What in the world?*

Frederic descends from his driver's seat without another word and crosses around the front of the horses to hold his hand up and help me down. He's acting peculiar. Was it something I said? Is he angry at me?

Taking my hand, Frederic's actions are gentle despite the obvious frustration on his expression as he assists me in stepping down from the wagon. "It's been a long day, Your Highness," he says as I open my mouth to ask him what's wrong. "You should retire for the evening and give yourself a rest."

"I—okay?" My response is a bit breathless, as if I'm a ship whose sails suddenly lack wind to push it forward. I say nothing more as Frederic gives me one final look, dips his head in deference, and then goes to the back of the wagon to help the others.

As kind and gentle as he is, I've never seen him with such an expression before. It doesn't help that as I watch him walk away, his long pale hair tied up at the back of his head swings back and forth like the pendulum of an old clock. Back and forth, over and over again, reminding me that time is ticking forward. Shaking my head to rid myself of the image, I turn toward the hulking manor. Though I know I should probably stay back and help the others unload what's left of the items they took to the village. Instead, I find myself moving into the front hall and taking the staircase up to the second and third floors.

More than anything, I want to talk to Solomon right now. Perhaps he can shed some light on Frederic's strange actions and attitude.

Solomon is nowhere to be found following our visit to the village. I search the dining hall and the parlors. I head to the training grounds and still find nothing. By the time I make my way back to my chambers later that night, I'm frustrated and sweating with exertion.

Celine greets me in the doorway. "Oh dear," she says as she takes one look at me and ushers me into the room. "You look exhausted," she tells me. "You should take a bath and rest, Your Highness."

With a sigh of frustration, I collapse into a nearby chair. I'm sulking, and I know it. "By the Gods, where could he be?" I mutter half to myself as I crane my neck back, trying to work out some of the kinks that have developed during the day's work. Keeping my back and neck bowed for so long as I'd tended to the sick and infirmed had done nothing for my own body's health, but I don't regret it.

"Let me draw you a bath," Celine insists as she hurries off into the adjoining bathing chamber alongside my room. She leaves the door open as she works, and I can hear her bustling around. Her soft footsteps lull me into a sense of serenity. The sound of her turning the spigots and the rush of water as she gathers drying cloths is calming. It brings me back to the present, reminding me of my current reality.

I have to talk to Solomon. It's not a want but a need. Yet, I have the strange sense that he's avoiding me, and I don't know why. Could it have something to do with Lord Frederic's irked mood?

As I think it over, Celine comes back into the room and urges me up from my chair. She leads me into the bathing chamber and helps me undress and step into the steaming water. I jolt at the heat when it touches my skin. I didn't realize how cold I'd gotten until the warmth of the water slides over my nearly frozen flesh. Sinking down until the surface grazes my chin, I pull my legs up to my chest and wrap my arms around myself.

"Celine?" I prompt as she takes a seat outside of the clawfoot tub and begins to soak my hair with the water surrounding me.

"Yes?"

I bite my lower lip. There's something I've been meaning to ask, something I've wanted to know for a long while from her. Now seems like the perfect time, and it will be a distraction from all of the other things I need to think about.

More water pours over my hair and shoulders. After several beats of silence from me after my initial start, Celine leans over and props her forearms on the lip of the tub. "Is there something you'd like to ask me, Princess?" Her voice is quiet and soft. Always polite. Always gentle. At least when it comes to me. My lips twitch at the reminder of how she acts toward Argyle.

Flecks of dirt and dust come off of my skin and disintegrate into the water as I look anywhere but at Celine. "Do..." I begin again. "Do you ever see things that you don't tell others?"

"You mean my visions?" she asks.

I nod without looking up.

"Sometimes," she answers.

I peer up at her from beneath my lashes, curious. Her eyes are tilted down though as she weaves the tips of her fingers back and forth through the surface of the water. I wait, knowing there's more to her answer than that singular sentence, and after a moment, I'm rewarded for my patience.

"There are an innumerable amount of paths that people can take in life," she says, her tone quiet and contemplative. "From the moment we're born, we've got the will of choice bestowed upon us by the Gods. Being born Noble doesn't necessarily mean you'll be good. Being born into a family of thieves doesn't necessarily mean you'll be bad." Back and forth, her fingers sway through the water. I'm locked on her now unable to look away.

"My visions aren't always accurate," she admits. "They show possibilities. Sometimes, I get a knowing that if I share my vision, it'll change. If the vision is a bad one, if it foretells troubled times, I share it regardless as a warning. But if it's good, then I leave it be. I want good things to happen and even if current times are tough, I've been given the gift of knowing it'll get better."

"Will things get better for Rozentine?" The question is out of me before I can call it back.

Celine looks up and meets my eyes. Her smile, though, is small and wane. "That is yet to be known," is all she says in response.

I curl my arms tighter around myself. "So much has changed over the last few months," I say. "I'm scared." No one knows how truly terrified I am. Not even Solo. To say the words out loud to someone who's not him feels like a betrayal, and yet, at the same time, I feel as if I can trust

Celine with my deepest worries. Looking into her dark eyes, full of such understanding and old pain, if anyone can understand me, I know she can.

We may be from two different backgrounds, two different worlds, but we are together here now. "Did you know that you would meet me?" I ask her.

Her lips quirk, one corner lifting. Just that small movement is enough to transform her usually stoic and calmly reserved expression into one of true beauty. When she smiles, she looks more regal than even I do. Lifting her hand from the water, Celine reaches up and touches my cheek. It's barely a brush, but the sensation is soothing, nonetheless.

"I knew one day someone would need me by their side," she tells me. "I didn't know who they were until I met them."

"Do you ever regret your ability?"

Her hand drops away and she turns her head. I follow her gaze, but there's nothing there. Just a chair where the drying towels sit and the wall. Her expression suggests that she's looking beyond them both to somewhere far away, somewhere I cannot see.

"Whether I regret it or not will not make it go away," she finally says. "I've learned to live with it and use it to the best of my ability." She turns back to face me and gives me another smile.

"I may have to ask you to look into the future one day," I tell her honestly. "If you stay next to me, I'll inevitably use you for your abilities." It's the duty of a Queen, after all, to use all within her means to protect her people.

Celine's smile widens. "I look forward to that day, Your Highness," she says kindly. "Now, let me wash your hair. It appears you come back each day covered with more dirt and grime than ever before."

Water pours down over my head with little warning other than that statement, and I cough and sputter as she soaks me through with a light chuckle. Reaching up, I part the wet strands that have run into my face.

I find my attention focused on the chair and wall that she'd been staring at before as she washes my hair thoroughly. Soap suds descend my shoulders. Though the scene before me and the room that surrounds me is one of familiar mundaneness, there is something beyond all of it. The Kingdom of Rozentine. The Sunfire Palace. Small places can hold within them imperceptible powers. Even ordinary people can do extraordinary things.

It doesn't matter if Nasir has managed to take over my Kingdom; he will fall, and I will reclaim my throne. That much I don't need Celine's seer abilities to know.

15
SOLOMON

As I shut my eyes, I'm transported into a world that has become all too familiar. The clouds beneath my feet clear away, revealing a stone-lined pathway. All around me, the light of the dreamland is muted beyond the clouds, as if the sun in this place isn't quite as powerful as it is in the waking world. I take a step forward, and immediately, the clouds swallow up the ground I'd been standing in, letting me know there will be no turning back.

With a heaving breath, I move forward. Following the path, I'm led through the foggy surroundings until I come upon a door. It's not special by any means. In fact, it appears every bit an ordinary wood door with an iron handle. Taking it into my grip, I turn it, finding the door unlocked, and enter the room beyond.

Stopping immediately once I realize where I am, the door behind me shuts and when I whirl, I find it suddenly gone and nothing but stone in its place. The figure on the bed across from me sits up.

"Solo?"

Damn the Gods, I curse to myself, but then it occurs to

me. This isn't real. I'm not physically near her, so this much contact is fine.

Slowly, I turn back to face Devonry as she slides her legs out from beneath the covers and moves to the side of her bed. She's dressed for the night in a long pale chemise that does nothing to hide the curves beneath. Curves that I've felt beneath my hands, beneath my tongue, and wrapped firmly around my cock.

As if awakened by the memory, my groin tightens and my cock lengthens beneath my trousers. Lifting a fist over my mouth, I cough into it and cant my hips to the side as I half turn away from her, hoping she won't notice.

"Is this…" Her question trails off as she approaches.

"Yes," I say, answering the unfinished query. "This is a dream."

"We're not…"

"No," I agree, moving my hand away from my face. I flex my fingers, opening and closing my own fists. "It appears we're in control this time."

"Is that so?" The sharp tone of the Princess' voice has me lifting my head and turning back toward her as she places her hands on her hips and glares at me.

"Princess?"

"I never imagined that I'd catch up to you in my dreams," she says. "But since I've got you here, as my captive audience, do you have something to say to me?"

My shoulders tighten. "I don't know what you're—"

Devonry doesn't allow me to finish as she stomps right up to me. Despite the obvious non-reality that we're currently in, though, the scent of her is as strong as it ever was. Soft and warm, it settles in my nostrils and only serves to harden my cock ever further.

"Where the fuck did you go, Solo?" she demands, glaring up at me with those flashing blue-hazel eyes of hers. They flicker gold for a singular moment before reverting to their calm state. Perhaps our ability to now control these shared dreams has something to do with her Awakening. No sooner has that thought occurred to me, though, than she slams forward, slapping a hand over my chest and pushing me back into the wall.

"Answer me, Solo," she snaps.

The heat of her palm slips through the thin tunic over my chest. It penetrates my very flesh and delves deep into the core of my powers. I feel chained to this place and her. A familiar hunger swells within my belly and my fangs tingle in the way they do right before they descend.

Turning my head to the side as I try to maintain my composure, I focus on a place above her head. "It will be best if you stay away from me for the next few weeks, Your Highness," I say.

"What? Why?" Her head moves back, the movement of her hair shifting caught in my peripheral vision and urging me to look directly at her. I ignore it and resist.

Frederic's words come back to me. Though I hadn't quite expected to tell her in this way, she must understand this is for her safety. "I— there was an incident at the village," I say. "I could be infected with this new epidemic and it would be better for you to—"

"So?" she interrupts, forcing me to glance down at her.

"So?" I repeat.

Her pretty blue eyes roll. "Solomon, I helped take care of Celine. Did you think I wouldn't take care of you too if you got sick?" My heart squeezes at her words.

"No," I snap, reaching out and latching onto her shoulder. I push her back slightly. "This new illness has changed. The man coughed up blood. We can't risk you, of all people, getting sick. Therefore, I must stay in isolation until we're sure that I'm not affected."

She stares back at me. "So, you want me to stay away from you ... for *my* sake?"

"Yes," I say.

"I was around dozens of those ill with this disease," she states plainly.

But none of them had coughed up blood on her. "It's for the best."

"I see." A moment passes, but there are no more outbursts from her. No panic. No more anger. Then she steps closer and I find myself with my back against the wall, quite literally, once again.

"Devonry?"

Her hand moves down my chest. My cock pulses. "I need to stay away from you for a while, but we're in a dream here," she says, her gaze moving down as well.

Fuck. There's no hiding my erection now. My teeth clamp down and my fangs itch to come out. I grasp her shoulders with both hands now. "It's not a good idea—"

"Give me one good reason," she snaps, cutting me off as her head turns upward once more and her eyes settle on mine. "You can't get me sick in a dream, Solomon. If I must be away from you for weeks, then fine. I'll do as you ask, but here, none of your reasoning matters."

"You have much to worry about," I tell her. "This is…" Inappropriate. Dangerous. Sanity-depriving.

"You didn't seem to care so much when you took me to bathe in the woods." Her reply is quiet and damn near pierces my chest.

I lower my head. "*Devonry.*" Her name is a plea on my lips. I cannot resist her.

Moving so that her chest is against mine, I feel Devonry's hands creep to my hips, both of them sliding beneath the hem of my tunic. When did my reserved Princess become like this? And why the fuck do I find it so Gods damned tempting?

"You're right," she breathes out the words. "There's a lot to worry about and we have a short while until the meeting of the Houses. I won't be able to be with you for the time being—not during the day—but why can't we have this?"

I grit my teeth harder. Despite that, my hands on her shoulders are gentle. The heat of her is against me, seducing me. I close my eyes. "I..." Have no reason to deny her. I've already fallen far from the grace of King Vernon. I've defiled her again and again and I've loved every instance.

"Fuck." The word bursts free from my lips a split second before my baser urges take over. I reach down and wrap my hands against the back of her thighs, lifting her against my chest with a single sharp movement.

A gasp of surprise leaves her lip, cut off only by my own as I dive down and take her mouth with the fervor of a savage. Hunger, deep and powerful, moves through me. She tastes of something divine and forbidden and yet still, I want her. I've had her, but I'll want her again and again. For the rest of my life and even beyond when the beating of the heart in my chest ceases. I will still want her.

"*Solo*." The barely there whisper of my name on her lips drives me to the brink of insanity.

Devonry wraps her legs around my hips as I stride forward, each movement bouncing her against me. We reach the bed where I set her down. Leaning back, Devonry's eyes meet mine. The glitter of desire in those crystal depths is like a lightning bolt to my spine of which she's the only cure to my pain.

My hands arch over my head, grabbing fistfuls of my tunic at the space between my shoulder blades. I drag the shirt over my head and off until the fabric collects at my wrists before I pull them free and toss the cloth away.

It feels real. Every touch. Every breath.

Slender, feminine hands move to the front placket of my trousers as Devonry begins to undo the laces there. I lift my palm and cup the swell of her breast through the thin fabric of her chemise. Her nipple pebbles hard beneath my hand. The sharp inhalation she gives raises her breast up and pushes it harder against my grip. I squeeze her lightly before letting my fingers move to the tip where I toy with the hard little nub. Pinching and twisting it, I smirk as her hands falter at the front of my pants.

"Something wrong, Princess?" I ask, pressing a chaste kiss to her temple as she bows her head.

"You…" She gasps as I pinch and twist her nipple once more. I love the way she arches and squirms, rubbing her thighs against each other as if she's trying to stop the feelings coursing through her. I could tell her, from my own experience, that repressing it all will only work for so long. "Solo!"

My eyes close at the cry that emits from her lips. When they reopen, I brush her hands away from my trousers and instead, reach for her chemise. She doesn't fight me as I slowly lift it up and over her head, tossing it away once her bare skin is revealed to my eyes. Pushing her back so that her spine meets the bed, I'm graced with an image that could rival any Goddess. Soft curves, round breasts tipped in the prettiest pink, a flushed face, and wet, parted lips.

As much as I want to take her mouth all over again, there's another taste I crave. With her eyes settled on mine, I lower myself to the ground knee by knee. Her next gasp fills me with masculine amusement. My lips curve upward as I grip her thighs and drag her to the edge of the bed, spreading her open so that I can find the new taste I desire.

I kiss one trembling inner thigh and then switch, offering the same to the other. Devonry's hands are shaking as they make their way into my hair and I look up, locking my gaze with hers right before I lean forward and take her into my mouth.

Juice, wet and hot, descends down my throat as she cries out again. I lick. I suck. I devour all in my path. The hunger for her is like nothing I've ever felt before, not even Bloodlust. This is something altogether different, something powerful. My eyes slide shut and with the sensation of her nails scraping at my scalp and her thighs over my shoulders, I allow myself to completely ravage her the way I've always wanted to.

It's different than the first time, more like the second. The first time had been out of my control. It'd been dark. It'd been incited by the Divine power emanating from the caves. Now, though, I can see her. I can control my own movements. I'm led by want versus a mindless need. I flick my tongue over the pearl at the top of her pussy and then delve inside, seeking more of her wetness so that it will flow over my lips to the back of my throat.

"*Solomon.*" She says my name—over and over again—as if she can't think of another word, another plea. There are no Gods here, just her and me.

Her body grows taut beneath my ministrations. The muscles in her thighs contract and release in repetitive motions, squeezing my head between them. Never has there been a man so turned on the way I am now. So inflamed by her taste and scent. I want to take her in an animalistic way that will eradicate any doubt she may have on whether or not I want her, on whether or not I will destroy this entire fucking world if it means she will be safe.

All it would take is one singular word from her, and I

would slaughter thousands. The human race itself would go extinct if she so wished it. Cities would fall into rubble and dust. Entire nations. She is my Master and I, her slave.

My mouth moves up to her beaded clit as it pulses with desire. I suction my mouth over the needy little bud as two fingers move to her entrance. Pushing inside, I feel her insides clamp around me as I suck and lick in rapid succession. My name falls from her lips as her hips lift off the bed.

"Ah!" She screams out and I'm rewarded for my efforts with a gush of wetness around my knuckles and the feeling of her arching up over me. A shadow falls over me as Devonry sits up and wraps herself around me with my head firmly grasped between her legs. Her whimpers are music to my ears.

I release her clit and lick at her, gently, soothingly, until her jolting trembles ease a bit. Once they have, she sits up straighter and lowers her legs from my shoulders, her chest rising and falling as she breathes through heavy pants. Her face is no longer the only thing that's flushed; her breasts are as well. The pink shade of her skin has descended, staining her throat and shoulders. She couldn't be more beautiful than she is in this moment.

A low, rumbling growl burns in the back of my throat. *Mine.* That's why I find her so beautiful now, because she's mine and she always has been.

Before I can contemplate the direction of my possessive thoughts, I jerk up and grip her face in both of my hands. Her eyes widen, blinking in surprise a moment before my head descends. I capture her lips with mine in an instant; the moment they touch, she relaxes again. Her hazy blue eyes slowly lower and she meets my kiss with one of her own.

It's not enough. Pushing her back onto the bed, I rip at

the front of my trousers and shove them down, freeing my cock from its confines.

"Open your eyes, Devonry," I growl, ripping my lips free from hers.

Her pale lashes lift as her gaze settles on me. Her breasts rise and fall with the harshness of her breathing. I lift one leg of hers over one of my thighs and then perform the same with the other. "Solo." Her voice is hoarse, clogged by pleasure. "What do you need?"

Soft fingertips, like a butterfly's wing, lightly brush against my rigid abdomen and I tighten all over. Beads of sweat pop up along my spine and shoulders. I can feel it at my temples as well. What does she do to me but turn me into a raving beast? I'm lost in her. So fucking gone and I don't want to be found.

"Look at me," I whisper as I move forward, gripping my cock in one hand and planting the other onto the bed behind her. "Look at me as I take you, Princess."

The head of my cock meets her entrance and despite all that work I did to make sure she was ready for me, she can't hide the wince that comes as I push forward. I split her open, delving deep into her core until I bottom out and there isn't a place where she exists without me and where I exist without her.

I leave myself there for several long moments, letting her adjust to my cock—it doesn't matter how often she takes me, her insides still clench around me in a vice-like grip. Her face twists and her hands flatten against my abdomen, pushing ever so slightly.

Reaching down, I snatch her up by her wrists and plant them over her head. With our bodies parallel to one another and my cock so deep inside of her, there's no escape. Petal-colored lips part. "Must you always be this *big*?" Her complaint makes me smile.

A chuckle rumbles up my chest before bursting free from my mouth. My head sinks down and I press a kiss to the side of her throat right before I sink my teeth into the same spot.

"Gods!" Devonry snaps out the word as her upper body arches off the bed and shoves against my chest.

"No Gods here, love," I reply, releasing her to lick at the mark I left. "Just us."

Her hands pull at mine as I lift up and look down at her. "Let me go," she murmurs.

I arch a brow. "Why would I do that?" I ask. "I've got you right where I want you." My hips cant back, sliding my cock almost completely out of her cunt before I thrust forward to the hilt. Her body shudders and her eyes roll back in her head.

Devonry bares her teeth and when she reopens her eyes and settles them on me, it's with a knowing glint in them. "You're tormenting me on purpose," she accuses, pulling against the manacled hold I have on her wrists once more.

I smirk. "Perhaps," I hedge, pulling out and thrusting back into her a second time.

Her lips part and she swallows roughly. "Why?" she demands.

I hum in the back of my throat. "Who's to say," I reply, leaning down far enough that I can lick a bead of sweat trailing down her collarbone. "Maybe I'm just repaying you for all of the years you've kept me on edge, *Princess*."

"Solo, don't—"

I don't allow her to deny me again. With fast movements, I transfer both of her wrists into one of my hands and then grip her hip with the now-freed one. Using my hold, I fuck into her with rapid thrusts. Her body moves up the bed as I power into her, her head arching back as she cries out in surprise.

She's squeezing me so Gods damned tight that I fear I won't be able to hold out for much longer, but if I have to stay away from her in the real world for the next while, then I'm going to get as much from her as I can here. Here, we don't have to abide by decorum. We don't have to be bodyguard and Princess, warrior and sovereign. We can be two souls colliding. We can be everything we were meant to be.

"Open your eyes," I snap again when she closes them. They pop back open immediately and I release her hands to grip her jaw. "Keep them on me," I order. "Don't you dare look away."

"Solo … Solo … I'm going to…"

"Come," I growl. "Come all over my cock, Devonry. Let me feel you squeeze me tight."

White teeth flash and sink into her lower lip, hard enough to draw blood as she does just that. My hips stutter, coming to a complete stop as I thrust myself as deep into her as I can and feel the way her inner muscles clamp down tight. She milks me free of my release, over and over again. I don't pull free. I don't have to here. Instead, I let myself unleash all of my darkness into her. Shuddering through my own orgasm as she reaches hers, I succumb to the glorious feeling of marking her in a way I know I've always wanted to.

Her nails sink into my shoulders as she squirms beneath me; they rake down my arms. "Solomon!"

Leaning forward, I lick the single bead of blood on her lip, a burst of dark spice and burning heat on my tongue. And like the ungrateful monster that I am, as I close my arms around her and hold her through her release, I think to myself … *if only this was real.*

16
DEVONRY

A halo of light surrounds Celine's form as she pulls the curtains back enough to peer outside. In the courtyard, I can hear masculine voices and the sounds of workers setting about their day. I peer at her, at the loose curls falling forward into her face as her eyes alight on something there beyond the window. Her lashes flutter, her lips purse, and then she turns to look at me. That pursing of her lips evaporates immediately, and her deep brown eyes blaze with excitement and no small amount of relief.

Relief at being off the road or feeling better? I don't know, and I don't want to remind her of the days all of us spent worrying that she would not be able to overcome her illness. I'm simply thankful for the warmth that has returned to her features, to the light of life now shining in her gaze. I can only pray to the Gods that soon I'll see Solomon's eyes with the same life and light, pray that he does not succumb to whatever awful disease has taken our continent and our people and made them all so … hopeless.

I sit up and give her a wan smile. "Good morning."

Celine drops the curtain and tucks her hair behind her ears. "I think the last of the Lords have arrived," she says. "Shall I help you dress so we might join them?"

Her words are followed by the sounds of crunching rocks beneath carriage wheels. My chest tightens. Today will not simply be another meeting. Today will mark the day that I take my first act as future Queen before all of the Houses and their representatives. I cast a look to the window before returning Celine's gaze, now more subdued than before.

"Yes," I answer. "Let's get ready."

Celine hurries toward me and stops alongside the bed to grab the rope alongside the headboard and tug it. Within minutes, the doors to my chambers open and a whole host of servants of the House of Caladrius enter. They carry into the room buckets of water, boxes of make-up and dresses, and all the things a Royal such as myself should now be used to and maybe once, what feels like a lifetime ago, I was.

Now, though. Now, I am changed. I remain silent as I watch them, with Celine at my side. I understand the formalities of meetings such as the one we're about to have. I understand the need for the elaborate gowns that the servants spread out for choosing at the end of my bed. Everything in this world of mine—in this political world—is a game. How you look, act, stand, speak. All of it can show weakness or strength. The masks we wear are as much an armor for protection as they are for disguise. Today, I have to walk into that meeting and stand as tall and unbroken as both my mother and then my father had before me, and as their ancestors before them.

No one but my closest friends, but the family I've made for myself along the way, can know the true depths of how I've changed. Of how the sight of jewels and crowns and tiaras and hair ornaments make my stomach queasy. I've seen the poverty across my lands, and now I find myself fighting back distaste and rage at the sight of so much opulence. Beautiful though they are, it's hard to accept the fact that they are needed. Because if I do not gain the support of the other Houses at this meeting, then I don't know where we'll be. I don't know where we'll go or what we'll do.

If I do not gain their support, then I do not know if there will be a Rozentine to rule anymore.

Once the servants are done, Celine dismisses them with a polite but firm command. They curtsey quickly and disappear out of the doors, turning and shutting them once they've all left, sealing the two of us inside. Alone.

I look to her, confused as to why they left before I was ready, and Celine cups my shoulder. "I thought you'd find it easier to bear with just me." Her words are quiet but full of understanding.

I reach up and clasp the hand on my shoulder, squeezing my fingers around hers. "Thank you."

That's it. That's all I offer and that's all we say to each other for the next few hours as she helps me bathe, dress in a gown of heavy skirts with a low cut against my breasts as the neckline cups my bosom and thrusts them upward. It takes at least half of the time for her to take hot irons and curl my short hair back away from my face. It's shorter now than it's ever been, but she still takes precious pains to get each and every strand and then pin certain parts with little pearls so it stays out of my face.

I force a smile as thanks once we're done. When I stand and turn to look at myself in the long mirror that had been brought in by the servants as well, I stare back at the woman in my reflection. Celine is at my side, a quiet friend taller than myself. I feel as if my whole body glows with an inner light. My pale skin no longer seems sallow, but bright, golden. My hair, which was once a choppy, uneven mess, appears purposefully that way. Curls swaying at my temples and slightly above my shoulders.

The dress is everything I believe my mother and father would have loved to see me in when I took my throne. It's a deep wine red with stitches of pale gold. Plainer than anything in the Bartoli Court that I'd seen, but perfect for a Queen done with the unnecessary frills and overwhelming luxury of Royal life.

I brush too-cold fingers over my pleated heavy skirts and suck in a breath that has my breasts pushing flush against the fabric at my chest. "Well, then," my words come out breathless and a bit nervous as I pivot to face the woman at my side. My friend. "Shall we go?"

She shakes her head slightly, causing me to frown as she moves away from me and back to the vanity that accompanies my chambers. "There's one more thing," Celine replies, picking something up and turning back to face me. My eyes fall to the belt in her hand, or rather what would be a belt if it were not far too short.

"What…"

Before I can finish my question, Celine comes back and kneels before me. My skirts are parted and a gasp escapes as I realize that there's a slit hidden within all of the fabric. She buckles the belt—not a belt, I realize but a harness of sorts with a dagger sheathed against it. Celine makes quick work of fastening it around my leg and tightening it until it's just enough to stay in place but not enough to hurt.

All of the remaining anxiety and fear at facing the Heads of the Houses fades into a little ball in the back of my mind. Still there, but not as prevalent or as overwhelming. I hadn't realized how accustomed I'd become to having a weapon on me. Even if it's not a quiver of arrows and a bow, the small dagger is like a symbol of my change, of all I've done to get here. It may be hidden, but I can still feel the heavy weight against my thigh, far lighter than that of the tiara now sitting atop my head, encrusted with the same pearls that adorn my hair.

"Now," Celine announces as she gets to her feet and fixes the folds of the dress that were once hidden to me and now sit as a secret access to a blade I hopefully won't need to use. "You're ready."

I push down the burning pain in the backs of my eyes and carefully reach up and touch a finger pad beneath the crease and sigh with relief when I feel no escaped tears. "Thank you." My gratitude comes out in a sharp breath full of roughness.

Celine says nothing in response, but merely inclines her head as if to tell me she understands, and I realize she does. She truly knows and accepts the new pieces of who I am, probably far better than I do myself. Even when she insists on dressing me, on treating me as a Queen, *her* Queen, never once has she made me feel like I'm wrong for refusing certain traditions now that my world has been upended. What would she have been like if she'd been born at my side, as a sister rather than a bastard daughter of a fallen branch of a Noble House? What will she be when she joins me in my Court after all of this is over?

A pillar of strength, I realize, as I gaze back into her doe-brown eyes. Eyes the color of the earth. Eyes like those of a wise forest creature. I don't think I've ever been more grateful for her presence than I am now. And as if she senses that too, she curtseys lightly and then joins me at my side as the two of us leave my chambers and walk along the corridors until we reach the great hall.

Every square inch of the manor has been dusted and polished until it shines as brilliantly as a diamond in preparation for today's meeting and those who are meant to attend it. The murmur of staff busy at work had been a comfort, so reminiscent of the Sunfire Palace I'd found myself thinking back to my old rooms, to Sheza, and the games I'd play with Solomon.

Now the halls are empty. Quiet.

Waiting.

As Celine and I near the entrance to the great hall, the thudding beat of my heart races in my ears. I pause just outside of the threshold, just out of reach.

Celine brushes her fingers against my elbow as my gaze slides to the closed door and then down. Solomon won't be here today. His quarantine has yet to end and no Lord would have taken the chance of infection, not after they had all ridden here through various methods to disguise this meeting. They were already risking enough with Nasir and his spies no doubt watching from anywhere, everywhere.

Celine, ever wise and knowing, speaks in a low voice. "I hear he is well," she tells me. "No sign of disease, thankfully."

"How long does he have before he can be released from his quarantine?" I ask even though I already know. I've been counting down the days since I was told. Counting the hours, the minutes. I just need to hear it from someone else now.

"Soon," is all Celine says.

My skin burns with the need to be near him. Because dreams do not do justice to what it's like when his flesh is flush with mine. The desire to see him in physical form, in the waking world, to assure myself that he is well and unharmed by the disease is a harsh boulder coated in flames sitting in my breast.

And if something happens to him ... if he *does* fall ill...

My insides ache with that familiar needling of guilt that's plagued me for days.

I had demanded we go. I had needed to risk our health to feel as though I was doing something useful for Rozentine, for my people. My fault. If he were to die from this, there would be no place I could hide from my shame. It would be *my fault.*

The sound of men's voices, low and tense, pulls me from my thoughts, banishing them away as I suck in a breath and realize that regardless of what happens with Solomon, to Solomon, I must play my part today. I cannot rely on him for everything and certainly not for this. The two doors leading into the great hall are propped open, and when I step into the entrance, I see a long table surrounded by mostly men.

They quiet as we step inside and Celine pulls the doors shut behind us.

Faces, familiar and new, turn to look at us. They look at me. But my attention only grazes over them, settling on one.

In a sea of people, I would find this man. Like a moth to a flame, I'm drawn to him. And suddenly everything rights itself as though for two weeks my center of gravity had been off.

Polished boots, new leathers, and shining blades strapped to his muscular frame, Solomon Winnett leans against the wall. Everyone else in the room is nothing more than a shadow in his presence. From my center, a swirling heat rises to my chest, over my neck, and to the tips of my ears.

The scuff of chairs against the floor breaks me from

the stupor I've stumbled into. Those gathered stand from their seats and lower into deep bows or curtseys. Only then am I able to shift my attention.

"Princess Devonry," someone murmurs, though whom I can't quite tell.

"Queen Devonry," I correct. Eyes of every color follow me as I come to the table and hover near the last available chair. "You may rise."

Lord Frederic smiles from where he straightens at my side. His attention drifts over me with clear approval before he pulls my chair back and offers me the chance to sit. "Queen Devonry," he starts, "it would be my honor to introduce everyone in the room."

The rest of the room waits until I've tucked my skirt under me and am seated before they lower themselves into their own chairs. Everyone except for Solo, who remains against the wall at the farthest point from me. I have to force a smile to my face to keep from frowning at the distance. We've had walls and closed doors keep us apart and even just this damn table between us raises the temperature of my blood several dangerous degrees.

"You are familiar with me as Lord of the House of Caladrius and Lord Solomon here, who is representing the House of Blood," Frederic starts, but I refuse to let my attention drift back to Solomon. Gesturing across the table, Frederic points to the other man at my side. "This is Lord Liriel of the House of Starfall."

With warm brown skin, hazel eyes streaked with silver —like lightning darting through a stormy sky—thick waves of hair framing his face, I find a resemblance to my friend in the slender shape of his face and those high cheekbones. I raise a brow at Lord Liriel, turning my gaze from him to Celine. Her mouth is pressed into a tense smile while something darker swirls in her gaze. Her father, perhaps? Who is this man to her?

Argyle's hand slips under the table, and I'm certain he's gripping her hand. And then my attention is on him. Argyle. He came.

Though his expression is missing that usual twinkle of humor or joy, he came. I can't help but smile broadly at that.

"Lord Liriel, any relation to my dear friend, Celine?"

The man stiffens but never once turns to face her. His ring-clad fingers curl into his palm on the table as he dips his chin. "She is my niece, your Highness."

Interesting. Or rather, fury inducing.

I don't hide my disdain for this man as I trail my attention over him, hoping to pour every ounce of my ire into it. Let him know how his Queen feels about their treatment of Celine. Perhaps he feels some of the depths of my annoyance as he leans back in his seat, gaze dropped to his lap.

"To his right, is my cousin and his wife, Ellis and Harlow of House Caladrius. Though I am Lord, Ellis often acts on my behalf when I'm called away or otherwise busy since I have no heirs as of yet. I thought it might be wise to pull him in on this conversation." Frederic beams at his cousin.

As with Celine and her uncle, there is a resemblance amongst the men, even if only slight. Ellis smiles the same gentle way I've seen Frederic do a thousand times. The woman at his side is petite. The cumulative of her features reminds me far too much of a bird. Her beak-like nose takes up most of her face making her eyes appear a little beady.

"It is our honor to be here," Ellis says. Even his voice is

shared with his cousin. Had I not watched him say the words I might have thought Frederic had spoken again.

"Here at my side is Baelenorn." Frederic turns in his seat. "From the House of Daemonium."

Violet eyes flick up to me under thick red lashes. The coloring of his gaze is a startling contrast to the rest of him. Pale, ashen skin and long auburn hair braided into two plaits. His cheeks turn a light shade of pink at my scrutinizing.

He slips a finger into his collar, pulling at it gently, before clearing his throat. "Most call me Lenorn, my Queen, as my full name is a mouthful."

"Lenorn," I repeat his name, eyes narrowed. How might he be related to Lord Byron? There is no clear resemblance here. Only the eyes. The eyes of a traitorous House.

Silence extends as I wait for Frederic to carry on with the introductions, if not for my own sake, then for the others in the room. When he's quiet for a moment too long, I continue for him. "Lord Frederic. Are you forgetting the House of Ravens?" Ellis and Liriel both turn with near-neck-breaking speed to look at Frederic. Solomon's boots squeak as he adjusts his stance and moves a fraction closer to our friends. "My first act as Queen is to establish the House of Ravens as an official House. Lord Argyle Toussaint and Lady Celine Dayon have been appointed to represent the House."

"House of Ravens?" Liriel starts. "You mean to tell me that the mockery of our true Houses is to be respected as one of us?"

"They *are* one of us." I lean forward, holding his stare, palms burning against the table. "Or have you forgotten that she is your niece sitting on the other side of this table?"

His lip curls at the statement, but he folds his hands into his lap and doesn't speak another word.

"Queen Devonry," Argyle's steady voice pulls the attention of the room, "is giving us what others have stripped away despite our birthrights. Though we are to be officially recognized now, the House of Ravens has been protecting and fighting for this country for years. We are hopeful for the future as we continue to do so with the blessing of the House of Sunfire."

Celine exhales but genuinely smiles. "As representatives of our House, we would like to make our support *very* clear. We stand behind the House of Sunfire and the Goddess Aerea. We stand with our Queen. What has taken place with the death of our King and the second Prince of Bartoli holding our Capital City will not be tolerated."

"As does the House of Caladrius," Frederic says, nodding in time with his cousin.

"And the House of Blood." Solomon folds his arms over his chest, the wicked gleam of his glare sliding from Lenorn to Liriel.

Liriel bows his head toward me. "The House of Starfall remains loyal to the Estand family and the line of the Goddess Aerea."

Skimming his fingers over the gold buttons of his amber jacket, Lenorn takes several heartbeats to finally speak. "I am not the heir of the House of Daemonium, nor am I the Lord, so I cannot officially swear my allegiance for my House." My insides start to knot. "But I, Baelenorn Loughtrey, pledge my own life to Queen Devonry and her rule."

Both Ellis and Frederic grin at a man who is clearly their friend. Their trust helps to melt some of the ice that surrounds my heart, but only a fraction.

"It is because of my House that I am here," Lenorn

continues. "I believe it is my House that is responsible for the disease. Many members of my family, as estranged as our relationship might be, have been open about their frequent visits to the Sunfire Palace and their communications with the Ambassador."

"And we are supposed to trust you?" Liriel taps a ring-clad knuckle against the table. For a moment I stare down at his hands.

Is Celine's uncle truly concerned for our country, or is he merely trying to get some of the attention off of himself by pointing out the obvious?

Frederic's chair groans under him when he moves to place a reassuring hand on Lenorn's arm. "Both myself and Ellis can speak to his loyalties."

Though Frederic's trust is a comfort, I can't help the worry that rises dangerously inside me. One word from the House of Daemonium and Nasir will be aware of our location and we will have lost the element of surprise.

"I've only just met Ellis." Those stormy eyes turn to Frederic's cousin. Liriel knocks his ring against the wood once more. "I can't trust him any more than I can a stranger on the street."

"We might say the same about you," Harlow speaks up from Ellis' side, a fierce protectiveness shining within her near-black eyes. She leans around her husband to stare down the Lord of the House of Starfall, who only stares back with a deep frown. "And yet we've been trusted to be here in this room with our Queen to right the wrongs that have happened in our great country."

"I am a Lord. I speak for my House. You ... both of you ... are merely here." Liriel sticks up his nose.

"A Lord terrible enough to throw your own niece from your House?" Argyle's free hand fists upon the table, knuckles straining until they pale.

"So now this has been turned upon me? It is not unusual for someone like her to be cast from their House. Without our standards, your House of Ravens wouldn't even exist," Liriel says, unaware or too stupid to notice the way Argyle's gaze darkens, as do the corners of the room. "We are not questioning my morals here, now are we? It is his loyalties that we must decide are true or not."

"You can take your standards and—"

"He's right," Celine says over the roar of angry men. Shadows flare but recede. "This is not judgment day for Lord Liriel. We've gathered to find a solution. To fight against Nasir and those who've betrayed us within the House of Daemonium."

My friend's face is flush, her jaw set with certainty. She locks eyes with me and perhaps only those of us who know her best can see the hurt she harbors, while the rest of the room only sees the perfectly composed woman she aspires to be.

As the room once again goes quiet, Lenorn's throat bobs. If this man can be trusted, if the entire House of Daemonium hasn't been poisoned by Nasir, then it can be assumed that it took much bravery on his part to be here today. To stand against his House and his family in the name of what is right and just. Those attributes alone are achingly familiar to those of the friends I've made since that Bloody Night.

Hope flares in my chest. I don't want to believe that an entire House has turned its back on me. And Lenorn might be proof that not all have.

"I am here because I want to help." Lenorn breaks the silence with a whisper.

"Then help us." I breathe the words out. "Time and trust will be the true test of your loyalties. Are we all in agreement though? We will come as one to remove Prince

Nasir. And we will burn away the evils that remain amongst our great country."

I will toss my own fire over Rozentine until every bit of Nasir's malevolence has been torched to ash. Then I'll cleanse the streets of the slave trade. And I'll burn down the last of the lines that separate the Ravens from their rightful place. When I'm done with this country, we'll have been reborn.

17
DEVONRY

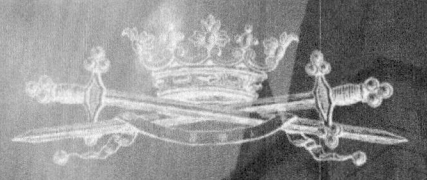

Conversation dwindles as everyone rises and moves to leave the room. Frederic, ever the attentive host, guides Lord Liriel and Lenorn, speaking of an array of finger foods waiting for them in the dining hall. Ellis and his wife reluctantly follow, exchanging momentary glances only they might be able to decipher.

Argyle pushes in his chair, holding his hand out for Celine. His shoulders remain lifted, tensed up to his ears. Though they ease when Celine's palm meets his.

"This was good, I think." Celine pats Argyle's arm, causing a muscle to tick along his jaw. "There is hope," she finishes, the sentiment pointing in my direction.

"There is hope," I agree, not yet ready to rise from my seat. They walk as a pair out of the room, pulling the door closed behind them.

Is this enough? With a sigh, I lower my head into my hands. I don't want to see Nasir's face when I close my eyes, but he's there. He's there laughing at my jokes, escorting me through the gardens, and offering me a gift from his travels. He's there in the letters he'd written me that I'd ripped open before returning to my room to read. Then he's there with blood on his hands and an expression I'd never seen him wear before.

Not only had I lost my father that night, but my best friend. Or perhaps we'd never truly been friends at all. Because the man I'd seen declaring his love for me had been a stranger. I mourn for them both.

"What are you thinking?"

I drop my hand from my face and straighten. Solomon pulls himself away from the wall, his steps a solemn *thud, thud, thud*, and he makes his way closer, closing the distance that remains between us. His eyes brighten as power pulses through his body. My own skin prickles with goosebumps and molten heat that rushes to my core.

Now I'm thinking of nothing. Or rather, I'm thinking of his *something*.

A strand of hair falls forward over his forehead. It curls over his brows and makes my fingers twitch with the desire to brush it away from his face. After two weeks without him around, having him so near sends my heart into an erratic sort of rhythm.

"Devonry," he says softer, stopping almost within arm's reach.

"I was just hoping. And worrying." I manage a half smile of my own. His lashes lower, his attention glued to my mouth as I speak. "You've been released from quarantine, I see? And you feel well?"

"Released with Frederic's blessing." He rounds the corner of the table and, in one smooth motion, pulls my chair backward, turning it until I'm facing him. Half his mouth lifts at the gasp that rips from my lungs. "I am well, but I am starved."

"Starved?"

Those large hands settle on the arms of my chair,

caging me in below him. Another curl of dark brown hair falls forward to join the first. His breath, warm and scented like syrup, fans across my cheeks.

"Starved," he repeats. "Two weeks is a long time to go without your touch, without the taste of you on my tongue."

"Oh." I bring my face up to his, our lips near brushing and he sucks in a sharp breath. "You don't want to talk about the meeting?"

"I don't want to talk." The words have hardly left his mouth before his lips are pressed to mine, tongue already sweeping the kiss more open with a desperation that mirrors my own. My body aligns with the back of the chair. Every inch of me is pressed between wood and the man who sinks his fingers into my hair.

A torrent of butterflies swirls in my stomach and a shiver goes down my spine before spreading to my extremities. Heat. Undeniable heat is coaxed between us, brought to flames at the push and pull of our kisses. In equal measures, we take and give.

I've missed this. The feel of his skin. The tender but firm brush of his lips. Gods, I've missed him.

Solomon breaks away, sucking the breaths we've denied ourselves, and presses his forehead to mine. His eyes flutter closed. "Dreams are not enough."

How could I ever get enough of him? In dreams or in reality. Even now, my body screams *more, more, more.*

I manage to open my eyes. When had they closed? And I'm caught in his crimson gaze. Those eyes stay locked on mine even when he pulls away, even as he lowers to his knees before me. The glint of hunger leaves me trembling.

He pins me to my seat with that stare. His large hands fall to the hem of my dress, fingertips brushing against my stockings. With every breath, my breasts threaten to heave themselves from my top.

"Solo," I whisper, attention darting to the very thin doors separating us from all the representatives of the Rozentine Houses. "They could hear."

"Then behave and stay quiet," he practically snarls, fangs pressing into his plump lower lips. "Or let them hear you. Let them know." With every heartbeat that passes, my skirts rise further. His touch stops along the strap of the dagger. He hums his approval with a "Good girl" before continuing. Sharp clawed fingernails skim over my flesh, finally reaching and pulling my undergarments down until the cool air meets me. Quickly though, the cold is replaced with the nearness of his breath.

Oh Gods. I am undone. Melting in my seat, torn between the fear of being caught and the relief of Solomon's hands on me.

His large palms find my ass and drag me to the edge of my seat. His face is lost to the layers of my dress and found again as he pushes my legs wider, pressing kiss after kiss up my thighs until he reaches my center.

"Gods, you're already wet for me," he says with another brush of his lips. The width of his tongue presses against me, opening me up further as he delves into my desire. His mouth chases every ounce of moisture that's pooled just for him, licking it up as if this truly is the only thing that might satisfy him.

When his mouth finds that bundle of nerves, my fingers bunch in my skirt, a quiet moan leaving me. The sting of his claws as he cups his hand around my thighs is the perfect balance to the pleasure setting my body ablaze. He teases small circles with his wicked, sinful tongue. His growl of appreciation vibrates against me, tightening all the muscles in my core.

Every pass he makes builds that thrumming thrill bit by bit until it blooms into euphoria. I start to cry out but manage to force my mouth closed. Wave after wave of bliss hits my body at full force. My shaking legs close around Solomon's face as I ride the sensation until it comes to its peak.

Solomon's touch disappears. I whimper.

"Hush now, my Queen," he says. Then his fangs plunge into the dip where my thighs meet my hip. A pinprick of pain is washed away as he pulls blood into his mouth and the rush of an orgasm explodes into something even greater. A moan is muffled against my lips, begging to be released. My breaths come in short and shallow pants. The edges of my vision darken.

Then he's sliding his fangs from my flesh, licking over the wound, and sitting back onto his heels. The sheen of our deed is obvious over his cheeks and chin. The scent of arousal, so uniquely mine, is thick in the air. All I can do is inhale and watch as he licks his lips and tilts his head up to the ceiling, exposing the length of his neck. The knot in his throat bobs.

He runs a hand through his hair, finally pushing away those fallen curls. Then, in silence, he takes his time pulling all my undergarments and layers back into their place. Every brush of his fingers or scrape of his nails against my flushed skin sends another tremble through my body.

Solo stands. His own want is clear while he adjusts himself in his pants and offers me his hand. But how can I possibly stand after that? If I rise, my knees will start knocking before I'll be tumbling into a heap.

Still, I let my fingers slip into his. Our hands intertwined have somehow become my home, the one place that feels so very right despite all the wrong going on in our lives. And even though my legs manage to hold me up, Solomon is right there waiting.

"Now, we can go," he says, offering me a cocky grin. It only does terrible things to the once steady beat of my heart. What a terrible, wicked man. What was once a familiar hate is long gone and replaced with a warm sensation I'm hesitant to give a name to.

"That's—yes. I need to speak with Lenorn." I run a hand over my dress, checking to make sure the material is back where it should be. If anyone with ears was within ten feet of those doors, they likely know what happened. But I won't be giving them any clues.

He hums, bringing his lips back to mine for a swift kiss. My mouth is still swollen and red. My skin is still flushed.

"You're distracting me." I swat at him, only for him to roll his eyes.

"I'll do more than distract you if you've got the time."

Oh Gods. "Promise?" I ask, brow arching in challenge.

"I'll get on my knees and swear it to you now." Solomon starts to lower to the ground, but I sink my fingers into his shirt and pull him back up.

"Later." I laugh through my exhale. Two weeks was plenty of time for me to imagine everything I've wanted to do to him and what he might do to me. Later can't come soon enough.

Together we walk out of the room, to a thankfully empty hall. It's enough time for my flesh to cool, though try as I might my cheeks still feel the heat with every glance I make toward my guard. The flash of his smirk is gone, but somehow, it's still reflected in his gaze as he watches me.

Before long, the scent of breakfast wafts through the hall, pulling us toward the dining hall. Voices carry but their words are not discernible at our distance. At least, not to me. Solomon pauses at the door, slowly letting me go, before offering a deep bow.

"I'll let you do what you must. I'm going to find Argyle," he says, straightening.

"I'm glad you're well," I whisper.

"Me too." His attention falls to my lips for several heartbeats before he turns away and disappears down the hall. It takes me far longer than it should to turn back to the room.

The long table is covered in trays of pastries, ranging from savory to sweet. An entire ham sits at the center, already thickly sliced and missing several cuts. Fruits garnish the plates and the wine glasses are already filled to the rim.

There is no sign of Lord Liriel, but Frederic and Ellis are already deep in conversation near the head of the table. Harlow leans back with a laugh, holding her napkin over her parted lips. Lastly, Lenorn sits quietly with the ghost of a smile.

It's him. I watch as I bring myself to the table. Only a few steps away, Frederic looks up, and the conversation pauses long enough for him to stand, followed by the others. "Queen Devonry, we are honored that you've joined us. Please, sit and eat to your fill."

I dip my chin but remain standing. "Actually, I was hoping that I might speak to Lenorn alone for a moment."

Everyone sits with the exception of Lenorn. His hands are clasped in front of him, fingers fidgeting, and I swear he pales a shade. Which is likely hard to do when he's already quite ghostly.

"Happily, my Queen. Shall we step out into the hall?" He moves forward, offering his arm, dropping it, then offering it again. "I'm sorry, I feel out of my element here," he admits quietly as I set my hand along his forearm.

I try to give him a reassuring smile, but what I manage only feels like a terrible grimace. After my last interaction with the House of Daemonium, I hadn't imagined I would be walking arm in-arm with another member of the House. Especially not this soon.

What I know of this man is so little. My trust, only extended by my confidence in Lord Frederic, already feels stretched thin. Lenorn isn't the heir to the House. But that doesn't mean he is a man without ambitions, and I would be an idiot to not have at least the passing thought that he may want to rid himself of any competition. Being on the good side of the Queen is a most advantageous place to be.

After everything Frederic has done for us, for me, for my Kingdom, it would feel wrong of me not to have faith in him. Frederic is our ally. He's proven that again and again. With the Lord of House Caladrius vouching for him, I have to give him a chance to prove himself. It would only be fair. Even if my body is tense with the memories of a particular, purple-eyed serpent.

I stop and pull my hand away, taking the step back my body so desperately needs. My hands shake, but I fist them at my sides and force myself to meet his attention. Lenorn is nothing like Byron. From his coloring to his twitchy, nervous mannerisms. It's enough to allow me to exhale some of the tension riddling my shoulders.

"Have you been to the palace, yourself?" I ask.

He blinks. "Yes, but only once."

"Does your House have any reason to question your loyalty? Might you be able to get back into the palace again?" Those aren't the only questions burning on the tip of my tongue. It would be all too easy to flood the man with a thousand more.

"I—" He swallows and I watch his throat work. "A few know my reservations about our House's betrayal, but if

I'd been any more vocal, I feared I might end up a member of the Ravens. I've stayed mostly quiet. Please don't let my fear of rejection sway you though, because I will do what must be done to help you back to your throne." Lenorn wipes his palms against his pants. "My family plans to be back in Court within this next month; it would not be out of place for me to ask to accompany them." He pauses again. "If that would please you."

It's easier to offer a reassuring smile the less I see the Ambassador in him. Lenorn is not determined to sway me one way or another. He's here as a servant to the crown in such a way that may cause him a great deal of strife from his House.

"It would please me. I've had the thought that if you might be able to go to the palace, we can use that to our advantage. Would it be too much to ask that you help us get inside?" Certainly, a Queen wouldn't ask though, they'd command. Perhaps I should have commanded him. It wouldn't be hard to demand that he get us inside, but after everything, I still can't bring myself to do that.

"Whatever you wish." He lowers, taking my hand to brush a kiss over my knuckles. "Shall I send word to Lord Frederic when I am aware of the dates?"

"Yes."

Lenorn lets my hand go and I clasp my fingers in front of me. The creases on his forehead formed by his nervous expression lessen as he smiles gently. "Then I will do just that. Is there more you wish to speak of?"

"No, thank you." My eyes follow him as he bows and turns to walk away. Those questions that still stay with me turn to lava in my mouth, needing to be spewed out for fear they'll burn me alive otherwise. "Lenorn?"

His back is to me and he's moved several paces away, but he stops and turns back.

"Yes, my Queen?"

"Were there any survivors from the Bloody Night? Is my maid—" Her name gets stuck in my throat, but my need to know is enough to get it out. "—is Sheza alive?"

His eyes widen. A softness takes over his features and his shoulders lower a fraction. Is it pity that I see in his gaze? Something else entirely? I ready myself to hear the worst.

"Many servants are alive. I don't know this Sheza by name, so I cannot speak to her specifically, but stay hopeful. Sometimes in the darkest of nights, hope is the light that will get you through."

Is hope enough?

18

SOLOMON

My footsteps are silent within the darkened corridors of Frederic's manor. Quiet enough that as I come upon a couple of familiar figures in a nearby alcove, illuminated by the sconces of fire upon the walls as well as moonlight streaming in through the window that backlights them, they don't notice me. Argyle's head rears back at something his companion says, but the reveal of his face gives me pause. Just the man I wanted to see, and yet, now that I know he's not alone, I don't wish to interrupt him.

My attention moves from him to the woman in front of him. Disappointment is heavy within me until I realize who it is. For the first time in a long time, I feel my lips spread into an amused smile. Argyle's expression—ripe with a hunger that I know all too well—combined with the obviously irritated woman before him make me realize I am not the only one currently struggling with wanting someone I should not want to possess.

Instead of leaving to give the two of them a bit of privacy to work out whatever is between them, I settle more firmly into the shadows and prop my shoulder against the wall just around the corner. Out of Celine's sight, but certainly, Argyle must know I'm here. If he does, however, he doesn't act like it.

Celine's hands push at his chest, and yet he still moves into her, pressing her further back against the wall at her back. Argyle's head dips, and he says something, his lips moving as he talks in a low tone only she is privy to. I could push some power into my body and pick up the conversation, but even I'm not that crude. This is something that has long since been coming for the two of them. My curiosity won't let me leave, but I also need to talk to Argyle.

If Argyle chooses to secret her away somewhere, I, of course, won't give chase, but he's not the type to take a woman in such a public place. Even if he were, Celine isn't the type of woman who would let him.

The cold of the stone wall seeps into my skin past the barrier of my clothes as I watch the two of them. At whatever Argyle says, Celine shakes her head and pushes against him again, though this time, she's a bit less forceful. She's caving. Whatever it is that Argyle wants, it's clear that he's slowly but surely going to get his way.

I wait, both curious and resigned. Then Argyle grabs Celine by her arms in a sudden movement. He pushes her against the wall rather aggressively and his head dips down. I turn my face away. I don't have to be as experienced as I am to know what he's doing. He's kissing her. A beat passes and then another. I peer back, curious about Celine's reception.

At first, she's stiff as a board. Denying him even a hint of her softness, but then—as if she can't help herself—the tension in her body slowly eases out. Her arms arch up, wrapping around his shoulders, and much to my surprise, she goes up onto her toes and kisses him back.

Slowly, but surely, I think to myself, *Celine is losing this battle between her and Argyle.* I almost feel bad for her.

Discomfort floods my system and I take a step back, fully intending to walk away. I'm no peeping bastard, after all. I'd been waiting on Argyle to finish things for a reason, but if Celine is amenable to his desires, then I shall leave the two of them to it. Turning my body, my head slams into the underside of the sconce on the wall and I come to a jolting halt.

"*Fuck!*" I cup a hand over my forehead and curse.

A soft feminine gasp around the corner of the wall echoes back to me and I release an internal groan as it's followed by a harsh flurry of footsteps—there and then fading away. Damn it. I wait a moment, wondering just how badly I've fucked my friend when I hear him call out.

"You can come out now," Argyle says, sounding rather exhausted. "I know you're still there."

I haven't felt quite this sheepish since I was a youth under my uncle's tutelage. Instead of running from the circumstances, though, I straighten, rubbing at the sore spot on my head, and round the corner to face my friend. "I didn't mean to interrupt your rendezvous," I tell him honestly. "I was planning on leaving when I saw the two of you…" Well, I'm sure he knows how long I've been here and just when I decided to leave. Argyle is nothing if not viscerally aware of his surroundings at all times.

Argyle blows out a long breath and sinks back against the wall as I approach. "It's fine," he says with a wave of his hand. "I didn't expect it anyway."

I arch a brow. "You didn't expect her to reciprocate?" I ask.

"Of course not." He shakes his head. "She's made it clear since day one how much she despises me."

How like him, I think. *To want the one woman who wouldn't so readily jump into bed with him.* We men are creatures like that—always wanting that which we cannot have.

"I'm not entirely sure what game the two of you have been playing," I say, "but it's clear there's tension building between both of you."

Argyle turns his head to the window, his profile only revealing the singular dark eye of his as he seems to gaze at something far beyond the glass—perhaps something even beyond the world outside. I pity the poor bastard. I understand him.

"I don't know what it is about her," he finally admits after what feels like an eternity of silence. "She enrages me and entices me all within the same breath. She can say something so Gods damned ridiculous and then a moment later, it's as if I've never met a creature so intelligent. She drives me absolutely mad."

If anyone knows exactly how he feels, it would be me. With a sigh of my own, I clap him on the shoulder. "I believe women were put on this plane of existence just to drive the male species to the brink of insanity," I tell him.

That garners a bark of laughter and Argyle shakes his head before looking back to me. My hand slips away from his shoulder. "Why did you seek me out?" he asks. "I know you weren't skulking around just to watch me try and seduce your precious Princess's little Lady's maid."

I ignore the precious Princess comment. "I'm worried for Devonry," I tell him.

He snorts. "When is that ever *not* the case?"

Though I can't deny that statement, I still level Argyle with a dark look. "She hasn't been sleeping well," I say. "Especially not since the meeting of the Houses."

"And the dreams?" Argyle rests back against the wall with his upper back spanning the column he leans against. He crosses his arms over his chest, stretching the dark material of his tunic as he eyes me. He is one of the few people I've ever told about the shared dreams between Devonry and me.

"I can sense her emotions within them," I admit. "So, I know for certain that she's frightened of something."

"She has a lot to fear," Argyle states. "Or did you forget that she's wanted by a rather insane foreign Prince who's recently usurped her throne after slaughtering her father?"

"Sarcasm might be your second language, my friend, but it is *not* needed here," I snap. "I'm being serious."

"As am I," Argyle shoots back readily. "She's a young girl. Yes, she is a Queen and a Royal, but that doesn't negate all of the other things she is. She must still be grieving the loss of all she's ever known. You cannot expect her to suddenly become the perfect sovereign overnight. I admit, I didn't expect much of her in the beginning, but she's come along quite nicely."

"Nicely?" She is practically a different person than who she was a few short months ago. Devonry has blossomed in these dark times. She has become stronger and every inch the Queen I'd expected and hoped she would be.

Argyle continues as if I hadn't spoken. "Devonry is still just a woman, Solo," he says. "She has every right to fear the future. Her life is at stake, but I don't doubt that she's more concerned with yours."

"She shouldn't be," I say through gritted teeth.

Argyle rolls his eyes. "Regardless, she is. You wouldn't love her so if she wasn't the kind-hearted girl she is. Being kind-hearted, though necessary, is difficult for a ruler. At the moment, she is faced with an enormous task—taking back her Kingdom. And even if she doesn't want to, there's still the decision of whether to shed blood to do so or not always on her mind. What I know of the Saintess Queen, pacifism was her way of life. Are you to tell me that doesn't still linger within her mind? Surely, you would know the Princess' mind far better than I."

He's right. Damn it, but I know it. Of course, Devonry still thinks of her parents and their expectations. One doesn't grow up surrounded by rules and expectations without making it a part of themselves. Even if I understand the need for the decisions she's made thus far, there has to be at least a part of her that regrets it all. I curse myself internally.

Argyle sighs. "I understand your worry," he tells me, turning his head down the corridor—the way I assume Celine had gone since she hadn't passed me in her escape. "More than most would, I understand. But you, too, need to understand that sometimes, you cannot rid the world of everything that may frighten the woman you care for. Sometimes, you just need to be there for her. All of the things that have hurt her have helped her to grow, and even if you wish she had not gone through such pain, even if you wish you could have stopped it, the fact is that it already happened. You can't change the past. You can only be there for her in the present and future."

His dual-colored eyes land on me once more and settle. I consider his words with the weight of the experiences and knowledge I know he has. I find myself cracking a smile despite my own frustration. "You've changed quite a bit from the drunkard I met all those years ago," I say. "You sound almost as wise as an old man now."

Argyle scowls. "Don't antagonize me, you damnable brute," he mutters.

I laugh, and the feeling of the light sound fills me with ease. More ease than I've felt in a long time. "Thank you, friend," I say honestly. "I hope this means you'll also be able to handle all of the other changes coming your way."

He harrumphs. "What changes?" he snaps. "After all

this is over, I'm going right back to my taverns in Carion City."

I shake my head. Even if I don't say it, we both know that's not true. "Your life has already taken a turn for the better, Argyle," I say. "I doubt you'd be able to convince the woman you just tried to seduce to follow you back to that city."

He stiffens and then shoots me a dirty look that makes me repress another smile. The two of us are quiet for several moments, but then the other reason that I sought him out creeps back up into my mind and my desire to smile fades.

"There's one more thing," I say. "I want to extract a promise from you."

He eyes me. "An oath?" he inquires.

"If you so choose," I say before drawing in a sharp breath. "Should anything happen to me, I want to ensure that there will be someone I trust by Devonry's side."

Argyle's expression becomes shadowed. "You're not planning on doing anything stupid, are you?" he demands, his voice lowering into an angry growl.

"No." My response is swift. "But you cannot deny that the future is uncertain. Just as you said that Devonry has every right to be afraid, so do I. I would damn myself to the eternal fires of the Afterworld's dark side if I didn't at least do something to ensure her safety should anything take me from her. You know it would not be my will."

Argyle is quiet for several moments. It is a heavy topic, I know. Perhaps one that he's never thought of himself since he's never had a family or close friend relying on him. Now, though, I can practically see the thoughts turning over in his mind.

"If something happens to me, I'd like for you to stay by her side as long as she needs. Even after she retakes her throne," I say. "She'll need someone who she can rely on for her safety and protection. She'll need an aid and confidant." And I doubt any man she marries will be able to provide that. There is no one more dedicated to her than I.

"She will be taken care of," Argyle finally says. "If you promise to do the same for Celine."

My eyes widen. "She means that much to you, then?"

His shoulders droop, and he drops his arms back to his sides before lifting his gaze to mine. "You already know the answer to that," he says. "I would not ask an oath of protection from you if she didn't."

I nod. "Understood. Of course, I will look after her in the event something happens to you."

Argyle exhales, expelling a long breath. "Good, that is … good. Thank you, my friend."

"Of course," I reply. "It's good to see you pining after a woman finally." A deep chuckle rises within me. "I know she'll keep you on your toes.

With a groan, Argyle slaps a hand over his upper face, scrubbing it down and pulling at his skin as he bemoans his interest in Celine. "That blasted female makes me want her like no other," he confesses, sounding rather angry about it. "I worry that she'll suffer if I'm gone though. So, should anything happen…"

He doesn't need to finish. "I shall treat her as if she were your widow," I say.

Argyle nods. "And I shall do the same for your woman."

As it should be.

19
DEVONRY

The sun rises into the sky, marking a new day. All around me, servants bustle about. Somehow, even though we're not taking much with us, there still seems to be a flurry of movement and things to do. I look up at the face of Lord Frederic's manor with its white stone and pillars. The ivy crawling up the sides, the flags of House Caladrius fluttering in the breeze.

Ever since that Bloody Night, it seems as if I've been constantly on the move. Just when I'd become accustomed to one place, it was time to progress to the next destination. With all sense of normalcy changing, the effect is dizzying. What was once routine is no more. Everything has changed—and I, half frightened by it all, am part of that.

"Have your thoughts caught up with you?" The familiar timbre of Frederic's voice makes my shoulders relax, and a smile comes to my lips as I hear him approach. Soft footsteps lead to the place at my side, and I don't have to look when I know he's already there.

"Yes, they have," I admit.

"Were you running from them or waiting?" he asks.

That, unfortunately, is a question I don't have an answer to. So, instead of responding, I finally turn to look at him. "I can't thank you enough for all of your help, Frederic," I say.

Today his pale hair is loose around his shoulders rather than tied back. It makes his already soft expression appear even softer. "You never have to thank me for doing what is right, Your Highness," he replies.

I shake my head. "No, I do," I disagree. "So many people struggle to know what is right, much less act on it. So, I thank you, truly, from the bottom of my heart. Were it not for you, I don't know how we would have made it as far as we have."

Lord Frederic is quiet for a moment, staring down at me with those enigmatic, yet kind, eyes of his. A small smile plays at his lips. "I shall see you once again on the throne of Rozentine, Your Highness," he says, his tone low and respectful. I blink at the reverence I hear there. It slides through my ears and into my veins. "When you call for me, House Caladrius will be there. I will be there. For you and for the people you care for."

My bones shiver at his words. It isn't as if I haven't heard them before. Maybe not spoken in quite this way, but that's essentially what Solo has been telling me from the moment it was decided that I would not run and hide and that I would fight back and take my Kingdom. Only now, it sounds … a bit more official.

At the end of this war that we will wage, there can be only one victor.

I lower my head back at him. "Thank you, Your Grace," I reply. "Your loyalty will not be forgotten."

"Even if it is," he says. "It will always remain."

My heart practically freezes in my chest at that statement. It reminds me that once, I'd been a Princess with no true knowledge of the world. Now I am burdened with the weight of my subjects' love and hope. Though I'm proud of it, I am also well aware of the heaviness of such a gift. Loyalty given to me simply because of my birth is one thing, but loyalty given because they view me as worthy is something else entirely. I can feel the burn at the back of my eyes, unshed tears dying to be released. I'm no longer naive, at least not in the same way I once was. I blink, trying to push the overwhelming tidal wave of emotion back.

"I will endeavor not to disappoint you, Lord Frederic," I say in response.

His eyes close as he lowers his head further, bowing as low as he can without drawing the interest or curiosity of those around us. I thank him silently for that. When he rises again, he turns away, striding forth to call for servants to send them inside.

The courtyard quickly empties until all that's left are Solomon, Argyle, Celine, and I, along with Lord Frederic and his closest aides—all of whom stay back as he approaches us. Solomon motions me toward him and I don't resist the call.

"Lord Solomon," Frederic nods to Solo, "if you ever have need of House Caladrius, I hope you know that we are always ready to provide aid."

Solo dips his head. "I thank you, Lord Frederic." I watch the two of them with no small amount of curiosity. Because of my relationship with Solo, I often forget that he is a Lord in his own right and as such, he has the knowledge of Noble etiquette. He just rarely uses it.

Frederic turns to me with a smile, but as he does, he continues to speak to Solo. "Take care of her, won't you?"

I blink up at him and part my lips to respond, but Solo

speaks before I can. "I will," he says. "Even if it means I have to lay down my life. She will be cared for."

Solo's words make my chest squeeze tight. His oath, one of protection, sounds like a far more intimate one. I peer up at him, but his gaze is squarely on Frederic. Maybe I'm wrong, but I don't want to think so.

At the very least, I think the two of them—Frederic and Solomon—appear far more at ease with each other than I've seen in their previous encounters. That's a good thing, considering Frederic is now one of the few people in Rozentine I am sure we can trust.

"Well, then," Argyle steps forward, breaking the moment of silence, "I suppose we should head out."

"Yes, I suppose so." Frederic nods before looking to our horses with a pinched face. "Though, I do wish you'd at least allowed me to give you a few more horses."

"We want to get through the mountains quickly," Solomon responds. "And with the supplies we have, it's best we travel in as small a pack as possible."

I press my lips together but say nothing as Celine also offers her thanks to Lord Frederic. The reason we won't be taking more horses is due to the fact that we may have to eventually abandon them. Turning my gaze out over the horizon of the Sevire Mountains in the near distance, I remember the last time we were forced to traverse them and how that had nearly resulted in our deaths.

This time, thankfully, we only mean to travel along the outside of them as we head toward the House of Starfall, the House of Daemonium's territory, and eventually, back to Sanctus City and Sunfire territory. It's been so long since I've been to the Capital City that I fear I've forgotten what it's like. Will it be like my memories, or will it now be tainted by all of the other places I've traveled to?

I'm so lost in my thoughts that I don't realize the others

have finished with their goodbyes until a pair of strong, wide hands grip me about my waist and lift me bodily up toward the back of the horse I'll be riding. A gasp escapes me, and I scramble to get into place, tossing my leg over the back of the horse's saddle and gripping the reins as the steed neighs and steps back and forth.

Ahead of me, Celine is already sitting, sideways on the back of Argyle's horse. He deftly grabs ahold of the back of the saddle as well as the front around her side and sets his foot in the stirrup before swinging onto the back of the horse's rump. I look down just in time to see Solo's hand come up and grip the front of where I'm sitting and perform the same. Heat slams into my spine as his chest meets my back.

All of my breath rushes out at once as he settles more firmly on the back of the horse and I feel my body slide back to his. The heat and hardness of him remind me of all of the things we'd done in our dreams when he'd been in isolation. My mouth goes dry as Solomon takes the reins. The space inside the lower part of my belly flutters, as if a million butterflies have suddenly sprouted and taken flight.

"Have a safe journey," Lord Frederic calls as he lifts his hand.

"Thank you!" I call back.

"We will see him soon," Solo reminds me quietly as he steers the steed after Argyle's horse, "in Sanctus City."

"R-right." My heartbeat kicks into a fast pace. *Sanctus City.* Where this whole farce will come to an end. Where I will finally face Nasir and Rozentine will become mine again, no matter the cost.

20
DEVONRY

Back again on a singular horse. One horse. One man. One girl with no room to move. *Me*.

Beneath my butt, the horse's movements sway from side to side as it clomps forward down the beaten path and back into the lower Sevire Mountains. Hours pass in silence after we leave Lord Frederic's manor. Even Argyle and Celine seem to realize there's a new tension in the air as they remain quiet, no arguing or even muttering to be heard.

Curious, I lean to the side and peek back at the two of them over Solomon's shoulder. I blink at what I spot. Celine is leaning against Argyle with her eyes closed and her head turned into his chest. Solo nudges me and my eyes shoot to his. A sparkle of amusement glitters in those dark crimson recesses.

"Give them some privacy, Devonry," he whispers. "They've had a long night."

My eyes widen. I whip my head around and peer at them. Celine wouldn't … would she? Argyle's arm lingers at Celine's waist, and whereas before, she might have been grumpy or particularly angry about it, she seems quite content to be in his hands.

Solo nudges me again and sighs when I still don't look forward. "If you don't face forward," he says. "I'll kiss you in full view of the two of them."

My body goes stiff in an instant as his threat penetrates my ears. Slowly, I tilt my head and look up at him. *"You wouldn't."* Even as I narrow my gaze on him, the side of his mouth curves upward. *Yes, he fucking would.* I sniff primly, with false decorum, and turn my head away from him. "You might be the Blood General, Solo, but I am your Queen. You'd never steal a kiss from your Queen."

Solo's wide palm releases one side of the reigns and my eyes widen as I stare at that hand of his as it moves back toward me. I inhale sharply as the heat of him brushes my side a moment before his fingers curve over my waist. He leans closer, his breath whispering over the top of my ear. "You're not crowned yet," he murmurs. "Would you like to make a wager about that, Princess?"

As if my head is on a string with someone else maneuvering my movements, I look up at him. Those ruby eyes of his meet mine. Do I want to wager a kiss with a man like the one currently holding me close to him, whose scent is occupying my every thought?

Nope. Not at all. I would lose in an instant and I would enjoy every part of my downfall. I flip around and face forward, crossing my arms as the horse's movements underneath us jostle me slightly. Solo releases me and picks up the reins. I resent the longing that lingers. "I thought they hated each other," I mutter. "I can't help but be interested in their newfound"—relationship?—"truce," I finish lamely.

The deep rumble of Solo's chuckle reverberates against

my back and I have to force myself to lean a bit forward to keep it away. The things that sound does to me. If I could, I'd press my thighs together right now. However, to do so would not help. I can feel a low throb in my belly as it arches up and when I close my eyes briefly, all I can picture are his hands on my flesh and his tongue lowering down into the space between my thighs. A shudder works through me.

"If you'll recall, you hated me as well," Solo says.

A muscle jumps in my jaw as I crane my neck backward, looking up at him as he looks down. "Just me?" I prompt. "You seemed to take great pleasure in tormenting me, Solo. You taunted me mercilessly."

He scoffs and shakes his head. "I did no such thing. I merely retaliated when you felt the need to make my duties difficult."

My lips part. "You liar!" As soon as the words erupt from me, I slap a hand over my lips and jerk my head over his shoulder again. Argyle's eyes meet mine once before his lips curve into a knowing smile. Thankfully, though, Celine didn't seem to hear me. A groan works up my throat and as I lower my hand once more, I send Solo a dark look full of retribution.

"You forget, Solomon," I say in a more reasonable tone, "you tormented me as much as I did you. What I did was retaliation. What you did was torture—plain and simple. Do you remember when you dyed my favorite dress that ungodly shit-puke green color and then hid everything else I owned right before a big dinner with the Houses and my father?"

"Ah, but I only did that because you purposefully fed my horse those ungodly treats that make him shit and fart right before a battle demonstration. I seem to recall you snorting and laughing so hard in the stands as I rode through the demonstration field with a horse that smelled like something had died and crawled up its ass."

I cross my arms over my chest, fighting back another snort like the one he claimed I'd made. "Well, what about the time you snuck a giant rat into my room?" I demand.

"It was harmless," he say. "Besides, that was retaliation for the night you attempted to trap me in a closet with Lady Zoela."

I bite down on my lower lip, teeth sinking deep as I recall that particular bit of memory with fondness. "She's a beautiful Lady," I say sweetly, tipping my head back as I flutter my eyelashes at him in complete and utter innocence. "I don't know why you were so upset by that. The Court Officials were asking when you'd be getting married anyway. Even my father had mentioned something about it. I was simply trying to offer my assistance in procuring a Lady of standing to become your bride."

"Oh, is that so?" Solo's chest rumbles again, and this time I lean back against him, letting the sound roll through me as my own lips twitch in remembered amusement. "Perhaps it simply slipped your mind that she was also forty years my senior and a three-time widower who had a knack for accosting any young man in her purview. I do believe my cock carried her fingerprints for weeks afterward. I had to practically pry her off of me with the sheath of my blade."

"A simple 'thank you' would have sufficed." I sniff, feigning dignity when all I really want to do is laugh aloud at the old memory of Solomon stumbling out of a once-locked closet and trying to ward off the older woman with heavy makeup and fingers that appeared to be stuck to the front of his trousers. "She's a well-respected Noble Lady of lineage."

"She was a molester, and you knew it," Solo replies tartly.

Why had I done that? I think to myself. Surely, it was in response to another torment he'd caused me, but as I relax against his chest, I can't recall. There were so many times we'd do those things—setting each other up to be embarrassed or humiliated. At the time, I'd found nothing but frustration in the moments when he'd managed to succeed in his plots. And as a Princess and heir unable to go beyond the walls of the Sunfire Palace except for very rare occasions, I'd practically lived for those brief moments of freedom.

"You know," I say, thoughtfully. "You were the only one I could do that with aside from Jacin. Sheza never approved, and all of the other handmaids were too frightened of getting into trouble."

"If I recall, Jacin helped you a few times," he says with a sigh.

"Yes," I agree. "He did."

Silence falls between us at that. The old memories I'd once thought so terrible and annoying are now happy ones. Yet, still, they are tainted by the sorrow of all that we've lost. We—not just me. Because as much as I cared for Jacin and even fancied him on occasion, he was Solomon's friend too, his cousin, and in many ways, a brother. My heart aches now.

We ride a bit longer and I'm so absorbed in my thoughts that the hours feel like minutes. It isn't until sometime later, I blink, recognizing the long shadow on the ground is ours and the day is waning. I look up and stare at the horizon, noticing that the sun has already disappeared beyond view, and now only the edges of its rays are visible.

"We should stop soon," Argyle calls out.

Solo looks back and nods his agreement. "We'll make

camp for the night a little ways off the path," he says. "We'll set out again at dawn."

"How far from Starfall territory are we?" I ask.

Solomon peers over my head toward the horizon and is quiet for a moment. After a beat or two passes, he sighs. "We made decent time today," he says. "Tomorrow, we'll have to find a village and make sure the horses are alright. We set out a bit later than I anticipated, but we'll need to water them this evening. If we don't run into any issues, I'd say within the next week."

A whole week? I bite down on my lower lip. "That's so long…" The words slip out before I can stop them and though I don't mean for them to sound like a complaint, I know they likely come off as one.

"It would be at least ten days with a carriage," Solomon replies. "Let us hope we don't run into any trouble."

I nod my agreement and tighten my thighs around the horse's saddle as he steers us off of the pathway and into the woods alongside it. The flat roads turn to rough terrain and I jolt forward, my hand snapping down and gripping onto one solid masculine thigh as the horse neighs and rears its head back when the incline changes.

The sound of Solo's quick inhale of breath reaches my ears a split second before I feel his hand on mine over his thigh. "*Devonry*." There is a whole world of meaning in that one word. Desire. Pain. Want. Need.

"I-I'm sorry," I say, quickly extracting my hand, realizing just how high up my touch had been. I hadn't meant to do anything, but now I'm viscerally aware of his sudden stiffness at my back and the way our bodies rock against each other. I close my eyes but stop just before inhaling deeply. He's so close I just know doing so would cause his scent to invade my nostrils. So, instead, I part my lips, open my eyes, and breathe shallowly through my mouth, silently begging the Gods to end today's trip sooner rather than later.

They must hear me and my pleas because not but twenty minutes later, the terrain evens out and Solo pulls our steed to a stop in a small alcove of trees. "This is good for the night," he says, looking up to the overhang of branches above our heads. It's hard to see the sky through the leaves. "If it rains, we'll be mostly protected here."

"Do you think it'll rain?" I hear Celine ask from somewhere behind us.

Solomon slips off of the horse and then reaches for me before answering. "There were clouds in the sky when we left," he says. "I'm surprised we haven't seen anything yet."

"They didn't get bigger or darker," Argyle replies. "Perhaps the storm is moving."

My hands land on Solo's shoulders as his palms settle against my waist and tighten. Our eyes connect briefly as he lifts me from the saddle and carefully deposits me onto the soft ground. It's not a big alcove at all, so he ends up standing rather close. Close enough that our chests meet and my heart rate picks up speed.

This is by far not the time for any of these thoughts and yet, I can't seem to help myself. As I peer up into his glittering crimson eyes, a lump forms in my throat that prevents me from talking. Solo moves away first, attending to the horse as he pulls woolen blankets from the satchels on its backside.

"I'll help," I say, taking the blankets from him only to have them quickly plucked from my grasp as Celine appears at my side and takes them away.

"Why don't you rest, Your Highness?" she offers.

Solo doesn't say a word. Instead, he turns back to the horse and takes up the reins to tie the creature to a nearby tree before removing his sword from its sheath and cutting a few of the lower hanging branches that linger around us. Tossing the weak branches into a pile, Solo re-sheaths his sword. "I'll go in search of nearby water for the horses," he says, and before I can reply, he's gone—leaving me standing in the middle of our not-quite-put-together-yet camp with a strange sense that I've done something to upset him.

As Celine bustles away and begins laying out blankets, I sigh and go in search of rocks. That, too, she tries to take over when she catches me, but I finally wave her away. "Out here, I'm just another traveler," I remind her. "If something were to happen to the three of you, I'd need to look after myself anyway. Please, Celine, let me do something." If she doesn't, I'll go out of my head.

"But, you—"

"Celine." The call of her name in Argyle's deep baritone stops her from any further argument. She still shoots him a rather irritated look, but after a beat passes between them, she concedes with a sigh.

"Alright, Your Highness," she says. "If that is your wish."

"It is," I say, and though her pinched lips and furrowed brow make it clear she's unhappy about it, she backs off and goes back to setting out the blankets.

I don't ask what Argyle's plans are. After his one word to Celine, he quickly ties their own horse and disappears into the woods—most likely to hunt up something small for our night's meal. Of course, we have rations in our satchels, provided by Lord Frederic, but if we're going to be traveling for another full week, we'll have to be mindful of our usage.

My lips twitch in amusement as I gather several stones from nearby and cart them to the center of our little alcove. Just a few short months ago, I was a Noble daughter, a Royal, who knew nothing of survival skills. Yet, here I am now and it feels natural to dig my fingers into the dirt, pulling free rocks to set up a fire pit that will keep the four of us warm through the night as the temperatures inevitably drop.

I carefully arrange the stones I procured into a circle and dig into the center before filling it with twigs and leaves and some of the smaller branches Solo had chopped off before he left. Once I'm finished, Celine comes up along my side with the striker stones from one of our satchels. I sit back and watch her start the fire, blowing lightly on the leaves that first catch the flame. Our silence is companionable. It's easy.

Minutes pass, and the sky above grows darker and darker until the main source of light comes from our fire as it builds. Both Argyle and Solo return. While Argyle is carrying a rather small squirrel and a sheepish grin, Solo is carting a couple of fish.

I gape as he slings them onto one of the blankets. "How did you fish without a poll?" I ask, astonished.

Argyle chuckles and lays his own catch nearby before going to untie the horses. "I have a sword," Solomon answers.

"I'll take these two to the waters," Argyle calls out. "Celine? Help me to gather some to bring back for our meal?"

Celine jumps up from where she's been crouched next to me, and for a moment time freezes, her body going stiff as she realizes how eager she seems. My lips twitch as I suppress a smile. If anyone understands the strange turmoil of wanting someone you thought you despised, it's me. It's amusing to see it happen to someone else.

Celine's cheeks turn pink as if she can sense my

thoughts, but she quickly adjusts her skirts in what I assume is an effort to hide her blatant enthusiasm. When she peers at me out of the corner of her eye, I direct my attention to Solo to give her the illusion that I hadn't noticed.

"You can't catch fish with a sword," I say. "What did you really do?"

Solo levels me with a look and then with one raised brow, he pulls his sword free, holds the sharp end over the ground, and jerks it down. "Stabbed it," he replies. "With. My. *Sword*."

"I'll take them," Argyle says as he peers over the newly caught fish. "If I smoke them over the fire right, we might be able to save some for road rations."

"No," Solo says. "Just cook it all. Two fish and a squirrel will hardly feed the lot of us. We've got to eat what we can when we can."

Argyle shoots Solo a confused, almost inquisitive look. Not for the first time, I wish I had the ability to read minds because whenever they do this—talk without actually saying words—I end up feeling left in the dark. With a grunt, I turn away from them and snatch up a stick before poking the fire and watching it flare up as the golden embers drift into the darkened sky.

Celine moves away toward Argyle, offering to skin and gut the small animals for preparation when they return with the horses. I frown as I look back at her, but it's Solo who appears at my side and answers my unspoken question in a low whisper.

"She's likely better at it than you think," he says. "Celine knows how to survive."

Right. Celine is so often soft-spoken and gentle that I forget she's not a real Lady's maid. She's a member of the House of Ravens, and in the end, the House of Ravens is full of survivors. Those who've fallen from Noble Houses, half-bloods, and the like. My chest aches, and I turn back to the fire, jamming the long stick I hold into the bottom and letting it go.

My mind whirls with that reminder and it makes my insides roil with the need to do something. I stand abruptly, moving quickly away from Solo as I head toward the horses. "I'm going to go practice," I announce, pulling my bow and stock of arrows free.

"Don't go too far," Solo warns, his voice louder than before.

"I won't."

He doesn't say anything more as I sling my quiver over my shoulder and he doesn't even insist on following me. Either it's a miracle, or he senses my need to be alone. Whatever the case, I'm grateful. Because I do need some alone time. I need time to come back to myself and remind myself that this Devonry, the one who practices shooting arrows and eats stream-caught fish over a fire in the woods and sleeps under the stars, is not the real Devonry.

After all of this is over, I'll be back on my throne, and this ... whatever this is between Solo and I could be over. While I have little interest in the Bartoli royals, there are other countries for which alliances could be made. I am supposed to be the furtherment of Rozentine. However, I'm not so sure my own desires match what this country will need of me now. I rub a hand over my breastbone, trying to stave off the ache that opens up a cavern of a hole inside my chest, right where my heart is.

21
DEVONRY

The rain held off for longer than any of us anticipated. Though I wish it would have held out longer still. My hood is plastered to my head. Every bit of my clothing is drenched thoroughly through. A fat water droplet makes its way down my nose and I sigh. Another day of travel. Another soggy pair of shoes.

Even Solomon's warmth faded as the rain brought with it a bitter cold wind. Now, where our bodies meet is hardly enough to fight against the uncontrollable shivers wracking our frames. Underneath us the horse twitches, occasionally shaking her mane, to dispatch some of the water. The squelching sound of hooves pulled from mud follows us along our path.

I lean back into the circle of Solomon's arm. With our bodies pressed together, the flush in my cheeks is a stark comparison to the frozen tip of my nose. I try to catch a glimpse of Argyle and Celine to our side but their silhouettes are only dark, blurred images against the downpour.

The storm brought with it the musky scent of earth. I'd thought eventually I'd turn nose-blind to the smell, but here we are, still trekking through, and every breath brings another fresh waft of dirt, pine, and something distinctly animal.

With no sign of the sun, my eyes search the shadows as our path widens even further to allow room for carriages to pass one another. Not that anyone other than us is out in this weather. Still, the road is just another reminder that a village is not far ahead.

Something sours in my stomach. Throughout the trip, we've done our best to keep to the outskirts of villages and avoid people suffering from this terrible disease. I grip the horn of the saddle until the skin of my knuckles stretches taut. My hands throb from the cold, the dry flesh threatening to crack. I've earned a couple of glaring looks from Celine over the callouses and the general poor state my hands are in at the moment. But what is there to be done? We didn't pack frivolous things such as lotions. Not that a lotion could fix the fresh callouses from my anxiety-driven practices with my bow.

Buildings appear through the haze of the storm. Vibrant red paint stands out even at this distance to identify the sickness that's rapidly working its way inward from our borders. We have yet to pass a town that hasn't been affected. How far has this disease spread?

Immediately, my thoughts wander to Lenorn and his declaration of his certainty that the House of Daemonium is the source of it all. Wickedness must run deep within this family for them to release this fresh, otherworldly darkness upon us all. And how much of it has been Nasir's influence? What if it had been his idea, to begin with?

I grind my teeth. Even after all of his betrayals, my mind still finds reason to defend him. I suppose after years of friendship and what I thought was trust, it's still hard to think of him as the monster I saw. I want to have imagined it all. If I had then my father would still be alive, so would Jacin, and I'd still have my best friend.

But I wouldn't have Solomon. I'd never have met Argyle or Celine.

My eyes would still be closed to the horrors the House of Ravens faces and the violent slave trade terrorizing Rozentine. Perhaps all these terrible things are predestined by the Gods. Most certainly think so, and if I was as devout in my faith as a Princess or Queen ought to be, then perhaps I wouldn't feel so sick when I think about it all.

Our road branches into two paths. A road straight through the town and the other arching away as though it, too, worries for its health. The men steer the animals away from the main road. For a moment, the rain lessens to a drizzle, and I can make out the crumpled forms of people huddling on stoops and bodies lying near the road.

All of this because I'd run. Another person dead because Nasir couldn't have me. What more might he do to claim me as his bride or to have my country for himself? How many lives is that power worth to him? What am I worth to him?

I shudder to think.

Solomon holds the reins with one hand, the other palm settling against my leg. He squeezes gently. And like always, it feels as though he knows exactly what I'm thinking. Maybe he's thinking the same thing. It's possible they all are.

I turn to look at Argyle and Celine again. Rain tracks their faces, looking far too similar to tears. Celine's lips are pouted, a resilient sadness darkening her gaze that, even at our distance, is easy to make out. Argyle's expression, though, is much harder to read. The man has practiced hiding his feelings for quite a long time, but these weeks together make it easier for me to find the small details that give him away. The muscle that twitches along his jaw. A thin wrinkle forming between his brows. Even the ever so slight way his body curls toward Celine as if he might shield her from the horrors.

Another crack forms inside my chest. The pain of it is becoming normal as my heart breaks a little further every day. I can count the terrible fissures and match them with the memories, each one a permanent scar.

It's impossible to look away from the town even as it gets harder to view through the trees. My eyes remain glued while my mind counts every person, dead or alive. The last form I see is so small it can be none other than a child. The figure shifts and then curls into themselves.

My fault.

By Aerea's flames, the thought keeps coming back.

My fault. This is my fault. I did this.

My fault.

Each time the thought returns louder than the next until the words are a terrible chorus of all the voices of the dead ringing in my ears.

A huff from our horse has me flinching as I'm pulled out of my thoughts and back onto the muddy path. The earthy aroma that surrounded us before is accompanied by an additional layer of sick that stings my nose with every breath. I release my fingers from the horn of the saddle and stretch the stiffness out of them.

"I hate this," I say, watching my words turn to fog in the air. "If I'd have given Nasir what he wanted, we could have avoided all this death."

Solomon's muscles tighten, the ripple of his reaction apparent even through our clothing. His fingers grip my legs. The fabric of my riding pants bunches under his palm. "Even if you would have given yourself up, I would have never allowed it." The brush of his words sends a rise of goosebumps down my neck.

"It's terribly sad, but you did the right thing, Devonry," Celine adds. She tugs her hood further over her face but manages to peer over to me with her large brown eyes. There is a sincerity in her voice, but still, I can't get rid of the nagging in my head that says they have to say things like that; I'm their Queen first and their friend second.

In our following silence, the rain comes to an end. The sun tries to make an appearance through the thick clouds, only managing to shine for a few seconds at a time before being snuffed out again. A chatter rises throughout the woods as animals come out of their shelters. Birds chirp happily, unaware of the piddly mood of the passersby.

"People are resilient," Argyle says, giving me a reassuring smile that doesn't quite reach his eyes. I swear I die a little more inside. "They will get through this. We will get through this."

"Nasir will fall." I turn my head at Solomon's word, leaning back against his shoulder and letting my hood fall back. He lowers his chin, speaking against my skin. "When he falls so, too, will this disease if it is caused by the House of Daemonium's abilities." The brush of his lips is a soothing balm to my queasy stomach. "Keep your head up, Princess." He finishes the sentiment with the brush of a kiss against my temple.

I close my eyes, trying to focus on the comfort of our bodies pressed so close together. I try and I fail. No matter how quiet the thoughts get, they remain. This could have been avoided. Every death is blood on my hands. All of this ... is my fault.

22
SOLOMON

Not even the small sweeping circles of my fingers over her kneecap seem to lessen the way Devonry's body is wound taut. Every village and town we'd ambled by only had her stiffening and shrinking into herself more and more. Honestly, I didn't know someone could do both those things at the same time, but here she is doing just that. Her body caves in toward mine as if she's trying to hide against me, and in the same breath, her muscles go rigid as if there's no softness to be found in her. Not anymore.

I know that's not true though. Know it as well as any man who has slid himself into the soft, waiting core of a woman's body and felt her go liquid around him. I want to do as much right now with the curve of her ass rubbing against my cock with each shift of the horse's legs beneath us. The urge, however, is more than repressed—it's shoved down and locked into a secret vault so deep inside of me that it won't ever see the light of day again unless I deign to let it.

Step. Step. Step. The horse's hooves clomp against the

hard ground. I know the reason for Devonry's wariness and fear. We're getting closer now, only miles away from where it all started, from Sanctus City. Her home. *Our* home.

The last of the small surrounding towns fade from existence, becoming pinpricks behind us until they disappear over hills or beyond trees. We reach the outer layers of the city and Devonry sits up, straightening her back even as she draws her head further beneath the hood that covers her hair and shields most of her face.

I can guess the emotions she's feeling because they're likely the same as my own. An odd jumble of turmoil and displacement. The city, itself, is no different than when we left it. Months ago now, we'd fled this place—rather, the shining beacon that is the Sunfire Palace that rests in the center of it. I can't say why, but I'd expected there to be change after us. I'd half expected buildings would have been caved in, relegated to nothing but dust and rubble. Though I am glad to see that everything still stands, it almost makes the lack of ruin seem like a bad omen, as if it's all a lie and there are worse things than destroying buildings and lives.

Citizens still linger in front of the businesses lining the main road. Several pull scarves up over their faces, fighting against the wind with every step. Past them, I watch as water splashes out of a shallow puddle when a man jogs by with a package tucked under his arm and a hat pulled low over his forehead. I sigh before inhaling the aroma of freshly baked bread from a bakery we'd passed only a moment ago.

Before me, Devonry's head turns on a swivel, eyes scanning the people, the stores, and the homes we pass. Another thing to be grateful for is the fact that amidst all of the normalcy in Sanctus City is another absence. Not just the absence of Nasir's rage and anger and rule, but also the absence of death. She lets out a long exhale that I feel in my very bones. There are no painted doors or dead bodies decomposing by the streets. The illness hasn't taken here. Not yet at least. Or possibly not quite as widespread.

I tug on the reins until our horse slows then stops just before a small inn. A vacancy sign hangs in the front window, swaying when the door opens and closes to let out a couple who giggle and turn toward the shops. I tug the reins to the side and follow an alley alongside the inn, going further back as I listen to the sound of Argyle's horse trailing mine.

Further and further we go until the streets become darker and the shops ... less charming. Though Devonry had grown up in this city, I know that these parts were hidden from her. So her quiet shock as she takes in the slums of Sanctus with each passing breath rolls off of her in sorrow-filled waves.

It isn't until we reach a dilapidated house that's more of a hut than a true lodging that I slow the horse to a trot and then a complete stop. I swing myself out of the saddle, adjusting my hood before Devonry's. Her eyes narrow as she peers out from under the fabric and slips down the horse with my assistance.

"What is this place?" she asks.

I take a moment to look up at the two-story wooden building with its grime-coated windows and the rusted iron handle on the front door. "A safe house," I reply.

"Yours?" she gapes at me in shock.

I shake my head. "No." She doesn't ask whose, and I don't tell her, but I have no doubt that our host will announce it himself when he, too, arrives.

My lips peel back from my teeth as I grab ahold of the horse's reins, and behind me, I hear Argyle help Celine off of their steed before doing the same. Together, he and I lead the animals around to the side of the house where a small—too small—alcove was built for just this purpose. There are no stables, but two stalls have been carved into the side of the house and filled with rotting hay. They will just have to do. I have no clue where the other's horses will go when they arrive, but that's not my concern right now. Getting Devonry inside and safe is.

When Argyle and I return to the front of the house, it's to find Celine and Devonry standing upon the rickety steps leading into the abode. Argyle pushes past the two of them, gently sliding both ladies to the side as he withdraws a key, long and iron and just as rusted as its lock, and opens the door.

The mass of weak wood creaks out of our way, but no one moves. I have to put a hand on Devonry's lower back and nudge her to get her going. Finally, the four of us step inside and the door shuts behind us once more.

Exhaustion clings to everyone. Despite the obvious discomfort with standing inside the strange and dusty front room of what looks like it was once a merchant's manor—long ago—Devonry stretches her arms over her head and then stifles a yawn. Her wandering gaze never pauses its perusal of the space as she takes in the bare floors and walls. No art or extras, despite there being pale places upon the walls where paintings had once hung. A sign that the previous owner of this house had been someone of quality, maybe before the slums had become what they are today, perhaps abandoned long enough for Lenorn to find it and take it for his own and keep it this way in an effort to hide a house that he could use later for a purpose very much like the one we now have of it.

Instinct has me motioning to Argyle to split up and double-check every inch of the space. He does. With quiet footsteps, we separate and scour through the house, finding nothing but threadbare sheets and old, sunken beds, and the barest of essentials. It's certainly not a house of luxury, but it is safe enough. For now.

When we return to the women, it's to find them in the small kitchen with a candle lit, but thankfully with the curtains drawn. Argyle stomps in after me and collapses into a chair at the table that looks like it could barely hold two plates, much less the candle that currently rests in its center.

"His place is a dump," he complains, adjusting his belt.

"It's safe," I reply.

Celine bustles around the room as if she's lived in this place her entire life, opening cabinets, finding what she needs, and then hurrying toward her next task. All the while, Devonry trails her as if needing something to do but very much aware that Celine will not accept her help.

Argyle watches Celine with cool, low-lidded eyes. "I'm glad to be off that damn horse," he says, pushing his hands into his back and hissing when muscles crack. "I feared another hour on that thing and my body might be stuck in that terrible position forever."

Celine appears at the table and sets down two mugs of water. "Drink," she orders.

Argyle grins as he picks one up and thanks her before turning to me and flicking a finger at her. "At least I had that pretty thing between my legs," he says.

With her back turned, Celine's spine stiffens and she turns and scowls at him. "Pig," she mutters before going back to whatever task she's decided needs to be done now that she's served water.

I blow out a breath and take a seat at the table as well, facing Argyle. His amused expression cracks and then leeches away entirely until there's nothing but cold, calm seriousness looking back at me. "How long do we have before Lenorn arrives?" he asks in a whisper.

"Not long enough for you to go out," I murmur. "So don't ask."

"I wasn't thinking of it," Argyle replies, sitting back in his seat as he lifts his water to his lips. One gulp, however, has him sputtering and spitting the stuff back out into his mug before turning accusing eyes on Celine. "What in the Afterworld was *that*, Celine?" he demands.

Devonry rests with her back against the counter, looking between the two as Celine dumps some of that water from a bucket—where she got it, I don't know, but it'd been here when we came back in—into the sink.

"Payback for pinching my backside on the ride here," she snaps.

Argyle gapes at her. "I was helping you to adjust so your back wouldn't hurt!" His defense might have been believable if he hadn't looked down at said backside, eyes glowing with something any man would recognize. *Desire.*

My own desire creeps up my spine as I swap my attention to Devonry. I run my tongue along my lower lip, all too readily wanting to press my mouth to hers and kiss away her worries. Celine harrumphs, the sound breaking through my thoughts, but she doesn't say anything more. With a curse, Argyle shoves the mug away from him and crosses his arms.

I busy myself by pulling a coin purse out and tossing it his way. He arches a brow at me.

"Why don't you go grab some essentials," I say. "Something to eat and … perhaps find yourself something *clean* to drink."

Devonry's choked laugh is like music to my ears and just hearing its muffled sound is enough to have me grinning as Argyle flings me his middle finger, right before picking up the coin purse and disappearing out the door.

A moment later, however, he reappears, glowering at me once before stalking across the kitchen to Celine. "What are you—"

"Don't argue," Argyle snaps, grabbing ahold of her hand. A sputtering series of angry sounds and undignified curses that prove that despite Celine's obvious need to cling to propriety, she too, had lived on the streets and within the House of Ravens for a long time, and follows.

Argyle ignores it all and merely leads her out, leaving both Devonry and me alone. In silence.

Devonry is quiet for several long moments. Then she speaks. "How long do you think it'll take them," she begins, sliding me a knowing look, "before they finally give in to whatever it is that's between them?"

I shrug, my muscles pulling taut across my back with the movement. "It took us years," I reply.

More quiet. Had it been the wrong thing to say? Maybe. But it was the truth.

After what feels like an eternity of that unending silence, I shift and stand up from the table that's practically using me to keep it upright. It wobbles and then sags, but thankfully, it doesn't collapse. Breath, quiet but full of something fiery, squeezes from my lungs as my legs carry me to where she is.

She's still wearing her cloak, but the pieces of it that she'd kept tight around herself now fall open to reveal the lines and curves of her body beneath it. I step closer. Her heat envelopes me. Her smell. Everything. I hunger for her. Want her. The beast inside demands to take her, to have her, to protect her.

"This isn't really Sanctus City, is it?" she asks, gesturing around the empty kitchen save for the two of us.

"It is," I say. "And it isn't."

Her blue eyes, flecked with gold, peer up at me, waiting. I sigh and scrub a hand down my face. "It's an outer part of the city," I answer her unspoken need for more information. "Like a town nestled against the actual city proper. It's close enough for us to get where we need to be, but not so close as to put you in the heart of where we'll likely have to infiltrate."

"You mean Sunfire Palace."

I nod. "Yes. Sunfire Palace."

Our eyes meet, those blue-hazels against my crimson ones. We're so close to the true Sanctus City that I'm beginning to fear that she and I will slip back into the familiar roles we've played for years. One look at her face and I know, though, that the naive Princess is gone. I am both saddened by that and proud of what now stands in her place. A Queen, ready to rule, ready to take her place, and ready to fight for her people.

The horror that she had to face to get here now, though, leaves my chest hollow. "We will get you home, Princess," I tell her, swallowing around a lump in my throat as I say the words. "You will see it again, the Sunfire Palace."

For a moment, she says nothing, and then, as if she's being pulled by an invisible string that only she can sense, see, or feel, she skirts around me and drifts back out to the main room, to the foyer where the windows are unshrouded. She pauses in front of one and peers out into the street as the sun above goes down and night takes the sky in a dark wash of ocean-colored clouds that grow deeper and deeper with each passing heartbeat.

"You know," she begins, "everything still feels so very new."

I'm too afraid to even take a breath, afraid she'll stop

talking if I do and I need her to keep talking. I need to know what pains and fears have claimed her gaze and made it turn misty and far away.

"I think everyone's forgotten that I was always stuck in the palace. I wanted to leave before this all happened. I wanted to know the world. My father said it wasn't safe, and because I was not yet Queen, his order was obeyed."

I had obeyed that order and kept her locked in the palace because it was not only what my king had commanded but also because I believed him to be right. To keep her safe and sequestered, I thought that it was needed. Now, though, with the pain in her voice as she speaks, I find that the only place left for those memories is in a chamber of regret.

"The furthest I ever managed to reach was Sanctus City," she continues, still staring out of that window. "Until we fled. Until Sanctus City and the Sunfire Palace were no longer truly mine. Now, the most I've seen of Rozentine is what I've witnessed while running away." She bites down on her lower lip, the skin paling beneath the pressure. "I wish there was more good to be seen."

Damn self-control, I close the distance between us. "There *is* a lot of good in Rozentine," I assure her. "We've just hardly had the time to see any of it." Then, because I'm too far gone for her, I take her hand in mine and rub my thumb over her knuckles. "You're the best thing Rozentine has, and when you're back where you belong, I'll take you to see all the wonderful things your Kingdom has to offer." My lips skim over her delicate fingers.

Vaguely, I'm aware of figures in the street, shadows of people passing. Her lips part ever so slightly on a breath. "Solo…" She gently pulls her hand away as the people don't, in fact, pass but instead pause. They turn toward where we are and I grab ahold of her, yanking her back as the door opens and a familiar face appears in the entryway. Even with his head covered in a hood, I recognize him.

"Hello, there," Lenorn's voice carries toward us and my shoulders loosen. My hold on Devonry eases.

Lenorn tosses his hood back, revealing that his red hair has been braided and tucked into a dusty hat resting beneath it. Previously, he'd worn fine clothing that gave away his Noble blood before his purple-hazed eyes could. Now, he's adorned in brown pants that have ripped mostly around the knees and a thin cream-colored button-down with several coffee-colored stains around the collar. A long gray jacket completes his commoner's look with fingerless gloves to match. At least he's playing his part.

The one man whom we trust the least is the one who can get me near enough to Nasir to end his life. Frederic's promise of his allegiance feels flimsy when I look into the eyes that belong to the House of Daemonium.

Lenorn smiles and turns to Devonry. "My Queen," he whispers, bowing only slightly; what with the door still being open.

"Hello, Lenorn. I hope your travels were not as soggy as ours." Devonry pulls her cloak tighter around her shoulders and takes a careful, purposeful step away from me. My eyes flash black and red as my ability pulses through me, but I quickly quiet it and my vision returns to normal just as quickly.

There is a wagon on the street behind him. I lean around and watch as another man takes the horse's reins and guides it toward the back, around the side of the building. "We've put our horses in your ... stables." Without a better word to describe the alcove, I give him what information I can.

Lenorn offers an amused smirk. "Don't worry, we'll take care of the rest," he says. He lifts the cap from his head, those thick red braids falling down his back, as he rings the hat in his hands. Water clings to the cap before he finishes wringing it out, and I note the trails of droplets dripping from his cloak.

"Would you like to take a look at the setup?" he inquires, coming further into the house.

Devonry stiffens as she's forced to take a step back, once more closer to me with the movement. Another sigh sticks in my throat. It's going to be a long fucking night.

"Yes, show me," I answer our companion as I take Devonry's shoulders in my hands and gently nudge her toward an open doorway. To her, I say, "Find a room you'd like to stay in."

She doesn't say anything, but I also don't wait for a response as Lenorn strides through the house toward the back door and I follow him. He leads me through the kitchen once more and to a door at the back of the dilapidated manor, where he opens it to reveal the wagon sitting amidst weeds and broken stones in a small space behind the building.

Without waiting for me or to see if his friend is ready, he jumps off of the stones and reaches the wagon in a few short strides. He only stops when his legs bump the wagon's edge and then, he lifts a flap of the wagon's cover to reveal several large crates before glancing back at me.

It's a fine wagon, not nearly as worn-down as the clothes he's chosen to wear. The bonnet is thick enough to protect the cargo from the elements as well as curious eyes. Even the wooden crates lined up neatly behind a bench are polished enough to be considered appropriate for a delivery made straight to the Capital itself. I hum in satisfaction and let the man continue.

"Weapons," he says, "as well as rations and food stores

should we need it. I'm hopeful we won't, but there will be more wagons coming in the next few days."

"Infiltration shouldn't be too difficult." But even as I speak the words, I know the truth. There are always things that could change a plan at the last minute. These weapons and rations are a good idea. Plus, there will be more men coming. If we're unable to infiltrate the palace and kill Nasir as we hope, then a second plan will have to replace our first.

"You'll send a letter for us before you go," I demand rather than ask.

Lenorn gives a curt nod. "Whatever you need."

"Good." The door behind me opens and as if she knows what I'm planning, what I'm about to say, Devonry pauses on the threshold and doesn't come any further. I'm thankful she's far enough away not to hear the hardness in my voice, the shroud over the fear that I feel deep within my gut. The fear that I might not come back, that I could fail her. If I do, she will still need protection.

"Send a letter off to my uncle, Lord Ahren, be discreet in what you say but make him aware of our plan. He's trustworthy and will come to our aid should we need it, and should we fail—he will take Devonry and get her out."

Lenorn's fingers tighten upon his cap at his side, but he nods his understanding. "I will ensure she gets out safely if I can, my Lord. Even if it costs me my life."

"Thank you." Gratitude fills my chest. Of all the promises he could have made, that is the most important and meaningful. To protect my Queen is to save me from an Afterworld of unending suffering.

Lenorn seems to realize that but thankfully doesn't comment as he explains the rest of the plan. He tells me of an increase in visitors to the palace—merchants, florists, bakers, and others. It's not just some of his own family from the House of Daemonium. Though he cannot figure out why they're coming and going at all hours, it gives him —both of us—pause.

The longer we talk, the more aware I become of Devonry standing there, watching us silently. My hatred for Nasir renews as my Queen's presence reminds me of what he's robbed our great country of.

What in the name of Levim is he doing? Familiarizing himself with the people of Sanctus City? Trying to sink his claws into our country a little deeper? No. It has to be something else, but what?

Fury becomes a violent thing in my chest. It raises its head and calls to the monster that always lurks beneath my flesh. I roll my shoulders as a ripple dances down my back. A sure sign that the monster might just decide to come out and play. That's the last thing we need. Shifting into the beast that Nasir has painted me out to be with all those damn wanted posters in the middle of the street will do us no good. So I numb myself to the violent emotion as best I can and reinforce the bars that cage my beast inside of me.

Finally, I hold up a hand silencing Lenorn. "It's late," I say. "We'll reconvene in the morning."

Lenorn blows out a breath but doesn't argue. His assistant or friend, whoever he'd been traveling with, has since disappeared and when I send him a questioning look, Lenorn gives me a small smile that doesn't reach his eyes. "Bartok is running errands for me," he answers my unspoken question. "Gathering other supplies and sending notes that I've asked him to get out to more of my people. He can be trusted, do not worry."

I nod and turn back to the house, only instead of finding Devonry in the doorway, I now see Argyle. His face is stiff and his arms are crossed as he looks between me and Lenorn. I approach.

"Where is Devonry?"

"With Celine," he answers before peering at Lenorn. He nods to the man, who in turn, nods back.

"Lord of Ravens," Lenorn says respectfully.

Argyle's face blanches at that title, but he doesn't argue against it. A blessing as I'm too tired now to do or say anything to fix any insult denying Lenorn would intend. Lenorn, wisely enough, senses that it's time for his departure and disappears into the house.

"Devonry will likely want to say goodbye to him," Argyle murmurs, watching the man retreat into the dirty house. He digs his hands into his pocket and pulls out a folded piece of paper. "I meant to show you this. We saw it on the streets on our way back."

I take the parchment and unfold it. Staring back at me is my own dark gaze. Thick brows over narrowed eyes. I have to give it to the artist, you can see the glint of hunger in my eyes. But still, the shape of my face is a little off, rounder than it is, and my nose might actually be too small. I groan and push the wanted poster back at Argyle. "At least no one will recognize me. I don't look like that at all."

"What do you mean?" Argyle spins the page and holds it next to my face. "The likeness is uncanny." I don't hold back my glare. "Yes, that's your expression, exactly. But that's not what I was going to show you." He points his finger lower on the page. I follow his direction, skimming the text. "The price for your head has gone up. You're worth a pretty coin now, thousands in fact. He might as well be waving a red flag in your damned face."

Thousands.

I can't wait to get my hands on Nasir and wring his bloody neck.

23
SOLOMON

The next day comes, and with it, more of that unsettling fear that had clung to me in the night. The sun rises and falls once more over Sanctus City, and the rendezvous manor that Lenorn had set up for us is suddenly filled with people. His people. Friends and trusted warriors who have chosen to follow him, to follow Devonry.

I am as much grateful for their presence as I am wary of them. With us so close to Sunfire Palace and the old memories of the last night we'd both been within its walls resurfacing in my mind, I'm on edge. Even if Lenorn trusts his people, I've only just begun to trust him. Devonry trusts Lord Frederic—as do I—and Frederic has vouched for Lenorn, I remind myself.

Despite their presence, however, Lenorn has the good sense to keep most of them on rotating shifts, guarding the manor, completing tasks to prepare for battle—to sneak into the palace or fight our way in if we must. Each hour draws us closer and none of us have received word from Ahren or Frederic on the status of their arrival. They're late, and we cannot wait much longer. There's no telling when the illness that has been spreading across Rozentine like wildfire will reach here. If it hasn't already and we simply have yet to see it.

As night falls on our second day back in Sanctus City, I, along with our newest and closest allies, find ourselves seated around a table that has mysteriously replaced the rickety one that had been in the kitchen when we'd first arrived. I don't have to look to Celine or Lenorn to know who'd done it. I'd caught the two of them talking quietly in the hall earlier that morning, and by the time lunch had come, the table had been there. If I wasn't so sure that Argyle would cut off the man's hands should they touch Celine, I'd say she and Lenorn might have been a good match.

Devonry steps into the room, her back straight and a determined look written upon her face. My attention seeks her out immediately, latching onto the way she shines in the darkened interior of the manor. Not even the fireplace, small as it is with its crooked mantle, can produce a fire large enough to keep the place warm. Yet the room feels brighter, less terrible, as she strides past the group of us that have arrived and taken our seats.

I stand abruptly and move for the head of the table to pull out the chair there for her. Her gaze lifts and meets mine. Blue hazel eyes flecked in chips of ice and gold reflect an emotion she's trying to hide. Nervousness. My throat swells, but I keep my mouth shut as she takes me up on my silent offer and moves to the chair I'm holding out for her. Once she's seated, I move to her side and sit as well. Argyle and Celine sit on her other side.

Now it's just the four of us, plus Lenorn and Aegis, Captain of Lord Frederic's guard, who had come ahead of Lord Frederic, just in case he wasn't able to make it before our plan was set into action. Still, I pray to the Gods and Levim that he will. As much as I dislike the obvious affection he and Devonry share, he is a good man and one I would trust with a sword at my side.

The six of us are quiet as everyone gets adjusted and Celine pours water from the pitcher sitting in the middle of the table. Her hand shakes as she brings the glass to her lips. I turn away as Lenorn begins to speak.

"We'll infiltrate the Sunfire Palace tomorrow," he announces.

"So soon?" Celine's hand creeps up to her neck. "Lord Frederic hasn't arrived yet."

Lenorn shakes his head. "We've gotten word that the illness has made it to the outer parts of the city," he says. "Some *in* the city. We cannot risk holding out here and waiting. If we do, we risk our own forces catching the disease and weakening us before we can even begin."

The grooves alongside Aegis' mouth and cheeks seem to deepen, but he still says nothing.

The silence stretches out before us. "Then tomorrow it is." Argyle sighs. "We wake early and we go before dawn."

Lenorn turns to the pack at his side and withdraws a map, a familiar map, I realize. It's one of the Sunfire Palace. Except it's not professionally done, but written in very fine printed hand. There are also passageways that no other map would have, no one save for someone who had lived and breathed that palace all their lives. My head slowly turns to Devonry.

She doesn't look at me, but still, pride swells in my chest. She's changed so much in the last few months. Though I loved her as a girl, as a sweet young woman with a bite of temper that never truly let me forget the fire in her bloodline, now I love her as what she is—a woman. As much as I'd hated it at the time, all of those times she had snuck away from me, giving me such trouble, is finally coming in handy.

"From what we've gathered, Nasir is still keeping the same rotation of guards—obviously, many are his own personal guards—but the system and shift changes are the same. We strike during one of those changes. We take the guards out and separate." I point to a place on the map. "Aegis will free anyone being held captive by him—Court Nobles, servants, it doesn't matter. So long as they are not loyal to Nasir, you free them." He nods once.

I shift in my seat. "Once we've infiltrated the palace, I'll find Nasir's chambers. Lenorn"—I pause and gesture to the man—"you'll come with me."

"Not me?" Argyle frowns as he leans forward.

Devonry's attention centers on my face before she glances at the rest of the room. I feel the heat of their stares, but the only one who seems to understand when I lift my head and meet his is Argyle.

"No," I say quietly. "I need you here," I don't look at the woman at my side, "protecting our Queen."

"*What?*" The word shoots out of Devonry's mouth like one of her arrows, quick and precise now that she's had practice.

Celine's mouth tightens, but neither she nor any of the males seated at the table say anything against my decision. Devonry's head whips around, the swaying strands of her strawberry hair swiping at her cheeks as she centers her glare on me.

"You can't be serious," she grits out. "I *am* going with you. This is not an argument to be had. As your Queen, I command it."

"Your Highness—" Lenorn's pained tone is cut off as Devonry grips my arm, silently demanding that I look at her. I do, and it hurts to see the rage in her beautiful face, to know that I cannot appease it, that if it means keeping her safe, I will not.

"It's too dangerous to take you with us," I state, forcing myself to remain unaffected by her fury, at least visibly. "You'll remain here with Argyle as your guard. Lenorn or Aegis will also leave a contingent just to look after the house, but hopefully, no one will suspect your presence here." In this trash heap of a manor on the outskirts of the slums of Sanctus City, no one would expect their Queen to be holed up, waiting. Not here. Her safety is the reason I can stomach leaving her in this hovel.

"It will be dangerous regardless," Devonry snarls, her nails biting into my arm. The gold flecks in her eyes flash and dance with emotion, glimmering like fire embers.

"What if they recognize you?" I ask. "If you ride with us, what if you are spotted and they—"

She cuts me off. "What about *you*?" she hisses, eyes narrowing. "What if men you've worked with or who you've trained spot you? What if whatever powers Nasir seems to possess have taken their minds, and they capture you and turn you in? What if they've seen your wanted poster?"

That damn poster. Its remains are scattered in the trash now. I'd shredded it between my fingertips after staring at it for far too long. But she must have heard of it from Celine. When I lift my gaze to the woman in question, she turns away from me, solidifying that answer.

As the Blood General, my name is known far and wide. My face, however, was only known to the Nobles and those within the palace security. She's right. The posters may have changed that.

"You don't need to worry about it; I'm called the Blood General for a reason. I know how to go undetected. I have experience in battle, Your Highness. *You* do not." My words are cool, unbending.

A line forms between her brows, and Devonry opens her mouth to speak, but whatever she means to say is interrupted as Argyle lays a hand on the table with a loud thump. "I will ensure her safety," he tells me, his bi-colored eyes settling on my face. "I will ensure both of their safety."

I nod to him, thankful that he's directed us back to the topic at hand rather than the fight that I can sense brewing between Devonry and me.

This is nothing, I tell myself. Her rage. Her anger. I'll accept it. *Compared to everything else, Solomon, this is nothing.*

But the quickening of my pulse in my ears suggests that it's more. I've seen war. There'd been days where I'd ripped men's throats out and watched as the spark of life in their eyes died. I'd spent time in enemy territory. And none of that holds a candle to the stress my body is riddled with thinking of Devonry being anywhere near the action.

We'd been so close to being caught when we'd fled Bartoli. Prince Enver and the Ambassador had been right there. Only by the grace of our Gods, and Devonry herself, had we managed to escape. It could have gone sideways at any moment. What we're doing now could too. If Lenorn isn't as loyal as he pretends to be. If I'm recognized. There are a thousand of other ways we could find ourselves at the wrong end of the sword and I refuse to allow her to be near that kind of carnage if I can help it.

The rest of the conversation follows, with Aegis and Lenorn offering commentary on which entrances would be best to infiltrate. How many weapons we need. Which soldiers will go, and which will stay.

The longer the night and the planning drags on, the hotter Devonry's silent anger grows. When it's all said and done and everyone has gone to their rooms for the night, I feel heavier than I ever have before. Weighed down and exhausted before the battle has even begun.

Before it does, there is another I must fight first. One I do not want to, but one that I cannot overlook before the morrow comes.

24
SOLOMON

Her fury is palpable. It vibrates off of her body in waves as I step into the small bedroom Lenorn provided to us in the manor, the one she'd chosen. The walls are made of dark wood with grooves of age wedged into their panels. Two thick woolen sheets are hung across from one another to ward off the chill that may seep through—one against the far wall across from the bed and the other above the headboard. A lone window has the curtains drawn, but they rustle as the cold seeps in with the breeze.

I take in the tiny bed shoved against the wall, and alongside it is a petite writing desk and stool. Both look like they'll collapse if I even get too close, much less sit on them.

Already on the bed, Devonry lays on her side, facing away from me. She's not asleep though. With the tension that tightens her muscles and keeps her shoulders around her ears, that much I know for sure. With a sigh, I quietly stride across the room to the desk. Dropping onto the stool, the damned rickety thing creaks, and I freeze for a moment, wondering if it really will shatter beneath my weight. The wood must be made of stronger stuff than it looks, however, because it holds. With slow movements, I reach down and pull off my boots one by one. In the bed, Devonry's breathing hitches.

Quiet, oh so quiet, I begin to speak. "I'm not denying you because I don't trust you," I tell her. Exhaustion flows into my veins, living, breathing, agonizingly heavy. Rolling my head on my shoulders, I try to work the tension from my neck as I think through my next words. How do I make her understand that I'm only doing what I must to keep her safe?

The sound of fabric rustling has me turning my head to see Devonry sit up and stare at me from her spot on the bed. "It's *wrong*," she says, hissing the last word with barely repressed anger.

Once, so long ago, she'd seemed to have nothing of the sort. After her father, after King Vernon had been slaughtered, I'd thought she'd wither away and it would be a blessing to have her disappear into the House of Blood territory. Now, though, I know that would have never worked. She's far too volatile and far too resilient to wither and disappear.

A wave of heat rolls off of her, reminding me of alcohol being poured on a cooling fire that suddenly flares bright and strong. That, too, is another reason I refuse to bring her with me. Her abilities are still far too new to her. I have years of experience with mine, a lifetime. She's had weeks. Even if the speed of her mastery is impressive, it's still eons behind my own.

"You're denying me what should be my *right*."

I grit my teeth at her words. "A right to get yourself killed?" I snap back. Regret immediately fills me as soon as the words are out. I hold up my hand before she can toss another insult my way. "No, no, please don't. I'm sorry. I didn't mean it like that."

Her round, blue-hazel eyes glitter at me from the corner of the bedroom. The slim light from the window stains the corner of the bed and the floor. "Then how *did* you mean it?" she demands.

I lower my head and rest my arms on my thighs as I stare down at the place between my feet. Even the floor is marked by scars as if someone had sat here on this very stool and chucked a knife into the wooden planks beneath their feet over and over again. "I don't want to fight tonight, Devonry," I say. *Devonry*. Not Princess. Not Queen. Just ... my Devonry.

"You'll be fighting tomorrow," she says quietly, the anger lessoning in her tone even if only slightly. "What's one more tonight?"

The chuckle that escapes me is anything but amused. "Let me rephrase," I reply as the grin flits over my lips, more of a grimace than anything. "I don't *want* to fight with you." *Ever*.

I lift my head and watch as Devonry crosses her arms over her chest and my eyes shoot to the thin, white fabric of her nightshift. I don't know where the hell she got it and I'm not going to ask. Though I suspect Celine might have had something to do with it. If anyone tries to remember that Devonry is a Queen used to the luxuries of life, it's that woman. Not that I mind. If I could, I would give Devonry everything in this world, including the sun. She deserves that much.

Devonry tips her face down and glares at me. That, too, I find attractive. Everything about her entices me. From the spark of anger in her eyes to her soft lips and the little furrow between her brows. I'm so fucking far gone and I don't want to be saved. Not from her.

"You're a Queen," I continue, reaching down and picking up my boots to set them together at the side of the desk. "You need to think of yourself. What kind of guard would allow his Queen to walk into danger alongside him? This is my job and you need to let me do it. If we lose you, then we lose everything. Trust me and stay here tomorrow. Argyle will keep you safe. Lenorn has also offered to leave a few extra men, and I agreed."

She's quiet and that does not bode well for me, but if she's not screaming and hurling insults then I'll take it. I stand up from the stool and reach back, gripping a handful of my tunic and pulling it up and over my head.

"What are you doing?" she finally speaks as my head breaks free of the fabric. I turn and deposit it on the top of the desk. "You're not sleeping here."

"Yes," I say, my tone firm, unyielding. "I am."

"No!"

"Devonry." I look up at her and arch a brow. "What did you think I was doing when I came in and started taking off my boots?"

In lieu of an answer, she curls her upper lip back at me and grips the sheets so tight that her knuckles turn white. "You can sleep on the floor," she gripes, jerking her chin in that direction.

I march toward her, unbidden. She scoots closer and closer to the wall as I approach. The movement only gives me the perfect amount of room to lift the corner of the bedsheets and slide in next to her. Devonry's body is stiff and straining as I reach for her, pulling her away from the edge of the bed and into my arms. She turns away, kicking back at my calves.

"Stop this," she growls, struggling against me as she bows her spine. "I don't allow this. I'm mad at you."

Closing my eyes, I hug her tighter, feeling the warmth

of her back through the sheer fabric of her nightshift against my chest. Without a second thought, I bury my face into the back of her neck and her hair, inhaling the soft, tender scent of her sweetness. Cool and soothing. At least, it is until my cock jerks against my thigh, stiffening.

Gods damn it. I adjust, pulling my hips slightly back as I try to hide my condition from her and still keep her close. After a while, she stops struggling, but I'm not so naive as to think she's fallen asleep in my arms just like that. Instead, she lays there—ramrod straight and unmoving— as time ticks by. My mind is weary. My body is tight. My fangs throb in my gums and the back of my throat feels the intensity of barren dryness.

"What happens," Devonry whispers after what feels like an eternity of silence, "if you don't come back tomorrow?"

My eyes open and land on her profile, the rounded paleness of her cheek and the soft freckles that dot her flesh, lighter than any freckles I've seen on another. They're barely perceptible, but I have better sight than most. I see everything.

"How will I know?" she asks.

"I…" I don't know what to tell her. I know what she wants—reassurance—but neither of us wants to lie to each other.

With stilted, still angry movements, Devonry rolls onto her opposite side to face me. The two of us are chest to chest as she tilts her face up at me expectantly. There are tears in her eyes, I realize. Glittering jewels that threaten to break free, but she won't let them. Not yet.

"Don't you fucking die on me, Solomon Winett." Her words are hoarse. Enraged. Scared. My arms immediately tighten around her.

"No," I say.

"Promise me," she orders. "Make an oath that no matter what, you'll come back to me. You'll survive whatever happens."

"Will you stay here?" It's a bastard move to use her care for me, her worry against her, but I'll do what I must to ensure her safety. Even this.

The corners of her rose-petal lips turn downward and she scoffs. "You are…"

"An asshole," I say. "I know. But will you stay here? Answer me."

She bites down on her lower lip and those trembling tears cling to her lashes. "You're right," she says through gritted teeth. "It's dangerous for me to follow you. So, yes, I'll stay here with Argyle and whoever else you decide is worthy enough to guard me. I'll be good and I will wait, but Solomon…" Fingers scratch against my chest and my cock expands further in my trousers. "You better fucking come back."

Desire. Hot and heavy swells within me. Not just my cock, but my whole body is consumed by the need for her. Withdrawing one arm from her side, I reach up and stroke her cheek with one finger and then lower it slowly down until I'm holding her chin in my hand before I lean down and press my lips to hers.

The kiss is desperate. She's already kissing me back before I've even fully opened my mouth. Her tongue invades, hungry and determined. *I love her.* Fuck, I love her so damn much, and it's the kind of love I know will kill me if I let it. Yet, still, I can't stop this. It's already too late for both of us. We crossed that line back in the caves of Bartoli and I don't regret a single moment of it.

"Don't die, Solo … I can't…" Devonry breaks the kiss before I'm ready, but both of us are panting heavily. I want more.

"It's going to be fine," I assure her. "It's all going to be fine. Trust me."

"I won't survive it," she says. "Not you."

For a moment, all of the breath in my lungs escapes, and I'm left a hollowed man with nothing but those words filling me up. I know, without asking, that she feels the same way as me. She might not have known what I was to her the same way I had, but none of that matters now. All that matters is that she loves me too. Those words prove as much.

I kiss her again, dragging her body into mine as my hands reach for her nightgown. She doesn't fight me. Instead, she arches one leg over both of mine before resettling against me. Pale, ivory skin is revealed to my eyes as I lift her gown over her head and drop it to the side of the bed. Her breasts, high and pink tipped, scrape against my chest.

There is hunger, but there is something deeper. There is devotion. Pure as a dove and unfettered by anything mortal. I know in my darkest parts that even if I am physically stronger than her, she will always hold the reins to my strength. I would sooner eat my own flesh than wound her.

"Solo…" The sound of my name on her breath is enough to break me. It stabs into my soul and rips me to shreds, opening up all of the old agony I buried long ago. I dip my head into her shoulder and clutch her to me.

I'm not afraid of death. I'm not afraid of what will happen to me tomorrow. We have an advantage in infiltrating the Sunfire Palace. I know it as well as my own territory. Despite that, it almost feels too easy. As if the travels through Rozentine were supposed to be much harder. That lingering anxiety won't relieve itself. I try to shove it down, but it continues to crop up when I give myself a moment of peace and silence. She's the only thing that can drown out the worry etched into my soul.

"Solo, kiss me," Devonry begs, distracting me once more. "Please."

I cannot deny her. Shoving the last of my worried thoughts into the back of my mind, I lift my head away from her skin and offer her my mouth. She takes it gratefully. Her hands clutch at the back of my head, sliding through the strands of my dark hair—longer now than they had been when we'd left this place so few months ago.

Reaching between us, I lift her up with a hand beneath the rounded cheeks of her ass. Her lips follow mine, a small whimper of desire escaping her mouth and making my head swim. She seeks me out, her mouth on mine, her tongue twining over my own. I practically rip at the ties of my trousers to free myself, and when my cock springs up and the heat of it touches her pussy, she sucks in a breath. Her belly hollows out as her lashes lift and she looks back at me, wiggling down a bit, silently asking for more.

My hands move along her back and sides. I kiss her chin and her cheek. "Do you know the ways I want you?" I ask, brushing my lips over her jawline.

"If it's anything like the way I want you then I don't know how you ever held back," she replies a bit breathlessly.

Fuck. My cock practically throbs in need. A sharp punch rips through my stomach at her words even as I withhold a chuckle. "You have no idea," I murmur.

She is silk in my hands against the roughness of my palms. How can anyone be so soft and strong in the same instance? Tiny, cool fingertips graze my abdomen and my muscles clench instinctively as the aching need for her ricochets through me. My fangs shift in my gums. The scent of her is fresh and heady. I lick her throat, tasting salt and smelling her arousal in the air.

"No more waiting," Devonry says, her tone tight as she scrapes her nails over the ridges of my stomach and pauses to gently touch the edges of a few of the scars there. "Take me. Please."

My throat closes, but I do as my Queen commands. I adjust her and reach between the two of us, holding my cock upright and directing it to the soft, swollen, and wet entrance of her body as she pulls her hands back and holds onto my shoulders. Her spine stiffens as I enter her slowly. Her head cranes backward, the feather-like strands of her tinted hair—both blonde and red—grazing the fingers I have on her spine.

The air between us feels too hot, as if we're in the middle of a volcano ready to erupt. Neither of us seems to mind it too much. Once she's completely seated on my lap, my cock filling up her stomach, she rights herself and looks down between us. Pink lips parted, cheeks flushed, eyes still shimmering—she's everything I ever fantasized about.

My eyes close as her inner muscles squeeze around me. A groan arches up my throat. "*Fuck...*"

Small, feminine hands land on my shoulders, and my eyes snap back open to see her gaze fixated on my face. I blink as she lifts up, pulling my cock up and out of her cunt only to suddenly drop back down. The pleasure slams into me like a tidal wave. Her body is so fine. She moves as if she's been invaded by the spirit of a dancer—gracefully, her hips roll into mine as she does it again, pulling herself up and then moving back down.

Panting breaths mingle between us as my fingers grip her hips and on the third descent, I help her, slamming her into my lap with a force that makes her cry out. "Solo!"

I lick a bead of sweat from her collarbone and then

press a kiss there as her hips begin to gyrate and grind. "You like it hard, Devonry?" I ask. "I can do that. I can do whatever you want. Give you anything—just name it."

Her hands rip away from my shoulders to slap my cheeks, a hand on either one. I freeze, startled as she directs my attention to her face. "*You*," she huffs out. "I just want you."

My tense muscles ease ever so slightly and I wrap my arms around her. "You have me," I swear it. "I am yours," I say. "Eternally."

With that, our bodies begin to move again. In sync, she lifts and I help her, filling her over and over again as I spread kisses along her chest, neck, and lips. She moans and rides me through it all, squeezing down on my shaft until I have to grit my teeth and shut my eyes against the beauty she presents with her breasts swaying before me as she takes me into her most inner core over and over again just to stop myself from coming too soon.

After several long moments, she begins to tremble with each time she releases and comes down. I take over, lifting her with nothing but my own strength as I thrust into her. "Come," I whisper into her ear. "Come on my cock and show me how much you want me, Devonry."

My words are practically a plea. A plea that she answers all too readily as she comes apart all over my lap, the wetness of her release leaking all over me. I don't care because the scent of her, the feeling of her insides contracting and releasing around me becomes too much. My body tenses and instead of pulling out as I know I should, I hold her tight. My fangs slam down out of my gums and my nails lengthen the barest of inches.

I didn't know then how it feels to have her attention and affection. I didn't realize what might truly be possible outside of the palace, and though, I despise Nasir—

though, I fully intend to cut his throat out and display his head for all to see—I am thankful. Grateful that I was given this much, this opportunity to be with her. To love her as I have, even amidst the dangers that surround us.

Through my own orgasm, I hold her still, forcing her body to accept me, to take my cum. Though I know it's wrong to not ask for her consent, I *am* marking her, *branding* her as my own. I want there to be something lasting between us. Should anything happen … she will have a piece of me forever. My heart.

25
DEVONRY

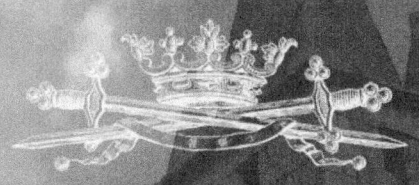

It's rare for Solomon to fall asleep before me, but he must be exhausted and wrung dry because that's exactly what happens. I lie there as the light of dawn peeks through the thin glass window across the room and I can't help but stare at him. The structure of his bones is sharp and angular. His brows throw shadows over his eyes when he stands, but here, like this, he's softer.

His lips are slightly parted as he breathes deeply. I want to run the pads of my fingers over the little pinpoints of stubble along his jaw, but I don't want to wake him so I hold the desire in. I snuggle against his chest, feeling his muscles automatically tighten and then relax as he pulls me closer. Time keeps moving, and the sun keeps rising, and after a while, I finally succumb to my own exhaustion.

Warmth. All I feel is warmth, and then that warmth turns into something new. Hotter and hotter, growing more and more uncomfortable until I swear there are flames licking at me from every side. My eyes snap open and as soon as they do, the oppressive fever-pitched heat disperses to reveal a strange layout before me.

I look down, moving my hands from my sides to the blades of grass that tickle the backs of my thighs. I'm naked in the dream as I was when I fell asleep. Mind and thoughts disjointed from the feeling of grass on my palm—slightly wet from morning dew—I glance up and peer around, seeking out ... something. Someone.

Perhaps one of the Gods?

No one else is here, though, and for some reason, I don't think they're going to show up. Every time before, in the dreams brought about by Aerea and Levim, I had a sense of anticipation. I don't have that sense now. All I have is ... comfort.

The heat is gone and warmth is in its place. It's not uncomfortable or too much. It just is.

A buzzing noise sounds right past my ear and I jump as a bee flies past, fat and swaying in the wind as it collides with a nearby flower and begins to greedily drink down its nectar. Slowly, I press both hands into the ground and climb to my feet. Shadows roll over the fields surrounding me and I glance up to see clouds rolling over the sun, pausing only briefly before moving on.

An old memory comes to me. A dream my mother told me about so long ago. What ... what had it been about?

I take a step further into the field and when nothing comes out of the trees and tall grass, I keep going. Birds chirp and sing. Crickets jump through the grass, releasing their own skittering noises. Despite all that, this place is peaceful. Serene. Something I haven't experienced in a long time.

There's no time here. Only calm. It's so perfect, I know that it can't be a real place. Still, I keep walking. Even without the anticipation, I feel like there's something I should be looking for. The grass brushes my calves and higher, tickling my skin.

Finally, I come to a stop as the grass parts reveal a pond. Hovering in the center of the water is a singular lily pad. I tilt my head at it as I come to the edge of the water and peer down. The *surface reflects my face as I know it to be—heart-shaped with the stain of reddish blonde hair and a few freckles here and there.*

A twig snaps and my head jerks up. "Hello?" I call out.

There, along the other side of the pool, a dark hulking figure appears. The grass sways in the wind, revealing the body of a small wolf. A pup. It's beautiful. Silky black fur, glowing ruby eyes, and straight ears.

I immediately feel a tug in my chest, as if a string has wrapped itself around my heart. I crouch down. "Hello," I say far more gently than before. I reach a hand out over the water. "I won't hurt you," I promise. "Would you like some water?"

The wolf pup tilts its head to the side and blinks at me. Instead of answering, it disappears back into the grass. Pain slices through me and I stand abruptly, meaning to give chase. I don't know why, but I can't let that wolf go.

Before I take even a step toward it, though, it appears again. This time, it's much closer. Its head pokes out of the grass, spots me, and then disappears again. I don't move, instead watching the tops of the grass as the pup moves through it—coming closer and closer to where I stand.

My heart pounds inside of my chest, echoing in my ears. Louder and louder. My fingers tremble as I hold myself impossibly still. The next time the wolf's face appears, it's so close that I can see that it's much larger than any wolf pup I've ever known to be. It's not quite grown, but big enough that lifting it into my arms will prove hefty. I don't care.

Slowly, I lower myself to my knees and watch it approach. I hold out my hand again. "Hello, there," I repeat.

The wolf pup pauses at the end of my arm and sniffs at my hand. "It's alright." My words are a whisper on the wind and I take a moment to realize that this creature probably can't understand me, but I hope it will at least sense that I mean it no harm.

A soft, warm tongue strokes my finger and I jolt before laughing lightly. It's head tilts, ears flopping over and tugging at my heartstrings once more. Gently, I touch one of his ears and then cup my hand under its head. The wolf steps forward a bit more and nudges my hand, demanding attention.

I bite down on my lower lip as tears fill my eyes. I couldn't say why, but this creature is so beautiful that it hurts. My whole body sways toward the wolf. The vision of the field and pond wavers as tears fill my eyes. Why does it hurt so much?

The wolf sniffs at me and then licks my hand again. I take it as a sign of permission to lift it. My hands wrap around the small animal under its front legs as I heft it up and bring it closer, cuddling it against my chest.

"You're so sweet, aren't you?" I coo as I sway the animal back and forth.

Wide eyes peer up at me. There's a clear intelligence within them. There's no way an animal could understand human language, and yet … something tells me that this wolf is no animal. Not really.

Swaying the wolf back and forth, I hold it closer to my chest until our heartbeats combine, becoming one. My stomach drops and an ache forms. I don't release the wolf though. Instead, I clutch it closer. It sniffs at me some more and licks the tears that break free from my eyes.

"Who are you?" I ask, staring into its knowing gaze.

An answer never comes. Only morning and the waking world.

"Devonry?" I jolt awake at the sound of Celine's voice on the other side of the door, accompanied by a hesitant knock.

Immediately, my hands reach for the opposite side of the bed where Solomon had lain the night before. My search, however, comes up empty and the sheets have long since cooled, suggesting that he left not long after I fell asleep. I wonder, distantly, if he'd so readily fucked me just to tire me out. With a sigh, I sag back into the pillow and blankets that remain, forgetting that Celine is waiting for an answer until she knocks again.

"Your Highness? Are you awake?" Celine asks.

I sit up again and call out to her as I reach over the side of the bed and grab my discarded nightshift. "Yes, sorry. I'm awake." The fabric descends over my head as I yank it on and weave my arms through the sleeves.

The knob turns and the door creaks open. Celine peers into the room, scanning the contents until she lands on me. Once she spots me, she slips inside and quickly shuts the door behind her. Her arms are laden down with what looks like new clothes.

Tension fills me at the concern etched into her features. "Is something wrong?" I ask.

Celine's lips pinch together before she opens them and releases a sigh. "You've been asleep all day," she says. "Lord Solomon said we should let you sleep, but it's almost night now and I was worried that you were feeling ill."

"Solo told you to let me sleep?" My earlier assumption comes back. Had Solo wanted to tire me out so damn much that I wouldn't try to follow him into battle? Did he truly think so little of me? Yes, perhaps it was stupid of me to demand to go in the first place, but that was only because I worried about him. I know that this is for me. That without me, there would be no battle. I'm hardly trained, after all, and no amateur bowman would be much help to him and the others.

"Yes," Celine answers before lifting the fabrics over her arm. "I brought you new clothes—freshly laundered." I peer at her curiously and she dips her head as she comes closer. "There wasn't much to do," she confesses, answering my unspoken question on how in the world she'd managed to clean my clothes when we have more important things to worry about. "I needed an activity to keep me occupied."

She leans over the bed as I turn and slide my legs from beneath the sheets. The strange dream lingers in the back of my mind as she hands me the clothes. "Thank you," I say, and mean it.

The white tunic is still somewhat gray, but it feels softer than before. It's such a small gesture but so kind it brings more than a small wave of emotion. I bend over the clothes and hold them closer as I fight back tears.

"Your Highness?" The bed dips as Celine takes a seat alongside me. The warmth of her hand reaches me before her skin does as she pats my back gently. "What is it?"

I shake my head. "It's nothing," I try, only to be stopped by her firm expression.

"I will not ask if you don't wish to talk about it," Celine states, "but please, do not lie to me. There is most certainly something bothering you. I will not pretend otherwise. If you want to keep it to yourself, that is fine, but do not deny yourself your own thoughts and emotions."

That, more than anything else she could have said, makes the tears break free. They slide down my cheeks one by one, and no matter how I press my lips together, I can't stop the sobs. Celine's face, once unyielding, becomes soft in her understanding as she wraps both of her arms around me and brings me closer. My face presses against her bosom and I let myself cry for what feels like the first time since my father died.

After a while, it doesn't feel like enough. Not enough of a connection. I need something to ground me. I drop the clothes, shoving them to the side despite all of her hard work in cleaning and folding them to bring them here, and I, too, wrap my arms around her. I cling to Celine for dear life as my whole body is wracked by my emotions.

"I'm scared," I finally manage to scrape out. "I'm scared that something will happen to him."

Celine's hands are ever-patient and soothing. She strokes my back, up and down, in long gentle movements. "It's alright to be scared," she tells me. "It means you care."

Too much, I think to myself. *I care far too much.*

For some reason, the wolf pup I'd seen in my dream reminds me of Solo. With its inky black fur and blood-red eyes, glittering like drops of liquid rubies, it'd seemed so similar to the man I'd spent my life both loathing and craving. The fact that the dream had ended before I'd known who it was hurt. It made my chest ache like a knife had been stabbed straight through my heart. More tears come and though I want to stop them, I can't. I just ... can't.

"You've been through so much," Celine says, her voice calm and melancholic. "You've been strong for so long, darling. It's alright to let yourself feel."

"I haven't been strong," I say. "I'm weak. Solo is the strong one. He protected me. He saved me. His cousin—Jacin ... he died protecting me. He died *because* of me."

"No." Celine jerks back, surprising me as she takes me by my shoulders and pushes me away from her chest so that her eyes can connect with mine. "That is *not* true." She stares back at me, her dark eyes hard. Her expression is far more severe than I've ever seen it and I've seen some of the death glares she's sent Argyle's way. "Nothing that has happened has ever been your fault," she snaps. "You are a victim of what Prince Nasir has done."

Victim. That word penetrates my mind and resounds. It echoes in my ears. Over and over again, getting louder until it's all I hear. Celine keeps talking, her words sharp and assuring, but I don't hear them anymore.

Is that what I am? I think. *A victim?* No. I can't be a victim. A victim can't be a Queen ... but a survivor can.

"You're right," I say, halting Celine's tirade. She blinks and stares at me. I shake my head and lean back, wiping my cheeks with my palms. She's not right about me being a victim, but she is right about one thing. "This is Nasir's fault," I say. "Not mine."

Celine nods. "Yes," she replies emphatically as she lifts my hands in hers.

My face feels stiff from all of the tears. My mouth is dry. "Thank you," I say. "For everything."

Celine shakes her head as her fingers cup over my own. "There are no thanks needed for doing what is right," she replies.

My lips part, but I have no words for her loyalty. I've never met anyone like her. No one as kind. No one with so much strength. I can't help but be grateful for the events that have led her to me or me to her. However it happened, I'm glad to have her in my life.

Sniffing hard, I withdraw my hands from hers and pick up the clothes once more. "I think I'll get dressed and meet you out in the shared room."

Celine picks up on my silent request quickly—it's not that I want to dress, though I need to, it's that I need some time to myself to gather my thoughts as I do. "Of course." Celine stands. "Argyle is here and there is some food if you're hungry. I'll be waiting out in the shared room."

I nod and wait for her to slip out of the door before I let the small smile fall from my lips. Turning, I stare at the thin window across from the bed. My eyes drop to the desk shoved against it and the stool. Solo's items are long gone. If I'm honest, I wish he'd woken me before he left so I would have at least been able to see him off. I chuckle to myself—I would have liked to see him off ... as if I were some newly married former maiden seeing her husband off to war.

With a sigh, I let go of the riot of emotions swirling around inside of me and I start getting ready. I rid myself of the nightshift and pull on the newly cleaned clothes, tucking the ends of the tunic into the loose trousers. I kept my travel boots in the room with me in the event of an emergency, and I pull them out from beneath the bed, putting them on, and lacing them up with skill I didn't have a few short months ago.

When this is all over, I'm either going to have to get used to wearing dresses again or I don't know … maybe I'll introduce trousers to women's fashion in Noble Society. Who would stop a Queen from wearing what she wants, after all?

The thought is still in my head as I open the door and step out into the darkened hallway. The sound of Argyle's baritone echoes back to me as I move toward it.

"—be calm and occupy ourselves until we get word," Argyle finishes as I step into the shared room.

I pause in the open doorway as Celine whirls away from Argyle and pastes a bright smile on her face at my arrival. "Your Highness," she says. "Are you hungry?"

To be honest, I'm not. The thought of eating right now doesn't sit well in my stomach, but she looks so desperate for something to do that I force another small smile. "I could use something to tide me over," I answer.

At that, Celine quickly bustles away from where Argyle is sitting on a chair against the wall with the perfect line of sight to the front windows of the house. He eyes me as his hands still over what he'd been working on when I came in —polishing his sword.

"Morning, Princess," he says lightly, smirking my way. "You sure slept the day away, didn't you?"

I roll my eyes. "Don't start," I mutter as I duck my head and move across the room. It isn't until I make it to the round wooden table and take a seat that I peer back at him again. "Where are the others?" I ask. "I thought Solo said he'd leave a few of Lenorn's men for backup?"

"He did," he answers before nodding to the door. "They're doing a patrol of the area nearby. They'll return momentarily."

Celine clatters through the bare kitchen, opening and closing cabinets as she bustles about. My stomach twists. Waiting is an impossible task. Every second that passes is another where I don't know what's happening, if Solo is hurt or if he's made it into the palace. Celine sets down a plate of bread and cheese in front of me before cupping her hand over my shoulder and squeezing lightly.

"Thanks," I murmur as I pick up a piece of the bread and nibble on it.

Argyle lifts his head and scans the outside through the windows before looking back to Celine as she goes around the room, lighting the candles that have been left behind. The sun quietly sets beyond the windows. Minutes turn into an hour.

I peer at Argyle, pushing the plate of only half-eaten food away. "I thought you said they would be back soon," I say.

Tension fills the room and Celine looks from Argyle to me and back again. It isn't until Argyle speaks, though, that I realize what my words mean. "I did," he says. Meaning they were supposed to be back soon, and now they aren't.

"Sh-should we wait?" Celine asks. "Or sh-should we go look for them?"

"Neither." Argyle stands abruptly and shoves his sword back into its sheath before strapping the belt around his waist. "I think we need to move. Gather your things quickly. Get your cloaks."

Argyle's cold words, combined with the fact that the other guards Solo had left behind for us have yet to return, have me practically leaping from the table, almost knocking the chair over in my haste as I hurry to the wall of hooks alongside the door. Celine makes it there first, ripping her cloak from the hook and then mine before passing it over to me.

"Where are we—" I don't get to finish my question. As I wrap my cloak over my shoulders and fumble with the clasp, Argyle releases a curse from where he stands to the side of the front window.

Without warning, he dives for both Celine and me, knocking the two of us to the floor in a heap and none too soon as the world around us explodes. The windows shatter and wood splinters apart. Above me, Argyle grunts. To my side, Celine screams and I know that sound better than most. It's sheer terror. It cuts off all too soon and I jerk my head, fear driving me to know if she's fainted or something worse.

But it's neither. Celine has a hand cupped over her mouth, muffling her fear as she presses her face into Argyle's chest. There's a buzzing noise somewhere, growing louder and louder with each passing second. I can't tell what's happening, but I do know that we're being attacked.

How? I have to wonder. *Is it Nasir?* It has to be. *But how did he find us? How did he find me?*

"*Fuck!*" Argyle's curse should be loud since he's right next to my ear. Yet, somehow it sounds far away. "Stay here!" he snaps a moment before he finally leverages up to his feet. All around us, the front of the house is wrecked.

The door is thrown off its hinges, and the glass of the windows is completely shattered out.

"What ... what was that?" I ask, though my voice sounds muffled—as if there's water in my ears. Confused and dizzy, I try to climb to my feet only for Celine to reach up, snagging the edge of my tunic sleeve. Her lips part and she says something, but I can't hear it.

"—explosives on the other side of the street," Argyle's voice has me turning my head. My whole body tilts, and I go down hard on my knees. "—I need to get out of here."

A hard hand latches onto my arm and I turn my head, expecting Argyle. It's not Argyle. A stony-faced man I don't recognize with a singular scar cutting down the outer side of his jaw stands above Celine and me, a sword in one hand.

I open my mouth to scream—to warn Argyle as I spot several more coming from the back of the house. Too late. It's far too late. The man's hand comes down—something hard slams into the back of my skull. Then ... there's nothing but darkness.

26
SOLOMON

I take a moment to memorize the soft lines of Devonry's face and the form of her curves as she lies in bed. Her eyes are closed, her lashes brushing the tops of her cheeks. My gaze though, is drawn to the shape of her lips and the way they part gently in her sleep. The need to press my mouth to hers swells within me until it becomes unbearable, but it's too much like a kiss goodbye and I can't allow that.

Careful not to make noise so as not to wake her, I pull the door closed behind me. Down the narrow hallway, another door opens and closes letting Argyle out. Our shoulders nearly brush the walls on either side. I find it hard to believe that Lord Liriel would ever stay here. Though Celine had mentioned that his room was on the upper level and this space was only meant for guests. How odd it is that Celine is only a guest in the house her family owns.

"Leaving without kissing me goodbye?" Argyle sings in a whisper as we emerge from the hall and into the sitting room. His shoulder bumps mine as he gives me that signature grin of his.

I roll my shoulders down and away from my ears. We round the furniture, heading toward the adjacent dining room. The warmth from the fireplace circulates the space and follows us into the next. "The day I take you up on that you'll be regretting it." Wiping the sleep from my eyes, I stop and turn toward him.

Argyle's collar is unbuttoned, his shirt stretched around his neck, and the hem of it not yet tucked into his pants. He tilts his head. "Is it because you'd ruin me for everyone else?"

"Yes."

My friend chuckles and plucks a cookie from an assortment waiting on a platter at the center of the table. He pops one in his mouth, chewing slowly. I frown at the idea of sugar so early in the day. Certainly, no breakfast would be better than this.

Will Devonry indulge herself with sweets after she wakes and finds me gone? Likely not. I can only imagine her beautiful features puckered with anger when she realizes I've slipped away. As long as she is safe, though, her anger will be worth it. I'd rather have a wrathful Queen than a dead one.

"Argyle?" I ask and he hums in response. "Do you remember our deal?"

He sets down his second cookie, his smile fading from his face. "I remember."

"At all costs. You protect her as fiercely as you would Celine. With the help of the Gods, I'll be back to get her soon." Refusing myself, I keep my attention trained on my friend instead of letting it drift back to the hall we'd come from.

Argyle grips my shoulder. "At all costs, brother."

Whatever words either of us might have added dry up on our tongues. The best I can give him is a nod before pulling away and heading for the door. Even for my friend, I can't find it in myself to look back. The curse of saying goodbye lingers at the back of my mind like a warning. If I say it, if I so much as think about it, this will truly be the last I'll see of them. So I don't turn around once as I weave through the house and out the back.

In minutes, I've mounted a horse and am trotting away from the gray safe house offered to us by the House of Starfall. And only when the house is no longer in my sight, my lungs are full of fresh morning air, and the leather reins are tight in my grip, do I send up a prayer for their safety and mine.

As planned, Lenorn and I are to rendezvous three blocks east of the servants' entrance for the Sunfire Palace. From there, we'll make our way onto the palace grounds, and Nasir will soon find himself at the end of my sword. I'll see his head roll from his shoulders for what he's cost me and Devonry. Though it would only be right to slice him open like they'd done to Jacin. My anger rolls through me like a wave. Muscles along my back, into my chest, and down my arms ache with the stretching need to give in to my abilities. Allowing Nasir to meet the true monster that lurks under my skin might be one of the most pleasant thoughts I've had about the man.

Pink kisses the sky and spreads to orange along the passing clouds. Few lanterns are lit in front of businesses and even fewer people walk along the streets. There's an eerie quiet to Sanctus City that only comes with the early hours of the day.

The city square, where I'd once found Devonry dancing on her birthday, sits barren of the streamers and flowers that had once decorated it. I can recall the way my

Queen's face lifted to the sky and her hair had fallen in dark dyed strands down her back. She'd been only a Princess then and held the attention of hundreds as she'd moved through a dance sacred to her bloodline. I'd been ... entranced *and* furious. Always torn between the desires of my heart and the duty of my oath.

Years of burying my love for her had hardened my heart, but it was in moments like those that every feeling I'd ever had for her came rushing back until I was sick with it. I wanted to hate her. I wanted to kiss her. It's easy to recall how hard it was to stuff my emotions back into the locked box I'd kept them in and let my fury overtake me.

Nearly anyone else faced with the wrath of the Blood General might have cowered before me. Not her. Devonry looked at me much the same as she always has, though her own anger was quite clear. She glared at me as though I wasn't the man who'd fought and won a war on her behalf, but like I was the boy she'd grown up playing with and hiding from tutors in much-too-small closets.

The memories fade as the city square is left behind me. My tongue draws over the points of my teeth, and for once, I'm thankful for this thirst to ground me in the present. When I am just shy of where I plan to meet Lenorn, I slow the horse to a stop.

The road is empty. I expect the bakery to have open doors, giving the street the aroma of freshly baked bread, but it's closed. Everything is practically reticent when I swing my leg over the horse and drop to my feet. Leather groans under my fingertips as I tie the animal to the nearest post before straightening.

On its own accord, my hand finds the hilt of my weapon and remains poised there. A breeze churns between buildings and ruffles my hair. I shuffle next to the horse after another minute passes with no signs of the House of Daemonium's non-heir.

Where the fuck is he? Hair rises on the back of my neck. My eyes swing from one side of the street to the other. No one and nothing waits for me. The awareness of his absence is a bitter taste on my tongue. One more minute I'll wait, though several more minutes pass as my thoughts begin to race.

Wrong. This is wrong.

I can't move fast enough to rid myself of the terrible notion of betrayal. Heat lances down my spine, my vision flaring a daring red as I scramble to undo the knot I'd tied moments ago. I think only of Devonry and the way I'd memorized her features this morning. Whispers of see you later but never goodbye and the reminder of my own stubborn need to protect her build inside my thoughts. I see Argyle's face as he nods and swears himself to our Queen.

My nostrils flare. The scent of sweat and metal becomes pungent. Men in armor, men come to—

I loosen the reins and turn. The tip of a sword grazes the flesh below my Adam's apple. Purple eyes watch me back, a Nobleman but not one I'm quick to remember his name. Not an heir of the House but a lackey.

"We weren't sure you'd actually show up. The Blood General isn't known for being especially trusting. And look…" He turns to look beyond me and up the horse. "Looks like you've forgotten your ward."

No.

My muscles stretch and strain under my thickening flesh. The flattened end of my nails lengthen to points to match the deadly edge of my fangs.

Boots thud against the pavement. The flash of weapons and armor shine with the morning sun. Men emerge from alleyways and shadowed shop windows alike to fill the street.

The violet in his gaze flashes, a sneer stretches over his lips, and then something ripples under his skin, reminding me of the Ambassador and his transformation into the serpent. "I've always wondered what might break a man as famous as you. Turns out we may find out after all."

Arrogant men truly do dare to parry with insults when they've got a dozen others to back them. It'd be humorous if I wasn't so fucking terrified on behalf of Devonry.

"It's truly a shame then that you won't live long enough to learn." My lips curl as his blade digs against my hardened skin. The point of contact aches but doesn't draw blood even as the flesh starts to split with the pressure. I wrap my hand around his sword and smile as the edges dig into my palm. Warm blood coats my hand, but metal hisses as it's bent out of place until his sword is the shape of a horseshoe.

With the iron scent thick in the air, I'm filled with a fresh rush of Bloodlust. The hunger that's plagued me for days comes back with an alarming need. His pulse rises and the current of his blood rushes through his veins in brilliant flashes.

I rip my own weapon from its sheath with my opposite hand, forgetting the reins and the animal at my back. The Nobleman is smart enough to take a step away and drop his now useless sword at my feet. Weapons sing as they're drawn from men's hips and poised for me.

I take half a step and revel in the fear that erupts in his eyes. My shadow lengthens. Power thrums through me as the monster rattles the bars of his cage.

Devonry's skin. Her strawberry hair sprawled across a pillow. The flash of her smile. The warmth of her kiss. Her heartache and the losses we share.

A *boom* shakes Sanctus City. Glass panels vibrate in the nearby buildings as the dirt under us quakes. Dark smoke pours into the sky at a distance. My heart stops beating. Air is caught on my tongue and frozen in my lungs. No one moves but the House of Daemonium Noble's mouth curves upward with a flash of teeth.

The haze of destruction rises as I calculate exactly where the explosion is taking place. My body knows the answer before my mind can even catch up. It's from the way I'd come.

They've found her. My Queen.

"To be fair, it wasn't easy getting answers out of my cousin. He'd bled quite a bit before we were able to get into that mind of his and pull out the location of the Princess." The Nobleman reaches for a short sword on his other hip.

A ringing starts in my ears. It vibrates through my head, into my chest, and outward toward my limbs. Only vaguely am I even aware that I've moved before my teeth sink past skin and muscle. Ignoring my hunger, I seek only death. The Noble's weapon clatters to the ground at his feet, never seeing me move from where I stood to where I bring his death before it's too late. Flesh strings between my mouth and his body as I yank away and let his body drop. His screams are taken by the gurgling of blood filling his traitorous lungs.

Then soldiers move all at once. It's a chorus of shouts and the pounding of charging footfalls harmonized by the roar of violence that rips itself from my chest as the beast stretches out of his cage.

My vision tunnels on beating hearts and coursing blood. I use the leverage of my weapon and let it swing in wicked arcs through the air. The blade meets steel and man alike. If I know their faces, they are unrecognizable to me now. Everything narrows until they're only that which stands between me and my Queen.

I snap my teeth as I twist and am met by the force of a soldier's strength. Metal slices against my ribs coming from another direction as I push the weight of my body into my movement and send his sword teetering out of his grip. Heat coats the side of my body. A growl rushes through my teeth as I turn and grab for the nearest man. Another soldier goes limp as I shred my fangs through his neck. The shape of his jugular flattens between the press of my lips.

Blood sprays across my face and I blink through it. There is only me and the death dealt at my hands. My monster and those who wish to test their luck against him.

If they have her … if they hurt her…

A shout born of desperation and fury tears up my throat. What barriers prevent me and my monster from becoming one crumble as another sword cuts across my shoulder blade and muscle tears.

Everything is red. Everything is blood. And no one is safe.

27
DEVONRY

It's been so long since I've woken up in a place I'm actually familiar with that when my eyes crack open and I see the recognizable gauzy curtains that flutter around my childhood bedroom, I'm sure I'm still dreaming. There is sunlight pouring in through the open balcony doors and a gust of cool air blows at the pale fabric that flutters around the glass doors.

The vanity I used to sit at every morning sits nearby, illuminated by the streaming light that glints off of the massive mirror framed in an elaborate golden outline and topped with the symbol of the Sunfire Palace and the Estand family: a sun.

I blink, waiting for the image to fade, but it doesn't. My muscles tighten in pain as I sit up in bed. I lift my hands to my face, staring hard at my palms. There are still calluses, freshly formed, on my skin and that tells me that this isn't a dream and neither were the last few months. Those calluses are from weeks of labor—of living from place to place and learning how to wield a weapon and how to take care of myself.

My head feels like it's filled with cotton and wool, heavy and light all at once. Confusing.

"It's beautiful, isn't it?" The soft voice of a man penetrates the space of nostalgia and bewilderment that consumes me. I've heard that voice in my dreams and then in my nightmares. It haunted me throughout my travels, and now it's here. Not a figment of my imagination, but a reality that I have come to face.

Turning, I lift my head and meet the eyes of the man who stands several feet away with his hands clasped behind his back. Something sharp floods my veins, a sense of urgency, a will to get away. *Fear*.

Nasir is dressed impeccably in a princely uniform made up entirely of smooth fabric, cut and tailored to his form. Long white pants and a buttoned burgundy coat with golden ropes and accessories only available to the select few elite of Sanctus City. His dark brown hair is just as long as I remember it, hanging just above his shoulders, with a slight wave at the ends. Fine trembles overtake my fingers and I dig them into the sheets surrounding me, stabbing my nails into my legs past the thin fabric as if that will wake me up from what I now know is no dream at all.

As my gaze wanders over him, I note that there's not a single speck of blood to be found. I don't know why I expected anything else. It's been weeks—months—since I last saw him covered in my father's blood. But somehow, when I'd run away from the palace, from my home and my throne, I'd trapped him in my memory in that final visage. Deep down, I'd expected him to arrive in front of me the next time we met as if no time had passed at all. Because, in my mind, I'd villainized him and created this perfect image of a cruel monster that *looked* like a traitor.

He doesn't though. That's the most terrifying thing for me to realize. He killed my father. Stole my Kingdom. Yet, he stands before me, with that stupid smile on his face as if I'll be glad to see him. As if the time between when I'd practically tripped over myself as I rushed to greet him was not buried in the past. As if nothing has changed between us.

Nasir doesn't let the fact that I haven't answered him or even spoken stop him from continuing. Turning his head, he gazes around the room before releasing the hands clasped at his back and striding for the doors. He stops just inside and catches a fluttering curtain, sifting the thin, transparent fabric through his fingers as he gazes outside.

"I've spent many nights here since you left," he finally says, "sleeping in that very bed." His eyes cut my way. The deep, soil-rich brown that I remember now looks like nothing more than deadened earth before winter. Cold. Unfeeling. Without life.

I suddenly very much want to leap out of my own bed and set it on fire. Instead, however, I gingerly edge myself closer to the side of the mattress and slip my feet out from beneath the sheets, keeping my body turned slightly. Instinct tells me that as long as I play along with his delusions, I won't be the one in any physical danger—but still, I can't help but not want to give him my back.

Because this man—Nasir—is no longer my friend.

He is my father's murderer.

My Kingdom's usurper.

My enemy.

"You're still beautiful," he says, his gaze moving to the side of my face. "Even with your hair cut like that, though I can't help but want to see it long again. I assume you'll grow it out now that you're home."

I reach up, fingering the strands. "I think I like it this way." I'm proud of the way my voice doesn't tremble, even when my insides do. My bare feet touch the floor and a shiver moves up from the balls of my feet, through my calves and thighs to the rest of my body. No matter the warmth of the sun pouring in through the windows and open balcony, the stone floor is cold, as is the air in the room.

"You'll grow it out again," Nasir replies. It's not a question, not even a request, but a command.

I stare at him. *How did I not see it?* I wonder now that it's so clear. How could I have been so blind to the obvious obsession in his gaze, to the possessive way he stares at my hair as if it's not mine at all—but his and I'm merely a part of it?

I decide it's pointless to argue with a lunatic, so I don't respond. Instead, I release the sheets and stand up from the bed, pivoting my body to face him fully as I move back toward the windows and wall.

"Where is Solo?" I ask.

Nasir's face changes immediately upon the sound of Solo's name. His lips twist, the corners curling down with distaste. His eyes narrow, the edges crinkling so that long lines are drawn tight into his skin.

"Your guard has been imprisoned," he tells me, as a matter of fact, "for kidnapping the Crown Princess."

My throat feels tight. "I wasn't kidnapped," I state coldly, glaring at him.

"Yes," he grits out, "you were." Soulless eyes find mine. "Because there's no way you would run away from me knowing what I've done for us to be together, now, is there?"

I shake my head, but no words come. I have no answer—certainly none he would like to hear. I glance to the balcony doors, but my bedroom has always been on the upper floor. There's no way I could make it out onto the terrace and manage to jump down without breaking a leg.

As soon as I recognize that flaw in my quickly deteriorating escape plans, I direct my attention to the doors that lead into the corridor. What's out there? I wonder. More guards? Those loyal to him? Those ... under his influence?

My heart leaps against the inside of my ribcage, like a frightened bird trying to get out. My lashes lower and then rise as I turn my attention back to Nasir. As if he can tell exactly what I'm thinking, his expression has since dropped away from the disgusted anger brought about by Solo's name and has smoothed into a calm, almost smug demeanor.

"It's no use, my love," he says, proving my assumption that my thoughts must be all over my face. "There's no escaping our destiny now."

"*Our* destiny?" I repeat. My hands slip over the stone wall at my back, fingers moving over the gritty crevices of the centuries-old structure as I slide along its exterior. One step, two...

A knock sounds on the door and it cracks open as Nasir calls for whoever is on the other side to enter. I freeze in my tracks as a vaguely familiar face appears. I inhale sharply when I recognize the face as Vierre—one of my father's personal guards. I thought they'd all been killed when I left, but here he stands, completely unharmed. His slightly longer than fashionable gray hair is pulled back into a low ponytail and the severe features of his face are lax. His eyes move over me, unrecognizing, as he turns to Nasir and bows low.

Shock riots through me. Vierre has always been one of the oldest and most loyal Royal guards. Why would he be bowing to Nasir, especially after all that he's done? Surely, Vierre knows the truth. My gaze travels from him to Nasir and back again as Nasir waves a hand and Vierre straightens.

"The preparations have been completed, Your Highness," Vierre says. He never looks my way. He doesn't even acknowledge my presence and keeps the sole focus of his attention on Nasir.

I lean against the wall for stability, my nails digging into the grain of the stone for something to ground me and assure me that this is, in fact, reality. Anger, fear, confusion—all of these emotions war with each other inside of me. Dust crumbles beneath my palms as heat fills my chest and then travels down my arms to my hands. I try to piece together what information I can.

Nasir claims that Solomon kidnapped me. Vierre is acting strange and ignoring the one he should be loyal to. Earlier conversations and thoughts come to me. My mind casts me back to the very night I'd escaped Nasir's clutches. My own guards—the guards of the Sunfire Palace had followed his commands. Why? What did Nasir hold over them?

"Vierre," I call out the guard's name but his attention remains fixed on Nasir. Nasir, in turn, however, looks to me as I step away from the wall. "Vierre, look at me!" I snap.

Still, nothing. *What the fuck?*

My head snaps to Nasir. "What did you *do*?" I demand.

Nasir sighs and flicks a hand at Vierre. "Thank you for the update," he says. "You may go. Do not come back unless called."

Vierre nods and bows once more before striding back through the door. I rush across the room, cutting past the end of the bed and even Nasir as I reach for the door. "Vierre!"

A hard hand grabs ahold of my arm and stops me as the door closes behind the guard with a resounding click that feels like the gong of a death bell. I halt in my tracks and look down. Pale fingers close around my upper arm and I follow the line of the hand and arm attached to those fingers until I find myself face to face with Nasir—so close I can see that there are no other lines of color in his eyes. Normally, even in brown eyes, there are various shades. Depth. In his, there is nothing but an opaque blankness.

"What did you do to him?" I demand again.

Nasir's hand clenches around my arm, coiling tighter and tighter like a snake holding onto its prey. I flinch as it begins to hurt and as if that small withdrawal brings him back, Nasir releases me and then sighs.

"The Nobles of Rozentine are not the only ones who've been afforded powers, Devonry," he says.

"You really are Awakened then." We had suspected as much, but it'd never been confirmed. Now, it is. His ability, his power—that's how he's able to control others, to turn them into mindless beings that only follow his orders.

"Yes," Nasir answers, stepping back as he adjusts the sleeve of his coat. He tips his head down, a lock of nearly black hair sliding over the side of his face. Even shadows do not play in his eyes—as if they, too, are terrified of him.

"I still don't understand." My voice is breathless, my throat tight. "Why all of this?" I gesture to the room, but I know he recognizes what I really mean. "Why did you kill my father? If you wanted to marry me—there were other ways."

As ashamed as I am now of my naive past, if he'd only waited a little longer, he would have had me in the palm of his hand and I would have been none the wiser. So, why? I have to wonder. I have to *know*.

When Nasir moves, I immediately step back, moving away out of sheer panic that he'll touch me again. He doesn't look at me though. Instead, he strides right past me, returning to the balcony doors and staring out over what I know is a beautiful view of the Eastern side of

Sanctus City. Every morning, the sun rises over those cobbled streets and terracotta rooftops. It was once the prettiest sight in the world to me, but right now, I'd give anything for this sight to be one full of those I hold dearest if only to assure myself that they're still alive.

"I heard you were taken to Bartoli," he says, his voice low. "I'm not shocked my family never even hinted at the truth."

"They knew?" I wrack my brain, thinking back—was that why they'd been so difficult to extract a promise of assistance from? They hadn't seemed to care at all what Nasir was doing, no matter how it hurt their political reputation.

Nasir chuckles. The sound is anything but amused. "No, they didn't know of my plans," he admits. "Had they, however, they likely wouldn't have cared. The Royals of Bartoli—King and Queen and even my own brother, Enver—they do not care for those like myself."

I frown, but before I can ask what he means, he tells me.

"I am not the Queen's child," he confesses. "But an illegitimate Prince born of a fallen Rozentine Noble—one of my father's many concubines and mistresses." His head tilts down as he lifts a hand to his face. Something sparks in the center, like a dark mist forming and dripping from his fingertips to create a small mass no larger than an eyeball in his palm. The mist twitches and spins around as if possessed by something *alive*.

I take a step back and bump into a trunk against the wall. It's disgusting. There's something so very wrong about it that even seeing it revolts me. "What is *that*?"

"Despair," he replies without looking at me. "Everything a person fears is contained within this ability of mine. Death. Hate. Pain. Loss. All of it resides right here."

Nasir turns to face me, his body outlined by the light that drips in behind him. "It's the ability to influence others," he continues. "It steals all hope—all light—within its grasp. It's ... painful without someone to ease the darkness."

Despite his words, he doesn't look like he's in pain. In fact, Nasir, himself, looks as if he's ready to be absorbed by the small ball of shadowy liquid in his hand. Almost as soon as I've seen the expression of wicked want enter his eyes, it's snuffed out. He closes his fingers into a fist and the materialized liquid mist evaporates and disappears.

"My ability pairs perfectly with yours, Devonry," he says, suddenly lifting his head as he gazes at me. "It's the true sign that you were meant to be mine and I, yours."

I shake my head and lift a hand to my chest, curling my fingers into my palm as I press down against my wild, beating heart. "No." The word is barely a whisper on my lips.

"Your sunlight," he says. "It will drive out the darkness within me. I knew you could feel it too—it's why you went to your father that night to ask to marry me instead of Enver, isn't it?"

"*No*," I say again, harsher this time. "That was a mistake."

Nasir moves away from the balcony doors, coming closer to me, and I have nowhere to go. The balcony is too far away and now I know for sure there are guards on the other side of the door closest to me. Guards under his influence, under his ... darkness. I hold perfectly still as he approaches.

"I'd hoped that your father would be willing to trade Princes," he says as he pauses in front of me. "Unfortunately, he seemed to be well aware of my abilities. He could sense it, and he was disgusted by it as many are."

"Why didn't you just influence him?" I demand. "Instead of killing him."

Nasir blinks. "You think I didn't try?" he asks, before shaking his head. "No, the Estrand line is a very powerful one. I couldn't control King Vernon for the same reason I cannot control you—your blood is too pure for this ability of mine, but it's okay."

I wince as his hand lifts to my cheek and his ice-cold fingers brush over my flesh. He smooths back a lock of my hair, the soft smile on his lips turning down into a disapproving scowl when he touches the strands of strawberry blonde. "Your powers have changed you," he says. "Your hair is turning red. How unfortunate. I always thought you looked as pure as fallen snow with your white hair." He rubs one of the locks between his thumb and forefinger thoughtfully. "No matter, though, you are still everything I need. I can't wait any longer—I need your body and your blood or else this power will consume me too."

"You … need my blood?" I ask. "Is that why you killed my father and rushed all of this?"

"Don't worry," he says, ignoring my second question. "I won't be taking it the same way that vile beast would." His upper lip curls back, revealing straight white teeth. "Solomon Winett is a disgusting monster who's defiled you too much. My sources say he drank from you." Nasir stares at me as if seeking confirmation, but I don't say a word. The less he knows about my relationship with Solomon and what it's become now, the better.

He hums in the back of his throat when I say nothing. "No matter, I suppose," he continues. "I will ensure that it never happens again. The Blood General will die by my hand once we're wed."

"No!" The word bursts out of me, stronger than any other I've had since waking. I rip myself from Nasir's grasp and slap my hands against his chest, pushing him back. "You won't hurt him! I forbid it!"

"You *forbid* it?" Nasir's hands close around my upper arms—far harder and tighter than they had before. My breath slips out between my teeth as I glare up at him, ignoring the pain. The heat from earlier rises. I've never truly *wanted* to kill—not like this. Right now, I fear I don't even comprehend the emotions roiling through me. The rage and sorrow. The need to protect.

"If you kill him…" My threat hangs between us with no conclusion. What will I do? Will I kill Nasir right here and now? I can feel the fire in my veins. I know I could. Yet … being in this room reminds me, too, of my mother.

My head turns away from him. She had rocked me to sleep as an infant in this room. She'd played with me and Sheza in this room. She'd taught me how to stand, how to smile, how to cry in someone else's arms when I was sad. And every time I'd let my anger get the best of me, she'd reminded me that anger was nothing more than the dark side of sadness. That anger could be tempered with healing. I don't want to heal, though, not in the way she would have wanted.

I've forgotten how long it's been since I heard her voice in my head. When was the last time? Was it before I'd killed the slave trader in Carion City?

Tears burn in the backs of my eyes. Standing on the edge of the dock, far away from everything I'd ever known, it'd been almost … easy to pull back my bow and let that arrow free. Standing here, in the wreckage of my past—of my Mother's past—makes it impossible.

"You *will* marry me," Nasir says with a note of finality that draws me out of my thoughts.

I shake my head. "No," I say. "You have no right to sit

on my throne, Nasir. Not as regent. Not as King Consort. Not as *anything*."

Fine tremors dance up and down the length of Nasir's arms. I can feel them as he squeezes me ever tighter until I swear my arms will break under his grip. I flinch but don't say a word of protest. Instead, I lift my head and meet his gaze, letting him see the resolution in my face rather than repeat myself.

Surprisingly, however, his expression is not one of anger. It's one of fear. I blink and focus on his face. Skin ashen, leached of all color, Nasir blinks rapidly down at me as if searching for the words necessary to get me to cave to his demands. What … is he afraid of?

"Solomon," he says. "That's it—isn't it?"

My heart nearly stops in my chest. "I don't know what you mean," I lie.

"He's the key." Nasir releases me so abruptly that I nearly collapse onto the floor. Before my weakened knees give out on me, I manage to reach out and keep myself standing with a hand on the wall. "You'll do what I want if he's in danger, won't you? Oh, I know you pretended to hate that bastard—he was annoying, so I'd hoped it wasn't pretend—but if you truly feel this way, then…" Nasir's words tumble over each other and he's not looking at me. It's more as if he's talking to himself as his voice tapers off. "Yes, that's it. If I just string him up above the chapel, you'll have to go through with it."

He closes his arms around himself, his fingers tapping incessantly against his own elbow. "I'd rather not keep that monster alive, but if we bleed him dry every now and then and don't provide any food, he'll never be strong enough to break free, but he'll be alive."

I don't like what I'm hearing. The words, the plans he's

making. Knowing it all revolves around Solo. It terrifies me.

"Nasir, stop," I say. "Just give up—it's not worth marrying someone who doesn't want you."

"*You do!*" he screams, startling me with the loudness of his voice as it ricochets up to the rafters and then echoes around the room. "You just ... you don't know it yet. It's *him*—he's the problem."

"He's not," I insist. "Nasir, you betrayed me, you killed my father—"

"*Fuck.*" Nasir's sudden stillness should alert me to the change in him, but I'm so shocked by his curse that I stop talking. My eyes dart to the door to the corridor and back to him. Nasir bends slightly and scratches at his arms. "Damn this fucking—" He stops himself and whips his head around. "Tomorrow," he snaps. "You will marry me tomorrow, and then we will have our wedding night, and it will all be over."

"I—" I don't manage to get a single word out before he's already pulling away from me and striding for the door. The refusal dies on my tongue as he pauses with a hand on the door handle.

"If you continue to protest, I'll be forced to kill him." His words are cold, without emotion. As if ice is growing in his veins and spilling into his voice. "The Gods will smile upon our union and finally, I'll be free." His head turns and he settles those brown eyes, altered back to normal and away from the powerful ebony that always comes with a resurgence of his abilities. They're still devoid of anything but indomitable knowing—as if his words are turning into prophecies as he speaks them. "You are my salvation, Devonry," he says. "If you resist ... I'll be forced to make it happen again. Don't ... make me do it, darling.

Don't make me kill in front of you and bathe our wedding in his blood."

I don't have to ask whose blood he's talking about. I know he means Solo.

Nasir rips the door open and leaves the room, slamming it shut with the resounding click of the lock turning into place from the outside; I'm left standing in a room that should bring nothing but comfort. Now, it's a prison.

28
DEVONRY

The first snow of the season blankets the courtyard of the Sunfire Palace, though it's a bit early for it. There are fluffy white piles on the railing of my balcony and frost on the windows. I stare through the etching of ice on the glass at the movement of a carriage rolling through the front gate. The wheels leave behind their mark in the snow, marring the once stunning purity of it. Even the changing of season seems to be rushing along in the same manner Nasir is rushing me with his traitorous plans.

I don't have it in me to stand from the chair I curled up into last night to make my way closer to see who emerges. Muscles in my neck are stiff as I turn my attention back to the flames filling the hearth. The heat warms my skin, less suffocating than the weight of the blankets on my bed. Frowning, I let my head fall against the back of the cushioned armchair. My fingers dig into the thick fabric of the arms.

While I'd been hiding from my own soldiers and then fleeing from Bartoli, Nasir had been here. In my palace. In my room. In my bed. Now that I know that, proof of his presence is everywhere. His scent lingers on my pillows, smelling like smoke and sandalwood. A long black strand of hair clings to my curtains. A single flower lays across my nightstand, dried out and fragile. I wonder if the smudge of someone's fingerprint at the end of my mantle belongs to him too.

This room isn't mine anymore. Is the palace? These people? The country?

I sink my teeth into my lower lip until pain blooms. He won't get away with this. He won't.

And what of Solomon? Of Argyle or Celine?

A soft knock comes from the door. I tense, my body sinking into my seat further. If I pretend to be oblivious to their insistency, then perhaps they won't enter, and this entire day—my wedding day—will never come. Power pulses through me and centers to a warmth in my palms. My eyes stay closed even as the door opens and the patter of someone's footfalls grows near.

"Shall I start your bath?" The words are spoken in monotone, no emotion or familiarity in them, but I'd recognize that voice anywhere.

My eyes go wide as I throw myself out of the chair and nearly stumble into the fireplace as my nightgown tangles between my legs. "Sheza!" I shout her name, surprising even myself at the intensity and rise of my voice.

Sheza doesn't so much as blink as she gestures with one arm toward the bathing chamber. Far more gray streaks in her hair than I remember her having. Dark circles stain the skin beneath her eyes and her hazel irises are haunted with black shadows.

"Oh, Sheza," I whisper her name like a prayer and reach out to cup her face. Delicate wrinkles deepen under my hand. *She's lost weight,* I realize as I take in her form and wonder if she's as fragile as she looks. Is the woman who switched clothes to save her Princess somewhere in there?

I lay my head on her shoulder, the fabric of her uniform scratchy under my cheek, and I wrap my arms around her slender body. One arm remains outstretched, pointing toward the bath; the other still rests at her side. She doesn't move to hug me back. Tears build in my gaze, blurring my vision as I try to breathe her in. Sheza's always smelled like home. As a child, I swore traces of my own mother's perfume, sweet like honeysuckle, clung to her clothes only to find out later that my mother had gifted her the fragrance. I've replenished the scent every year on Sheza's birthday since my mother's passing. She still smells like that perfume, but something greater mutes it. Something smoky and dark. I scowl as I fight the sob working up my throat.

"Shall we start your bath?" Sheza repeats.

Stepping away, I shake my head. "No. Do you remember me? Sheza, can you hear me? Fight him. Whatever he's doing to you, fight him…" Emotion clogs my throat and strangles the word. "Please."

"Your bath." Sheza blinks and reaches for my arm. Her fingers curl around my bicep, tugging at me. I shrug out of her touch. I hate that it's come to this, that I have to fight her. If anyone could understand why, though, it would be her. She wouldn't want this for me either.

"Nasir is controlling you." I want to scream the words at the top of my lungs but they come out with the trembling pitch of my sorrow. Of all the people he'd brought to bow to him, I'd never truly thought he'd be able to do it to her. Like I'd thought he'd never be capable of killing my father, taking control of Rozentine, or forcing me to marry him.

Her darkened gaze lingers on me for only a moment

before she turns and looks away in suggestion. "We have little time before you must be ready for," she pauses, "this wonderful day."

The short break in her speech is enough to give me hope. Sheza is still in there, fighting against Nasir. She wouldn't give up. Never. Not for me. Not for the country she's sworn her life to.

I stare at her, searching for a flicker of emotion. Rather, the swirl of shadows in her eyes clouds over the entire color of her irises. I suck in a breath. My sadness, frustration, and fury mingle together in the deepening pain stabbing my chest. My vision flickers gold when Sheza reaches for me again. This time, her fingers dig into my arm with the painful intention of force. Under Nasir's influence, she'd drag me to that damn tub.

"No!" Her withering strength is no match for mine and the power I'd built since she'd last seen me. I yank myself away and take a step to create even more distance. The back of my legs brush against the chair behind me. "I will not go. Please," I beg, "Please come back to yourself."

No matter what, I couldn't hurt her. How would I live with myself if I harmed her? I just need her to listen and break free of his abilities.

"Your bath. We'll need to start your bath now." She shifts forward. Her movements are rigid. Gone is the grace of the woman who helped raise me. Everything that made Sheza herself is smothered by Nasir.

That knowledge burns white hot in my stomach. It erupts up into my chest and blazes toward my throat. "Sheza!" I snap, desperate as the sensation of wicked heat licks its way through my limbs. No sooner has her name left my lips than a sob manages to escape. My shoulders shake with the force of it.

He's taken everything that I loved and tainted it. My

skin fevers as I stare back at Sheza. Hatred is a hot ichor crawling up through me and dragging power through my veins. I try to breathe through the blistering of my abilities churned by overwhelming emotion. Every breath I draw in isn't enough to soothe it.

Her eyes meet mine, but she doesn't see. Not truly. Even as her brows furrow in confusion and new lines crease around her puckered mouth. Wherever I look, I cannot escape the gold glitter of my ability or the thoughts of Nasir's betrayal. There's an urgency in every frantic beat of my heart and a twist of revulsion deep within my gut. The contents of my stomach go sour and the need to vomit rises, though I push down the urge and welcome the flood of anger instead.

"The future King requires swift preparations for his wedding—" Sheza starts to speak, though her words are quiet compared to the rush of blood in my ears.

"He will *never* be the King." I snarl. Placing my hands on either side of her face, I try to force her to meet my eyes to really see. "Can he hear me? How deep does his magic run in you, my friend? Nasir, you'll let her go. You'll release her from this." My arms tremble, my touch somewhere between a firm hold and a gentle embrace.

"The King—"

"Sheza!"

What little control I'd had on the fire of Aerea flowing through me isn't enough to contain me. Fire licks up my back. Sparks spit from the fire in the hearth as it jumps to nearly double its size and threatens to pour out onto the floor. Flames dance down my arms toward my fingers.

Her hazel eyes widen. I gasp and yank my touch away. Shadows string between my fingers and her skin. Smoke rises where the darkness clings to my hands before it glows red and burns away as I try to shake it off. Sheza stumbles forward as though the thing between us is holding to her with all its might as it drains from her eyes and mouth.

The darkness lets her go, jumping and writhing at our feet before the last of it burns away. Chest rising and falling as I try to catch my breath, I lift my gaze to hers. The sheen of tears makes her eyes glassy. Her ragged inhale pulls me back to reality as my flames die down.

"Devonry," she whispers before her eyes roll to the back of her head and her body crumples to the floor with a sickening thud.

I scream in terror, dropping to my knees. My fingers press to her throat and then her chest as I beg the Gods for her next breath. *What have I done? Oh Gods, what did I just do?* The shallow lift of her bosom is a relief so immense I collapse at her side. Hot tears fall freely from my eyes now. They streak my face and fall in fat droplets into my hair and onto Sheza's gray dress.

"I'm sorry, I'm sorry, I'm sorry," I chant. My hand strokes the side of her face. "Please wake up."

Had I hurt her with my abilities? My gaze rakes over her fragile form, looking for signs of burns on her skin. Though she looks older as her face relaxes with unconsciousness there are no marks of my touch on her. But my power had gone to my hands. It had forced itself into her body ... didn't it?

I replay the last couple minutes in my head searching for answers and praying to the Gods. Whatever I'd done had burned away Nasir's hold on her, eating away at his dark magic. Nasir's comments about needing my blood lingers in the back of my mind, darting to the forefront in a matter of seconds. Had it been my blood that did this?

Nasir can control those around me, but he can't control me. Is it my blood, the line of the Goddess Aerea herself, that keeps him from flooding me with his twisted darkness?

Does my own power combat his? One question after another fuels the flood of tears.

Distantly, I'm aware that the door opens and several bodies step into the room. I reach for Sheza's hand, gripping her fingers when I look up. Four maids sway with the same lifeless look in their gaze. One of them squats down to the ground and looks Sheza over from head to toe before stretching her hand out to me.

"Princess, we must get you into your gown," the woman says. I stare at her palm. "We must hurry."

And what if I touch her and what I've done to Sheza happens to her? What are the chances that they drag me away and I hurt them all? Pain knots itself above my heart.

"Will someone come for her? Will they see that she is well?" I ask, not sure that I can let Sheza go.

"We need to leave now," the maid repeats. She rises, but her hand remains waiting for mine. The others take another step toward me.

The wood in the fireplace is nothing but cinders, burned away under the rapid flood of my power. The last of the final embers glow as the heat flares bright before succumbing to darkness. I stare at the opening of the fireplace, at the black marks staining the stone and mantel. It leaves streaks charred into the floor just past where we lay. With excruciating slowness, I sit up. My gaze remains fixed. The fire is gone. Dead. I swipe at my cheek and my fingertips come away with smudges of ash.

"There is no more time to wait, Princess," another maiden says. Their eyes all drift over me and then above my head, watching and waiting but never fully present.

They have little to no control over themselves. They won't answer my questions, nor will they understand why I'm denying them the one thing they've been commanded to do. Worry nags the back of my throat, tasting like lead on the back of my tongue.

I force myself to pull my fingers from Sheza's lax grip. Her body retains the warmth of life and I remind myself that she's still here, she's still alive. These women know not what they do and I can't bear the thought of hurting them as I have her.

Nasir will not get away with this. He will pay for every injustice he has forced upon myself, my family, and my friends. That's the thought that steels my spine and pulls me to stand.

If I'm to marry him, it will be the last thing he ever does.

29
DEVONRY

"Oh dear." The woman next to me, another Lady in waiting sent by Nasir, pats my face with a starchy handkerchief as a tear escapes my eyes and slides down my cheek. She puckers her ruby-red lips into an unattractive smirk and raises one brow at me as another tear slips free. I want to shove her away, slap at her hand, slam her face into the ornate double wooden doors that stand before us.

Dressed in lavish Court attire I haven't seen in months, the woman appears every inch the Noble daughter I *should* be. I recognize her, but only as a passing Court Lady. She's no one of consequence, but she must be here under Nasir's orders. Perhaps she is his way of trying to be kind and give me a sense of normalcy in what is supposed to be my home but now feels like a prison coiling tighter and tighter around my throat.

My gaze slips to the doors again and moves down the grooves of carefully carved wood. There is no regular doorway; this one is larger than most doors and thicker. A beautiful nature scene has been etched into the front side of it, birds dancing along the top rim and trees arching along either side. Given life, it would be like looking between the two trees straight into a glen with grasses of the deepest green high enough to flutter at my knees and a distant pond with jumping fish rising from its depths to catch a glimpse of the sun.

I haven't been here since my mother's funeral, haven't seen these doors since I said goodbye, and she was sent off into the Afterworld and the arms of Aerea. I swallow a particularly hard lump sticking in my throat. This place is *her* chapel, a monument to the Gods that my father had added to the palace as a wedding present for her. It's supposed to be a place filled with only Holiness and reverence to the Goddess Aerea and her descendants. Now, I can hear the sound of foreign voices—voices that should *not* be in there—speaking in low tones beyond this blasted door.

"I know it's a happy occasion, but you'll ruin your makeup," the Lady next to me murmurs as she finishes wiping my face and then bends to adjust the long, cream skirts of the dress Nasir sent for me. I wonder if she even knows what she's saying. She seems to be the most animated of the servants allowed to roam the Sunfire hallways, and yet, at the same time, there is a hollowness in her gaze. A clouded look that tells me she's not quite aware. Perhaps she's in the middle of some dream and doesn't realize the treason she's committing by assisting a usurper who is holding her Queen captive.

Looking down at my hands, I curl my fingers into fists next to the fabric of the extravagant dress I'd been forced to put on. I haven't attempted to pull the strange darkness out of this woman or anyone else, for that matter. I'm not sure what will happen. Seeing Sheza collapse like that, and being unable to help her, has left me with a terrifying hole in my chest. What if I didn't free her from Nasir's control?

What if I'd simply killed her? I hadn't been able to check her pulse before they'd rushed me off, hadn't been able to touch her, hold her, or assure myself that she'd still been breathing. It would have been a simple kindness, but in this place, under Nasir's rule, there seems to be a great lack of that, of kindness.

My heart thuds in a consistent beat inside my breast, but it feels weak. Broken. Is this the end? Am I really going to marry Nasir? I'll do it. I know I will. As much as I don't want to. I know that I'd do unspeakable things to save the others, to save Solomon. The mere thought of his name makes my chest clench.

No matter what Nasir promises though, I hold the truth in my heart. Even if I marry him and gain back my Kingdom in this way, it won't be real. It'll be a betrayal of my actual namesake and my position. A Queen under the control of another is nothing but a puppet. She is not a Queen at all. My mind writhes with sorrow and desperation to find a way out.

My lashes flicker as I unclench my hands at my sides and then fist them once more, nails digging into my palms. The dress I'm wearing is long and elaborate. Ivory and cream, etched with gold stitchings that create an elaborate design down the front of my chest and over my backside. In another time, perhaps another life, it would have been nothing but beautiful to my eyes. The length of it curves over each side of my hips before releasing my legs and steadily flowing out and down, spilling onto the floor behind me. Little lace flowers dot the fabric over my chest and stomach. The beauty of it, the exquisiteness of all it represents, is harrowing because it, too, is a lie.

It's a Gods damned wedding dress and the groom, a traitorous murderer. My breath shortens, becoming shallow in my chest. Everything has gone to the flames of

Aerea. My allies are in chains, held against their will to keep me humble and obedient, and I don't know what to do to stop this.

A ringing gong sounds on the other side of the door, causing me to jump and my hands to release. My palms ache and I know without looking down that I've pressed little half-moons into the skin of my hands, likely to bruise with how hard I'd been holding them there. The woman next to me straightens and tutters with a phony sound of excitement. "It's time," she announces.

I close my eyes as tingles race down my arms and legs, pinpricks stabbing into my flesh. Cold. I feel so damned cold. As if all of the heat I've grown used to, all of the fire within me, has been put out. Water washes over my head, cooling me further and turning me to ice.

The doors creak inward and my eyes open to take it all in. I don't move, not immediately, not until the woman at my back nudges me with her hand. Only then do I lift my gaze and step forward. I stride into the room, one step, then two, and I stop as a familiar face appears at the back of the furthest pew to the right side. My chest opens and my lungs inflate as I inhale sharply, deeply.

"*Celine*," I say her name like a prayer. She's alive.

Celine lifts her eyes to mine, and I'm relieved to see that she hasn't been put under Nasir's strange spell. No, instead, there's a combined mixture of fear and relief in her red-rimmed gaze as she takes me in. There's a bruise on the side of her face that's been poorly covered by some makeup. It doesn't quite match her skin tone but has turned what would be purple into sickly green. Anger bolts through me like spreading fire one moment and the next, it disperses—as if someone has leaned over and blown it out. Shock evaporates the breadth of my ability. It's not the figure I already know is waiting for me down at the end of the aisle that does it though. Instead, it's the woman standing to the side just inside the doors. I look upon her in horror.

Celine.

She's dressed in a long, too pale, too pink gown that appears almost garish against her earthen skin. My eyes rove over her body, seeking out more wounds and I find them. Little cuts and more bruises along her arms and chest. Other than the bruise on her cheek, though, it appears that the rest of the wounds must have been caused by the explosion. I see no fingerprints. Perhaps the bruise on her face had been caused by the explosion, too, but something tells me not. The cuts and wounds along her arms and chest are left bare for all to see, but the one on her face has been deliberately covered—however poorly done.

Still, though, I'm relieved to see her standing before me. *Alive. She's alive,* I tell myself. That's what matters. In her hands, Celine clutches two bouquets of wildflowers. They're sorry, wilting masses crumpled against her cut hands and shaking fingers. I take another step toward her before I can help it but come to a halt when I sense someone's attention on me. Footsteps sound upon the hard marble floor. My gaze darts to the man who strides toward me—Nasir.

It isn't him, however, that stops my blood cold in my veins. It's what's behind him. Shock and horror. I thought I'd become accustomed to the feeling, but it has nothing on the scene that lies ahead at the very end of the aisle and behind the priest's altar. If I could breathe through the raging of my heart, I'd be screaming. Solomon's body is splayed like a disgusting trophy of war, his arms are tied out, spread wide, and held up by chains that are bolted into the walls on either side of the room, the only things holding him aloft.

As if that couldn't be bad enough, his chest has been stripped bare and there are wounds, many of them, some still bleeding as the ripe red rivulets run down his flesh to stain the torn trousers clinging to his hips and thighs. With his dark head tucked toward his chest, I don't see the expression on his face.

There are burns on him—his arms and chest and abdomen. Wicked-looking grooves cut into him as if someone had taken a red-hot iron and tried to pierce him with it, again and again. *Nasir*.

I lift one hand to cover my mouth. *No*. Fresh tears come to my eyes. *Gods … no*.

Solomon's skin is paler than I've ever seen it, more than ashen. It's practically the color of bleached rocks. It makes the bruises ringing his wrists and whipping over his forearms stand out. Above all of that, there stands the twin horns protruding from his forehead. I know enough of the Awakened to know what they are. They are a part of him, the darkest part of his abilities, the basest nature of the beast that resides within him. The horns themselves appear to be made of bone. They're blackened at the tips, and the color of that dark ebony stretches cruelly down into his face, as if it's paint dripping into his eyes.

I've never seen something so horrific and, yet, so beautiful at the same time. The horns arch up, taller than I've ever seen on any animal before curling back and delving into the roots of his hair as it hangs over his face. A sleeping monster, he appears. And just like the stretch of ebony on his horns and face, his fingers, now claws, look to be dyed that same deadly color. Where the paleness of his flesh finally stops, it's spread halfway up his arms, veins of darkness appearing, stretching the rest of the way up his biceps and into his chest.

He hardly looks human, and more terrifyingly, he doesn't move for so long that I don't even know if he's breathing. There are long gashes across his chest, diagonally down, open and unhealing.

Nasir steps in front of me, blocking the image. "I warned you, Devonry," he says, voice low. "I know everything now, darling. Just do as I say, and this will all be over quickly."

"*This is barbaric!*" I hiss back, tearing my gaze away from Solo to glare at my enemy.

He doesn't even react to my angry tone. "This is necessary," he says without feeling before gesturing to Celine. "Come."

Celine jumps forward and, though trembling, takes a step closer to him. He practically rips one of the bouquets she's holding out of her hand and it's then that I see her hands are bound by silver cuffs and linked together with a thick chain. My upper lip curls back away from my teeth, but I don't get a chance to curse Nasir before he shoves the stolen bouquet into my grip.

One hand lands on my shoulder and tightens over my bare flesh. "They are here to ensure your obedience, Devonry," he says, lowering his voice. "As well as your protection."

"The only thing I need protection from," I growl, "is you."

He doesn't bother to respond. So, I chance something else. Something that's confused me since the moment I laid eyes on Celine. "You're not controlling her." It's a statement, not a question. It's not that I want Celine to be under his control. I'm glad she's not, but I am curious— *why* isn't he controlling her?

Nasir's expression darkens. "Fear is just as controlling as my abilities, Princess," he snaps. "She's here for the very same reason your guard is."

It takes effort not to look back up at Solomon. Instead, I settle my gaze firmly on the man in front of me. I bite down on my tongue and grind my teeth. "You sure had me fooled, didn't you?" I grit out. "You seemed so genuine ... I almost believed it." I *had* believed it. I'd wanted to marry him at one point and had been ready to beg my father for it. "I guess no one can keep up the facade of kindness forever."

Nasir's lips curl downward and when he scowls, his entire face tightens at my insult. The hand on my arm becomes bruising. I repress the urge to flinch even when I can feel my bone aching under his touch. "Not everyone is as blessed as you, *darling*," he seethes. "I am only doing what I have to. As long as you do as I say, everything will be fine in the end."

Will it, though? I want to challenge him. Will he ever be able to come back from all of the things he's done? The lives he's taken? *No.* If I can't, then neither can he.

As if he can read my thoughts, Nasir's face softens and he releases my arm. Turning his hand around, I jerk my head to the side as he brings his knuckles to my cheeks. He doesn't bother though and simply moves his knuckles to the other side of my face and this time, I don't move.

"I do love you," he says. "You know that, right? I'm truly in awe of your strength, even now. But I need you, and I cannot risk you running away again."

"I thought you said I was kidnapped," I remind him.

"Yes, and that is what the rest of the world will believe. You were kidnapped and then you were rescued and brought back to me."

I shake my head. He can't truly believe to fool entire

nations, can he? Not when I'd already traveled to Bartoli and told them the truth. Though, I suppose if I'm to marry him, they'll also get everything they want. "This is lunacy, Nasir. Even you have to realize that," I say.

His hand falls away from my face. "Sometimes giving into the madness is the only way to keep yourself sane."

His words hold a note of finality, of sorrow so deep that it gives me pause. "Nasir—"

"I can't wait anymore," he states, cutting me off. "It's too late now, regardless. If I want to survive my own ability, I need yours. I need *you*."

"But—"

Nasir looks behind me and addresses the Lady who led me here. "Assist her to the altar," he orders. "And if she tries to flee…" He looks to Celine. "You may kill that one as punishment."

"As you wish, my Lord." The woman at my back responds. I don't know if I even have it in me anymore to hate her, not when I know she, too, is being controlled. But if it comes to it, if I have to choose between her and Celine, I'll save Celine and kill her. I've killed once, and even if I don't want to, even if I'm standing in my Saintess mother's own sanctuary, I'll kill again to protect those I love and those I am responsible for.

Nasir turns and strides back down the aisle toward the altar where Solomon is strung up like some ancient human sacrifice, backlit by the rays of twilight that pour in through the glass window behind him.

Celine releases a shuddering breath. "Are you okay?" I ask, glancing back at her.

Her eyes cut to the woman behind me and back to me once more. "I'm alive," she offers as a response. That, at least, is a blessing. She's alive. Solo … is as well. Though for however long, I don't know.

"Where's Argyle?" I ask. "Do you know what happened?"

Celine looks over her shoulder and stifles a sob. I follow the direction of her gaze and stop when I see a figure on his knees to the left of the altar. With his face so cut up and bloodied, and his usually large body folded nearly in half as he sits with his head hanging low, red droplets falling from his forehead, his eyes swollen, and his hands chained behind his back—I hardly recognize him. If he's awake, I can't tell. His eyes, even swollen, seem to be closed and the rattling breaths that come from him are even.

"E-extra precautions," Celine says. "We weren't told why, b-but…"

I shake my head again, stopping her. She doesn't need to finish her sentence. I know why they've both been brought here. I know why they, as well as Solomon, are all tied up and about to bear witness to this tragic play that Nasir has brought about for all of us. They're here to keep me in line. One wrong move—one more refusal or rejection—and they'll pay the price. Not me. Them. He couldn't have chosen a better threat.

The invisible scars that are etched into my soul deepen. They hurt more, too, since I once trusted him. The man I'd called my friend, my best of friends in fact. He'd been my ally in a sea of glittering gems and Noble children, all of whom had been taught from birth to lie, cheat, and steal from one another in the most political of ways. I'd thought he was different. Honest. The pain of his betrayal runs as deep as it had that night so many moons ago when I'd rounded the separating wall in my father's chambers to find him with Nasir's blade protruding from his chest.

The worst wounds, after all, are the ones given to us by those we once loved, those we once trusted.

"How did he know about you and Argyle?" I ask,

lowering my voice as I keep my gaze on Argyle, searching for some sign that he is better than he looks.

Celine's response is just as quiet. "I don't know," she answers. "But from what I gather—anyone under his abilities will confess any truths he asks of them."

I close my eyes. "Lenorn?" I inquire. "Solomon wasn't alone when he left the safe house." He wouldn't have been if he'd gone along with that ridiculous plan of his.

Celine is quiet and when I open my eyes, I note Nasir has arrived at the end of the long aisle and has turned back to survey us. No doubt, he knows everything already—all of the questions I'm asking her and the information I'm gleaning. I need to know, but I don't exactly have the luxury of hiding it. I glance back to the woman standing still and stiff at the edge of my dress's train. Her eyes are locked on Celine and me, as if she's waiting for the one wrong move that will have her attacking.

Celine shakes her head at my question. "I haven't seen any others," she confesses. "Not in the dungeons or otherwise."

What does that mean? I have to wonder. Were we betrayed? If not, wouldn't Lenorn be here for this? A glance around, though, assures me that he's not. In fact, the chapel itself is nearly empty. Other than the guards stationed at all exits, alongside each outer pew end, Celine, Argyle, Solomon, Nasir, the priest, and the woman at my back ... there are no guests to this farce of a wedding.

"You may begin," Nasir calls out. His voice rings through the rafters.

Fabric shifts and I look back as the Court Lady behind me picks up my train and holds it expectantly. Celine clutches onto the remaining bouquet in her hands. I look down at mine. He's thought of everything. From the dress to the Ladies in waiting to the bouquet. I lift my head, and down the long length of the chapel, I meet his gaze.

There's nowhere else to go. Nowhere to run. If I want Celine, Solomon, and Argyle to make it out of this alive, then I have no other choice.

"Y-your Highness?" Celine looks at me with such hope and I hate that I'm about to snuff it out.

"Let's get this over with," I say sharply.

She looks from me to the altar. "You can't be actually considering…" Her words trail off, choking to a stop as more tears fill her eyes.

"This isn't the end," I tell her, "but I can't risk the three of you. Not you or Argyle. Not Solomon. If I don't do this…" I swallow roughly, hating with every thread of my being the words I'm about to say. "He *will* kill you." She sobs and I reach for her, taking her chained hand in one of mine. "As long as you're all alive, everything else can be healed." No matter what he plans to do to me once this is over. As long as the three of them still breathe, then it will all work out. I will make it so.

"*Devonry.*" Nasir's impatient call resounds against the walls of the Gods' chapel. With one last squeeze around her fingers, I nudge Celine toward the center of the aisle.

"Go," I order her. "You know what to do."

She sobs again but squeezes my hand back just as strongly before releasing it. A moment later, she sniffs hard, and turns sharply, clutching her flowers like they're a lifeline holding her to this room. Her body moves jarringly, an awkward puppet on a string as she marches down the aisle in the way of a true Lady's maid at a Noble wedding. I hold my breath, waiting for her to reach the end.

Her head turns once she reaches the last pew, her long tangled brown locks shifting along her upper back as she does. I know she's looking at Argyle, whose head remains bent. I think he's actually unconscious and I'm thankful for that. The moment passes and Celine moves into place, turning back to face me. Tears track over her cheeks, clearing away the makeup and revealing more of the bruises on her flesh.

It's my turn. I take the first step forward, breathing through my teeth. The second ricochets up my legs, making my calves ache. The third, I look up and past Nasir and the dead-faced priest. Solomon's body hangs limp and lifeless.

It isn't until I grow closer, my steps gliding over the stone flooring, that I see the light rise and fall of his chest. My own heart throbs in sorrow and pain at seeing him like this. His eyes remain shut, though I can see the twitching of his muscles.

I stop a few feet back, aware that Nasir is glaring at me, but I can't stop myself. I can't help it. "Solomon..." I call out to him. His eyelids tighten. *Can he hear me?*

I go to call out to him again when Nasir speaks up. "Come, Devonry," he commands me. "Let us bring an end to this game of ours."

The chains holding Solomon still creak as he begins to awaken, to move.

Hope is a dangerous thing, I realize. Life breeds hope and death breeds sorrow. Between the two, I am trapped. As long as he's alive, even if it hurts, I know I still have hope.

30
SOLOMON

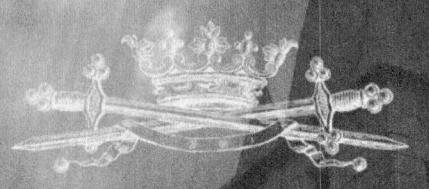

Hunger. Pain. Lust.

The baser of human emotions and instincts whip through me, cutting lashes across my flesh from the inside. Violence fills my every limb. It writhes inside of me, a living, breathing creature that marks the inside of my bones with its wickedly sharp talons.

I struggle to get a sense of where I am. To sense without my sight and attain a single hint of my surroundings. Quiet. There is nothing inside of me but that deadly quiet. I know it won't last. My arms have long since gone numb. There is nothing beneath my feet save for open air. My muscles ache with a memory I can't quite reach. Something I should know, should be able to recall, but suddenly can't. My body hangs in a large open space—nothing around me, nothing touching me but the rings of metal around my wrists, pulling my arms taut to either side. I sway back and forth as the beast that I've shared this form with for so long rises from the depths of my soul. The creature slithers into my veins and then takes over, fighting and struggling against that which holds us immobile.

My throat is dry—drier than any sun-caked desert, parched in a way I know all too well, in need of quenching. Blood. I want blood. I want it so badly—far more than I ever have before. My veins sing for it, skittering beneath my flesh, wrapping around my bones and practically vibrating with the need. I fear that if I do not get it, I'll explode into ash and fire and let the painful longing for it consume me until I become nothing of who I was.

No Solomon Winett. Only the beast will remain, lost to his own raving lunacy.

Why was that such a bad thing again? I wonder. If I just let it take me over, I doubt it will hurt anymore. Something in the back of my mind—a thin tendril of sanity—clings to my soul, ripping me away from that darkest of places.

Why? I demand again. Why, if not to release me from this agony, must I continue to maintain any semblance of humanity? Humanity is weak, and I am not. I am beast. I am Blood. I am God.

A low growl rumbles up my throat, coming from somewhere deep down in the recesses of my stomach. A soft scent, floral and calming, invades my nostrils. Even the beast within me subsides for a moment as we turn our head up and sniff, inhaling the aroma of petals and water. A gentle breeze that cools my fiery throat and makes my mouth water.

Mate. Mine. Her.

I've been reduced to single-syllable words even in my own mind. How pathetic.

"Solomon…"

I still, not out of fear or curiosity. No, the sudden stillness comes from a knowing so intense that it coils around me, tighter than these damnable restraints and chains. That voice, a light, almost lyrical note, is ripe with sorrow and despair. It's *her* voice, I recognize, the one of my mate.

She's sad and in need and I—I stop and take stock of where exactly I am and find that I'm trapped, a creature unable to move, unable to reach for her, unable to comfort her.

Yanking against my bindings, I roar aloud. The sounds of several quick inhalations of breath let me know that there are others in the room aside from her and me. Those who would keep me and my mate apart. My lips spread into a cruel, dangerous smile. The points of my fangs punch out of my gums, jumping down and slicing over the soft skin of my bottom lip. My flesh is harder, that of an animal's tough hide versus a human's feeble exterior. I can feel the rippling waves of the beast's prowling rage and need to protect swell beneath that layer of flesh.

My forehead throbs where I'm sure my horns protrude. The truth of my power. I am not human. Not deep down. They have not captured a mortal, but a living, breathing monster and *We. Are. Angry.*

Another raging roar screams out of my throat. A demand to free her. To stop whatever ails her and causes the foul stench of her terror to cease. Were I free, I would take her into my arms and pull her close, allowing her to feel me as her shield, as the one thing she will never have to fear.

Her choked sobs break me in a way I never thought possible. No loss. No grief could ever contain the agony I feel at the harrowing sound of her uneven breathing and anguish. It makes me want to rip my arms clean free to rid myself of the chains binding me. It makes me want to flood this very space with the blood of my enemies so that she may be reunited with me, so that she may cease her sorrow.

There has never been a worse torture than to hear my beloved's cries and be unable to touch her.

Dimly, I hear the voice of another. Deeper. Male. My upper lip pulls back away from my fangs. Though I cannot decipher his words, the sound of him and the scent of vile arrogance rolling off of the man in waves makes me want to rip his head from his body and drain his blood down my throat to quell the thirst that so overtakes me.

Bad. Evil. Dangerous. His desire is potent in my nose—desire for that which is not his. Desire for what is mine. *Mine!*

Metal creaks as the bindings holding me and keeping me from my goal struggle to contain me as I yank against them. There is a low throbbing in my ears that fills up all of my hearing, growing louder and louder until I cannot even discern the sound of her voice anymore, much less the man who wishes to have her for himself.

Still, I cannot forget her call. Her cry for me. She needs me.

Rage. Pure and unfettered releases from my throat. I bellow and roar, the howl of my own thunderous fury raking through the dried inside of my throat until it breaks off too abruptly, and no more sound escapes.

Tiny little daggers stab and poke at my insides, agonizing in their reminder of my inability. My head turns from side to side, seeking out her scent. I cannot be this way. I cannot be this powerless. Not when she needs me.

How did we come to be this way? I cannot recall. Surely, there was once a time when we were side by side, that we were one. In my hazy, faded memory—that of my human self—I can still taste her on my tongue. She is a light that fills my body when it is dying. My greed for her goes beyond the same greed of mortal desires.

The world could end. Humankind could cease to be. And still, I would know her, still I would want her.

Her fear is palpable to me. It pains me worse than any

blade. I pull once more against my bonds, propelling myself forward through sheer force of will, but nothing comes of it. No ground grazes my bare feet. I simply bow up and struggle against both my own insanity, the descent of red covering the area I see behind my eyelids.

Blood Madness, I realize. It's truly upon me, and once I succumb, there will be no coming back.

31
DEVONRY

Celine's eyes are hot on my face. I feel almost dead inside, but I fear it would be worse if not for the fact that Solomon seems to have woken from whatever oblivion was holding him in slumber. Like a wild creature, he struggles against the chains holding him aloft over the sacred altar of the Gods in my mother's chapel. The roar he unleashes whips through the air, angry and dangerous. It rattles the glass in the window frame behind him as well as the armor worn by the guards that stand silently along the sides of the chapel. The Noble Lady at my back inhales, as does Celine.

A low groan, however, comes from the man positioned on the floor. My gaze cuts from Solo to Argyle as he releases another, his chest swelling with the sound. Celine's soft sob is one of relief. Unfortunately, however, despite his earlier unconsciousness, Argyle still must contend with the gag wrapped around the lower half of his face, keeping him from doing much more than emitting those grunts and groans.

My gaze cuts away from him to Nasir. "Tell me the truth," I snap, needing a distraction as well as an answer. "Why do you need to marry me?" He already has the Kingdom. Everything is under his command. Rozentine fell easily to him and his powers.

"You know the people will not accept an outsider on the throne," Nasir says with a scowl. "They believe in the Goddess' bloodline, and you have that bloodline."

I shake my head. "You said you need my blood," I remind him, gaze narrowing on his face as if I can pick apart every minuscule change in expression. "What did you mean?"

Dark eyes move from me to Celine and back again, dull, lifeless, unyielding. "You're stalling," he states, tilting his head to the side before he sighs in exasperation. "Do you *want* me to kill her?"

If Celine is insulted or further terrified by his words, she bites it back. She doesn't release a single breath, much less a whimper or sob. "Answer the question," I reply coldly.

The growls from Solomon grow louder and are soon accompanied by the snapping of teeth and the creaking of metal chains. My gaze flickers up to him to see that his eyes are open, the blood-red color of his irises glowing with an unnatural brightness. My stomach churns when they connect with mine. The ruby rivulets in those irises seem to pulse brighter, squirming under my gaze.

I blink and return my attention to Nasir. He stands before me, grinding his teeth. Instead of answering me, however, he marches forward the last few steps, reaching down and latching onto my wrist. His fingers curl around my limb, tighter and tighter, until I grit my teeth at the pain.

Firmly locked onto me, Nasir yanks me after him as he turns and strides back to where the priest is standing, stony-eyed and empty-faced. "Nasir!" I wrench against his grasp. "Answer me!" Desperation tinges my yell. I have to know the truth as well as give Lenorn more time to arrive. He and Lord Frederic would not abandon us like this, I know it in my heart.

"Enough," Nasir barks out the command, ripping me forward and shoving me into the altar. I release my hold on the wildflower bouquet to catch my fall, but my knees slam into the bottom half of the altar and I go down hard. The woman behind me gasps as the back of my dress is tugged free of her hands.

Once I've caught my breath, I look back to find that the back of my gown has been ripped, starting at the center of the train and arching up to the left at my calf.

Nasir doesn't seem to notice, or if he does, he no longer cares about keeping up appearances. "Begin the ceremony," he practically growls at the priest.

A moment later, an old tome is split open, dust rising from its pages to tickle my nose as the priest lays it upon the altar. I stifle the urge to sneeze, blinking away the sudden tears that also rise to my eyes as my nose twitches in protest. No one notices or cares about my struggle. The priest's deadened voice begins to recite the text, speaking in the old Gods' language. A language few people have learned within Rozentine, a language that is meant to be sacred and certainly not to be heard by outsiders and traitors such as Nasir.

Rage pours through me and in an act of rebellious anger, I reach down and grip the opening of the dress and pull the sides of the fabric apart, tearing the dress straight up the side until my thigh is revealed. At least it makes the gown much easier to move in as I get back to my feet and turn to face Nasir.

All around us, the wilted petals of the wildflower bouquet flutter across the stone floor. As if the pathetic, flattened husks of the flowers create an impassable line that separates us from the rest of the room. The scent permeates our surroundings with the smell of soil and sweetness.

"I will *not* be complicit in this." I bite the words out.

Nasir arches a brow as the priest continues to speak, not even stopping in the face of my refusal. He looks back, directing his attention meaningfully to the room still lined with his guards, all of whom hold the hilt of their blades. Sheathed or not, they are ready for bloodshed.

"You will," Nasir states. "Or your friends will die."

"If you kill them, then I will spend the rest of my life trying to kill you."

Nasir laughs. "You are your mother's daughter, love," he replies. "You are not a killer."

My lips part. Oh, how he doesn't know. I'd assumed because he seemed to know everything. He knew of Celine and Argyle. He knew Solomon had drunk from me, but he doesn't know this. He doesn't know the truth of my words.

I try a different tactic though. Reaching out, I grab ahold of Nasir's hand and drag him toward me. His brows go up in shock. "Nasir…" I look up at him through my lashes, repressing the itchy feeling of insects biting at my flesh as his skin rubs against my own. "Tell me why you need my blood," I practically beg. "If you want my help, why not give me that much at least?"

Cold black-brown eyes dart between mine and then over the rest of my face. Searching for sincerity? Maybe. But I hope to the Gods he's not searching for love or forgiveness because I know he will never find that in me.

"Please, Nasir," I move closer even when the act of

doing so makes my skin crawl faster with those invisible little insect bites, "tell me the truth."

The priest drones on and on—as if he's completely unaware of the whispered words between us. He likely is. He's got that same blank look on his face as everyone else under Nasir's control. My heart thuds rapidly in my chest. Distantly, the sounds of chains and growling echoes up to the top of the chapel. I repress the urge to look at Solomon. I can't. Not now.

"You want the truth..." Nasir's gaze fills mine. I think I've got him. I truly do. He's not moving away. He's caught right in my grasp—his hands in mine, his eyes. I have *everything*—at least, I think I do.

Until I don't.

"With no pain, there is no light, no feeling at all," Nasir whispers back. I watch as the voids of his pupils expand wider and wider, swallowing every ounce of dull brown color in its path until his eyes are nothing but twin black holes that bore into me. More than simply into my body, his gaze seems to penetrate my very soul, going further into my heart and my past.

All at once, images flash through my mind. My once-long, white blonde hair curling as rain falls over me. My mother's caress as I lay in her bed with my head on her chest. Solomon's adolescent face, soft in youth, but cold and unfeeling after returning from battle.

Nasir leans closer, his breath warm against my cheek as he turns his lips toward my ear. A shiver skitters down my spine and too late, I try to tug my hands free from his. He doesn't let me go.

"I embraced this power not knowing what it would do," he says. "How much it would take. If I can't find light, then it will consume more than me, Devonry. It will consume you, too, and then the world. I need your blood because if it is already controlling me—drawn to you by your purity." His words are coated in a new tone—one far deeper and more terrifying than any other I've heard before.

As he pulls away, I realize that his eyes haven't returned to normal. He smiles down at me, knowingly. "You are the Goddess, Devonry," he says in that chilling reverberating voice. "The Goddess is the only one who can bring flame to the eternal dark."

The priest's voice fades away. Everything fades away. The sound of Celine's uneven breathing. The rattling of Solomon's chains. My mother once told me of an old story, one of the Gods' history. I've known of Aerea since I was born because it is from her that the Royal House of Rozentine was born. I know of Levim because of Solomon's bloodline. Thevaros, the God of the House of Starfall. Caladrius, the Healing God who named his descendants after himself. But little is known of the God of House Daemonium.

Etia. The Goddess of the Afterworld and Darkness.

Now, that old God's tale returns to me.

There were once two sisters—one of light and one of darkness. They loved each other to the ends of the world. They laughed. They cried. They created. They loved. Everything that they were, they shared.

My mother's voice rings soundly in my head. It's as if I've gone back in time, and she's alive again, right there before me, telling me this old story with a soft smile on her face.

The world was created to be balanced, and these two sisters were the core of that balance. Their existence created harmony and thus, the human race was born. Aerea, the daughter of light, created a Kingdom for these precious new beings. Several Gods came to admire Aerea's new treasure. Each of them gave a piece of themselves to help

Aerea create the perfect world. Even her sister, the daughter of darkness, participated. In response, Aerea created a House for each of her Godly friends.

The rays of light in the chapel slowly descend, throwing the room into darkness as the priest drones on. All around me, fires are brought to life as the guards stationed down the room turn and light the sconces upon the walls.

But as Aerea became more and more interested in watching her Kingdom, in bringing them miracles and blessings, she didn't recognize her sister's loneliness. Etia attempted to create a Kingdom on her own —to understand the love her sister felt for the humans—and found that she was incapable. Humans cannot live in the darkness because the darkness consumes all. Therefore, only when Aerea's creatures perished were their souls sent to her. By then, it was too late. They could not provide the same love for Etia as they had for her sister, as many were filled with regrets.

I look up at Nasir, wondering how I never saw it. From the beginning, the House of Daemonium was always secluded, choosing against maintaining properties in Sanctus City. Instead, they stayed either within their own territory or traveled abroad. If Nasir is the illegitimate child of a Rozentine Noble and the Bartoli King, then his darkness likely comes from them. Did Lord Byron know of Nasir's relation? Is that why he'd betrayed Rozentine?

Etia grew colder and angrier toward her sister. She grew jealous of the light Aerea possessed. The longer she spent in her realm of the Afterworld, the more lonely she became.

I close my eyes as I think back to the time when my mother told me this story. Almost as if her ghost had returned, a soft wash of warm air brushes over my cheek, mimicking the feeling of a hand stroking me. The biting pain of loss swells within my breast. I, like most children, feared the dark.

Light and darkness are needed to create harmony, my little dove, I hear my mother's voice say. *Without both, there would be no balance in the world.*

My eyes open once more as the priest's words come slowly to a halt. I finally think I understand. If Nasir is an Awakened of the House of Daemonium, if he has the power of Etia in his veins and I have the power of Aerea—then he's right. He needs my blood. Without it, he'll simply be consumed by his own darkness.

"You may seal these sacred vows with a kiss."

A ringing echoes in my ears. Vow? What vow? I never spoke, and to my knowledge, neither did Nasir. Nasir doesn't seem to be bothered by the priest's words or the missing vows. He steps closer, his hands coming up from mine to latch onto my arms and keep me from pulling away.

Distantly, I hear metal clashing. Shouts. Agonized screams. Is it in my head? Nasir's head comes down, his eyes closing.

No. I think. *No!*

Just before his lips touch mine, an animalistic roar echoes through the room, so loud and ear-splitting that it rattles the chandelier hanging above the pews. Crystals clank together. On the other side of Nasir, Celine drops her flowers and tries to cover both of her ears, but it's useless with her chains. She can only manage to tilt one side of her head down to her shoulder and cover the other ear as her face pinches tight.

Behind me, I hear a low groan from Argyle and a mumbling curse.

Without waiting for a second chance—and despite the aching of my ears as the world tilts—I shove Nasir away, stumbling back. The sounds of fighting grow nearer. Nasir finally seems to take notice and as his head turns toward the end of the chapel aisle, he lifts a hand to his guards.

Down the chapel room, at the end of the aisle, the doors fly open and whatever Nasir was about to say turns to silence and dust.

32
DEVONRY

Everything becomes chaos. It's fast, the change. It takes over the room and crashes between me and those around me. No one and nothing is spared. Metal screeches against stone, echoing up into the bare wooden beams above our heads. The clomping of boots and the clanking of armor rattles in the air.

War cries scream through the chapel and almost instantly, what was once a serene and beautiful room meant for some of my mother's sweetest memories has turned into a battlefield. Within the mass of armored men brandishing swords that swarm the room, I spot a few familiar faces. Hope blossoms in my chest.

Among the familiar faces, Lord Frederic strides through the throng of incoming soldiers along with Aegis, both of their faces smudged with dirt and blood. Frederic makes his way to the center of the chapel aisle. Had they been fighting outside this whole time? My heart leaps from my chest as Frederic is stopped midway when one of Nasir's guards launches forward and their blades clash.

Sparks dance along the length of the swords. Lord Frederic's long, pale hair has been pulled back into a high ponytail, creating a more severe look.

In this moment, I see how such a young Lord has managed to maintain his hold on the House of Caladrius despite his age. A healer and a warrior. He is both sides of the same coin and I've never been more relieved to see him. Pale hair flying, Frederic's head lifts. His eyes connect with mine for a brief second before he turns his head and slashes his blade across another of Nasir's guards as they dive for him.

He made it. *They* made it, I realize as I spot Lenorn in the crowd of men pouring into the chapel as well. My eyes fill with tears, but I push them back as I release the breath that has been building in my chest. Another recognizable face appears even higher than the rest—more so than Lord Frederic and Lenorn. My heart stutters in my chest.

Lord Ahren.

His face is reddened with fury as he stares above the heads of those fighting down the aisle—pews being overturned and shoved aside and climbed over as if this wasn't supposed to be a sacred place. I bite down on my lip hard enough to split the soft skin. Blood flows into my mouth, over my tongue, tasting of rust and fear. I know what Ahren is seeing. *Solomon.*

Metal screeches out of a scabbard right next to me and I stumble back as Nasir shoves me to the side and practically roars his fury at the scene before him. All thought of what Lord Ahren must be thinking and what he's planning flees my mind. Nasir's anger is a palpable thing and dark swaths of mist are forming against his hands and shoulders, dropping from his body like he's leaking power to curl around the tips of his boots and back up his ankles like wild, living snakes. I take advantage of his distraction and leap away from the altar.

"Celine!" I scream her name, and in a flurry of heavy skirts, I plunge down the short steps of the altar on my way to her. All the while, the priest stands there, empty-eyed, as if he's a mere doll with no life if Nasir isn't giving him commands. The man doesn't blink or do anything to even hint at the fact that he's aware of the battle going on around him.

"Your Highness!" Celine rushes toward me only to stop as the woman who had been following us down the aisle attacks her.

"Shit." I stop abruptly and turn back. Without thinking, I snatch up one of the candlestick holders sitting at the side of the altar. Gripping the cool metal, a growl unleashes from my throat as I take one large step, then two more, and swing it at the woman. Even as Noble as she appears with her pale skirts and done-up hair, her round eyes flare with panic as she looks up at me. She doesn't seem to even notice the candle holder in my palm as that panic dies with a glossy, glazed-over determination. Her hands lock onto Celine's shoulders, and as she tries to throw her to the ground, the side of the candle holder connects with her temple. Skin splits. Blood flows and she goes down in a heap against the slim steps leading up from the aisle to the altar.

Panting, sweating, with tear streaks and droplets of blood sliding from scratch marks on her upper arms and chest, Celine struggles to get to her feet, placing both—still chained—hands onto the ground. I drop the candle holder and help her.

"Are you okay?" I demand, running my fingers along her arms. My eyes glance over her, searching, checking, but thankfully, there don't appear to be any wounds deeper than the scratches.

She nods and then inhales hard. "I'm okay," she assures me, taking me by the arm. "We must get you out of here."

"No." I shake my head and bend, retrieving the candle holder as her hand slips away from my arm. "Take this and go to Argyle." I shove the candle holder in her palm. "Free him and then get out of here."

Celine's doe brown eyes widen as she stares at the spike on the end of the candle holder, where normally wax would sit. "Y-your Highness?" Her brows pinch down, but despite all of her bluster and irritation, I can also see the way her gaze moves immediately to the man in question. Concern is etched all over her features and it's very much clear how she wants to go to him.

I cup her shoulder. "I'm fine," I say. "Now, go. I'll get Solomon."

At his mention, her gaze moves back to Solomon, who remains suspended above the altar. His eyes are illuminated by a power within, glowing a brilliant red as he snarls at the proceedings before him. He's locked on the battle behind us, his muscles tensing with rippling waves of his veins bulging each time he tries to rip himself free of his shackles.

I direct Celine toward where Argyle kneels alongside the altar, pulling against his own chains that keep him locked in place and unable to move more than a few feet either way. Once I'm sure Celine is doing as I've asked, I finally face my own task.

With no sword and no other weapon at my disposal, I scan my surroundings to figure out a way to break those damnable chains that keep him locked in place. Along the right side of the altar, down the steps, and just outside an alcove, I spot one of the hanging flags—or rather, I spot the pole that the flag rests on.

My foot hits the leg of the fallen Noble Lady, and I stumble, nearly going down in a heap, and that's when I realize that there's no way I'll be able to move as well as I need to while dressed in this Gods forsaken gown. Bending down, I lift the already ripped fabric to my mouth. Using my teeth, I tear at the frayed edge until the stuff gives way.

I grunt and sigh as the rending ends and I'm left with bare lower legs and a jagged line of skirts around my knees. The rest of the white material is left abandoned on the steps, and I use my newfound freedom to get to my goal. My eyes lock onto the top of the pole, at the point of the spire etched in gold above the hem of the flag. That's what I need. The length and that sharp edge. With it, I might be able to at least loosen the chains embedded in the stone walls—weaken the rock around the metal, and—

"Devonry!" I come to a jarring halt as I look back at Argyle's shout.

He's still covered in blood and bruises, with one eye swollen shut, but with his one good eye—the blue one—he's glaring at me from where he sits prone on the floor as Celine stabs at the chains holding him bound with the candle holder. His gag sits around his throat like an ominous noose.

"Get out of here, you dimwitted woman!" he screams.

Really? And here I thought we'd gotten closer. Ignoring his shouts, I turn back to the task at hand. Locking my fingers around the pole, I plant my feet and yank upwards—pulling the damned thing from its holder. The flag slides down as I lift it higher and higher. I let it fall at my feet, rippling waves of crimson and gold with the image of a sun folding over itself.

"Gods damn it! Celine!" Argyle appears to have given

up on reasoning with me and has instead turned to Celine. "What are you doing? The both of you need to get out of here before—"

I've drowned out Argyle's angry ranting as I heave the heavy wooden pole toward the closest wall where Solomon's chains are shaking as he bucks and bows against them. Solomon's growls grow ever louder and more violent. Nervously, I glance toward his face as I jam the sharp end of the flagpole into the wall around where the metal links are locked. Dust rains down over my face and I sputter, turning away and spitting out the bits of grime and rock.

Solomon's horns stretch out from his forehead, evolving from mere nubs to ashen antlers dipped in ebony. His hands have long since lost their human exterior and are now animalistic claws with long, sharp nails twice the length they normally would be. Even his body seems to have swollen with the pulsating veins beneath his skin visible as they run up over his bare stomach, sprouting from somewhere beneath his trousers.

The rigid, shadowed lines of his abdomen appear deeper. His claws contract into fists as he roars his displeasure. I flinch at the sound. It's both terrifying and relieving. He seems almost completely lost to his Awakened form— something I've only heard of but never truly seen before now. I'd never truly gotten a good look at him in the caves when I thought he might have been changing. This is altogether different. It isn't desire making him this way. This is pure, unfettered rage.

Pulling back, I punch against the stone wall with the end of the pole in my hand again. My arms shake. My muscles scream. Sweat drips down the side of my face. "Almost there," I say, half to myself and half to the maddened creature that is Solomon. "I'll save you, I promise." And I pray that it won't be too late for his mind.

Fury has a way of making minutes feel like hours. I don't know how long I'm at it, swinging and poking and jabbing away at the locked metal that's welded to the fucking wall. It feels like an eternity, but there's no way the battle behind me could take that long. I'm half tempted to look back and see who's winning, but I'm too scared to find out that we're not. As long as I'm not being stopped from trying to free Solomon, then I'll keep going.

At least, that's what I plan—until the sharp sound of Celine's terror and pain echoes back to me. Freezing where I stand for a brief second, I whirl around just as a dead-faced, bloodied soldier rips Celine up off the floor and away from Argyle. He's certainly not one of Lord Frederic or Lenorn's men because he doesn't seem to recognize either Celine or Argyle.

"Fucking Bastard!" Argyle curses and rips himself up off the ground as he attempts to throw himself at the man. The attack is cut all too short, though, as Celine's efforts to free him seem just as useful as my own with Solo. He's dragged to a halt just out of her reach.

Celine's skirts fly around her hips and calves as she swings her hips, trying to kick and buck against her captor. I drop the flagpole and sprint across the distance between us. The guard cants his head to the side and upon realizing that Celine isn't something he needs, he carelessly tosses her to the side.

I watch, spellbound by the horror of the scene before me. It's almost as if the things happening all around me are part of some twisted play, and I am a trapped audience with no power to prevent it. Celine's body goes flying past another of Nasir's guards fighting with one of the armored men. Her head slams into the wall with a sickening thud and she crumples. Just like that, she goes from a vocal, spirited fighter to an unmoving body on the ground. A patch of blood marks where she'd connected with the stone and then droplets slowly ooze down to where she's fallen ... unconscious.

Oh please, by the grace of Aerea, please just be unconscious.

A beat of utter silence passes through my mind. Although I'm dimly aware of the clashing of swords nearby, the male grunts, the shouting and cursing, my ears don't pick any of it up. Then, the dull quiet erupts and everything slams into my head the moment Argyle opens his mouth and releases a roar so angry ... so agonized ... full of such fear that it makes my heart squeeze in my chest with sympathy.

The sound is so beastly, it doesn't sound human. It's the audible embodiment of pain, of sorrow, of rage.

With his arms still pinned behind him, Argyle somehow manages to use his fury to bolt up to his feet and launch himself at the man. Metal scrapes against stone, and for a moment, it's just enough to hold him back, but with the momentum he's built up as well as the height of his anger, the links keeping him bound break free. Bits and pieces go flying across the ground, skittering beneath the altar and down the steps.

Now freed, Argyle's body is propelled toward the soldier and he takes him down, fists flying. Bones break. Blood flies. My eyes return to Celine and her collapsed form, unmoving.

"No..." My knees hit the ground hard when I reach her side. My hands shake as I hold them over her, both wanting to lift her into my lap and afraid to move her for fear of causing more damage. "No, no, no..." This cannot be happening. My heart thunders in my breast, in my ears.

Tears aren't supposed to burn. It's not natural, and yet,

they do. They fucking *hurt* as they squeeze out of my eyes and roll down my cheeks. "Celine?" I tap her cheek lightly, hoping against hope that she'll at least open her eyes.

I've not had many female friends my age—the Ladies of the Court weren't true friends, not in the way that Celine has become someone so greatly important. "Please…" I practically beg, though I don't know who I'm talking to. Perhaps Celine herself, or even the Gods. Whoever has the power to bring her to open her eyes and look at me.

My fingers feel cold as I tap her cheek again on the other side and then gently weave them behind her head to lift her up. My hand comes away wet with blood. My nose twitches. More tears pour down my face.

The dull, nauseating sound of Argyle's repeated punches—flesh against flesh—finally comes to a stop. Footsteps sound behind me as I brush the dark wash of chocolate brown hair from Celine's face. "Is she—" Argyle's voice is hoarse as he begins to ask what we both fear but only to cut himself off.

I shake my head as I press two fingers to her throat. "She's still alive," I breathe with relief.

He, too, collapses at my side and I find that I can't fight him as he takes her from me, lifting her body and moving her head and his own legs until he's beneath her, propping her up slightly on his thighs.

He's bleeding, wounded. Breath wheezes from his lips, sounding shallow and uneven. It's clear he's got some internal injuries, and he must be in a mass of pain. He ignores it all, though, in favor of cradling Celine against him. He whispers something to her, something I can't hear. Then—as if I couldn't be any more surprised by his gentleness—he presses a kiss to her pale lips.

Argyle's one good eye gazes down at her lovingly,

forlornly. "Do not leave me, *brat*," he murmurs. "You've threatened to make my life nothing but misery and I plan to hold you to that."

I've never heard Argyle so choked up, nor have I ever heard him use that term before. Despite the fact that one might expect the term 'brat' to be one of derision, the way he says it tells me he's used it before and it's nothing to him but an endearment.

My eyes land on Celine's hands and how they hang to the sides of her stomach and thighs, limp but still chained. I look down at my own hands and push all of the anger and sorrow and pain and fear that I have in my chest into them, hoping … waiting … praying.

They begin to heat up, and the remaining blood against my skin bubbles up, clumping together and growing sticky. A warm glow emanates from my fingertips and then down into my palms. I reach forward and take the chain links into my hand, holding tight. I squeeze them, wanting them gone. I want nothing more than to see them disintegrate before my eyes. They don't disintegrate. Instead, they melt. The heat doesn't bother me, but the fact that I should have done this to begin with does.

Celine's hands fall to her sides and I shake away the melted metal that fell into my hand. Little pings of the hardening links now morphed into balls hit the stone and roll away. Argyle cups her cheek. "She's still breathing," he says. "She's still breathing." I know he's not saying those words for me but for himself.

"Yes," I agree. "She is." I lay a hand on his shoulder. "It's okay," I tell him. "Lord Frederic is here … he can heal her." If he was able to save Solomon and me after that horrid cliff fall, then this should be nothing. I believe that … I *have* to believe that because I cannot bear that, it's not possible. I cannot think of a different reality, or I will break further than I already have.

Without looking at me, eyes entirely focused on the woman in his arms, Argyle opens his mouth to respond. I don't get to hear what he has to say. One moment, I'm there at his side and the next, a harsh grip locks into my hair and rips me away—back into the horror surrounding us, back into the fray.

33
DEVONRY

A scream lodges in my throat and stays there as the hand at the back of my head tightens, ripping several strands of my hair out in the process. The pain ricochets over my scalp and down the back of my neck in sharp tugs. I press my lips together, cutting off the startled sound. Tears prick my eyes as I arch my back and stumble under the weight and pressure of being forced up to my feet and away from Celine and Argyle. Somewhere behind me, Solomon roars—taken over completely by his Blood Madness.

When will it ever stop?

Out of my periphery, I see Argyle get to his feet—despite Celine's position—but before he can even take a step toward me, two of Nasir's guards step between us. Whirling the two of us around, Nasir growls and holds out his sword in his free hand as he stands in the center of the now-destroyed aisle.

All around, the wooden pews have been dislodged, some on their sides, more of them practically shredded to bits by the cuts of swords—as if they'd been used as shields. My heart aches at the sight. This place—once so holy and serene—has deteriorated into a graveyard. Blood stains the stones underfoot and bodies lay here and there and at the front of the soldiers on the other side of the room, Lord Frederic, Lenorn, and Lord Ahren step forward like three generals preparing for their last war.

The scream in my throat thickens until it chokes me. "Prince Nasir," Lord Ahren begins. "Let the Princess go. It's over. You've lost."

Nasir shakes his head, and the hand behind me loosens, only to contract and rip out several more strands. I wince and reach up, latching onto his wrist to keep him from pulling out more. He takes a step back and then another and another, rounding the altar and placing it between us and the Lords of Rozentine.

"No," he says. "No, it's *not* over!"

"Nasir, don't make the same mistake twice," Lord Frederic says. I've never seen him look so cold. His normally casual and pleasant demeanor has been completely eradicated and in its place is a hardened man. His expression is dark, brows drawn low, and lips pressed into a straight line, slightly curving down at the ends. "Rozentine has been taken back. You no longer control the Sunfire Palace."

I feel his muscles stiffen behind me before anything else, but in response to Frederic's words, Nasir growls and turns. His sword swings out, catching the neck of the priest who stood by with no expression, as if he were no more than a puppet without strings. What little breath I have catches in my chest and turns poisonous.

The priest's body falls under Nasir's child-like anger and once it's down, Nasir doesn't stop. He stabs the man's belly with the tip of his blade, leaving the weapon sticking straight up through the priest's fallen form. It's grotesque.

Then, as if he truly can't believe what's happening, the

seriousness of his circumstances, Nasir begins to laugh. The sound echoes up the stone walls, sounding both manic and hollow. "I didn't do any of this for Rozentine," he finally responds. "Rozentine can burn in the Afterworld for all I care. I have what I want."

He punctuates his last statement by pulling me back harder, pressing his chest into my back, and reaching up with his now-freed hand to wrap it around my throat. Lord Frederic and Lord Ahren jerk forward only to be stopped by Lenorn as he reaches out and latches onto their arms.

"Careful," Lenorn says.

"Yes," Nasir continues to chuckle. "Careful … or I might just snap her neck."

"You wouldn't hurt her," Lord Ahren snaps. "You just said you did all of this for her. She's what you want, isn't she?"

"Yes." Nasir's laughter dies in an instant. His head dips and he presses his face into my hair, inhaling. "Devonry … my Devonry."

A low, dangerous growl erupts above us and I tilt my head back further, alleviating the pain in my skull as I see Solomon rattling his chains and snapping his jaws at us. The horns have grown, curling back over his skull. His fangs have lengthened into the size of tusks. My stomach drops out from beneath me. *What happens if he changes fully? Will he ever be able to come back?*

I jerk my face away from Nasir as his breath hits my ear. "*No,*" I bite out. "I am *not* yours and I never will be."

"Yes, you are!" Nasir roars into my face, spittle flying from his lips and landing on my cheek. I clench my jaw and rear back, kicking at his shins. "You're mine! You were supposed to be—"

"No!" I scream back at him, struggling and fighting against him. I don't care if he takes me away here and now, if he somehow manages to escape the three Lords with me. So long as breath is left in my body, I'll fight him.

"—mine! We were supposed to be together forever," Nasir continues, his voice changing. As he talks, it grows lighter, almost as if there's a woman's tone beneath his own, naturally deeper one. "You're the one that left. You left me…"

The hand in my hair drops away so suddenly that it sends me reeling and I stumble backward as Nasir straightens away from me. "Why did you fucking choose him and not me?" The woman's voice in the back of Nasir's throat grows stronger.

Confused, I turn and face him only to see that his eyes are no longer the natural brown they've always been, but pure darkness as he stares down at his own hands coated in blood. My lungs inflate. It's never good when I see his eyes change like this. Dark mist seeps from his lips with every word and trails over his chest and arms. "After all we've been through … you would willingly choose someone else, and when I asked you for my own Kingdom, you gave me nothing but the dead."

I frown, bewildered by both that oddly familiar voice and by the words coming from him.

Nasir lifts his gaze away from his hands and looks straight at me. "Tell me why, Aerea. Tell me why you abandoned me."

Aerea.

It's that one—that name—that catapults me from the Holy Saintess' chapel to a place far away and long ago. My body may be my own in this realm but my soul is not. It is shared, a spliced piece between me and … *her.*

. . .

"I LOVE HIM, ETIA." I PIVOT—MY BODY YANKED AWAY FROM the real world and into one that has long since stopped existing on this plane—to face a woman who looks like me. Only her hair is much longer than mine is now, and instead of the light peachy strands I possess, hers is fiery and a mass of waves that seem to stick out in every direction.

The woman in front of her, tall and thin, appears very similar in features, but different in coloring. Where Aerea is soft and rounded, freckled and skin warmed, Etia is willowy and slender, skin unmarked and a smooth white. Her hair, dark and severe, cutting down her back like the shaft of an arrow.

"Why?" Etia demands, glaring at her sister. "Why him? Because he helped you with your damned humans? I helped too!"

Aerea's face scrunches in pain. "No, it's not just that," she says. "I don't know how to explain it, but—"

"If you can't explain it then it isn't real love, Aerea," Etia snaps, cutting her off. "Because I can explain why I love you. It's easy—you're my best friend, you're my sister."

In response, Aerea's expression softens and she moves toward her. "I know," she whispers. "I love you too, but just in a different way."

"Why ... don't you want me anymore?" And just as I suspected, Aerea's heart clenched upon hearing those words, and mine gave a responding squeeze. The pain in her voice echoes through the chambers of my chest, dives deep beneath my flesh, and stabs at me.

"No. No no no." Aerea rushes toward Etia and grabs her by the shoulders. "I will never not want you," she swears. "But if we are to be true to ourselves then we must grow. The humans have taught me that if we stagnate and stay the same, then there is no honest progression."

"Progression?" Etia shakes her head. "What was wrong with how things were?"

"Nothing was wrong with it at all—oh, Etia, please." Aerea embraces her, pulling her tight, and side by side, the differences in their appearance are even more startling. Two sisters, almost opposites in

nature and power, and yet ... they are supposed to be the balance of the world.

There's no evil, only pain and sorrow and loneliness.

"You'll still go with him, won't you?" Etia asks even as Aerea clutches her against her chest.

"We need to grow," Aerea repeats. "To leave our old selves and create new ones, new families. I want to create a family with him."

Etia screams, the sound breaking through the fog of this old memory—one that has been in my soul for centuries. *"I'm your family!"* Etia wails. *"I'm your sister!"*

I cover my ears as the echo of her angry cry resounds, reverberating through my skull in a way I didn't know was possible. Over and over again, I hear those words. The pain in them is so precise it cuts like a blade.

"Etia, I love you! Please don't do this!" Aerea's voice and words are swallowed by the winds of Etia's pain and rage. The shout goes on and on and on, never-ending, only growing louder as time passes.

Aerea tries again. *"This isn't the end of our friendship,"* she yells. *"We will always be sisters!"*

"And yet..." Etia speaks once more and the winds go silent, ceasing their harsh dance around the three of us. The calm, however, is even more chilling. Etia lifts her gaze and I stumble back a step as my heart pounds within my breast, consumed by a need to escape. Her eyes are blacker than the darkest of nights, colder than any wintry season. Her final words, when she speaks them, hold nothing but hate.

"You still *choose* him."

34
DEVONRY

Etia's screams continue, lingering, echoing even as I'm slammed back into my body and the present. The undying cries and pain-filled sounds don't stop. Only this time, it doesn't come from the beautiful, ethereal lips of an ancient being so full of pain and sorrow that it tinges on each breath. Instead, her voice, loud and agonized, comes from Nasir. The sound bites into my ears, angry. Hurt.

"Devonry!" Argyle's shout at my back is followed by the grunting of guards. I assume he's taken those separating us out in an effort to get to me, but I'm not sure what to do now.

That memory ... it makes the reason why Nasir did all of this so clear and instead of being angry, I'm ... sad. No, maybe it's not my emotions or feelings, but hers. *Aerea's*.

"Not fair. Not fair. Not fair. *Not fair!*" Nasir-Etia screams out, clutching their head and shaking it back and forth as if it can dispel the rage and fear clear in their tone.

"Nasir ... that's not you," I say, reaching out. "It—"

"No!" He flings my hand away and whirls around, snatching the sword he left still sticking up within the priest's belly. "I have to kill him! If I kill him, you can't leave me again."

The words and their meaning hit me a second too late and I shriek in horror as Nasir turns, gripping the handle of the blade and stabbing the sharp end of it through Solomon's gut as he hangs suspended above the altar.

"*No!*" The horror shoots through me. Nasir is in a frenzy, eyes unclear, mind half taken by a Goddess'. He withdraws the sword, only to stab at Solomon again and again.

I launch myself forward, grabbing ahold of his arm. "Stop!" I scream. "Stop it!"

"Die! Die! Die!" Nasir is lost to reason. His voice is no longer his own. His actions are uncoordinated and jerky. Fire builds within the fear that resides in my gut. It erupts into harsh flames that consume my body and limbs.

I can't stop him. I have to stop him. If he doesn't stop, Solomon will die regardless of his Awakened form and I can't … I can't lose him.

Under the force of Nasir's blows, Solomon's hanging body swings back and forth as he growls and roars. His fists, now claws, curl and pull against his shackles as he tries to break free from the restraints to no avail.

My head pounds. My stomach cramps. The room around me spins. I hear screaming that isn't my own. Multiple male voices. Argyle's. Frederic's. Ahren's. Lenorn's. They all fade away, but not like before in the memory of Etia and Aerea. This feels different. It feels almost like burning.

Nasir jerks his sword free of Solomon's stomach and without looking behind him, his elbow slams into my chest, knocking me back. My legs crumple. My back hits the stone floor. More fire spreads through my limbs, up my arms, and into my fingertips. It travels faster and faster still, down my legs and up through my back. I thought burning alive would feel painful, but all I feel is warmth. Comfort.

Power.

The ache in my skull grows ever greater and I struggle to breathe. It's as if every single one of my veins has been suddenly filled with volcanic heat. It swarms me, and the stone beneath my back feels like ice. I squirm as my bones melt away, my skin dissolving into pure fire.

Succumb, Devonry. This time, it's your choice.

I recognize that voice. It is both mine, and it isn't. It's Aerea's. I don't know what she means, but I do know that I can't keep fighting the power in my veins. Sunfire bursts free—finally, blessedly, and then I'm rising from the ground.

I cannot feel my legs; it isn't until I rise higher and higher above the floor that I realize they're gone completely. I'm no longer human, but a fiery feathered creature. My arms lift and fall—*no, not my arms*—my wings.

They've broken free of my back, and somehow, unlike when they sprouted from my spine back in Bartoli, they don't ache nearly as much. Instead, it feels like I've shed a heavy cloak that kept me concealed and I didn't even know I could be so light.

"Dear Gods ... the Phoenix of Aerea..." I don't know who says it. Their reverent voice pales in comparison to the raging echo of screams through my head as I turn my head down to find that Nasir still hasn't stopped.

He's continuing to stab at Solomon, through his belly, his leg—wherever he can reach. Without thinking, I tuck my wings and dive down. My flaming body crashes into him, lifting him off the floor. The sword clatters to the ground and he rages below me, fighting the hold as my claws latch onto him, lifting him higher and higher than ever before.

This must end. It has to end. One way or another.

Release him, Etia. I hear Aerea's voice in my head.

Never! Is her response.

I don't know what to do, but Nasir's body is heavy, weighing me down as I try to hold him despite his struggles. He lurches one way and then another and suddenly, without warning, one of his hands latches onto the edge of my wing. The two of us spin through the air, and as I flap my one free wing to keep us up—we slide beyond the altar and the chapel, further back even than Solomon's wounded body, hanging suspended and raining blood down on the dead priest.

The flames of my body hit the stained glass window and instead of breaking, the very material melts—sending both Nasir and me into the night sky. Twilight has long since fallen and the fire that envelopes me burns over Nasir's body. He screams—agony, pain, and sorrow welling up within that one singular sound.

All life has meaning. My eyes slide shut as those words penetrate my mind. They're not Aerea's nor Etia's, but my mother's. I know that ... I know, but if Nasir lives—Solomon will never be safe, and neither will I.

A sharp bite of pain slides through my wing and I cry out—the sound like that of an echoing bird. I look down to find that even half burned, Nasir has pulled free a dagger from his boots and stabbed at my wing. I'm not entirely sure if he's even aware of what he's doing or if it's his survival instinct kicking in. It doesn't matter, though, because in the next instant, my hold loosens.

No! I try to contract my grip despite the pain, but it's too late. Nasir slips through the clawed feet of my Awakened form and falls down ... down ... down.

His back and skull collide with the ground below, crunching inward with a sickening thud.

Gods...

Slowly, I lower myself to the ground. My arm, my wing, aches. Blood oozes from my wound. Another kill. Another death. As I watch above Nasir's body—with his eyes still open and now staring into nothing, a ghostly figure separates from me.

The feeling is like nothing I've ever experienced, both invasive and oddly tingling. Aerea appears alongside Nasir's body and looks down sorrowfully, her lips trembling slightly as her brows pinch together.

"Etia," she calls before reaching down past the flames that still linger on his flesh and clothes, eating away. Her hand disappears into Nasir's chest and a moment later, when she withdraws it, she drags with her the same form of the Etia in my soul's distant memory. Sobbing, Etia collapses against Aerea. Her smooth skin is unblemished save for the tears streaking her cheeks and the strain upon her face. Where Aerea is rounded and soft, Etia is slender and willowy. Aerea is beautiful. Etia is stunning. Together, they are otherworldly. The sight of them together makes my heart clench.

"Don't leave me, sister," she begs. "Please ... it's cold without you. I cannot bear it any longer."

Aerea doesn't hesitate to wrap her arms around her sister. That's when it hits me—the true cruelty of this all. It was never about us—me or Solomon or even Nasir. It was never about Rozentine, but about these two. A Goddess unable to leave the past behind. Nasir had been nothing but a tool.

My eyes move back to his body. *Could I have saved him?* I wonder. *Could any of this have been changed?*

In the end, we were merely their vessels.

"Devonry." I look up as Aerea calls my name. Still

holding Etia against her, she speaks. "Do not feel so torn, my daughter. You have done all you can."

Her words echo into my mind, through my heart. I want to reply, but nothing comes out. Nothing can come out. Not in this form.

"You are so brave, child of my soul," Aerea tells me. "You are everything I hoped you would be. And with him…" She drifts off momentarily, her eyes turning somewhere back in the direction of the crumbling wall at the side of the palace. When her gaze connects with mine once more, they are filled with unshed tears. "You will have all that I never could. You will love and live and feel the grace of mortality, giving all your souls to each other. As a fragment of my own soul, I will love again through you."

Aerea's attention drifts back to her sister as she continues to cry and hold onto her. Softness overtakes her features as she strokes a hand down Etia's back and brings her closer than ever, pressing a kiss to her sister's temple. "I will take it from here," she says. "It's over now. I will take Etia, and there will be nothing more for you to do. Your life is your own once more."

I want to ask more questions. What about Nasir? What about Solomon? Will Solo live? Will Celine? But as Aerea and Etia's forms fade, becoming more and more translucent with each passing second, my body grows heavier. Try as I might, I cannot remain upright any longer. Falling to the side, my wings stretched out toward Nasir's body, I blink rapidly as the world turns to nothing. No more Sunfire. No more darkness. Only … oblivion.

35
DEVONRY

Droplets of rain turn to mist the moment they touch my skin, creating a haze of steam that blurs my vision. It separates me from the rest of the world. I'm alone. Empty. Solely myself.

The bite of stone under my palms brings the promise of stability against the rain-soaked ground. My body is light as I press my hands against the rock to ensure that I've not lifted into flight. The chill of the solid ground is another balm to the blistering heat of my flesh.

Water clings to my lashes but is blinked away like tears down the curve of my cheeks until they, too, have turned to mist. Forcing breath into my aching lungs, I get to my knees before the charred form of a body. The stench of burnt flesh is pungent. It invades my nose and sticks to my insides with the stink of death. A halo of blood surrounds his dark shape and when I look at my hands, the reminder of it still stains my skin.

Nasir. A terrible pain in my chest starts up as it all comes rushing back to me. Etia. Aerea. We are all extensions of what happened so many years ago. Was anything

Nasir did even done by his own will or by Etia's? My lip quivers. No matter what has happened, Nasir had indeed been my friend for a time, and I've mourned the loss of that friendship for months now. All of it surfaces with near-crippling agony and the knowledge that perhaps he hadn't betrayed me, but the Goddess Etia had.

"Nasir," I whisper, wanting to reach out and touch his body before it totally dissolves to ash. A shiver sends goosebumps across me as the wind turns and fresh rain touches my exposed flesh. What clothes I'd had were burned away in the flames of Aerea's Phoenix. So now it is only me, my shame, my sorrow, and my nakedness.

What anger I'd harbored for him is stripped away by quarrels far greater than him and I. Without the fury of his betrayal to fuel me, the delicate walls I'd built around my raw emotions are crumbling. A sob breaks free of the loose hold on my composure.

All the death, the worry, and the heartache slam into me. My father. Jacin. Nasir. My chest is cracked open and anguish oozes from the invisible wound.

"Devonry!" a voice calls through the pounding of rain. Boots slam against the pavement headed for me, coming closer with every feeble beat of my heart. The nearness of the movement breaks through the fog of my thoughts enough that I have the sense to wrap my arms around myself to cover my nudity.

Clothes soaked through with his hair clinging to his features and raindrops dripping from his glasses, Lord Frederic comes to a skittering halt at my side. His throat bobs. "Thank Caladrius, are you okay?"

He takes another step closer, falling to his knees at my side. There's movement behind him, others who'd come for me. His eyes skim over my flesh with the critical view of a doctor looking for signs of injury. I dig my fingers into my arms, knowing that the only real hurt I have cannot be seen.

Frederic's cheeks heat as if only now, in my silence, does he realize that I'm naked. His deft fingers work to undo the buttons of his top before he slides his shirt off his body and drapes it over mine. The material is wet but warm with his heat as I push my arms into the sleeves.

"Let's get you inside," he whispers. "Can I help you up?"

I nod. With his help, I rise. My legs shake under me, threatening to topple me back to the ground next to the corpse of the Prince. Could I have saved him? Was he always meant to die? How much of what transpired here was written into our fates by the Gods themselves?

And what of Levim? What of Solomon?

My blood runs cold. "Solo," I breathe out his name. Frederic leans closer as if he can feel the panic bubbling up in my blood and taking control of me.

Solomon had been strung up with chains, bleeding out at the altar of my wedding. Solomon had been dying as Nasir stabbed his blade into his gut again and again. Crimson blood stains my memories as it stains the Sunfire Palace floors.

"Solomon," I say his name louder this time. But it wasn't just him who'd been wounded. Celine's face flashes in my mind as I shrug out of Frederic's arms and stumble forward. Gold shimmers at the edge of my vision, what power I have left hums just under the surface of my flesh as I sprint through the courtyard, leaving Frederic behind. The ability is still there—not stolen away—but drained. The steady pounding of his boots is never far, even as I shove my way into the palace and past the startled faces of men as they watch their Queen dart past in nothing more than a wet shirt.

I weave through bodies. Puddles of rainwater are replaced with shallow pools of blood and I leave red footprints in my wake.

The guardsmen linger. Those who had once fought me and the other Nobles stand dazed. Their questioning glances frantically try to take in the scene around them as confusion darkens their expressions. With Nasir gone, the shadows have disappeared from their eyes. Their freedom is only now dawning on them.

The doors to the grand hall are thrown open, revealing more men who'd fallen. Death is everywhere, clinging to my home with its dark, sin-coated fingers. What decorations were put up for the wedding are splattered crimson, their delicate luxury ruined. I step over limbs bent at odd angles and the spill of organs next. Bile stings at the back of my throat.

It's the blood-soaked strands of dark hair fanned over Argyle's arm that give me pause. Argyle's eyes are squeezed shut, his lips moving rapidly as he cradles Celine in his arms. Her body is limp, her skin paling by the second.

The air in my lungs seizes. "Lord Frederic." I stop so suddenly his leather soles squeak against the floor as he comes to a halt at my back. "Help her. Celine first."

"Let me check you thoroughly first," Frederic says, trying to reach me. I take a wide step back, pulling myself away from his touch.

"No, I'm fine. Her first." Gold brightens in my vision. Frederic's eyes widen as he sees the flair of color and nods, turning quickly to my friends. His hands brush over Celine's skin and Argyle looks up with frantic worry marring his gaze.

Then I'm moving again past the blank open stares of the dead and over the blood splatter across the fine tiles. A cry rips out of my throat as Solomon's limp form comes into view. The monster still claims him, the blood of Levim the only thing keeping him from death. His flesh is gray and hardened, jagged blackened veins weave under his skin, making him look like a statue moments away from shattering. The steady drip of his blood trickles onto the floor.

His head lolls to the side, black strands of hair flattened to his forehead. His chains chime together as Lord Ahren works to undo the restraints. My bare feet slide through the blood, Solo's blood, as I make it to his side.

"Solomon," I say, my hands finally on him. My palms curve around the shape of his face, lifting his head. His skin is still warm but not hot in the way his powers usually keep him. My thumb skims over his cheekbone, leaving a smear of red. "Solomon."

Wake up. Please. Open your eyes.

I place a hand on his chest, desperate to feel the rise and fall of each breath. Blood soaks through Frederic's shirt as Solomon bleeds out onto me. My fingers tremble against him.

Please be alive. Don't leave me. After all of this, you can't leave me.

His chest moves in a slow, shallow inhale.

"Solomon!" My voice rises. "Get him down, get him down now!" My shouts echo through the room and over the noise. "Don't leave him here like a sacrifice to the Kingdom!"

Chains clatter to the ground. Ahren leans into Solomon's body, wrapping his arm around him and taking part of his weight. He reaches for the other side and moves to let him through, but I can't stand to be far away or to take my hand off Solomon's face. My arm rests on Ahren's shoulder as he works.

"My Queen," Ahren whispers, letting the other chains

drop and catching his nephew's full weight. He grinds his teeth at the mass of Solomon's monstrous form and lowers him to the ground. "Do not wake him. He is far past the point of Bloodlust. It's dangerous for yourself and everyone here if he should return to consciousness in the midst of his Blood Madness. He is weak and needs blood, but he will live."

I kneel in the puddle of blood and drape myself over his chest. The need to feel his every breath consumes me and my body tenses in defense as Ahren reaches for me. His hand stills as tears spill over my eyelids and down my cheeks. "If he needs blood, then I will feed him."

"You will not," Ahren says, his words a rush of fury. He takes a deep breath before continuing. "Devonry, if you so much as try, you'll be dead before he even realizes what's happened. Don't do that to your country. Don't do that to him."

Blood Madness is all-consuming. It's the wild thing that left his wrists marked from yanking at his chains so fiercely. It's the terrible thrashing of his fangs and the lengthening of his twisting horns until he's no longer recognizable. But my soul knows his. I'd recognize him no matter how his power changed him.

"I'll make sure he gets blood. Then, he'll need time to heal and rest. Don't worry for him because he'll be back to normal so long as you are there. He needs you at his side more than ever, my Queen."

I sit back on my heels and drag my attention to Lord Ahren. His expression is serious, his eyes pleading as though I'd be anywhere other than Solomon's side.

"What do you mean?"

He closes his eyes so tightly creases appear. His brows furrow as though he's in pain. "He hasn't told you. You don't ... know?"

Silence stretches between us. What is he trying to say? What do I not know? My mouth goes dry, my palms get sweaty. "Ahren, please."

He looks at me, attention scanning over my features. Is that pity in his gaze? "I've known for quite a while," he starts, his voice softening to a whisper, "Solomon's known since he was a young boy; being Awakened so early as he was will do that. He met you, and he knew the two of you were soulmates. He was drawn to you. He needs you like he needs air to breathe."

Mates. Solomon and I ... we ...

As shocking as it is to hear, perhaps I did know in the deepest parts of myself. It feels right. It rings like truth with each passing moment.

"Your father knew. It was the King that forbade Solomon from speaking or acting on the notion. He was always meant to be your personal guard and your guard only. Together you're stronger. Your power lends strength to the other by your mere proximity. But you've always been promised to the furtherment of Rozentine. You were never truly his."

I lay my palm against Solomon's arm. Power hums between us, that ever-present wild thing. My mind races through my memories. Of all the times I'd felt that same pull toward him, never knowing why. I think of the days I hated him but painfully noticed his absence when he was away. His skin on mine and the way we needed each other despite how hard we tried to refuse it. Then there were the dreams.

Everything had been so real. It *was* real. My mouth drops open with a gasp as it settles in. We were always meant to be, just as Aerea and Levim. Their love. Our love. It's all the same.

I snap my mouth shut. Why didn't he tell me? Even

after my father passed, after he'd sworn himself to me, after everything? He should have said something. Anything.

"I—" But the words never really come. I can't bring myself to hold Ahren's attention any longer. Shame warms my face. I should have known. He should have told me.

"I'll take care of Solomon. While you wait, go get yourself cleaned up and I'll let you know the moment you can see him." Ahren lays his hand over mine, gently taking it and pulling my touch away from Solomon. "Rozentine is going to need to see you strong."

With a nod, I look down at my guard … at my soul's mate. His monstrous form is still unconscious. Only his broad chest lifts and falls gently. The perfect shape of his features is stretched into a terrifying mask, but under it all, he's just Solomon.

For years, he hid the truth from me. Why? Why didn't he just tell me? How much time had I lost to this lie?

I swallow, desperate to rid myself of the dryness in my throat. On shaking legs, I stand. Dressed in nothing but Frederic's shirt, drenched in Solomon's blood, I drift like a ghost through the halls of my home, haunted by the certainty of my reality.

36
SOLOMON

The memory of pain echoes through my body. Though there is a numb quality to my ethereal dreams, my hands skim my abdomen searching for the wounds that don't exist here. I tongue my teeth, feeling for that stretched point of my fangs, but they remain retracted and snug against my gums.

Devonry. Her name is a snarl emitted by my monster, but the beast is not in control here. Though I'm not sure I'm entirely in control either.

Stringy white clouds tangle around my feet and drift up my legs like reaching hands. They circle my hands before drifting up and out. My gaze follows the smoky lines until my eyes meet a returned crimson gaze.

Red glows dangerously bright in his gaze. A scattering of dark brown hair has fallen across his thick brows and the rest of his hair sticks up at odd angles. Shadows darken the hollow cut of his cheekbones. I frown and his mouth turns down in time with mine.

"Solomon," my own voice greets me.

I look down at my body, the same as it ever was, but the person before me ... the man talking ... is me.

"Solomon Winnett," he says again. When I drop my hands, so does he. I take a step back and he creates double the space as we both furrow our brows. The man extends his hand behind him. A slender form that my own body has memorized every curve of materializes at his side. "We've come to say our goodbyes. You will no longer see us though we will always watch over you." This time, when I reach up and pull my hand down my features, he doesn't mirror my movement. "It's time for you to wake up."

Levim. Aerea. There is no doubt in my mind that I stand before my God and Goddess. Fear tightens the muscles in my shoulders. If I'm here standing before them, then I have failed. My mortal life has ended and I've left my Queen alone.

"What do you mean I'll never see you again?" The bite of frustration has me spitting the words. I can hardly look at myself, at him. My attention is fully centered on the woman at his side. The likeness to Devonry is uncanny though her hair is longer and darker. Fiery red, it cascades over her shoulders and frames the perfect oval of her face. Sparkling gold outlines her otherwise gray-blue irises. Those full lips of hers lift into a gentle smile. Though her stillness and poise are missing something; it's missing the gentleness of *her*. The certainty that this isn't Devonry herself is as unnerving as talking to the likeness of myself is.

Yet I still find myself wanting to reach out and touch her. My fingers ache with need. My muscles strain to keep me planted amongst the drifting haze of clouds that surround us. It's in these heavens that I've seen her and spoken with her through dreams. It is in these heavens where our bodies have intertwined without the consequence of reality.

"Solomon Winnett," the woman speaks, "you and your mate have done what we could not do. This life you live will be yours again."

Levim gives the Goddess a better smile than I've ever been able to muster in my life. "The two of you have given us our greatest wish. You are one. We are one."

A growl vibrates through my chest. My fingers curl into my palms until my nails dig into my flesh. "What are you trying to say to me? What does any of this mean?" I move a step forward but I'm not closer to either of them.

The clouds rise up between us. Their bodies become nothing more than silhouettes amongst the white. I shift forward again, then again. But no matter how quickly I move or how much of the fluffy haze I push through, the pair never appears any closer.

"Tell me what's happened. Is Devonry okay?" My desperation clogs my throat with unwanted emotion. I try to swallow past the lump.

"You've left your mate for long enough," Aerea sings and I stop in my tracks. Her voice resounds all around me, coming from every angle. "It's time for your rest to end."

I open my mouth to question them more. But they're gone. So are the clouds. All that surrounds me is darkness. I inhale slowly and wince at the ache in my gums and the pain deep in my stomach. The awareness of my eyes being closed settles in and I blink several times until the blurred edges of my vision sharpen.

Overhead the sheer fabric of a bed's canopy blows lazily in the breeze of an open window. A feather-stuffed mattress is soft under my back, a full pillow propping my head. I move my arm, only to be caught by the cold metal of chains against my wrists keeping me down. The same cut of cuffs against my ankles tells me there is little I can do to move. I yank again, only to release the warmth against my side when a body presses tighter against me.

Devonry's mouth is parted ever so slightly; her lashes curl against her cheeks, and her eyes closed in sleep. All the tension leaves my body as I melt against the bed and let the chains hold my weight despite the pulse of pain in my joints.

She's alive. She's okay.

Levim's words come bounding back through my thoughts. *The two of you have given us our greatest wish. You are one. We are one.*

No matter what our Gods mean for us, we're alive and together. Whatever else happens to us, we will survive that too.

37
DEVONRY

The baby wolf is back. It's a cute little thing with hair so ebony it reminds me of a raven's wing and eyes the color of rubies that glitter with a brilliant intelligence I've never seen in any other creature. It reminds me so much of Solomon that it makes my chest squeeze. After everything that's happened so far, though, I welcome the sweet dream of the little animal.

It crawls into my lap as if it was meant to be there and nuzzles against my stomach. Curling my arms around the warm creature, I cuddle it closer and bury my face into its soft fur. It's so smooth and silky, not something I'd expect a wild animal to feel like. My head throbs and strange butterflies are mulling around in my lower abdomen. For some reason, I really want to show this wolf pup to Solo. I want to lift him up and hold him out to Solomon as if I were the one who created this beautiful little beast.

As if it senses my thoughts, the wolf pup lifts his head and licks at my face. A grainy little tongue pokes out and slides right over my nose, making me scrunch my face and laugh. More butterflies break free inside my belly and swarm the rest of me. I do believe the wolf likes me. I'm glad because I have the oddest sensation of liking it back. Very much. Almost as if ... this animal is something that I could not bear to live without. I don't just like it. I love it.

The dream I'm having is so sweet and warm that when I feel something jostle me and a big hand touches my shoulder, I shrug it off. No. The real world is painful. It's sad. It's a fucking wreck. I'm so tired. I just want a break.

If I open my eyes, I know I'll have to face the truth—that Solomon is still unconscious. That Nasir is dead and I'm the one who killed him.

I just want time. Time away from all of that. Time with this little one because it seems to be the only thing keeping me together. I hug the wolf pup tighter, but instead of returning my affection as I expect, the creature wiggles from my grip and bounces to the floor.

"Wait," I frown after the animal. "Where are you going?"

Pausing, the pup looks back and a glimmer of something knowing shines in those familiar red eyes. It turns around without even a hint of an answer and begins walking away, back into the shrouds of clouds hanging over this dreamy place.

It's going to the waking world, I realize, and it wants me to go as well. Lifting my legs up until my thighs are pressed to my chest, I curl my arms around them and lay my head on my knees. I know I'll need to wake up at some point. I know I'll need to go back to the waking world, but is it really so bad to want to stay here? Just for a little longer?

"Devonry..." I press my forehead tighter to my knees as my eyes burn. I shut them and inhale through my mouth, filling my lungs with air over and over again, trying to focus on that.

I don't want to wake up. I don't want to be in pain anymore. I don't want to look at Solomon and wonder if he'll ever return from the Blood Madness. *I don't want to be alone.*

"You're not," a voice replies. "Open your eyes."

"No." I shake my head without looking up. More tears leak out of my closed eyelids.

"Devonry…" The deep voice that calls out to me is familiar, it's warm and inviting. It's a trick. I tighten my hold on my legs.

"Let me be," I beg that voice.

"Never, love," it replies. "Now open your eyes, or I'll take you while you sleep, and when you wake, you'll find yourself full of me and know the truth."

The truth? What in the Gods could he mean? What truth is there to know? The truth is that I am a failure of a Queen, and I don't even know if I deserve my throne anymore. If I can't protect those I am closest to, then what's the point of having that position? How can I protect a whole Kingdom if I can't protect those I love?

"Devonry … please, open your eyes," the voice continues. "You are torturing me. Don't you think I've had enough torment to last a lifetime?"

Who is this man to talk of torment? If anyone has dealt with enough torment, it's me and Solomon. With all of the pain and obstacles that have buried the path that should have been easy for us, it's a wonder how we're still all together in one piece at all. The wolf has left me, and Solomon remains unconscious. My stomach cramps with pain and my head throbs with sorrow.

There's only so much I can take.

"I know," the man's voice from before says, responding to my thoughts. I don't know how he can hear them. But it *is* a dream, so who am I to question it? "You've been so brave, Devonry," he says, that deep baritone of his comforting in a way. "You've been so strong, and I am so proud of you. You're everything I knew you would be and more. My heart. My soul. Please, my love, open your eyes. I miss you."

He misses me? Does he know me? What does he know of me? His heart? His soul? I don't understand. The voice, however, is growing deeper and more familiar with each passing word. The warmth in it reminds me of the warmth of the wolf pup.

Though I don't want to, though I fear opening my eyes only to be disappointed once again, something tells me that it's time. No more running away. I've had my reprieve.

"Devonry…"

My eyes, when I lift them, feel as heavy as boulders. They're burdened by sleep and exhaustion that goes beyond the physical realm. Light pours in through the curtains and over the tile and stone floor. A warm hand lays upon the side of my head, gently stroking through my hair. It's so comfortable that, at first, I don't even consider moving. Then, I remember where I am.

Jerking upright, and unintentionally away from the gentle petting hand, I turn my attention to the bare-chested man sitting upright in the bed. A shadow of beard growth covers the lower half of his face and down his jawline, but the same ruby-red eyes as the wolf from my dream shine from his face. His unmorphed face.

"Solo?" I can't believe what I'm seeing. I blink fast and furiously as if this image will disappear. It doesn't.

"Good morning, Princess," he replies, lips twitching for a moment before spreading into a full smile.

Oh, how he fucking takes my breath away when he smiles like that. It's criminal. Before I can think better of it —and of the effect it might have on his wounds—I launch myself up from my place at the side of his bed and throw myself at him.

"Solomon!" He takes my weight with an amused grunt and strong arms band around me, holding me against his chest.

Fresh tears find my eyes, but this time, there is no pain accompanying them. "I … I wasn't sure if you'd ever wake up," I confess.

"I could never leave you," he replies, burying his face into my neck and hair.

"The Blood Madness…" I start, choking on the words as my throat grows thick with emotion.

"I've overcome it now."

Yes, that's right. He's overcome it and nothing else matters. Thank Aerea. He's awake and alive and for that, I am grateful. Still, though, I cling to him for the longest of minutes. My hands rove over his shoulders and arms, feeling their strength and heat, reaffirming the truth that he's awake and well and truly breathing.

"What happened?" Solomon finally asks.

I swallow and sigh. "A lot," I tell him. "Lenorn made a deal with his House. I think they sensed that Nasir was losing power and they wanted to be spared."

A thunderous expression overtakes Solo's face. "What was the deal?"

I flinch. When Lenorn had told me, he'd looked so stoic and uncomfortable that I hadn't had the heart to force the answer from him. "I'm not sure," I admit. "But I suspect it has something to do with him rising as the next head of the House of Daemonium." Noble politics are something I will have to deal for the rest of my life, and already thinking about it makes my head ache.

With careful movements, I stroke his shoulder. Looking down at him and feeling a happy fluttering inside my chest.

All I want to do is crawl onto him even more than I already am and bring him inside me so that we may never be parted again. No one will likely ever know the true horror doesn't happen during battle but in the hours and days following—when you're not quite sure yet what all you've lost.

"What of the disease?" Solo asks.

I tilt my head at that. "It's gone," I tell him.

"Gone?"

I nod. "Yes, it was Nasir's doing and now that he's no longer ... well, he's dead and the disease seems to have stopped spreading. From what information we've gathered"—that Lenorn and Frederic and Ahren had gathered—"anyone who was sick, who wasn't already on the verge of death, is either fully recovered or on the mend."

Confusion and disbelief crease Solo's brow as he gapes at me. "Just like that?" he demands before shaking his head. "How in the world was he able to spread a disease like that without ever leaving the Sunfire Palace? Was it attached to his abilities?"

I blow out a long breath. "I don't know," I admit. "I think there are a lot of things we simply will never know the truth about." And the reasoning? That was another thing that confused me, but perhaps it was Etia's power leaking across Rozentine, pushing us to hurry along, as if another threat was all we needed to get back to Nasir and the Sunfire Palace.

"But..." Solomon's heat sears into my body as his hand touches my hip. "You have a theory?"

I sigh. He truly knows me far too well. "I think it had something to do with Etia," I confess. "You weren't quite sane during the battle, but when I attacked him, I pushed her out of his body and ... I don't think Nasir was in control of himself. All that he did, none of it was about us, about me. His abilities—if he had Rozentine blood in him—didn't come from a specific House like we might have thought. They came from *her.*" The disease too—or so I assumed. It was the only logical conclusion.

Solo goes quiet for a beat. My hands land on his chest and when I move to push away from him to answer the question, he resists. "Solo?" I peer up at him and instead of releasing me, he drags me further onto the bed, turning me until my ass is seated firmly in his lap.

"You attacked Nasir," he says, voice quiet. "I have more questions about you throwing yourself into the battle like that and just thinking of it … I don't think I'll be able to stop holding you for a while yet, Princess." His arms squeeze me tighter as if to punctuate that admission.

My heart stutters and then speeds up, taking flight, and then soars. "Solomon…" I whine half-heartedly, but the responding grin he gives me tells me he knows my true feelings.

With a weary shake of my head, I settle into his lap and rest my head against his chest. "Oh, fine," I give in—rather gracefully in my opinion. "I'm not hurting you, though, am I?"

"You?" Solomon scoffs as if the very notion is ridiculous. "Just answer my questions, Devonry, and keep your absurd questions to yourself."

"It's not absurd!" I argue. "Nasir chained you and hung you up, and then he stabbed you! You were wounded, and you've been unconscious for—"

Solomon stops my tirade with a single finger pressed to my lips. "Hush," he says.

Of all the pig-headed, stubborn, stupid, overly masculine—my internal dialogue is cut short as well when Solomon lifts his finger away and replaces it with his mouth. My eyes slide shut and I lean into the kiss as if I've been dying of thirst in a desert and the Gods have finally graced me with a drop of water.

Solomon's lips move over mine, soft and then firm. His mouth opens and so does mine. A shudder works its way through me. My hands land on his shoulders, nails digging into his skin despite myself. I need to stop this. I need to pull away. He's still recovering. Yet, trying to drag my lips from his is like trying to kill a typhoon with more rain.

In the end, it's Solo who ends the kiss and only, I suspect, because he wants answers. "Tell me," he says rather gruffly as he slips a hand under my legs and adjusts me against his lap once more.

Ignoring the telltale feeling of his rigid erection against my side, I clear my throat and begin. I tell him of Nasir's death and, more to that, of the strange power he possessed that allowed him to control multiple people by invading their minds. I confess the dreams and visions that Aerea had shown me and the sorrow of Etia and how she tied into all of it.

I go on to tell him of Nasir's growing madness—not unlike Solomon's—and how he believed that being married to me and using my blood would free him from his madness, the very madness that I believe Etia was feeding him in order for him to do her bidding. All the while, Solomon's hands never leave me. He strokes my back, cups my shoulder, and keeps me warm as he urges me to lean against his chest.

I recount the battle, the failed wedding, and Solomon being hung above the altar as a threat to me. Then I tell him of Argyle and Celine. Recalling the fear of thinking Celine had perished in the fight brings back the fear all over again and when I cry, he holds me closer still, stroking my hair and whispering sweet words I never knew he was capable of into my ear. Everything I ever needed to hear, he tells me. It's so perfect that I worry that I haven't really woken up at all and this is all still just a beautiful dream.

As if sensing my impending panic, Solomon squeezes me and speaks, redirecting my attention to our conversation. "So, Nasir is dead then?" he clarifies.

I nod. "Yes, he is."

"Who ended it?"

My eyes drop to my lap and I latch onto a piece of skin to the side of one of my nails, pulling until the pain ricochets up my finger.

"Devonry." Solomon tucks his hand beneath my chin and lifts my face to meet his gaze. "Answer me."

I swallow reflexively. "I did." The words feel cold and wrong coming from my lips, but they're the truth. "I killed him." How many lives is that now? Two on my hands? Or more if I count those who were lost trying to protect me?

Solomon's brows lower over his eyes and his lips pinch tight. "I'm so sorry you had to do that," he whispers. "But I am fucking proud."

"Proud?" I repeat the word, confused.

"Yes." His hand gentles against my chin and drops away, but I peer up at him still.

"My mother would have been ashamed." The words come out in a whisper. "She practiced pacifism," I remind him. "I killed that slave trader, and now..." I can't even bring myself to say the words again.

A soft sigh leaves Solomon's lips. "Did you ever wonder why your mother practiced pacifism?" he asks.

"She was a Saintess," I reply.

He nods. "Yes, but before she was a Saintess, she was a Princess like you and then a Queen."

"So?" What does that have to do with anything I've said or done?

"Finding peace is not easy, Devonry," Solo says. "In

fact, I'd wager it's one of the most difficult things to accomplish. Your Mother was called a Saintess because she found it. In herself and in her Kingdom and in *you*."

"Me?" I shake my head. "What are you saying?"

"I know I'm not much older than you," he says, "but I remember your mother, and I remember that she began practicing pacifism when you were born, not before."

"You think she started … because of me?" More confusion fills me. What would having a child change? Why would she—for some reason, the memory of the wolf pup in my dream comes back to me mid-thought.

"Peace is hard fought and hard won," Solomon continues.

"I know that," I say. If anyone understands that, I do—especially after all we've been through over the last few months.

Solomon bends his head toward me. His forehead brushes mine. He closes his eyes and speaks. "There is a darkness in everyone, Devonry," he says. "Even those who are blessed by the light. Your mother gave birth to the one thing that she knew would send her into that darkness because when you open your eyes and see your soul and heart in another's face, you realize you would do absolutely anything to protect them. Steal. Torture. Murder. As ironic as it is, to know no more violence, blood must be shed. To know peace, you must first know war."

Solomon opens his eyes once more and leans away, reaching up to cup my cheek. "Your mother would not have been ashamed of you," he tells me. "She would have been proud of the woman you've become. You have not killed recklessly. You have only done so when the lives of others were at stake and when you had no other choice. Don't let those actions define you. You are so much more than a bow and arrow and a crown."

Slowly, my lips spread. The smile is watery because more tears linger in my eyes. "I've missed you, Solo," I confess. "Thank you."

His head dips and this time, when his lips meet mine, I know I have no intention of stopping so I hope he doesn't either.

38
DEVONRY

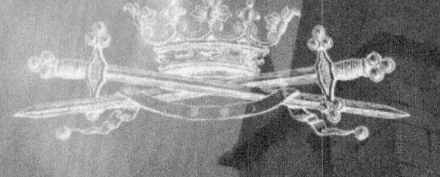

Solomon's breath is hot against my flesh. He kisses me back like a man consumed by lust. I groan and arch my back, my breasts pressing outward against him as his hands wrap around me. I can feel him against me, all over me. Now, I want to feel him *inside* me.

I thought I wanted him before, but nothing compares to this moment. Because now we're free. Free from the running and the danger. Yes, the world will have to collect itself, and the system of Noble Houses will need to be addressed, but for right now, there needs to be no other thought than him and I. Than the fact that we survived and that we're still living and we're still here, together.

"Devonry…" Solomon's voice is full of raspy want as he flips us both over. My hips lift up from the mattress as he climbs over me. His massive body slides down mine as his lips descend from my mouth and to my jawline and then my throat. "Devonry…" He says my name reverently, pleadingly.

I thrust my head back as his teeth scrape over my jugular and then to the side. My pulse flutters against the inside of my skin, tapping in tune to a rapid beat that I couldn't stop even if I tried. The question hovers in the air between us as his fangs touch my flesh. The answer is already alongside it.

Tipping my head back further, I smile as he hesitates and doesn't move. My hand arches up over us and slides through the midnight locks of hair at the back of his head, and I press him closer. "Do it," I say. "Make me yours."

He freezes, unmoving for several long seconds, and just when I think I've made a mistake—that I've assumed too much—I feel his responding chuckle. "You have always been mine, Devonry," Solomon tells me. "You just didn't know it until now."

With that, he rears back and strikes. His fangs sink into my flesh and my lips part on a startled cry. My thighs rub together as warmth pools low in my belly and then floods my insides. Tears prick behind my eyes and I realize, a bit belatedly, that I've closed them.

Not for long, it seems, as they shoot open again when Solomon's firm hand grips my thighs and spreads them wide. His hips drive forward and the hard shaft of his cock rubs insistently at the place between my legs. If it weren't for this damnable fabric between us, he would already be inside me.

I'm on fire, burning up from the inside out, yet it never reaches the surface. The Awakened power that rests within me seems to sense that Solomon is the reason for these volatile emotions. It never touches him.

He groans, a desperate sound low in his throat as he swallows my blood. The rush of it and the sting at my neck only send more pleasure coursing through me. How it's possible, I don't know, but I'm not exactly in the right frame of mind to contemplate the science of Solomon drinking my blood and how it makes me feel. All I can do is let that feeling overwhelm and consume me.

The place between my thighs swells and wetness oozes out of me, down the inside of my thighs. My head pounds in time with the suctioning pulls at my throat. I lock my hand against the back of Solomon's skull and then wrap my legs around his hips. I tilt my groin upward and rub against him, hungry for something of my own.

He pulls back, releasing my flesh with a wet sound. When his face appears over mine, his lips are painted a brilliant red, slightly darker than the glowing irises of his eyes. I want to consume him the same way he does me. I want to bite him and suck him down, drain him dry, and take from him everything he's willing to give me.

Leaning up, I nip at his lips, tasting rust and liquid heat. His pupils expand, nearly consuming the entirety of the red in his gaze until there's nothing left but a thin ring of ruby color. My chest rises and falls in rapid succession and Solomon, in response to my nip, reaches down and cups a hand over my thigh while the other is pressed into the bed, holding him suspended over me.

I drop my legs from his waist and press a hand into his chest. "What are you planning, Devonry?"

My lips twitch in amusement at his question. I kiss the side of his mouth and push lightly. "Instead of telling you," I reply, "let me show you."

Solomon follows my silent command as I push him over onto his back. Switching our positions, I climb over him. Straddling his hips gives me a strange sense of arousing authority. I can feel how hard he is beneath me, the strain of his cock against the inside of his trousers and I know I'm the reason for it.

I can't wait anymore. I've wanted to do something for him—to him—for so long, and now I have the opportunity.

Reclining and scooting further back on his legs, I reach for the front of his trousers, pulling the strings out in fast movements. His jaw tightens, a muscle jumping beneath the surface as I reach beyond the fabric of his pants and curl my fingers around his hard length.

He's hot to the touch and thick enough that it's difficult to wrap around him, the tips of my fingers not quite touching together. "You're going to drive me to fucking madness, Princess," Solomon swears through gritted teeth.

My lips twitch and curve upward. I hope so because I already reached that same point long ago. I stroke him a few times, running my hand up and down his shaft as pearly white fluid bubbles up from the small hole at the top of his cock. Tucking the choppy strands of my hair back, I lean down and blow a light breath over his head.

He jerks and hisses out yet another curse. "*Fuck!*" He squeezes his fists into the sheets below and I grin as I move closer, letting him feel the heat of my breath against his sensitive flesh. "By the Gods, I swear if you don't—"

I don't let him finish. As he curses my name, I part my lips and drop down over him, taking his cock into my mouth. He cuts off his words as the shaft against my tongue pulses. He tastes like salt and warmth. I close my eyes and sink further, taking him deeper. A squirt of fluid shoots out over the back of my throat, and I shudder as I lick at the veiny underside of his cock.

I'm hungry for more than my own pleasure. I want his as well. I want to taste him and consume him in this new way. I want to see him lose his fucking mind over me the same way he makes me lose mine. Withdrawing until the tip of his shaft is against my lips, I press a soft kiss to the underside before opening my mouth again and taking him deeper still.

Down, down, down I go until he stretches my lips and

billows out my cheeks. He's massive. Are all men so impressive? From what I heard in our travels from both the whores we'd run into and from Celine herself in some very quiet and rather uncomfortable conversations on the road —that's not the case. I lick at him, lapping up the salty taste of him and relishing in the heavy groans above me.

When a firm hand locks onto the back of my skull, I jump only to grin and push myself deeper. I breathe heavily through my nose as I try to go down as far as I can, taking him all the way into my throat. Unfortunately, his cock hits something it shouldn't and I choke, withdrawing immediately as I cough and hack.

"Alright, that's enough of that," Solomon growls as he lifts me away from his wet cock and flips us back over. "Any more and I'll explode."

Still coughing, eyes teary, I try to catch my breath. "That's…" I cough some more. "What I wanted, though."

Solomon glares at me as he reaches for the hem of the day dress I'm wearing and rips it up and off of me. The slip beneath goes along with it, both dropping off to the side of the bed with little more thought. I touch Solomon's chest, running the tips of my fingers over the valleys and dips of each of his abdominal muscles and the scars that linger in between.

"You're playing with fire, Devonry," Solomon snaps, snatching my hand away and slamming it against the mattress.

I smile in response. "I am the fire, Solo."

When his only reply is to glare at me some more, I grin and lift my hips against his, rubbing my naked flesh against the bobbing cock between us. "Are you going to leave me like this, Solo?" I ask him. "I'm hungry … feed me."

"You devious little creature." The words are a hiss that escapes his lips, but they lack any true anger. I know he wants me. The evidence is as clear as the thick monstrosity between his legs. There's no point in resisting anymore.

"Solomon…" I breathe his name as I arch against him once more. My breasts feel heavy. My nipples are pebbled and throbbing. The fingers locked around my wrists that hold me trapped against the bed do nothing to quell the raging fires inside. "Please…" I'm not too proud to beg.

"Shit." Solomon's head dips for a moment, and I pray I'm going to get what I want. I hope that the Gods are at least that kind after all we've been through. When his head lifts once more, I know I'm right.

He releases my wrist to reach down and spread me open beneath him. Locking my legs beneath each of his forearms, Solomon drags me closer until the opening of my cunt is beneath the underside of his cock. I feel it rubbing against my wetness, teasing me with its presence. I moan and arch upward.

"Please, Solo…" I whisper. "Take me. Fuck me. Please me…"

"Damnable Gods…" I don't know if the curse is a prayer, but it sounds like one as Solo lets my legs fall over his thighs and reaches between us to set the head of his cock to my opening. My insides clench automatically in preparation, in want and need. "You're going to be the death of me, Devonry Estand," he whispers as he rubs against me, up and down in maddening motions. "What a beautiful, delirious death it will be."

With that, he shoves forward, penetrating me in one single thrust. A scream shoots toward my throat and gets locked inside. No sound escapes. My back flies off of the mattress as he fills me to the hilt. All of the breath within my lungs evaporates as if it never existed in the first place. My eyes slide shut and my brow pinches down as I try to adjust to the pressure within me.

"Don't close your eyes," Solomon's voice deepens as he speaks. The moment hot fingers touch my jaw, clamping down, my eyes shoot open once more. "Look at me," he commands. "Look at the man taking you, Devonry. Tell me what you want, and I will make it so."

"I…" I can't speak. The ability has abandoned me, and all I can do is release a low keening sound as he withdraws, pulling his cock out of my insides before shoving it back with the same violence as before.

It's fucking wonderful, better than anything I've ever experienced before. I'm overwhelmed by the sparks dancing beneath my flesh. The fires take root in my lower abdomen and expand outward. I release the sheets and reach for him instead. My nails clutch at his arms, latching on for dear life.

Just as I'm holding onto him, my insides reach for him too. My inner muscles clamp down as he thrusts back into me, squeezing tight to prevent him from leaving again. Stars dance over my gaze, speckling my vision with little pops of brightness and colors.

"You have to say the words," Solomon says, his voice low and amused as he bends over me. "If you want something, you should reach out and take it."

Asshole, I think to myself. He's taunting me. Bringing me to the edge of a wonderful precipice of pleasure and then backing away. If my nails bite hurt, he doesn't show it either, not even when they draw blood.

Wetness slides down the crack of my ass with each thrust as Solomon penetrates me—over and over again, completely disregarding the cling of my inner muscles as they try to hold him in place. My chest squeezes tight and finally, after what feels like forever, a fresh moan bubbles up out of my throat.

I gasp, I moan, I cry out with each pass as they drive

me further up the crest. All the while, Solomon hovers over me, his eyes darkening as his own breath quickens. A flush spreads down his neck and chest and over the ridges of his muscles. Even through my own pleasure, I find a sick sense of gratification in knowing that I affect him in a similar way.

His hands shoot downward, cupping me under my ass as he lifts me up and away from the mattress. With a cry of surprise, I reach for him, wrapping my arms around his shoulders. I cling on for dear life as I leave the bed entirely and find myself held aloft by him and him alone. His thighs slap against mine as he hefts me up and drops me back down onto his cock. Each pass as he fucks into me hits somewhere deep. A sharp ache begins to spread throughout my abdomen.

Sweat clings to my temples and slides down my jawline. Breathless, I lean forward and collapse against his chest. I'm so tired. Exhausted really. My belly feels swollen with the thickness of his cock pummeling my insides. A lightness invades my mind, picking me up and carrying me away as my eyes roll back into my head and I feel myself come to a shuddering, trembling peak.

Humiliatingly, my cunt floods around the length of his shaft, and my muscles contract all at once. Tears pour from my eyes and down my cheeks. My lips scrape against his shoulder as he continues to thrust through it all.

Stop, I want to cry. *Please. Wait!* A break. I need a break, but I can't voice any of it.

Solomon fucks me like a man possessed. In and out, punching his cock into my lower belly as if he plans to make a hole inside of me in the shape of him. Still, despite all of that, I latch onto him, holding tight. Afraid to let go.

More tears prick my eyes and flow over my face, wetting his skin. He, too, is consumed by his actions, and sweat clings to every muscle. Solomon keeps one hand cupped under my ass as he lifts me with nothing more than his own strength and then slams me back down over his lap. With his other hand, he reaches up and slides his fingers through the uneven strands of my hair.

Locking on, he brings my head back—forcing my face away from his shoulder so that he can see me in all of my teary-eyed embarrassment. His gaze softens, though, when he sees my expression and instead of teasing me as I half expect, he brings me forward for another kiss. Lips part and his mouth takes mine. Tongues twine together. My eyes slide shut and all I can do is *feel*.

"You take my cock so well, Dev," Solomon whispers against my lips, his breath blazing against the sensitive skin of my lips. "You were made to take me, love."

More moans spill from my lips at his words. What he does to me should be criminal. He is my lifeline, my everything. How had I not seen it before now? A fresh wave of emotion overtakes me and I open my eyes to blink blearily at him through my watery gaze.

"I love you," I whisper.

His hips stutter to a stop as his brows shoot up. A moment passes and I think I've made a mistake in my confession. Then he closes his arms around me and the world tilts. He slams me against the bed and lifts up, his cock withdrawing and slamming into me.

"Of course you do," he grits out. "You're fucking mine. My fucking soul. My Devonry…"

He fucks me harder than ever before. A scream echoes out of me as I claw at his chest, my nails scratching across his nipples and muscles. "Harder," he snaps. "Scratch me, claw me, make me feel you."

A hand snakes its way down between us, and I feel the rough pads of his thumb and forefinger pinch down over the bundle of nerves above my cunt. All at once, the world explodes and Solomon's body stops, hovering over me, buried deep within me. Hot jets of warm fluid fill my insides and I clamp down around him, wanting to keep it all within me.

When the trembling of our bodies ceases and I can see once again, I peer up into glittering blood-red eyes. I blink, confused. "Are you … crying?" I reach up, cupping Solo's cheek as concern slaps me in the face. "Why? What's wrong?"

"You love me," Solo says, the words a whisper.

My concern immediately abates and I laugh. "And that makes you teary-eyed?" I ask, teasing. "Who knew the great Blood General would be brought to his knees by a woman in love."

"I have loved you since before you were born, Devonry," Solomon confesses. "Since the moment I set eyes upon you, I knew only what devotion was. All that I am. All that I will ever be is yours."

Invisible chains wrap around my heart and etched into the metal links is his name. "Solomon…" I don't know what to say to his words. They both hurt and feel like the greatest blessing of all.

"I was prepared to live my life in your shadow as your guard and nothing more. I was prepared to see you with another, no matter the pain it caused me. Now that I have you, though, I can't do it. I can't see you with another."

To that, I know exactly what to say. "I think we've both lost enough," I whisper to him. My father. My mother. Jacin. "So, trust me when I say … you'll never have to see a day come where I am not yours."

A single tear slips from his eyes and rolls down his cheek. Keeping my gaze locked with his until the very last moment, I lean up and touch my tongue to his skin. I lick the droplet away and press a kiss to his lips.

"Marry me." It's both a plea and a prayer.

I clasp my arms around him and hold onto him as if the two of us are waiting for a great storm to carry us away. "Yes," I whisper back. "Yes."

39
DEVONRY

A few weeks later...

All of Rozentine has been drawn to the center of Sanctus City. In the days following the great and terrible battle within the Sunfire Palace, word had spread over what happened, over what Nasir had done. His crimes, even if they hadn't been known to many citizens, were paid for by his death.

Some nights, I wake screaming, thinking that I've once again turned into that fiery bird, only this time, my body is still human and the flesh over my bones melts as I slowly descend into a madness far worse than any I've ever known. On those nights, I'm woken by firm and gentle hands, Solomon's hands. I haven't been able to sleep without him by my side; I've refused to. He had almost died. I'd almost lost him and that was something I wouldn't think of, couldn't bear to think of ever again. So if he wanted to help me, he had to sleep by my side so whenever my dreams came, I could wake and know I wasn't alone. That he was there and that he always would be.

Now, weeks later, I face my people and see nothing but our future. A future with them and, most especially, with *him* by my side.

The people of Rozentine, from all Houses and territories, stride through the streets of Sanctus City, having flocked from their homes to witness what will be a new era of our Kingdom, to witness my coronation. The evidence of their enthusiasm is clear as they crowd the streets waving flags of burning phoenixes. Children weave their way to the front of the crowd or sit high on their parents' shoulders, all for a glance at their soon-to-be crowned Queen.

The heavy stomp of boots from the guardsmen before and behind my carriage is drowned out by the cheering of the people. Hands reach for me on all sides, waving frantically or tossing flowers as I pass. Red petals flutter to collect on the streets.

A glimpse of the Sunfire Palace comes into view as I adjust myself in my seat. I force my smile to remain planted on my cheeks despite the way my face aches. There is real joy here, in this city, at this very moment. Yet the deep reminders of my sorrow remain. I'm told the grief will come and go and then eventually ease as time goes on. As if those I've cherished and lost are small enough to be forgotten or time itself is big enough to fade my love. I see my father in the beginning of lines that crease my eyes when I smile. I hear Jacin's laughter in the brief moments that Solomon lets himself go to a deep chuckle. Every day, I walk past the cracked stone where Nasir's body had fallen. The ash has been scrubbed away, but I often wonder if the spirit of the man who'd once been my friend remains, a spirit beyond the palace walls. My heartache and happiness go hand in hand, clinging to one another like frantic lovers.

I search the faces of the people, trying so desperately and quite impossibly, to remember all of them. It's for these citizens that I will bring great change. Rozentine has never been meant to stand still, and I refuse to be a stagnant leader. Though I'll never be the Saintess Queen, soft and peaceful, I'll carry her gentleness and mercy with me always.

As every great member of the line of Aerea has before their coronation, I'd ridden through the streets of the Sanctus City since dawn. Though today is a day for traditions, the custom of taking this trip alone is possibly my least favorite part of the day thus far, even though it's only just begun. It would be a good time to think about what sort of ruler I wish to be, but truthfully, I've been thinking about it since the moment my father died in my arms.

I know exactly who I'll be for my country. I'll be the Queen to rid the slave trade from the streets of Rozentine. I'll be the Queen that welcomes the House of Ravens. I'm the Queen who will see my people safe, happy, and thriving.

As the carriage rounds the last corner, heading for the palace, I exhale and lean back into the seat. The pins that hold my hair on top of my head poke at my scalp as I tip my head back. Small clusters of rubies adorn the strands gathered back from my face.

The sound of horns breaks through the humming of the crowd. Men draped in red and gold stand tall at the palace steps trumpeting my arrival. My body sways as the carriage slows to a stop. Cheers rise as the door is opened, a hand outstretched and waiting for me. I place my fingers in his, feeling his warmth, letting it soak into my very soul, and I smile.

The train of my gown trails behind me as I step out of the carriage and into the waiting entourage of guards. One representative from each House, dressed in their respective colors, waits in one of two lines on either side of me. My eyes lift to Solomon first. His expression is soft, though he does not smile as he bends forward in a bow. The burgundy ropes that hang around his waist sway with the movement, as do the war charms. His black suit fits the broad width of his chest and molds to the shape of his muscular body. It sets my heart into a steady gallop. He lifts his brow when he straightens, a smirk pulling one side of his mouth.

"I know." Argyle leans in from my other side with a bow of his own. "We look good." He winks and runs his hands down his navy suit embellished with black embroidery. A pin of black wings glints from its place on his chest as the sun stretches over the Sunfire Palace. The others, men from the Houses of Sunfire, Starfall, Caladrius, and even one from Daemonium stand at attention.

"Are you ready, my Queen?" Solomon asks.

"Yes." I pull my shoulders back and with Solomon and Argyle at my sides, we take to the steps. The horns continue their song and the shouts of the people follow us, only muffled when the palace doors close. Music drifts from the throne room, the same jaunty tune played for the men and women who'd worn the crown before me. We step in time with the beat, a slow march toward the inevitable. My fingers brush against Solomon's as we near the final stretch to my waiting throne.

The large open doors lead to the gold carpet that stretches up to the dais. Red flower arrangements sit atop shimmering vases on either side of us, leaving only enough room for the men and me to make it around them. Scattered petals soften underfoot. Every inhale I take is perfumed with the floral scent.

From all angles, bright glowing eyes watch as their next

ruler ascends. Nobles from all the Houses gather before the throne in support. Gazes glistening in silver, red, blue, and a few lavender. The House of Daemonium has dwindled to only a few of those proven loyal to the line of Aerea. Lenorn dips his head in respect when our eyes meet. At his side both Frederic, Ellis, and Harlow stand tall. Frederic's smile is soft, but it brightens when my attention reaches him.

I'd never have made it here if it wasn't for the support of these people. I might not have saved Rozentine from the rule of Etia if it hadn't been for Solomon. My hand reaches for his. If I'm to take the throne, then I'll always have my soulmate at my side. His palm opens for my touch, but his shoulders tense as he sends a sideways glance in my direction. The fatigue of my facial muscles is easily forgotten when all I can do is beam up at him.

Each man from the Noble Houses breaks off to stand at either side of the throne at the base of the dais. Solomon takes a step as though he'll join them, but I hold his hand tighter in mine.

"Come with me," I whisper.

His eyes bounce over my face. I can already hear him internally cursing me for putting him in a position that, per his current title, is not proper. The Blood General's place is at the foot of the throne to bow at the feet of his Queen. But I know with certainty that Solomon's place is at my side. I bite my lip as he sighs into the stretched silence.

My soon-to-be husband. Future King Consort.

"Solomon Winnett, stand beside me." I try again, squeezing his hand.

His mouth twitches. "Forever."

"Forever."

Together, we take the final steps to the throne. Once a Princess and her guardsmen, now a Queen and her mate.

The crown rests upon a velvet pillow stuffed with down positioned on a pedestal for all to see. My mother's crown and her mother's before her. The threat of tears stings my eyes as I try my best to blink it away and turn to face the crowd. Both Celine and Sheza follow behind us, gathering the train of my dress and lay it delicately in its place before they step behind the throne. My next exhale is shaky as I glance at Celine, who gives me a reassuring nod before I face the crowd again.

Solomon's thumb rubs a gentle circle against my skin, a reminder of our togetherness, before he looks to the priest waiting at the side. "May I?" He gestures to the crown then back to me. The priest frowns slightly but only looks to me for an answer.

"You may," I say.

The sound of the music softens to a low cadence as gentle as a lullaby. Every Noble quiets. Each *thud* of Solomon's steps as he crosses to the crown matches the beating of my heart.

"Today, we welcome the next ruler of Rozentine." His voice resounds off the walls, filling the room. The crown sparkles in his hands as he lifts it from the cushion and turns back to me. His expression is soft, eyes wide as he looks down to take me in. I lift my chin, waiting. "Queen Devonry Aerea Estand."

Solomon blocks my view of the Nobles with his broad shoulders. Butterflies bubble up in my stomach and flutter up into my heart. With a gentleness no one might think the Blood General capable of, he sets the crown upon my head. Then his touch glides down the side of my face, creating a ripple of goosebumps. I scoop his hand up before he can drop it back to his side and intertwine our fingers. He smiles, truly smiles at me, just briefly before he turns back to the room.

"To the Queen of Rozentine, Devonry Aerea Estand. Long may she reign!" He bellows the words and the room breaks out into applause.

"Long may she reign!" they echo.

"Long may *we* reign," I whisper to Solomon. His eyes drift close as he bows his head.

Between crown and sword, I am the first and he is the latter. Together, we will rule. Together, we will reign. Until time calls us home to the Divine Plane and our lives start over again. In each life, we will find each other. We will love each other.

There is no parting, even beyond death.

EPILOGUE
DEVONRY

Some months later...

I thought I knew what pain and fear were the night my father was slaughtered in front of me. I thought I knew so much of the world after the weeks that followed and I was forced out of the only home I'd ever known. I'd spent so much time on the run, in danger, and fleeing from a friend I thought I could trust. Now, though, I know the truth.

None of that could compare to *this*.

Another wave of agony ricochets up my spine and I grit my teeth, reaching out and latching onto the ropes the handmaids had tied to the two posts closest to my head. It fucking hurts. Why didn't anyone tell me it would hurt like this? One might think that hundreds of years of this shit and they might at least give their Queen a little bit of warning, but no. I went into this blind as a bat and now I regret *everything*.

I've never been present for a birthing and now, not only am I present, but I'm the one lying prone on a bed with leather between my teeth and a giant baby's head trying to make its way into the world through my insides.

"Almost there, Your Majesty!" Sheza exclaims as she and the midwife settle between my trembling legs, spreading them wider. Apparently, propriety doesn't matter much when you're shoving a Gods damned baby the size of a small elephant out of your nether regions. I'd never actually seen an elephant in person, but the paintings and drawings had me believing that they were massive creatures and so is this child. Massive and causing me a great deal of pain.

I blame Solomon's size. *I* am barely a few inches above five feet. *He*, on the other hand, is a monstrously tall and broad-shouldered warrior with barbarian blood running through his veins. The size of our child's head is all his damned fault.

Celine, in response to my muffled grunt, leans over the side of the bed and worriedly pats my face clean of the sweat currently pouring off of me. Unable to give her a thank you due to the massive weight of pain that slices through me, I manage to give her a half nod of appreciation. Her lips twitch in amusement before she shakes her head.

Her eyes scan down my form with a crinkle of anxiety. Yes, I don't quite blame her. The small, rounded size of her own belly is enough to make her worry. Argyle is just as big as Solomon and that means their fucking babies are both likely to be monstrous. In a few short months after my current predicament, she'll be in the same position and it'll be me wiping the sweat from her brow.

"Push, Your Majesty," the midwife commands.

Push? I think. *Again?* I've *been* pushing and we've gotten nowhere.

Spitting the damned leather out of my mouth, it falls to

my chest with a plop and I turn my attention to Celine. "Where's Solo?" I practically beg, breathless and near sobbing.

Her worried eyes soften and she reaches forward, laying a gentle hand on my shoulder. The slender band around her neck swings forward and slips from her collar. The wooden heart, carved by Argyle's own hands, hangs between us. I blink at it, half focusing on it to keep myself from going insane or screaming as another bolt of pure, unfettered pain nearly slices me in half.

"Lord Solomon is on his way," she assures me.

"Why the fuck isn't he here now?" I half cry out as I writhe against the bed, closing my eyes briefly and blocking out the image of that wooden heart.

"He didn't want to leave you in the first place," Celine reminds me.

Of course he hadn't, and truth be told, he wasn't the one who needed to attend the meeting with the House of Ravens—it was supposed to be me. Due to my *condition*, however, we'd had no choice. I flop back onto the pillows behind my head and groan as another wave of unending pressure rolls through me before seizing my insides in a tight grip. They're coming faster now, closer together, and I'm scared.

I didn't think I'd be doing this alone—and though I recognize that I'm not truly alone, not with Celine, Sheza, and the midwife here ... I want Solo. I want my husband. My eyes start to water and my grip on the ropes tighten all over again as a racking bolt of fire shoots up my back and down again.

"Ah!" The scream I release is full of emotion and the tears break free, rolling down my cheeks.

"Please, Your Majesty, you must push," the midwife reminds me.

Push. Push. Push. Fucking fine! Leveraging up, using my hold on the ropes, I bear down and struggle through my muscles contracting together around the baby in my belly, trying to urge it toward the place between my legs. I maintain the pressure, pushing and holding my breath as I do until I can do it no longer.

By the time the latest wave has ended, I collapse back into the pillows and groan as Celine wipes my face again. Her hand is cool against my heated skin and I close my eyes, leaning into it. A moment passes, and I can only barely feel the hands of the midwife as she moves my legs out of her way and checks my insides again to see how far along the baby is from being born, I assume.

"How long has it been?" I wonder aloud, breathless.

"A few hours," Celine answers with a wince.

My eyes pop open. Hours? No wonder no one warns expecting mothers. If they knew how painful the process of childbirth was, they wouldn't do it. Even now, Celine's obvious concern for me is somewhat mollified by the fear in her gaze and the way she's been restlessly cupping her own belly after each of my contractions, as if she's mentally preparing herself to go through the same process.

A low groan erupts from me. "Never again," I pant. "I'm not doing this again, I can't." Solomon will have to keep his cock far away from me. I didn't think it was possible to live without sex now that I knew what it was— especially how it feels with him—but if I have to bear this again, I just might die. Honestly, I might die with just this one.

"They all say that, dear," the midwife says, sounding amused. I'm not quite sure if I've said my last thoughts aloud until I figure out she's responding to my earlier comment. "You'll feel quite different when the babe has arrived and is laying in your arms, suckling at your bosom."

"Then it's his turn next," I mutter. "Solomon can do this instead of me and he can have the damned babe's lips on *his* bosom!" A scream lodges in my throat as fresh muscle spasms ripple over my stomach sending shoots of icy hot fire through my hips.

Sheza gives me a half-amused, half-sympathetic glance, her face pale. "If only we could pass off this job to the men folk, Your Highness, all women would rejoice."

Isn't that the fucking truth?

"Another one's coming," the midwife announces a moment later. I don't know how she knows before I even know it myself, but she's not wrong. As the next contraction overtakes me, I bear down and grit my teeth. More tears leak from my eyes and I pray to the Gods that this ends sooner rather than later. As much as I want Solomon here, I also just want this to be done.

Just as the last tendrils of pain fade away, a commotion sounds in the corridor. Celine turns away from me, and I catch sight of her frown in my periphery. "Is something wrong?" I ask, nervous. It's just the sounds, right? It has to be. It's definitely not the babe in my belly. It can't be ... can it? "What's going on?" I demand, breathless.

"I'm not sure, Your Highness," she replies, and then blessedly, she answers my unspoken concerns with her next comment. "I'll take a look." Definitely about the commotion outside. I almost sag in relief.

No sooner have the words escaped her lips, though, and she's taken a step toward the double doors that lead from my bedchamber than those doors fly open, and a tall, broad-shouldered male appears. Tears prick my eyes as red-faced, panting, and sweating Solomon's eyes lock onto me, his nostrils flaring.

"Devonry!" Still in his leather riding clothes, hair askew, and eyes wild, Solomon sets his sights on me and then barrels forward, only to be drawn back by a slightly slower Lenorn.

"You cannot!" Lenorn cries, appearing almost as red-faced as Solo. "This is a woman's place—we must not interrupt."

Oh, for the love of the Gods ... I open my mouth to tell Lenorn just where he can put that outdated notion—preferably up his backside—when Solomon beats me to it.

With a dark look, Solomon looks down at the hand on his chest and snarls. "I suggest you remove your hand from me and allow me to be with my wife as she gives life, if you know what's good for you." His words are low and more than a little threatening.

I don't see the full brunt of his expression as he turns his head slightly down and back to glare at Lenorn, but whatever it is must be terrifying because Lenorn's features pale and his hand slides off of Solomon's chest immediately. In response, Celine quickly hurries toward them. I don't know what she says to Lenorn as he—with his eyes wide and frightened—backs out of the room, but hopefully, it's to mind his own damned business and stay in the corridor.

Solomon turns back to me, his expression easing and brows creasing in concern as he takes me in. I must look a mess with my hair soaked in my own sweat and my face flushed with heat. It only takes a few seconds—all of which are far too long for me—for him to reach my side.

"I'm sorry," he says immediately as he falls to his knees alongside the bed and reaches for my hand. I unweave my fingers from the ropes and let him take it. He presses my hand to his cheek. "Thank the Gods I made it in time."

"If you hadn't, I might never have forgiven you," I tell him honestly.

He closes his eyes and presses a kiss to the center of my palm. "I'm here now, my love," he whispers. "I will be here until the end."

I know he doesn't just mean the birth of our child but so much more. My heart squeezes. No matter how many times I hear it, it still makes me queasy with joy. Solomon's eyes open again and he arches up over me to press a kiss to the center of my forehead.

"What do you need?" he asks.

"You," I confess, tightening my hold on his hand as I feel the flutterings of a new wave of contractions start low in my belly and expand outward. I peer up at him, feeling both weak for needing him and afraid of the fact that this has already lasted so long. I won't voice my fears, but in my head, they roll over and over. Are all labors supposed to be this long? Is the length normal? What if something is wrong? "Hold me?" I gasp as the pain heightens.

"You never have to ask," Solomon says. He gently helps me forward and I release the opposite rope to allow him room to crawl behind me. Now, with his back against the headboard of our bed and mine against his chest, I feel better. His presence as well as his warmth and touch gives me much more relief than I ever knew possible.

"Bear down, Your Majesty," the midwife says sharply, her gray-haired head popping up over my legs briefly before she disappears back down beneath the sheets covering my lower half. A few steps behind, Sheza orders Celine to hurry and grab a few more towels and bring some warm water.

"Solo?" I tilt my head up, seeking his eyes with my own as my belly contracts and the pain starts again.

"Yes, my love?" Solo's red eyes glitter like rubies as he

looks down at me. How had I never noticed the reverence in that gaze? It's a wonder I didn't see it during my childhood. It's so obvious to me now.

"Distract me?" I plead as my hands latch onto his arms and my nails dig deep. Thank the Gods he kept the leather on, or else I'd be scouring his forearms with long scratches.

Pressing a soft kiss to my temple, Solomon cradles me closer and rocks us—not enough to disrupt my entire body, but just enough of a sway that the contractions don't seem to be that bad. "Have you thought of a name yet?" he inquires.

I blink and realize … no, I haven't. "W-we don't"—I answer through low gasps—"know if it'll be a boy or girl yet."

"You haven't thought of one for each, just in case?"

I clench my jaw and bear down, pushing and holding my breath as Solo gently brushes my hair out of my face. I feel too much—all of it, all around. I both want to clutch him against me and smack his hand away. Oh, by the Gods, it's so not fair that men don't have to bear this responsibility.

"I see the baby's head!" the midwife exclaims. "That's it, one last time, Your Majesty. One more push, and it'll all be over."

Oh yes. Everything within me strains for this horrible process to be over and done with. Nine long fucking months, I grew this child inside of me, and if they aren't born today, I fear they never will be or that something terrible will go wrong. Fear gives a mind far too much kindling, and it's always rotten.

"I've got you," Solomon says, wrapping his arms around my shoulders and chest. I hold onto him, digging my nails into his forearm as I squeeze my eyes shut. The next contraction wraps around my insides and squeezes against the baby wiggling against my bladder. I swear to the Gods, if I pee myself right now, I'll toss Solomon and his too-big cock off of the nearest tower.

"I hate you…" I mutter without heat as I feel something just about to give way. There's so much damned pressure. It swells low over my abdomen and between my legs. Right there. If I could just…

"I promise you, my love," Solo replies—sounding pained. "You cannot hate me as much as I hate myself right now. I wish I could bear this for you."

Me. Fucking. Too.

As soon as that thought pops into my mind, however, the dam of agony finally gives way to relief. The stopped-up dam within me bursts free. I drop into Solomon's waiting arms, sagging as my legs give out and slide down. Dimly, I hear the midwife's exclamations and Sheza's excited cheering. Exhaustion clings to my entire body. My eyes droop.

Celine returns with a bowl of water and towels thrown over her shoulder just as the midwife does something below, her fingers brushing my trembling thighs, and then holds up a red-faced infant. I blink as the baby is swept away before I can truly get a good look at them. Solomon cups my cheek, tipping my face up as he presses a kiss to my lips.

"You've done so well, my love," he whispers, voice strained. "But perhaps this will be our one and only child." In the time since he entered and climbed behind me, that red flush on his face has seeped away to reveal pale, clammy skin. His eyes jump from me to the infant crying across the room and then back again. "I don't know if I can bear to see you in such pain again."

The chuckle that leaves me is weak. Before I can work up a response, though, Sheza returns to the side of my bed with a bundle in her arms. With tears in her eyes and the wrinkles that line her features deeper than I've ever seen before, she sniffles and looks at me.

"Would you like to meet your son, Your Majesty?" she asks on a choked whisper.

"Son?" Despite my weariness, I lift up slightly, my eyes locked on the small bundle in her arms.

Sheza nods and holds the child out. Solomon helps me to take him, his arms sliding along the outside of mine as I bring the baby to my chest. Pale skin, reddened and ruddy cheeks, with a mess of black hair darker than a raven's wing, our son parts his lips and lets out a rather annoyed yawn as his eyes squeeze into the tiniest little slits.

All of the breath in my chest rushes out at once. "He's ... beautiful," I whisper.

"He has your nose," Solomon says.

I tilt my head. Right now, his nose looks a little smooshed, but if Solomon sees it, I guess that's fine. I pull the bundle closer and lean down, pressing my cheek to the smoothest skin I've ever felt in my life. It's ... amazing. All of the pain I'd just felt, even some of the soreness that still wracks my body, it all pales in comparison to this. To *him*.

Tears fill my eyes. I think I get it now. Why my mother became a pacifist after she gave birth to me. Violence around a creature such as this—so perfect, so innocent, a new life in a world full of it—it's unthinkable. My hands start to shake. What will this little one think, though, when he grows up? What will he think of me and all that I've done?

"Don't." Solomon proves that he knows me better than any other as he presses the word softly into the side of my face. It slips from his lips like a secret. "Don't think of anything else, Devonry," he tells me. "Just hold him, and love him, and know that there is nothing in this world I would not do to protect the both of you."

Damn him, I think. He knows just what to say to calm my racing heart.

The small baby boy in my arms opens his eyes, wrinkling his nose as he stares up at Solomon and me. A gasp lodges in my throat. "His eyes," I whisper.

Solo is quiet for a long moment as both of us take in the eyes of the child in my arms. Red as a blood-filled sea. Sparkling and then there's something else that stems from them. Those eyes are glowing, filled with a familiar power.

"He's Awakened," Solo says, his voice barely above a whisper.

"Just like you were," I agree.

Solomon, as if he can't quite believe that the tiny little creature in my grip is something that the two of us created, leans over my shoulder slightly and strokes the baby's face with a single finger. He jerks slightly and then smiles.

"What is it?" I ask.

Solomon's lips stretch wider and wider. "He knows who I am," Solo says. "He sent a spark of something into me when I touched him."

I frown and look back at the child. "I don't feel anything." What if I can't feel anything? What if it's just Solomon? That's not fair. I'm the one who carried him and birthed him and—

As if sensing the direction of my worrisome thoughts, Solo chuckles and nudges me. "Touch his face and you'll know what I mean," he says.

Hesitantly, afraid to find out that I won't in fact know what he means if I follow his instructions, I lift a hand and gently graze it over the babe's forehead. Just like that, a fire bolts from where my skin touches his. It's crude and strange, like pressing my fingertip to the edge of a poker that's been sitting in the hearth for too long. But it's there—power. *My* power along with Solomon's glowing red eyes.

"Do you think he'll have wings?" I ask quietly. Wings like mine? Or will they be different? Will they make me think of Solo? Sun and shadow. Light and dark.

Solomon hums low in his throat as he once again strokes our son's soft full cheek. "Perhaps," he answers. "There's no telling what a son of the House of Blood and House of Sunfire will be. He might just surprise us and have wings that possess both of our powers."

I release a watery chuckle. "I swear he'll be just like you," I say. "He already has your eyes. Of course, he would take after you when I did all of the work."

Solomon nuzzles me and releases a low laugh of his own. "I believe I helped with the conception part," he murmurs.

"Oh, sure, take your credit with the pleasure and none of the pain." I roll my eyes.

He stiffens and hugs me tighter. "I would have taken it," he replies. "All of it. I'm sorry."

I shake my head. "It's over now," I say. "Forget it." I know I will. Because there is nothing more important to me now than the little ruby-eyed infant that nudges at my chest and wrinkles his nose at me.

"He's likely hungry," Sheza says with a sniffle as she smiles down at us.

I look up at her. "How do I…" I don't know how to ask, but my breasts do feel heavy and swollen. I know from what the midwife has taught me how, precisely, but I've never done it before.

"We can get a wet maid," Sheza says, suddenly turning away. A nursemaid … I don't know if I want that. For some reason, I have this urge and this feeling that it should be me. I know it's common for Royalty and Nobles to hire wet nurses, but I want to be the one to feed my child.

Before I can call Sheza back and say as much, though, Celine approaches the end of the bed. "So," she prompts, "have you yet thought of a name?"

My thoughts instinctively switch back to that and my gaze returns to the infant. I think back. Months ago, long before I even knew I was pregnant, I'd had dreams. In my mind's eye, I can recall it almost exactly. That tiny little wolf pup curled in my arms. It reminded me so much of Solomon at the time, but now I know … it wasn't Solomon at all, but this little one.

"Yes," I say, knowing exactly what he'll be named. "Wolfe. I want to name him Wolfe."

"That's a strong name," Solomon says. "I like it."

My chest squeezes with happiness and relief. Yes. Wolfe. Our son. Our future. That is who he will be. A strong, brave, red-eyed boy who will carry on the will of our souls. Whatever his decisions are, whatever he decides to do with his life, I know that no matter what, our love will always carry on in his existence.

This, I realize, was the true reason Levim and Aerea were reincarnated in Solomon and me. They never got to have a child of their own, and now they do. Through us, they have him.

ABOUT LUCINDA DARK

Lucinda Dark, also known as USA Today Bestselling Author, Lucy Smoke, for her contemporary novels, has a master's degree in English and is a self-proclaimed creative chihuahua. She enjoys feeding her wanderlust, cover addiction, as well as her face. When she's not on a neverending quest to find the perfect milkshake, she lives and works in the southern United States with her beloved furbaby, Hiro, and her family and friends.

Want to be kept up to date? Think about joining the author's group or signing up for their newsletter below.

Facebook Group (Reader Mafia)
Newsletter (www.lucysmoke.com)

ALSO BY LUCINDA DARK

Fantasy Series:

Mortal Gods Series
A Sword of Shadow & Deceit
A Reign of Storm & Madness
The Blood of Gods & Monsters
TBD

Awakened Fates Series (completed)
Crown of Blood and Glass
Dawn of Fate and Valor
Wings of Sunfire and Darkness

Twisted Fae Series (completed)
Court of Crimson
Court of Frost
Court of Midnight

Barbie: The Vampire Hunter Series (completed)
Rest in Pieces
Dead Girl Walking
Ashes to Ashes

Dark Maji Series (completed)
Fortune Favors the Cruel
Blessed Be the Wicked

Twisted is the Crown
For King and Corruption
Long Live the Soulless

Sky Cities Series (Dystopian)
Heart of Tartarus
Shadow of Deception
Sword of Damage
Dogs of War (Coming Soon)

Contemporary Series:

Gods of Hazelwood: Icarus Duet
Burn With Me
Fall With Me

Sick Boys Series (completed)
Forbidden Deviant Games (prequel)
Pretty Little Savage
Stone Cold Queen
Natural Born Killers
Wicked Dark Heathens
Bloody Cruel Psycho
Bloody Cruel Monster
Vengeful Rotten Casualties

Sinister Arrangment Duet (completed)
Wicked Angel
Cruel Master

Iris Boys Series (completed)

Now or Never

Power & Choice

Leap of Faith

Cross my Heart

Forever & Always

Iris Boys Series Boxset

The *Break* Series (completed)

Break Volume 1

Break Volume 2

Break Series Collection

Contemporary Standalones:

Poisoned Paradise

Expressionate

Wild Hearts

ABOUT REBECCA GREY

Rebecca Grey leads a busy life. Somewhere between raising two kids and daydreaming about being a reality television star, she writes. As a reader she enjoys books filled with arrogant boys—who she would never waste her time on in real life—and large fantasy or paranormal novels. Much of her love for these things is reflected in her books.

Learn more at Rebecca's website below!

www.rebeccagreyauthor.com

ALSO BY REBECCA GREY

Awakened Fates Series

Crown of Blood & Glass

Dawn of Fate & Valor

Wings of Gunfire & Darkness

The Prince's Games Duology

Vengeance

Vanquish

Brothers of the Otherworld Standalones:

Chasing Boston

Hunting Devils (Coming Soon)

The Darkest Queens Series

Made From Death

Kill The Queens

End Of The Sword

The Last Royal

Ruined By Fae Saga

Ruined

Madness

Heartsick

The Cursed Kingdom Series

The Cruel Fae King

The Cursed Fae King

The Crowned Fae Queen

The Twisted Crown Series

The Shadow Fae

The Iron Fae

The Lost Fae

Made in the USA
Coppell, TX
06 October 2025

60893263R00239